THE ORIGIN STORY

ROAR ANIMAL UNIVERSITY

There are animals with a small 'a' and Intelligent Animals with a large 'A.'

This is the narrative on how Intelligent Animals changed the world.

S.P. GROGAN

Animal Farm Re-Imagined

FIRST EDITION

10 9 8 7 6 5 4 3 2 1

Printed in the United States of America

Published by Roar University Press

ISBN 979-8-3507-5733-0

RoarUniv@Gmail.com

Books by S.P. Grogan

Vegas Die, a Quest Mystery

Captain Cooked, Hawaiian Mystery of Romance, Revenge, and Recipes

Atomic Dreams at the Red Tiki Lounge

Lafayette: Courtier to Crown Fugitive (1757-1777)

Crimson Scimitar: **Attack on America** (2001-2027)

Cookbook Passion (Editor)

Roar Animal University, the Origin Story

Required Reading, *SPG* unpublished memoir

ACKNOWLEDGMENTS

A Heartfelt Thanks To
Our Special Animal Friends
Blackie, Shasta, Meowie, Kona, Polo, Mercedes, Cooper
Our Special Human Friends
Jamie & John K, Jim & Nancy, Keith & Jessica,
Rick & Nancy, Kamal, Kammie, LN & P
Dr. Mike & Pam

Editing by: Sheila Grimes and Rica Graphics
University crest and podcast logo by Kure Designs
Eliza & Banyan tree sketch artwork by Isabelle Osborne

This work of our past educational journey containing individual transcribed interviews supported by public record research documentation has been collected, collated and published by permission and under the authority of the National Scholastic and Literary Review Board, and is graciously presented to the reader in this approved official collegiate edition by S. P. Grogan, Dean of Administrative Affairs, Roar Animal University.

A work of fiction…today

“We can judge the heart of a man by his treatment of animals.”
— Immanuel Kant

“Some people talk to animals. Not many
listen, though. That’s the problem.”
— A.A. Milne

*The general species name, *orangutan,* is derived from the Malay language, *orang*-people; person and *hutan*-forest, translated as ‘person of the forest.’

Animals Speak...and Write

*About a decade ago, a remarkable event was the medical transformative invention and selected implementation of **ITSE** (pronounced: *it-see*), the acronym for *Implant of Thought-Speech Enhancement.* This name is far better than the researchers' lugubrious terminology: *Neuronal Oscillation Magnetic Intracranial BCI (Brain-Computer Interface) Stimulation Transmitter for Enhanced Cognitive Response.* Patented and tightly controlled by a quasi-public licensing board known as the *ITSE* Governing Committee [ITSE-GovCo]. This astounding medical technology worked satisfactorily to help human strokes, Parkinson's Disease, and debilitated patients to process thought brain waves into recognizable speech patterns. Several years later, and in more advanced new models of *ITSE*, they discovered that Animals could likewise benefit, and again strictly monitored by certification, the small computer devices were implanted in so-called intelligent animals who served humans in such capacities, first in further medical and educational research, then for guide and service animals, and finally entertainment animals, those in circuses, motion pictures, and television. Regulations dissuaded affluent humans from acquiring these devices for their pampered pets, as obnoxious incidents revealed that dogs would invariably whine, sulk, and beg incessantly until their needs were met, and cats would tell their owners where they could go in the foulest of language.

Corollary progress also included writing by ITSE Animals, and there was no issue with this skill. Verbal dictation was entered into a computer or iPhone, converting speech into a screen display. AI then auto-corrected to the proper syntax and sentence structure, followed by email or printing, and archived in the Cloud. No further scientific updates are required to enhance the Animal writing format. And as time has progressed writing itself as displayed among humans finds cursive and highbrow prose writing short of extinction, with many humans dispensing with writing altogether except as text abbreviations and symbolic emojis. Post-it notes and graffiti with its abbreviated hieroglyphic scribble verbiage and requiring pic-click AI translation and interpretation has become high literature.

[* **"New Science & Technology That Led to How Animals Came to Use Human Speech"** —See Author's Notes in Appendix]

Publisher's Note:

With over 100 million animal species on this small planet, and where in this year nearly 18,000 of these animals are currently facing extinction, occasional *RoarUni Facts* will be provided for your surprise, thought and edification.

CONTENTS

ELIZA

Two years ago

She knew she had a thinking mind but could not express herself in their language. If so, she would have told them what they did and what they were doing was wrong.

Another day, and again, she knew they would come for her; it was her routine for the last two years. Repetition. And they did. The side door slid back so she could shuffle into the larger cage. Her fruit bowl, half-filled, her show cage water-hosed, barely cleaned, leaving scattered feces to dry and mold in the humidity. Flies everywhere. The water fountain worked. Of course, that was her act, what they had trained her for—an entertainer of sorts.

She could see the others, similar to her kind, primates, but small monkeys off in the distance, on their island, on display for those humans who came and paid to watch the wild antics of the distressed. The monkeys, Capuchins, could not escape, surrounded by a moat of fetid water, the island their open cage, their prison; but at least they could swing upon real trees, nearly bare, the leaves torn away for food or in frustration. Each morning, she counted the monkeys to keep alert, guessing their correct number. Difficult from their scattered play-jumping. Twenty-one this morning was her tally. Four were missing. That happened; their numbers fluctuated. And those gone, taken, never came back.

The human families soon arrived, and when they came to her, one of her captors would bang on the cage bars, and she would run back and forth, making outrageous faces at the humans; then, when she heard the whistle, she would run to the water fountain, gulp water and go and spit on the humans. They all laughed, took photos, and moved on to the other few exhibits, usually to see the baby monkeys. After all, this compound with its cages, island, and two corrugated-tin warehouse buildings only housed monkeys. And lots of baby monkeys.

But, in her two years here, she never saw anyone that looked like her, a pouchy face, dark skin, reddish body hair, with arms twice as long as her legs, an arm span of 8 to 9 feet. The humans did not let her climb trees or take her to play with the island monkeys, and these monkeys never even acknowledged her with a wave. Deep loneliness became her only companion.

She had been doing this for two years. The repetition. Before that, from a fogged recollection of the past, she remembered trees reaching the sky, far away in a jungle where she could swing free, climb high, and eat fruit until her belly gurgled. Then, humans came, with their nets and cages, and she found herself pushed into one cage after another, sent to this place, where they taught her to spit at humans when the whistle blew. If she wanted food.

At the end of the day, they prodded her back into the smaller cage for the night, her hovel home, offering a ragged blanket and a little more food, the bare minimum. When she was in the jungle, she would build a nest in a tree and sleep 40 to 60 feet above the ground. Safe from predators. But in her cage, restless sleep brought ugly, misty images, and over time her mind and body weakened, listless. Even the chatter of the small monkeys on the island died away at night, as if they feared the morning. And so again, she would count those newly arrived and those who had been removed, to where, she never heard. This was her entertainment to keep her thoughts of her past and what they had taken from her at bay.

ROARK

Two years earlier.

This was to be expected of his life at that moment. Roark was an Animal with a capital 'A. Roark, the movie star orangutan, was the highest-paid Animal celebrity. This evening, he was being chauffeured to the première of his new film, *Mad Monkeys of the Universe*. The studio had taken care of everything, even providing him with a female orangutan from a San Diego wildlife preserve the previous night as a thank-you. He was not impressed; she was uncouth, an animal with a small 'a' who believed that sex (and female orangutans were the aggressors) by rote offered unremarkable, slapdash coupling. He did not feel that she had mellowed out his butterfly anxieties towards *Mad Monkeys of the Universe*, the high-budgeted extravaganza, his greatest accomplishment to date.

And once again, he was in the opening credits, even if placed after his human co-stars; nevertheless, impressive recognition when scrolled: 'and featuring Roark.' He was at the top of his craft.

Public relations razzle-dazzle at the theater was at its best—the press was out in force, cameras clicking like chattering bird beaks, questions chirped around him, fans hooted, cheered, and applauded. With the other stars, he walked the red carpet and was interviewed about the movie, about to seen for the first time with the ensemble cast. One human reporter, bending down with her microphone (as one had to do due to his short stature), asked, "Do you think there will be a sequel?

"Let's not get ahead of tonight," responded Roark with a deep-throated laugh. "If the audience finds the story, with all the action, and my character as a far-seeing oracle compelling, then I can envision more." He, being an 'A' grade Intelligent Animal (IA), could, through a high-tech medical implant, speak English. The reporter, seemingly at a loss for words talking to such a well-known star, hemmed and hawed out of embarrassment before forming another question.

"Do you have an opinion on this law they are proposing that will ban live Animals from circuses? It seems to have a lot of people interested. Do you see that happening in the entertainment industry? Films like we're seeing tonight?"

Just like the press, he thought with disdain, *seeking a 'gotcha' question that could jeopardize his fan base if he gave a political opinion and they spun it the wrong way.*

With his trademark smile, he answered as graciously as possible, "I am only interested in the success of this motion picture, and I hope you enjoy it also." He walked in with the other stars to find their assigned seats. But in the back of his mind, the reporter's question bothered him. *Why would they want to take out real Animal stars in the movies? What would they replace them with? Back to humans in costumes?* To his surprise, he would see a taste of this very unpleasant future on the silver screen as the theater lights dimmed to one spotlight.

The director came on stage and spouted platitudes about how hard everyone worked, giving credit to the hero, the human male lead, as the rebel Space Cowboy, and faked enthusiasm for the attractive female co-star, the princess of a threatened galaxy. Finally, a quick nod to Roark, who waved to the audience like the other cast members, and, like the actual celebrity he personified, sat back relishing in the applause of recognition.

The movie began. And Roark was shocked.

The ending climax.

The destructive fire of neutron disruptors from the last of the Mad Monkeys had pinned down the mysterious Space Cowboy and Princess Aruhu from the star Earendel in the Sunrise Arc Galaxy in the destroyed city of Ozyman.

"This might be our last rodeo, Princess." Particles of building stone from blasters rained down on them.

"We can't give up hope," the princess's voice strained yet strong. "Do you think Oracle Cavor can bring help back in time?"

Space Cowboy fired back at the attacking Mad Monkeys. He knew his weapon was almost empty. "Darlin', I don't know. He was trying to rally the Selenites to your cause."

The small battlefield went quiet. Firing stopped.

Space Cowboy never hid the truth. "The Monkeys are preparing their form of blind courage to rush us. Princess, I won't let them take you alive."

Princess Aruhu understood his meaning and quickly bent to kiss him.

"You are a special man."

"Yes, I know," replied Space Cowboy, expecting the killing charge as he heard the Monkeys build their shrill cries into a symphony of death-chilling screams.

Fifty diseased primates rose and rushed toward them, their leader Kobal among them.

But a new sound entered the approaching maelstrom of howling madness.

"By the Flaming Sword of Deschain," cried Princess Aruhu, "It is your friend Oracle Cavor! And with a tribe of Selenite warriors."

Space Cowboy sighed in relief. "Good buddy, that Cavor."

Across the broken city came a wave of Selenites and, in their lead, the orangutan oracle, scientist, and mystic Cavor. With both hands, he fired antimatter projectiles from vacuum-pressured pistols at the surprised Mad Monkeys, decimating their ranks. He was shouting as he mowed down the enemy.

"Eat space dust, monkey shit!"

[At this point, the audience erupted in cheers.]

The battle resolved in slow-motion scenes of bloody gore. As Oracle Cavor [Roark] walked up to the two now rescued, his lethal cosmic pistols smoking, the evil ones vanquished.

Princess Aruhu threw her arms around Space Cowboy. "How can I ever repay you for rescuing my planet and my fellow Earendals?"

Space Cowboy [looked into the camera] and gave one of his leering smiles of knowing the answer [as did the audience].

Oracle Cavor grunted, "Another Universe saved, eh, Cowboy?"

Fade out to credits. And a teaser (with the son of Kobal) towards a possible continuation of the Space Cowboy adventures in a sequel to this first *Mad Monkeys of the Universe.*

Shocked, Roark reeled. Shocked at the whole movie. It was not *he* on the screen. It looked like him; all the features were his, all the mannerisms. But in the plotting, he spoke with a 'hick' accent when he was supposed to talk in a lilting upper-class voice and act as the Wise Oracle, dispensing advice to give courage to the human warriors before the battle against the Mad Monkeys. And worse yet, his co-starring role had been modified, and he turned out to be a raging 'attack dog' to support the hero and blow away Mad Monkeys with a brace of advanced anti-matter pistols. They had transformed him Rambo-like, from the wise, into an angered, reckless primate. He cursed at the betrayal to his art; they re-created him like a flawed human.

When the film ended, the guest attendees applauded the result. A blockbuster, they all gossiped as if in one voice—*Mad Monkeys of the Universe,* destined for box-office success in its general release into hundreds of other theaters. The departing crowds, especially fellow actors living in Tinseltown, hid their jealousy, silently acknowledging that another sequel was destined to follow, making the key film team quite wealthy. They all remembered the first *Star Wars* film and the franchise goldmine that followed, the merchandising and branding. Millions and millions of dollars to be banked.

From his limousine on the ride home, Roark called his agent, a human named Sammie Leibowitz, and ranted and wailed to the agent that they had taken the scenes he had shot on a green and black background screen in the studio and without his knowledge had rewritten key scenes, digitizing his body and persona movements and CGIed (Computer-Generated-Imagery) the hell out of him. It was him, but not him.

He lamented to Sammie, slamming down a bottle of coconut water. "They took all these camera shots of me, then digitally altered them, probably ran some AI program. They altered all my features and even how I walked, making me a different Animal. They lip-synched a new voice, not mine. Seriously, I know my talent has been damaged. If this goes on and this film makes as much money as they say it will, they'll crank out a series of these space zombie movies." He could voice his contempt, but he had to accept a rosy financial future where he would get, fractionally, salary and royalties, being recast a part of the sequel. "They'll still use my character, as they should. In the end, they left my character alive, essential for future plotting—so what? No other studio or producer will offer me a serious role. And let me expand my talent. I once played '*The Creeping Man*' on television. Hell, I'm on the Walk of Fame. I am an awards contender. I could do *Richard III*. Now, I'll always be the violent sidekick to the superhuman hero. They Chewbacca-ed me. My fans will forget all my previous early-year roles, and then the ten films that made everyone money. They'll remember me as a face on t-shirts and coffee mugs. And no memorable lines except: 'Eat stardust, monkey shit.' I was unaware of all this; they hid it all, defrauded me, and lied to me. They think just because I'm an Animal who thinks for himself, they can dismiss me as being unintellectual and primitive!"

Sammie, his agent, had no chance to calm down his client.

Roark, the star who had spent his career building an image, knew his talent had been compromised. He would be wealthier than he was, but he knew he had been pigeon-holed and his career probably stalled into shoot-'em up fantasy adventures. He felt wronged and sought justice.

A day later, he did what any normally affronted human being, and in this case, an aggrieved Animal would do in this country—he filed litigation through his attorney for damages based on the unauthorized use of his image—He sued the director, producer, studio, distributor, and even the CGI AI who went by the name of Hal.

That was the beginning of his downfall. You don't fight the bosses of Hollywood. They didn't seem to care about Animals even those who were an 'A.'

Stubborn, blinded by his pride and ego of stardom, his belief that his cause, indeed, was righteous, would prevail. Against all other cautionary warnings from his highly paid advisors, he learned too late: power lunch moguls can be more vicious than a pack of jackals.

And all that is demeaning of social media became true and he was eaten alive by vitriolic tug of wars between the click-bait tribes. He had his supporters, but few with a voice to sustain a bulwark crusade. Roark found himself ostracized and belittled in the culture zone which had given him accolades and comfort. As the legal morass oozed along where court dates seeking his vindication became months out, he retreated into below-the-fold, back-page obscurity, his fame diminished.

To the final resolution, not he but the fictional character Oracle Cavor saved him, or rather the consumer demand for the sequel. *Mad Monkeys of the Universe: Part Two: Space Cowboy's Revenge.*

Revenge would likewise set Roark on a new path.

THE CIRCUS ANIMALS

"Did the law pass?" inquired PennyRae, the elephant, moving herself into the line of pachyderms.

"Yes, unfortunately," grumped Emperor penguin, Balfour. "A close vote, though." He waddled back and forth, corralling the smaller penguins. "On the first of the year, all circus animals will be banned from circuses. Proponents said it was for the best, protecting us Animals, but it's forced retirement for us."

"Perhaps our lives will change for the better," this plaintive wish, from Hazel, one of four zebras, each of the striped equines now prancing in place with a monkey on their back, waving miniature streamers.

"Who knows," said Balfour, his voice rising to compete with all the performance prep cacophony. "But above all, we must stick together."

"All right, Animals," shouted Benny, the brown bear wearing a top hat and a collar of red, white, and blue satin ruffles encircling his neck. "Whatever will be, will be. So, let's make this our best performance ever."

Inside the arena the band struck up the martial music, '*Entrance of the Gladiators*', the theme for exaggerated pizazz pomp, and the inner tent flaps opened with a flourish as the clowns entered first, followed by the Parade of Animals.

The circus had begun—the stirring of happy souls.

The entertainers lived for applause, yet as word of the new law spread among them, they sensed the magic under the Big Top slipping away to where memories grow cold and fade.

WILDERNESS VIEWS

Current Day

One morning, Eliza's routine changed. As the sun began its arc, where through the hanging Spanish moss the mist slipped away, other humans arrived—in uniforms—the strangers shouting and waving weapons. And the bad humans disappeared. Her life improved slightly.

She no longer had to spit on humans who laughed at her. The monkeys on the island were all the same number day after day. The strangers took care of all the monkeys and gave her pills. She felt better and more alert. Two months later, a small sign was placed on her cage. And they took her photograph. Could she have read human writing, she would have known that the little sign stated: "Federal Forfeiture Seizure. Asset Auction of Anndwell Monkey Farm; Inventory, Lot #25, Female Orangutan. Born: Borneo. Age 7 years. Genus Species: *Pongo pygmaeus*. Name: Eliza."

Her life was about to change, but she had no say in the matter and could do nothing about her circumstances. Animals like her were animals, with a small 'a.'

* * *

It had been two years since Roark's last personal screen appearance. He felt himself no longer relevant in the eyes of the fickle public's appetite for heroes and resolved happy endings. He spent his days cooped up in an invisible cage. Of course, this 'cage' was his five-acre estate in the San Gabriel Mountains, which he had purchased during his whirlwind days of stardom and fat paychecks. Outside his gated property were plenty of trees where he could go, sit, and brood. Being mostly pine trees, swinging proved awkward with their sticky resin and needles, but pinecones were a delicacy.

Within Roark's inward turmoil, a festering resentment had grown over time, morphing into revenge against the Hollywood establishment, those producers he had initially trusted, who saw him as a mere uneducated animal and treated him as such until the audiences loved him. Quickly beyond those heady days of hustle and after ITSE, he could negotiate better scripts, becoming the recognized sidekick to human stars, finally achieving an increased salary commensurate as a second or third A-lister, and ultimately separate screen credits. It was not superstardom but recognition in the Animal fandom sphere, akin to that of a Rin Tin Tin, Lassie, or a class musical production like Director Billy Rose's *Jumbo* the Elephant. He looked back to the days when he ranked above the actors in more recent films: Frank the Pug dog in two *Men in Black* movies and Crystal, a Capuchin monkey (*Hangover II* and *Night at the Museum*).

Most valuable was the power of ITSE freedom, which allowed no owner or trainer to hold power over Roark. Career decisions were made by him, whether film contracts or promotional tours. Yet still, all decisions were made in concert with and handled by his human triumvirate: his agent, Sammie Leibowitz (commissioned), his Century City attorney (high hourly billing), and his Big Eight CPA firm, the latter to fight the federal audits each year against IRS agents who could not understand how an animal could earn as much as humans. The government intrusion assumed, without evidence, that such a salary resulted from money laundering by unknown human production companies. All outside challenges, with attached publicity paid for by the studios, battled in the courtroom trenches and eventually won.

Certainly, his promising career headed for better opportunities. Not so far along as to sport ostentatious wealth, yet easy street big bucks were coming in, most tucked away in tech stocks. The future looked bright.

Until it wasn't. The premiere of the multi-million-dollar production of *Mad Monkeys of the Universe* undid his world.

He sued the film studio for stealing his likeness by using AI, creating a CGI look-alike to do action scenes that no sane Animal would try. Three years of a legal morass, parties worn out, the case, which was settled out of court only six months ago, involved a non-disclosure agreement. However, according to the tabloids pieced together from leaks, Roark got a huge cash settlement and a royalty on any future use of his image. The studio paid off because they got caught—they thought they could pass off his image as any general-looking average orangutan, not realizing all his distinct facial features were prominent to his Tapanuli species and set him apart as a heartthrob, if not a recognizable brand. The studio was caught in a bind because they had green-lighted the second installment of this series of ape-AI-simulated films, retaining the orangutan character, the first *Mad Monkeys* now doing exceptionally well on streaming cable release. The studio, with a new script, had signed the past actors, Roark, in a legal bravado of defiance, being the only holdout.

Roark won but lost. In the undisclosed settlement, perhaps closer to the truth, it was reported in the media that Roark made nearly five million dollars to allow the studio and producer to continue using his features in the film series. One third paid to his legal team. By this settlement he would not directly act, but the studio-producer could manipulate his image to their heart's (and cutting room floor) pleasure. However, according to the gossip mill, within the terms, he could not participate in any other TV or motion picture as an actor for five years until all sequels ended. He would still have his screen credit as a featured player, a Screen Actors Guild check at a reduced scale (still substantial), and royalties on any brand marketing of his features as a toy or in any AI-generated kids' book. This ten-year merchandising side contract would probably bring in a few more million dollars over this period.

I do not need to work for the rest of my life. Roark sought to make this his new mantra towards future living, but…

Roark grumped around miserably. For the first time since his career launched ten years earlier playing an extra in a Dr. Doolittle remake, he had no direction. Boredom did not suit him. *I am a creator, and I still have talent.* He felt lost as to purpose. *Where to, what next?*

Orangutans, with their facial expressions, make moping into a fine art.

FORCED RETIREMENT

The passage of the SOCA law constituted a life-threatening challenge to all circus Animals' settled existence. This government-passed law outlawing Animals performing in circuses arose from the power of public persuasion from humans. Several examples of abuse in the past were documented by undercover investigations exposing circus Animals in crowded cages and mistreatment when training them. The most outspoken advocates against such Animal harm were humans, mainly consisting of empathetic animal lovers and owners of dogs and cats, who considered that they knew best. These humans rallied under the banner of '*Save Our Circus Animals*' [commonly referred to as *SOCA*]. Over the years, this non-profit organization rose in influence because of the well-placed social media outcry with their exposés and graphic press conferences. Eventually these do-gooders lobbied their cause to victory.

Most impacted among all circus Animals within this busker circuit, the most esteemed were the entertainers of The Cody and Bonfils Travelling Circus, the 'C&B' as it was known in the trade. These acclaimed impresarios of this classic visual art, like their ancestors before them, were integral revenue generators and prided themselves in providing delight to all who visited the side shows, petting zoo, and main circus tent as they traveled the country throughout the summer season. They delivered nostalgia and good memories: *The Circus is Coming to Town* being the historic town crier's mantra, or artistic posters -- *Notice of Coming Attractions* slathered on walls. Children and their parents got their money's worth from an attendance ticket to The Big Top. Novelist Ernest Hemingway once said, "The circus is the only fun you can buy that is good for you."

In the most recent years and during the cold months, The Cody and Bonfils Travelling Circus, the 'C&B,' struck tents, packed equipment and entertainers onto special trains, and wintered in southern Florida, where many other circuses found residences near Sarasota to replenish their stamina and learn and diligently practice new tricks to excite audiences for the next season.

The C&B Animals were the ultimate show performers: talented, smart, and, above all others of their kind, quite shrewd. They were model citizens, erstwhile employees, never demanding. Still, with their ability now to speak English, they wisely maintained a loosely organized Animal representation team known as the Executive Committee. They had power, more a perceived pride of their worth, but not to any extreme. Yet, beware, if they felt wronged, they might institute a mass lay-down, or after some slight or grievance, as the displeased employee, they might piss on a customer.

Such events were few and far between, and quickly arbitrated to resolution. Wisely, both circus owners and the Animal stars negotiated for appropriate conditions related to their status and importance. Enclosures were enlarged, and special dietary food offered. And, without prejudice, all were provided with the latest in veterinary medicine, and any new members hired to this artistic company gained free ITSE insertion. With this back-and-forth communication and fair contracts, there had never been a scandal with the human handling of C&B Animals or a complaint from the Animals themselves. Their bond was not that of master and servant, trainer or beast, but as co-workers.

The best example of their 'intelligence' could be observed when the C&B Animals established a Rainy-Day account, managed by them, where a small deductible cash percentage based on their food cost was invested in Certificates of Deposits, not to be touched except in an emergency. Over the last few years of circus operations, this token contribution had grown to be a sizable deposit on call against any stormy deluge that might wash out show performances. Fortunately, no weather or labor dispute shutdowns had occurred, but SOCA created the tempest and, in the end, forced the circus Animals into retirement.

Many circuses forged on, seeking relevance, and several even tried to go virtual, with artsy fake AI-generated screen displays of Animals or with no animals employed, instead using only human gymnasts and contortionists. Sadly, they found they could no longer match the flair and ambiance of an actual old-fashioned Animal-celebrity circus. Most operations folded their tents for good. Several circuses sold out their animal inventory to wildlife sanctuaries or city zoos. Animal brokers suddenly blossomed. The worst were under-the-table transactions involving individual humans who ran 'hunting' preserves or individuals seeking to own their own 'wild' animals, to be housed in a bedroom or basement, hardly under the best conditions.

C&B Animals took an entirely different and progressive route.

In a mass meeting, adamant and unanimous agreement passed in a quorum vote by all C&B Animals to work on a solution where they would not split up their Animal family and be 'resettled' apart [sold off like common farm animals]. General consternation followed such a brave decision. *What to do?*

Fortunately, Board Members, Hazel, the Treasurer Zebra of the C&B Animals, and Events & Publicity Chairman Mercedes, an elderly orangutan, believed they had a solution.

RoarUni Fact

Hear them. Communication exists for all animals. Bees perform a 'waggle dance'; chimpanzees greet each other by touching; gorillas signal anger by sticking out their tongues; many animals release 'smell' pheromones to attract mating partners; Fiddler crabs wave large claws to attract females, and peacocks display elaborate feathers for courtship. And affection, elephants entwine trunks, giraffes press their necks together. To suggest playtime dogs, bow their front legs and stretch out. And today, Intelligent Animals speak to humans.

THE EXECUTIVE COMMITTEE

C&B Animals, as was reported, operated under the auspices of an Executive Committee. It would be mistaken to assume certain beasts held leadership roles ranked by size or ferocity—or the hierarchy of the food chain--not so in a circus.

In this instance, the Intelligent Animals (IA) of the C&B were consistently recognized universally as elite and highly selective talent, not a menagerie but a troupe of specialized actors. Such acclaimed circus animals do not generally act as humans (except when perhaps in showtime costumes). They do not take on human personalities and foibles, naming themselves as characters who desire to mimic the traits of humans. They are their own creatures with hereditary habits of nature, of the 'wild,' unique unto themselves. They are not cartoons nor AI movie-generated monsters (as shall be seen). They are not overweight creatures who can fly with large ear wings, nor do they look like teddy bears, go looking for honey, have a piglet and donkey as friends, and hold banal discussions on depression and friendships.

In truth, Intelligent Animals abhor anthropomorphism.

What is perceived as a human attribute placed on a fictional animal is invalid, with circus Animals presently transformed by *ITSE*. They are intelligent to their quirks. The circus IA leadership structure is an example against this misperception and a nod to individualism. Look at the Executive Committee: *

Balfour, Emperor penguin (Chairman)
Larry, lion (Vice Chair and Association Secretary)
Skye, brown eagle (Operations & Building Committee)
Mercedes, orangutan (Publicity & Events Committee)
Hazel, zebra (Treasurer & Finance Committee)
Huntington, elephant (Rules & Regs Committee)
Benny, black bear (Building Maintenance)

---

* *Historically, naming an animal (usually a pet) might receive multiple names, the humans trying to be 'cute' or pretentious, whereas circus Animals received only one stage name—single names simplified circus inventory listings. As events unfold, this timeless single-name moniker would soon transform the IA world dramatically.*

DECISIONS MADE

In early November, as the C&B Circus made its winter camp for the last time, the meeting of the newly-formed Association was held in one of C&B's large tents near the town of Sarasota, Florida, where, as mentioned before, most of the past historic circuses wintered.

Chairman Balfour called the meeting of the Executive Committee to order and asked Secretary Larry to read the minutes of the last session.

Larry cleared his throat. Within the C&B, the lion pride consisted of Larry and four lionesses: Calypso, Calliope, Clio, and Sekhmet. The latter being the strongest and assuredly the dominant mate in the group's hierarchy. The other three, never born in the wild, would never be defined as 'huntresses,' and today, no longer entertainers, they spent their time each day basking in the sun or watching television, attracted to novella dramatic romances, where they sang and danced out the various episodes.

It was Sekhmet who decided that Larry would serve on the Executive Committee to report all happenings back to her. She would decide what Larry's vote would be and what was best for the entire pride regarding any significant votes of the Committee. Instead of watching trashy television, Sekhmet preferred to watch international news on the internet, as well as the local news, a devourer of human political culture.

Larry, quickly adapting to his retirement mode, as he had when not on the circus stage, treated each day as a day to be wasted in languid style. He did not relish his position on the Committee, though it met infrequently. Instead of paw-slow note-taking, he digitally recorded the meetings, then had Orville, the only C&B chimpanzee, later transcribe the discussions and votes into readable notes, which Larry would then edit down to succinct paragraph points (the fewer, the faster) for his report. However, today's reading of the last meeting's deliberations had been momentous for the Animals and required some historic demonstrative showmanship. Larry brushed his mane with a flair for regal emphasis.

"It was agreed that we would file the formation of the 'Southern Florida Herd Association' with the State. Chairman Balfour has already taken steps with our outside human legal counsel to trademark both 'The Herd Association' and the shortened version: 'The Herd.' Around the table, there was mutual agreement. This key decision severed the cord, the final dissociation from the Cody and Bonfils name, and thus the relationship with those humans of the circus family. It had to be done, though the parting retained fond memories for many. They were to be on their own, and their independence must be reflected as such.

Larry continued: "The Executive Committee then approved the establishment of the Operations and Building Subcommittee, with our colleague, Skye, as its head, responsible for defining and securing our future home for all Association members.

"Finally, we had a report from Rules & Regs; a draft of the Association's by-laws and rules was circulated, and a vote is expected today." At the end of the table, Huntington, the bull elephant, nodded and pointed to the 30-page document before him. He stood near the table (no chairs had yet been constructed for him).

"Huntington," intoned Chairman Balfour in an officious voice. "Your trunk is leaking on the table."

"Sorry, Balfour," said the elephant, removing his dripping nozzle appendage. "I have a cold."

Larry, as Secretary, finished his report, and Chairman Balfour asked Skye to update them on the exciting and anticipated plans for their new home.

Skye was a brown eagle. The C&B had hoped to acquire a bald eagle to play the part of making a dramatic entrance during the grand 'ring parade' during the show's finale, with all participants taking bows with patriotic martial music and the swoop of an eagle with an unfurled flag in its talons. Skye had bested all contenders during the audition try-outs, and the show owners felt an eagle was an eagle, and his ability to make a grand entrance, wings majestically flapping, was what counted, not necessarily the color of one's feathers.

Skye hopped from his perch to the table and began beak poking through his notes as he brought everyone up to date. One of the great things about eagles was their ability to spot prime real estate locations while skyborne.

A map lay open in the middle of the table, the central focus on the coastal tourist town of Short Skiff Key and the surrounding area, located on the Gulf side in Florida, south of Tampa Bay, south of Sarasota, north of Venice Gardens, off Highway 41, towards the ocean between small boat canal waterways.

Skye pecked at the location.

"The Kure Steel Fabrication Plant is 35 acres within the Short Skiff city limits, but on the east side in a more rural section with access to the highway. The plant had been shuttered since 1974 due to stagflation and could not handle higher interest rates, nor could it service debt against offshore, cheaper steel marketed in the U.S. Back then, the country had a 2% economic contraction, and the Dow hit its historic low that year. The city's Urban Renewal

Authority bought the property about ten years ago, but its citizenry could not decide what to do with it. The real estate has sat vacant for years, overgrown with weeds and vandalized by graffiti. Then, we came along.

"It suits our purposes to a T. There is a major common area within the old plant, and there are multiple rooms that can be divided to fit tenant needs. Several rooms have high ceilings for the giraffes and a cooling room that we could chill for your brethren, the penguins, Mr. Chairman.

"There are two attached storage warehouses, one where I feel Huntington and his friends can comfortably move around, and the other could be a lion house." Skye glanced at Larry and got a smile in return. Larry, of course, would have to run their new housing by Sekhmet. She would probably direct the other lionesses to decorate. The brown eagle offered a compelling concluding point. "There are ten acres used in the past for finished product outside storage. The rusted pipes and coal bins can be cleaned off and broken into various roaming pastures as they fit our membership. The question is, are we near a sign-off between Short Skiff Key leaders and ourselves? I believe we are."

Skye looked to the Sub-Sub Committee members. Besides himself, this included Chairman Balfour and Treasurer Hazel of the zebra contingent. Hazel interjected as if it were her cue.

"We have reviewed the documents with our counsel and are satisfied. We will purchase the property with a down payment of $800,000. Our Rainy-Day Fund can afford this, as well as the money for clearing the property and at least half of the estimated pre-remodeling construction in a minimalist concrete style. The Association membership will pledge, as rents, half of their

Government Trust stipends* received to service the mortgage. Regarding renovation costs, the First National Bank of Short Skiff Key will advance with a short-term loan. I support this project and move that this Committee approve the proposal, contract, and financing." Skye flapped his wings, his way of seconding the motion.

The motion passed without dissension. Instead of English-voiced cheers, the Animals resorted to their original noises of excited approval, a cultural release of tension, suggesting deep-felt satisfaction. They were now the owners of a future home, an apartment complex with a diverse tenancy to be housed within.

---

* *As part of the SOCA law, the Government set up a trust fund with a 10-year monthly stipend for all ex-Circus Animals to assist in their transition to private living.*

MERCEDES

Thus, it came to be that the Association renovated the Kure Steel Fabrication Plant into the South Florida Herd Apartments, known as *The Herd.* The move-in, at the end of Spring, came off as a well-choreographed event, placing everyone into a 'no-cage environment' better than they had ever hoped.

The only sadness, though more an awkwardness, was separating themselves from the Cody & Bonfils Circus, where they had spent their years entertaining. In the same way, by government law, the trainers and 'animal handlers' also found themselves forced into retirement; some but not many would re-educate and run new carnival amusement rides brought in to replace the animal acts.

All seemed well in the new housing environment, and the Herd Apartments ran efficiently from the opening day. Sadly, as it is to be, six months after opening, the female orangutan, Mercedes, Newsletter Editor, Publicity and Events Chairperson, and a member of the Executive Board, died in her sleep.

It was not unexpected as she was somewhere in her early fifties, which is quite old for a female orangutan. As she had told her friends, she could not remember a birthday or anyone to remind her of one. Of all the circus Animals of the C&B, it would be surprising to know that she was native-born to her heritage habitat as a pure Tapanuli from the Batang Toru region of Sumatra, Indonesia. All other C&B Animals were born as third- and fourth-generation naturalized locals, never knowing their ancestral roots nor hearing stories of the old country.

Mercedes had been 'captured' as a baby and, through various traders, sold to a circus that prided itself on an 'ape show' of performers. During this time, after 8 years, she became sexually mature, and two years later, from another Tapanuli primate, gave birth to a baby male who grew up to have a Tapanuli mate and bore another male child, still retaining pure Tapanuli genes, a rarity in captivity, and quite a valuable asset. Mother and son became featured performers until bad management closed the primate show, and the 'livestock' was dispersed and sold off at auction.

Heartbroken at the loss of her son and his family, which, in turn, split up, Mercedes went to the C&B with her cries of loss unheeded (Animals, even the entertainers back then, did not speak conversational English). The circus owners only heard untranslatable moans and grumbles. Years afterward, through the circus grapevine, she learned that her son had died from an unexplained illness, most probably indigestible food trash offered unwittingly by a human child. Near the end of her life, she had only one living direct relative, her grandson. And as a prized property, at an early age had been sold; this time not into a circus but to a company that trained animals for motion pictures and television programming based in a city called Burbank in California.

Over the years, Mercedes started collecting her memories of her circus career, and in her faded scrapbook of clippings, she included pasted highlights of her grandson's burgeoning career. She was proud when he first appeared in a newspaper entertainment section. One sentence mentioned him as a contract player in jungle features, and later she scissored out more tidbit stories when he graduated to sidekick roles, usually along a Great White Hunter actor in swashbuckling films, always shot on the lots of a Burbank studio.

Mercedes could see, first by watching his bit parts on cable during downtime at the circus, and later on Movie Night at The Herd Apartments or in the movie fan magazines, that her grandson showed talent and was going places. Over his formative years as an actor in training, he had grown, his physique developing, part of a male testosterone surge, prominent mustache, large side flanges covered in downy hair from cheekbones to temple, and a noticeable skin sack beneath the chin, which gave his voice strength in vocal commands, primarily a strong frequency long call, louder than his cousin Sumatran and Bornean orangutans. These features inspired adoration among the female orangutan population, with words like 'star' and 'idol' being applied to him. A handsome male orangutan with dominant oozing sexuality has that effect, and a rare Tapanuli at that (only 750 of the total pure population survive today).

Her grandson's stage name was Roark, just Roark, strong and beautiful. Yet of his personal life, his grandmother knew little, and because of their separate situations, no effort sought to establish a relationship with him. Lineage tracing among Animals never caught on, being too traumatic, with most internet searches quoting: 'Bred/Eaten' or 'Shot/Eaten.'

Mercedes knew he was family and that he was safe, comfortable, and doing exceptionally well. For herself, after years of entertaining crowds with C&B, management retired her from further showmanship exertion and let her be an interesting sideshow exhibit. In her free time, Mercedes became one of the founders of the C&B Animal Benevolent Association long before the SOCA law was even imagined. When the legislation eventually passed, shaking up the industry, the Association formalized its Executive Committee and granted it central power. Mercedes continued with her responsibilities, now living a simple life, running the Association's monthly newsletter called 'The Heard', and when the Herd Apartment Complex opened, she relished in planning social events within the complex, and puttering around the community garden cultivating durian fruit for herself, and eating ants to protect everyone else's planted plots. With her passing, all at The Herd mourned her with deep sadness.

In her will, she had made a bequest.

Out of nowhere, and totally unexpectedly, Roark received a letter from the attorney of The Herd Apartments in Florida. His grandmother had died and named him as her sole beneficiary. Among her few assets, now his, was a valuable lease-tenancy apartment in The Herd.

THE DILEMMA

The Executive Committee of the Association had been informed by their counsel that Mercedes had bequeathed all her estate assets, including rights to her apartment and contents, to her grandson, Roark. However, they were surprised when they received a letter from a law firm in Beverly Hills bearing a *very* long list of partners emblazoned on its letterhead, informing the Association that the grandson wished to move into his grandmother's apartment at the earliest convenience.

A special meeting of the Executive Committee convened to address this unexpected and challenging issue.

Chairman Balfour, a prominent Emperor penguin, made the issue serious with his usual act of hopping on the table and stomping around. In preparation, earlier, he had asked Huntington, the elephant board member, to look at the Rules and Regs, and the eagle Skye, to do a background check on this 'Roark' orangutan. However, several Association members and tenants had spoken to their representatives (the Executive Committee) and excitedly explained that Roark was well known nationally as a successful performer, an entertainer *like they all once were.* Still, to the Chairman, this Roark was an outsider, an interloper, not one of their Circus family.

By utilizing Huntington's research, they had dealt with death and estate disposition among other Association members, but this bespoke an anomaly. All previous members who had passed on were part of a group and housed communally, as was their preference. Mercedes, as The Herd's only circus orangutan, saw herself as distinct and had always been separated from the troop of monkeys who chattered endlessly and swung among tree branches crafted in The Monkey Garden to their architectural design.

Mercedes, one of the few residents with her own apartment, a large one with an extra room to house her memorabilia. Piled sealed boxes spoke to years highlighting performances of a noted actress known for her many caricatures of face manipulation.

As an elephant, Huntington did not have to glance at the thick documents of the Rules and Regs nor the gobbledygook quicksand of the 'Save Our Circus Animals' legislative law. As expected of his reputation, he had a good memory.

"By the law," explained Huntington to the Committee, "when a circus animal dies, whatever the circumstances, then the government stipend amount paid to the recipient ends and disappears."

"We have made provisions," offered Hazel, the zebra Treasurer, with further clarification, "for this possibility with our Rainy-Day Fund to cover any shortfall. Nevertheless, to the Association, it is a monthly loss of revenue, and such funds, as we know, go towards mortgage reduction."

Chairman Balfour said, "If we don't have an immediate need for the cash, I say, let's keep the apartment vacant until a committee is formed to find another use or a new tenant among ourselves." Perhaps the underlying thought was that Balfour might, as Chairman, believe he was worthy of such an upgrade. He had often groused that in his colony, all his fellow penguins, the lesser King penguin variety, seemed beneath him, enjoying their carefree waddling without responsibilities, frolicking in the icy bathing pool, and munching sardine sushi with wasabi. Not said aloud among many tenants, but given Balfour's status as an Emperor Penguin, some felt his Chairman title might be going to his head.

"Let's not be too hasty," squawked Skye, not wishing to see another committee formed. "My internet search and a few calls have brought to my attention that this Roark is quite wealthy. Four years ago, he was the highest-paid animal actor in the country."

Growled wistful Larry the lion, perhaps with a tinge of envy, "That would have been the aspiration of any one of us back in the day if we just had a good agent and a social media influencer to promote us." All around the table agreed. A circus animal could no longer achieve mega-stardom when faced with the obsolescence of their career due to unwanted legislation.

"I've been thinking," said Hazel, using her financial mind and quietly counting under the table with her hoof as a type of equestrian abacus. "We should offer this Roark his grandmother's place. I see advantages, not just the money, but perhaps added new blood, hearing fresh stories of his career to entertain ourselves at our group events. I am tired of all the repetitive on-the-road tales and the show gossip we've heard dozens of times."

"I agree," affirmed Skye. "And he does have a family tie; that's one strong criterion he meets. If he wants to move from Hollywood to a Florida apartment, that's his choice. And such a relocation can be to our benefit."

Chairman Balfour saw that he might not sway the discussion his way and conceded in fake humility, but with an idea.

"If we offer him the open apartment, we should do so at the full stipend amount for his rent. Maybe even more. As you say, he can probably afford it. And let's make this a one-year lease with extension options, with the provision that the Association can deny him an extension if he doesn't fit with our membership. Circuses and Hollywood might be alike, having a plethora of entertainers, but they are distinctly different worlds and cultures. And there may be a failure to communicate for the good of us all."

RoarUni Fact

Animals have strange group names. A group of parrots is known as a 'pandemonium'. Buffalo form an 'obstinacy' and rhinoceroses a 'crash.' The collective noun for porcupines is a 'prickle'. There is a 'murder' of crows, but what about an 'exaltation' of larks?

THE CLOWN

The Executive Committee felt this would be a good offer, and they delegated Skye and Hazel to exit and make the call to the LA law firm representing their client, Roark. A quick recess, and when they reconvened, a few glitches arose from the long-distance negotiations.

"The attorney accepted the lease amount and length of the term with the one caveat: that Roark bring along his employee," explained Hazel somewhat hesitantly, "From the description, he acts like a butler, a jack-of-all-trades, to handle this Roark's needs."

"Well, I guess another orangutan can be viewed as a tenant with this Roark," affirmed the Chairman. "Let's adjust the lease cost, add another half for rent." Chairman Balfour saw dollar signs in this transaction, a slight bonus to offset an actor's frippery of requiring handholding to any West Coast whims. The Chairman wondered to himself, *What else might they squeeze out of this piggy (monkey) bank?*

"No," said Skye with slow emphasis. "I've learned from Roark's attorneys in this matter. *Not* another orangutan, but a human. And not just any human. This fellow was a Hollywood stuntman before he was injured and became a domestic servant to Roark. Because of his injury, he can't speak. Or perhaps he can't speak well. Not sure I heard correctly. And strangest of all, he was a circus clown before he worked in movies. And while in that job, ironic to his injury, he never spoke while in character."

Hazel jumped back in.

"Roark's attorney said that back in the old days on the circuit, he was known as the clown, Silent John Bertuccio."

"Silent John," nodded Larry in remembrance. "Isn't he the black human clown who wore whiteface?"

"That's him," agreed Skye. "I got a brief bio emailed to us. [Skye glanced at a print-out.] He's not African-American. He's an immigrant of North African colonial lineage. Maybe Italian-Ethiopian. He came up through Italy in pantomime farces, and in the States, he joined the Circo Atayde, then Sparks Circus, before Ringling bought it when they consolidated a few other circuses. He gravitated to California, where he started as a bit player in movies excelling as a gymnastic and pratfall stuntman. His story is somewhat vague, but from a trade magazine source, I read that in a Tarzan movie remake, as an African warrior, he took a death scene fall from a cliff, and somehow, a sharp rock hit him in the face, crushing his throat. Something like that. Uses a type of voice modulator on the larynx." Skye chirped out a joke, "He's a half ITSE." They all chortled, laughed, and whinnied—a human who was less than human.

"Bummer for him," Larry said with his trademark low growl but with understanding. He knew the dangers of being an action entertainer. In his younger days, he used to jump through fire hoops at the crack of a whip—a lot of singed hair.

"We can't have a human in our apartments," the Chairman's firm opinion.

Hazel put forth a heartfelt observation. "If Mercedes instead of a quiet passing had had a stroke and required in-home care 24/7, under the circumstances, the nurse would be human, probably a live-in." She looked to the Chairman. "Or would you put her in a convalescent home, away from us? No, we are family forever and together."

The Chairman gave her a stern glance, trying to mask his disapproval. It was not that he was for sending anyone, like one of the prancing horses, off to the glue factory. It was just that 'rules were rules.' And the Association must operate under one spirit of obedience.

Larry must have read his mind. "There's nothing in the rules forbidding live-in help," said Larry, looking at the Chairman. "At least not one yet on the books." He continued, "We haven't had to deal with this situation before. We might consider it a one-off exception. After all, this Roark is not an original Association member. An exemption does not undermine current Rules and Regs. To me, a silent servant does not suggest he'd be bothersome." That was the most Larry had ever spoken outside of reading past Board minutes. He was a 'nay-or-yea' sort of lion. Sekhmet, his outspoken mate, made the hard decisions. He wondered, *Should he confer with her and ask for a postponement? Or call her during a bathroom break? Yes, he would do that.*

"And he's a former clown." Skye put in. "Seems sort of coincidence or fate to come into our enclave. Look at the bright side: Silent John will take care of any eccentricities this film star brings with him; he must be one of these celebrity personal assistants I hear about."

Trying to seek a middle ground, Huntington put in his peanut's worth. "Well, it's not as if Silent John is seeking his own apartment."

"Maybe we should ask more for the apartment?" suggested the Chairman, testing the Committee's temperature.

The Executive Committee eventually rationalized the exception to the unstated rule of Humans in Residence by qualifying Silent John as a required member of the medical staff. Maybe the truth was closer to this Silent John being an *emotional service companion*.

* * *

"Why didn't you just put all these animals down and be done with the headaches?" the auctioneer's comment on first viewing the stock of the Anndwell Monkey Farm. "They're a sorry mess."

Eliza heard the human's voice but had no comprehension of what was being said.

"That came under consideration," came the response from the government agent coordinating the sale of assets. "But the damn animal activists got wind of the plans and raised a shitstorm."

"All I know is how to present the junk I'm selling in the best possible light. We have one month until the auction, and you people need to put a little weight on these apes. Fluff them up, if you want to get a good price."

"I couldn't care less", said the government man. The place stank; it was drenchingly humid, and even his eyeballs were sweating. He wanted to find a bar nearby, not be involved in shutting down this back-country rip-off. But he had bosses to report to, and he could make himself look good. "Okay, I will bring in some vets to shoot them with vitamins, and we'll increase their food."

"It'll help. In one month, I could sell them all." The auctioneer had been staring at Eliza.

"Whatever. They're just animals," said the government man, and he sought the air conditioning of his car.

EXILE

"Who are you?"

How the mighty have fallen.

Roark, the actor, the star, still in his primal youth, beaten but not physically, arrived at the Tampa Bay Airport, an orangutan on a mission—one of revenge. Roark was here on sabbatical, a retreat, an escape, whatever it was.

In career limbo in his industry, he had been blackballed and blacklisted, a pariah to those close-knit moguls of power.

It did not show in his countenance. He could play many characters, and his outward mien at this moment was one of indifference, seeking no attention. Impartial to the curious. His face held a smile and a nod if the humans stared too long as they tried to guess who he might be, then accepted that his dismissal as an accepted celebrity might do, except for the kid with his mom, who, at the baggage carousel, had asked innocently enough. The boy must be tuned in. He wore a 'Teenage Mutant Turtle' t-shirt.

"Who are you?" The small boy repeated his inquiry. Roark ignored him.

The answer came from a vibrating voice nearby: "He is Roark, the star in ***Mad Monkeys of the Universe…*** and other films."

The boy looked at the man just arriving, pushing a cart laden with luggage, each stickered with distant destinations, several of which were from international film festivals.

The boy jumped in terror and cowered behind his mother.

That was understandable. The man, a black man, was a clown of sorts. His face was painted white, his lips in red paint exaggerated in an upturned smile, Joker-like. But what heightened the boy's fear was that this man's face was half-covered by a white plastic mask, not a Halloween-type mask tied on with a rubber band but affixed at an angle as if glued on flush to the skin, perhaps in the style of the *Phantom of the Opera*, if the child had seen the show. The mask left half of the clown's face showing.

Finally, below the man's head, wrapped around his neck, was a white plastic tie-sized wrap of the same material as the mask, and centered in the middle of his neck across the throat was a strange square of black patches like a soft metal quilt, about four inches by four inches.

The clown's face had no expression as he asked in a mechanical-like vibrating voice, "Would you like a signed Roark photo?" And Silent John took a pre-signed studio photo of the star from a satchel draped over his shoulder and handed it to the boy's mother, who reluctantly took it. Backing up, she was likewise startled by this costumed aberration. She noted that this white-faced black man had addressed them and spoken, but his jaw, mouth, and lips barely moved. The neck wrap delivered the voice. Mother and son quickly departed, to the worrisome look of the other onlookers, many of whom were distancing themselves; was it shock or uncertainty about what this man represented?

"Is he a movie star?" could be heard from the boy being yanked along, pulled quickly by his mother, seeking a greater distance from a perceived threat to her child.

"No," said the protective mother, "He's just an animal." To whom was she referring?

Roark signaled to John and climbed onto the baggage carrier. An airport porter pushed the carrier towards the waiting limousine.

Roark did not like walking in public spaces. Though he wore a silk shirt and tan cotton slacks, he wore no shoes. What shoes would be comfortable…or stylish? Besides, airport floors were dirty from travel and slobs. He would have to bathe when he arrived at The Herd Apartments and his new residency.

Roark's exile had begun.

RoarUni Fact

Orangutans are highly intelligent; they share about 97% of their DNA with humans. Infants nurse on their mothers for four to five years and stay in their mother's nest for about seven to eight years. Females raise their infants alone. Orangutans can live 40 years in the wild, over 50 years in captivity as an 'a' animal, and 62 years with an ITSE implant.

HERD APARTMENTS

"A splendid edifice," remarked Roark from the limousine, taking in the view. What he saw was a grouping of several attached structures, like building blocks with a six-story central feature resembling an upturned shoe box and descending in a building-block manner from three stories to two to one story of various concrete square and rectangular shapes. What brought the hodgepodge into a cohesive unit design was the color scheme; all buildings were painted white except for the extruding edifices of window edges, roof lines, or accented protrusions, which were painted in soft angled variations of aqua, orange-yellow, and light cherry red—a circus tent visual effect.

Roark looked for the proper description. "Historic Miami shares the same palette, or likewise, white with blue accents found along the Greek coast, or candy-colored Dutch Colonial on Curacao in Willemstad. It's like Art Deco slams into Bauhaus architecture."

Then came Silent John's rasping voice, "But is this a place of refuge or a prison?"

"Let us hope neither."

A formidable mesh wire fence surrounded the building assemblage and acreage grounds, tied every fifteen feet to concrete pillar posts. New landscaping had taken root, and trees, larger than saplings, were interspersed with hedge plantings that would, in years to come, form a formidable visual barrier. Passersby strolling the outside perimeter sidewalk gawked to catch sight of any residents—the Animals--usually a rarity.

At the vehicle entry, a shiny brass plaque announced: "***The Herd Apartments.***" The main gate opened inward, and the limousine entered a circular courtyard drive, stopping under a newly constructed classical porte-cochere.

"Your warders are here to greet you," said Silent John, presumably with a smile under his make-up. Roark couldn't always tell the hidden significance of the man's words.

At the building's entrance were a bear and a zebra. Roark and Silent John noted that the two Animals were moving back and forth, a sign of nervousness.

Silent John offered a reflective comment with prophetic elements.

"Perhaps they see *you* as the new warden."

SCRIPTED TOUR

The Welcoming Committee consisted of Helen the zebra, an Executive Committee member and Association Treasurer, and Benny, a rust-colored brown bear, who introduced himself as Director of Facilities, Operations, and Maintenance.

Helen made herself sound officious. "We are pleased that you will be a resident at The Herd, our community of elite talent, of which you will now be a member. Benny here and I will give you a tour of our exclusive apartment conclave. There will be a small get-together greeting held later, around 4 p.m., in our common lobby area. All residents have been invited.

"But first, let me personally extend the condolences from The Herd Executive Committee and all residents for the loss of our dear friend, Mercedes, your grandmother."

Roark merely said, "Thank you. I knew little of her or her career. I will have to learn more from you about my grandmother's qualities." He offered no more, looking at the building, and the welcoming committee took this as a hint.

As they begin walking the premises, neither zebra nor bear cast their attention to Silent John, who followed behind Roark.

Benny carried a thick folder with him as he walked and talked.

"I have brought a copy of our Rules and Regulations for The Herd Apartments. We encourage our residents to read this document thoroughly and familiarize themselves with its contents.

We believe that since we have a diverse Animal population, we all strive to live as a cohesive unit to gain mutual harmony."

Roark nodded, not in total agreement. To harmony and peace, yes. But living by set rules, not so much. In his past career, accepting limitations was not part of his vocabulary. Now, here, on his part, his behavior would require artistry in acquiescence.

As they strolled through the buildings, Benny explained the amenities and how to use them. Roark was impressed—the modern equipment of the exercise room and the eating areas was indeed impressive. However, he noted several troubling approaches in the presentation, primarily the overall Association's operating philosophy.

Human interaction with the Herd Animals (the IAs) was to be discouraged or kept to a minimum wherever possible. Humans were not encouraged to be in proximity to the apartments themselves, and the buildings were finished by design so that no humans could see the Animals enjoying their daily lives.

As Benny explained to Roark, showing him an outbuilding off the major interior thoroughfare, veterinary services were offered here where Animals requiring check-ups or medicine would have to go and meet human medical personnel on a private and selective appointment schedule.

In a sympathetic voice, Hazel pointed out an enclosure where a variety of small animals slept or, if moving, did so in a stupor. The Animals viewed included a small donkey, a miniature horse, goats, geese, and a few pigs. A camel and an elephant, both female, stood in support, talking to the smaller creatures in soothing tones. Within the enclosure, on a television screen, repetitive ocean waves rolled in and out, their motion varying with light rain falling and flute music playing in soft tones. Hazel proudly explained. "These resident friends of ours were in the C&B petting zoo, and most have been diagnosed with stress issues caused by human children's 'over-touching' abuse. We seek to bring them back to appreciate their worth, not as human playthings."

The tech media integration most impressed Roark, but with mixed thoughts. Television sets were everywhere, in all living units. Free-to-use computers and iPads were in all the common areas, and first-run and classic movies were shown twice a week in the lobby arena.

Hazel was proud of this social media communication system, even saying with a smile, "There has been a recent demand for access to the entire library of your films, Mr. Roark. There may even be an invitation for you to give a lecture on your time in Hollywood if that is acceptable."

"Roark is fine. That's the only name I use. And I would be happy to make myself available, but I would like to wait until I settle in." That was the tactful response, and Helen seemed pleased.

As the tour wound down, Roark's realized the residents' dependence on social media. Everywhere he saw Animals, they were absorbed with their tech devices, and most of the entertainment he saw being watched seemed to be animal shows, with nature documentaries being the most popular (a *suggested* Rule on what to view, but not mandatory, he was told). Even when he saw the exercise grounds set aside for running animals or another enclosure for climbing animals, he noticed that though they could exercise or bask in the sun, such activity gave them ready access to television screens scattered everywhere, outside and inside. Notably, there were no commercials or advertisements since the Animals did not require human contact to purchase marketed products; therefore, the space between shows was reserved for news and announcements by the Executive Committee, such as programs announcing group events or veterinary scheduling. However, most posts reminded all residents of the Rules and Regulations that they must follow to maintain a cohesive and happy community.

The last stop, off the elevator, on the top floor, and down the corridor: his grandmother's previous residence, his and Silent John's new abode. Before the apartment was a small wagon carrying Roark's (and Silent John's) luggage, which had been off-loaded from the limousine at the entryway by Elizabeth and Darcey, two tapirs, acting as porter-messengers. On the tour group's arrival, the tapirs slipped their harness apparatus and went their way. Roark was expected to take in his own bags. Silent John stepped up to unload.

"The resident gathering get-together is in about an hour," explained Hazel. "We look forward to introducing you to the entire assembly of residents." She paused, then said pointedly, "It is an Animals-Only social event." No invitation for Silent John.

"Your two-bedroom apartment was designed as a mini-suite," said Benny, finishing his tour, "Being located in this wing has quite a bit of privacy as many of the other apartments are vacant for future use, though Orville, a chimpanzee, is two doors down, and his and your apartments each have a back door into our Primate Garden. The other primates are housed as a troop across the garden in their own group enclosure. You will find the garden pleasant and perfect, with mature trees for climbing and sitting around. We have even placed TVs on poles so you can view TV shows from a high perch."

Benny unlocked their apartment and handed over the keys to Roark, along with the Orientation Packet with Rules and Regulations, and various announcement memos, which Roark passed to Silent John. As Benny and Hazel began to leave, for the first time, Silent John spoke in his gravelly tech voice and addressed Benny specifically.

"In the C&B Circus, you were the star as the Animal Ringmaster?"

Surprised at this recognition and not knowing how to talk to this human, presumed to be Roark's 'Man,' Benny stumbled out a reply.

"Yes." He felt that would not be enough. "They wanted me to lead the bears as a dancing ensemble, but I could not learn the steps, regardless of how hard they pushed my training."

"You were quite featured in the poster advertisements."

Benny did not know what to say next, and Hazel snorted a whinny. The tour was over, and bear and zebra departed after Roark had thanked them for helping him acclimate to his new home.

The door opened, and Roark entered a drab and sterile interior. His grandmother's personal effects were piled in the corner in taped boxes. Furnishings were basic, although, for orangutans, various mock and rigid plastic tree limbs were built into the living room and bedroom walls. There was a modest kitchen, but since food was supplied and not cooked, most of the appliances were dusty and unused. The refrigerator, however, had been recently stocked with water jars for sucking and what looked like plastic containers of leaves, durian fruit, and assorted fresh vegetables. One container held gourmet pickled grubs and ants—a pleasant 'Welcome' perk.

"Somehow, John, I intend to make my stay pleasant."

"This is more a convalescent garret than what you have been used to."

Roark sighed at this truth. "A little discomfort will make me stronger. I, *we*, shall endure until our triumphant return." He headed to his bedroom and jumped on the mattress, testing it. "I shall take a shower and then go see our new hosts. I would appreciate it if you could handle the unpacking."

Silent John nodded and began his task of arranging all that they had brought with them.

RoarUni Fact

Animal extinctions are more recent than you think. Golden toad (2019), Pinta Tortoise (2015), Mountain Mist Frog (2021), Chinese Paddlefish (one of the largest freshwater fish (2019), Po'ouli, also known as the black-faced honeycreeper (2019), the Brazilian Alagoas foliage-gleaner, a small bird species (2019). Just to name a few of many.

CURIOUS CRITTERS

After pleasant introductions were made to all the key members of The Executive Committee, Chairman Balfour asked the all-important question: "And what are your plans with this residency? Any hobbies to enjoy, or is it merely a well-deserved retirement sojourn?"

Roark absorbed the Emperor Penguin's inquiry as a fear that his arrival and stay would be troublesome to their carefully orchestrated anti-human agenda. Roark had no desire to be an intruding activist. He was here to revitalize himself and plot his return to Hollywood. He sought to assure his small audience that he would be a model citizen.

"I am here to rest, recuperate, enjoy beautiful Florida, and also to lock myself away and write my memoir."

"I have always wanted to write my own story," said the Chairman. "But so much more to accomplish."

"You hold a worthy position," smiled Roark, turning to others of the Executive Committee as they raved about the wonderful life to be experienced at The Herd Apartments.

Roark, with the Committee as his gatekeepers, formed a variation of a receiving line, and the general population of the Apartments trekked by and, as entertainers themselves, puffed their importance in their introductions, many querying him with questions of the curious or ignorant and/or rude. He knew his responses had to be sensitive and politically astute since, no doubt, any answer would be broadcast quickly as opinionated gossip among all residents.

Said one, an ostrich named Ralph, his head bobbing with an agitated tic. "You brought a human with you. I think that is incompatible with the Association's charter."

"In Hollywood, we must work closely with humans. John is my associate and researcher for the writing I will be focusing on."

A pack of four white poodles approached him, and their spokesperson made the point, "We noticed you arrived wearing human clothing—The Association has a rule that we all should feel free enough to go au natural."

"Of course," another poodle added, "dress is accepted if one ever goes out into the human public and away from our buildings, but we only go out on special occasions and in supervised group tours, approved on a trip-by-trip basis."

Roark listened attentively. "I have no problem going without clothes (he wore none for this event) in this great setting, though I am surprised you are not allowed to wear the entertainment costumes of your circus days."

The poodle leader scratched behind her ear as she responded, "The Association decided that since we have retired from our circus life, we should dispense with any vestiges of those days." As an afterthought, she said, somewhat wistfully, "We were part of the famous Dancing Diamond Poodles, and while within the ring, dressed like royalty. But those memories are behind us. Besides, two of our dance line, a male and a female, were adopted by our trainer. That destroyed our close-knit unity."

And so it went, with Roark being gracious, answering questions as he could, listening to those who wished to relate their past careers.

The gathering ended with everyone feeling all would be right and that the movie star Roark, as a new resident, would be a positive addition to The Herd.

RoarUni Fact

The pangolin, a small scaly anteater, is the worlds most poached and trafficked animal due to the high demand of their scales and meat in Asian cultures. 70% of Chinese citizens believe pangolin products have medicinal value, though scientifically proven to be false.

CASUAL ASSISTANCE

For two weeks, Roark indulged in his self-imposed hermitage, seeking new directions and desiring that special mental light bulb to click on, sparking his Creativity to a Plan of Action. One direction was not going well. His attempt at starting his memoir hit the proverbial wall of writer's block—*when your imaginary friends refuse to talk to you.*

His discarded memoir openings included: "I spent much of my childhood listening to the sound of humans striving and animals being told what to do."

Or "I am the Invisible Orangutan."

His last effort stared back at him on his computer screen. Only the first sentence: "Call me Roark." He turned to review his life, accumulated press clippings and news stories that John had cataloged and placed into a timeline series of folders. For sure, there was something of him that deserved a new stage to reanimate his hibernating fans and gain a fresh audience.

During the early days of his residency, the first honest friend that Roark had become acquainted with was Orville, the chimpanzee, who had taken over his grandmother's position as editor of *The Heard* community newsletter. Orville became Roark's news (gossip) source on what was happening around the compound and outside the Apartments in local town activities, and beyond to greater world events. Orville bore insecurities, caught between his desire to be a published creative storyteller and the easier, more comfortable job as a part-time journalist dealing with press release facts. Orville and Roark quickly became simpatico in their talents and mutual interests and could easily discuss current literature on best-seller lists or explore Animal issues in the human-controlled world.

According to ITSE, all tech-modified Animals were limited and controlled in what and how they could work as employment, primarily in service positions to humans, where they could take orders. Restrictions were not legal forbiddances, but for years were unstated as 'that's the way it is.'

Listening to Orville's intense heart-felt opinions, Roark found the chimp's dialogues too idealistic, leaning to radical ideologies, specifically his views expounding that all Animals must be free of humans, the Herd's catechism position, but realizing all are animals (humans being of the homo-sapient variety), the first step in goal attainment being: Animal rights must also equal all rights enjoyed by humans.

Roark himself held no set beliefs except in his career, where his primary and central focus was accepting how the game was played. He had to get along convivially with humans, though many of those he worked with treated him as 'lesser', a 'minority.' Survivability and flexibility might best describe Roark's floating philosophies.

To believe in a better Animal future, Orville, though he would not admit it, had to accept living with current hypocrisy, accepting his new circumstances of being at The Herd, on the human government dole (the monthly stipend), while subscribing in print to many of Save Our Circus Animal's (SOCA) pro-animal welfare positions. This human support group for improving Intelligent Animals' best interests supported Circus Animals becoming 'free but cared for.' Orville readily endorsed their new campaign, the

'Back to Africa' movement. The root of this movement was that those ITSE Animals and lower animals who were not inclined to assimilate into the human world could opt to be repatriated back to their ancestors' home country. Of course, most animals interested in a resettlement program no longer had immediate families or relatives in Africa or South America, but it was a solid battle cry that created public interest. This *Back-to-Nature Animalism* rang of idyllic romanticism. Orville, who had gained the advantage of a better life, being an Intelligent Animal who could talk, and importantly, *think*, assuaged his guilt by speaking out for lower animals, those unrepresented, disenfranchised without a voice.

The Herd Animals held no desire to return to a foreign land. They appreciated the country they had grown up in, enjoyed the current standard of living (from the Government), and the Apartment standards of self-seclusion. They would go nowhere internationally, let alone away from Short Skiff Key. The amenities were too good, and what if, where they migrated to, there was no internet connection and bad Wi-Fi service? Heaven forbid!

One early morning, a floral-scented crisp breeze drifted before the day's humidity descended and pushed residents to the beach or air-conditioned living. Orville checked out the Herd's self-driving AI-programmed street golf cart and gave Roark the basic tour of Short Skiff Key. Their leisurely travel took them through the two-block historic downtown area fronting the oceanside roadway and a turn-of-the-century small boat harbor, with a rock dump constructed breakwater featuring a photogenic wooden pier and rusted iron piling. A palm-lined parkway led away from this varied commerce of insurance companies, sea-themed restaurants/bars, and tourist tee-shirt/beach product shops, taking them winding through the residential neighborhoods ending at the freeway, where, if going further east, the lost tourist might discover the rural area of scattered vegetable and fruit farms bordering swampy sloughs.

Orville had no real agenda to present to Roark by this tour, but he did not need to verbalize what the 'star' could see for himself. Short Skiff Key consisted of the usual Floridian humans, those seeking a slower, calming lifestyle. For the animals, the few seen by Roark were employees taking care of cleaning stores or grooming gardens and lawns. If they were on the downtown street, they were running errands and in a hurry. Homes for ITSE-speaking animals were small apartments concentrated near the freeway. Of course, when they were noticed, humans and animals stared at the two primates gliding along, seemingly with no cares in the world. Reactions, if any? Were they seen as simple-minded oddities or arrogant interlopers?

"Yes, Manor Farm, located across the freeway, had a few speaking animals, and they tried a farm-to-table café. Tourists looked in, but few stopped to take a closer look. I think the animals did not have a business background or lacked customer service training to make it work."

Roark acknowledged the answer and thought no more of what he had seen. At this time, given his circumstances, he gave it no importance. His distracting thoughts were about his own problems. He might even admit to himself, if he even considered it, that, as a celebrity, he had come from and still lived in a 'bubble', oblivious to the outside world and its realities.

Another day, while in conversation with Roark, Orville said, "Did you see that article I emailed you on the Anndwell Monkey Farm in Mississippi? They were shut down under a federal seizure declaration, and the court ordered the liquidation of all their assets, which included the animals they owned. The owners are out of the picture, already found guilty and sentenced to prison."

"Remind me, what did the owners of this Farm do?"

"They were masking their tourist tour farm for animal trafficking in rare endangered species and running an illegal monkey baby-mill factory for research labs." Orville handed over a paper copy of the news story. Roark perused the article.

"Animal abuse by the human owners?"

"Yes, most certainly, but little details of their crimes." Orville paused before launching into his real reason for bringing the subject to Roark's attention. "Several animal rights groups are banding together to try to save these animals. SOCA wants to acquire any of these animals at auction and put them into their 'Back to Africa' program. However, they don't have the financial resources or have yet to establish a placement system to send them back to their countries of origin. I spoke to Chairman Balfour to see if the monkeys from this Anndwell Monkey Farm could be housed in our primate troop apartments, but he refused outright. Even if temporarily, he saw this as a 'pollution' of ignorant monkeys versus the current entertainer-educated ITSE residents."

Roark understood Orville wanted something from him, and he sought to short-stop any request for involvement with SOCA causes. He was no card-carrying member or affiliate supporter of fringe causes like Orville.

"I could probably make a small donation, maybe for the auction or help your friends find housing somewhere for displaced animals."

Orville handed him another piece of paper. "Of course, any amount would be helpful. Here is a list of the animal inventory the government is auctioning off. I thought the animal listed, #25, might interest you."

Roark scanned down.

#25 Female Orangutan. 7 years old.

"When's the auction?" Just curious. Roark was not heartless. He could feel empathy, at least to his own kind, while at the same time maintaining an aloof rule: no desire to get involved. He had been constantly battered by fan requests, most of which were turned over to a studio secretary to send out a formalized decline.

"The auction is this weekend," responded Orville, holding his breath.

"Well, you know, I am not an activist. Certainly, I'm concerned and abhor any animal abuse, but I can't be a savior to everyone. And I assume she is not even ITSE."

"Probably true. The owners couldn't care less about her. These humans were lowlifes, but since this was a 'front' using a tourist show, and she's the only orangutan, I'm guessing they used her as a showpiece attraction. If so, she could qualify as an 'entertainer' and be eligible for the ITSE operation."

Roark read more about the inventory and this primate named Eliza in the sale notice.

"Who knows," said Orville, sensing he had Roark's focused interest and shrugging his shoulders with fake indifference, "these animals will be sold off to, maybe another wildlife farm with poor conditions, maybe stuffed in small cages, or to an unlicensed zoo. The government gives lip service but is not the best enforcer of animal health and safety."

"Well, why don't you and John look into maybe helping out somehow? Nothing over the top. And leave my name out of it."

Roark's attention shifted away from saving distressed animals to the underlying currents of his own dissatisfaction and writing his memoirs without self-excitement.

WELCOME MAT PULLED

Roark's basic plans, his return to Hollywood, and revenge against the elite power brokers aimlessly wandered as loosely undefined structures mulling around in his thoughts. He decided to spend a good half year thinking of his best strategy. He needed to plan a strong public relations campaign, rebuild his fan base, and create or discover a 'hit' script—a film vehicle he could personally star in with no stunt people and no artificially digitized look-alikes, but where he was *real* and the sole and primary star.

He and Silent John spent their time in seclusion, making their apartment livable and decorating it with Roark's art collection, original poster renderings featuring his movies, and a few signed lithographs of artist Henri Rousseau's jungle primitivism, which had been shipped to him shortly after his arrival. His grandmother's boxes of personal items were stored in John's room, several boxes piled up as legs to support a work desk.

A few weeks later, Roark decided to take advantage of the Monkey Gardens and do some shuffle exercising and tree swinging.

At his entrance, he was immediately accosted by some very unhappy monkeys, a mixture of Capuchins, Mantled Howlers, Yellow Baboons, Vervet, Spider, and Macaques. Their aggravation was apparent as they chattered and jumped around, screaming as if they had been confronted by a hungry leopard.

"Why did you portray us in such a bad light as evil killers?" asked a scar-faced primate Capuchin, who went by the name of Edgar.

It turned out that in their curiosity about the new tenant, they had recently viewed, just out on cable, the first *Mad Monkeys of the Universe*.

His excuses gained him no respite: "It's a work of fiction." He even threw out, "I had no control over what they did in editing."

Others cried out: "Do you feel primates killing primates [his AI character wielding destructive monkey-slaughtering weapons] is fair to us peace-loving creatures?" They jumped from tree to tree, shouting abuse, "Mad orangutan, mad orangutan!"

When some flying poop hit him in the back, he retreated to his room.

His next venture out went no better. Roark arrived in the common space area to sample the 'Happy-Hour' hors d'oeuvres and found himself facing a lioness with attitude.

Her immediate complaint. "Your presence has the local town council wanting to interfere in our desire for privacy. Since we are low profile, they want to encourage your involvement in promoting their Chamber of Commerce tourism."

"And you are?" Roark tried a disarming smile.

"Sekhmet. Larry, my mate, is on the Executive Committee."

"Well, you can tell whatever human you feel will listen that I appreciate that they think I still have promotional value, but like all of you, I am here to be a recluse, to seek anonymity." (Believing it would be 'only temporary anonymity'). I will draft a letter for me to sign, and you can mail it to them."

Sekhmet growled. "No, that will not be necessary. I will speak to whoever is in charge. General human contact is avoided. Our general population seldom goes out."

"Everyone is confined. Like a zoo?"

She gave a low growl again. "Our Rules and Regs give everyone guidance, and our enjoyment of freedom is the right not to intermix with the human world. Privacy is security."

"Well, since I am not too restricted in that regard. I will be going to the beach with John to exercise, eat bananas, have conch chowder, and take a siesta."

"There is the Monkey Garden for you to enjoy."

"It seems an exclusive club, and I have been asked not to apply for membership. I have been in similar circumstances where I came from." Roark belonged to no human private clubs.

The lioness tried to glare him down, as her ancestors might have evil-eyed a gazelle on the Serengeti, but Roark gave her back a wide-toothed smile, gums folded back, and ambled away without having tasted any of the charcuterie munchies on the buffet table.

Sekhmet had her power, but with frustrating limitations, through controlling Larry to voice her opinion. The orangutan drew out a sore subject. The former circus Animals were still adjusting to their new surroundings and the imposed Rules & Regs. And not totally to her regal liking, the self-appointed Kings and Queens of the Herd were the Executive Committee.

SAND AND SUN

The afternoon trip to the beach was not that wonderful. Roark and John became the curiosity of those seeking the sun-kissed sand. Short Skiff Key residents may have had circuses wintering nearby in Sarasota, and recently, in their village, there existed an apartment complex full of exotic ex-circus Animals (all unseen). However, the curious and some obnoxious humans could only stare hard, making the outing awkward.

The orange primate and masked clown did their best to enjoy the ambiance, sitting on Tiki Shark motif beach towels, and protected from UV rays under an umbrella featuring *Shellfish – the Movie* designs (Roark had an ape cameo in this motion picture).

Both sought to ignore the rude or frolicking, sun-roasted humans. Yet, one visitor in particular did catch their attention. Along the wet sand of the incoming tide, a disheveled man walked slowly, trailed by a scraggly mutt—a dog without its hind legs—tied in harness to a small wagon on skids, awkwardly pulling, front paws digging into the sand. Occasionally, the man would bend down and pick up a discarded soda can, beer can, or other surf detritus and place it in the wagon. When he did that, he would pet his dog and continue his beachcombing ritual. Another man's trash…

Roark saw a homeless beach bum with a handicapped animal and prayed he would never fall so low as being destitute or without a limb.

John saw man and beast as symbiotic, dependent upon each other's needs, but wondered if there was not a better life for either, separate.

It was on this day at the beach that one of the local humans snapped a photo of Roark, his back to the camera, sitting on the beach by himself, staring out at the flat, untroubled Gulf waters. Whether Roark was resting, contemplating, or in spiritual meditation did not matter. The photo was uploaded online, picked up by the West Coast tabloids, and plastered in many gossipy publications with headlines like: "Star Flees to Florida. Is Career Over?" Or with more half-news scrutiny, "Roark Marooned. Living with Ex-Circus Animals."

As to the celebrity in him, if not diminished by the paparazzi's glossy ridicule, Roark could understand why some of The Herd Animals felt reticent at themselves being out in the town trying to be normal, meaning, like humans. He accepted that enclaves did have a purpose. Like millionaires in guard-gated compounds or celebrities in tight industry pecking-order circles of award self-congratulatory ceremonies. Clans, sects, class, or fraternalism. This effect of tribalistic crowd security was that they mattered only to themselves and no one else. And there was that separation because of ITSE, animals frustrated for direction, handicapped with limited human traits.

Not Roark. Even in his doldrums, he had an inner core of self-belief. He accepted his stardom as self-achievement and fan recognition as his due. Always the loner, he never held membership in groupthink nor subscribed to bad press as the final chapter. A setback is a pause. To Roark's mantra, a primate of talent is never defeated. Roark was aware of his strengths long before ITSE gave him the voice to articulate what he already knew of himself.

Though he accepted the general assumption that other animals could gain advancement, Roark had not really paid much attention as to why they had not. Maybe the lack of fire-in-the-belly, or the better metaphor to his kind: their failure to reach for the best fruit at the highest branch in the tree.' Bluntly, Roark looked inward only to his goals and held little concern about others' ambitions.

He was here, at The Herd, among his own 'creatures' solely to strategize and discover how best to prove his abilities weren't atrophied, that with the right showcase, his career would burst into standing-ovation resurgence, both to the public and to himself, more than ever before.

But sometimes, even for an actor, life can change the script.

RoarUni Fact

African buffalo herds display voting behavior, in which individuals register their travel preference by standing up, looking in one direction, and then lying back down. Only adult females can vote.

CATALYST #1: THE AUCTION

The Auctioneer moved quickly through the list of mobile equipment, the beat-up cars and panel trucks, then on to assorted tools. The buying crowd dwindled. A local hospital bought the medical equipment for pennies on the dollar.

The highlight of the auction, the animal inventory, became anticlimactic when it was announced that the monkeys, from the island, would be offered not individually but as a lot. Four bidders raised their numbered paddles, and the purchase soon went to a human named Harold, standing between a black man with a hat pulled down to his eyes and a medical mask across his lower face, obscuring his features. The other attendee present was Oliver, the Herd's chimpanzee, but here for his own purposes, at this point, trying to bolster Harold's courage. The human, holding a bidding paddle, looked nervous and fidgety, as this was a momentous occasion for his group, SOCA, for he had been chosen as the representative to bid on all these island monkeys, for it was hoped they would be the first trial group to be repatriated to Africa.

Orville encouraged Harold that he would become a hero, and in the midst of fevered bidding, SOCA's bid was accepted with the cry of 'sold', paying perhaps more than anticipated, and with no real game plan of what to do next. Orville offered the advisory support of Roark the movie star, though the famed orangutan had made no such commitment.

As the auction drew to a close, #25 went to bid, and the auctioneer primed the diminished audience with all Eliza's glorious traits, mostly made up on the spot. Harold thought he should bid for this female primate with the sad face, but Oliver dissuaded him, explaining that she might be a distant relative of Roark, and Oliver was instructed to see what might happen.

The auctioneer felt a little disappointed with the action when only two active bidders went against each other – a bidding war between the auction number paddle raised by the chimpanzee and a scrawny-looking Chinese fellow standing next to what seemed to be his interpreter. The dollar amount moved up, thanks to the skill of the auctioneer's baited sing-song cry. At one point, it seemed the Asian man would prevail. But at that heightened moment, the black man quietly glided away from the chimpanzee, walked close to the other bidder, and stared, removing his hat and facial covering to reveal a crooked smile. The Chinese bidder, a believer in omens and huài yùn [misfortune]shuddered, turned away, and the auctioneer, anxious to be done with it all, his eyes locked on the paddles and seeing one bidder's hand lowered, slammed down the gavel, declaring the victor. Orville felt pleased at his victory, yet smartly gave accolades of 'well done' to Harold of SOCA for his purchase of a troop of 'untamed' monkeys.

Eliza had been in a state of quivering fear all day, not knowing what was happening, who these ugly humans were who crowded around and gawked at her. She hid her eyes and only started to look up when she heard the jungle talk, not English but noises of a fellow-like creature, though she could barely comprehend.

Her gaze fell on a chimpanzee, dressed as a human, smiling at her, and she was even more shocked when the chimpanzee turned to two humans, one man, the color of dark rock, wearing a mask, and another human, conversing with them in that English tongue, as if they were friends.

She wondered to herself if she had heard right. The chimpanzee had told her, making a chattering expression, in orangutan pidgin, something like: "You are safe now. Be brave."

What is going on? she wondered, which turned to fear as two other humans dropped a covering over her cage.

* * *

Several days later, Orville sought out Roark and said matter-of-factly.

"Well, what do you want to do with *her*?"

"What? Who?"

"Eliza. The female orangutan. You were the top bidder at the auction. Congratulations." Orville gave the animal benefactor a bemused look, realizing Roark had forgotten about his offhand comment that led to a commitment to 'rescue' this unfortunate fellow creature.

Roark did not need the headache. His agent had just sent him a bundle of scripts to read. One could be *The One*, his comeback vehicle.

"Ok. Ok. I suppose I don't want to see an animal story end tragically. Keep on it. Get her somewhere safe in the System."

"You're the boss." Oliver left.

That would be that. Roark turned his attention to his scripts.

CATALYST #2: THE TREE

Silent John provided the next catalytic change of direction in Roark's life. John, tired of nit-picking fighting to check out the Herd's only golf cart to run errands, had gone to an auto dealership and leased a behemoth SUV for him to drive as the chauffeur and go-fer companion to Roark.

Driving back to the Apartments using a back road, avoiding traffic congestion on Highway 41, his drive took him on a crumbly, pot-holed asphalt road past a swampy area bordered on dry land by older commercial buildings now shuttered.

A catastrophic human epidemic years ago killed 40 million people worldwide, and to the detriment of animals, an investigation blamed monkey lab testing. The subsequent quarantine shutdown bankrupted many small businesses across the country, including in Short Skiff Key. The block of buildings that Silent John now viewed consisted of a long row of failed shops, several detached stand-alone office buildings, and one dilapidated Victorian house, previously a funeral home. Among the buildings, what Silent John saw made him return with Roark. But not to see dilapidated structures.

Near the backwater swamp, a large banyan tree squatted magnificently behind the boarded-up funeral home, next to and against what had been the employee parking lot for the strip center buildings. Roark marveled at the tree. Immediately, he jumped out of the SUV and swung into the foliage, a happy primate.

Unknown to Silent John and Roark at the time, which they would later learn, banyan trees are rare in Florida. Their origin is from India and surrounding humid countries, where temperatures would never drop below 55 degrees. Historically, manufacturer Harvey Firestone brought a banyan sapling to inventor Thomas Edison in Fort Myers in 1925. As nature often reproduces, birds eat the fruit and spread the seeds. One seed fell, planted, and flourished more than one hundred plus years ago in Short Skiff Key.

Roark romped within the tree, easily hiding himself in the branches and drooping vines—hidden privacy, a key stimulant to Roark, as well as substance. A banyan is a fig tree that develops accessory trunks from adjacent prop roots, allowing the tree to spread outwards indefinitely. The Great Banyan tree of Kolkata, India, has 2,800 such dangling roots and is the largest tree specimen in the world.

Roark only saw a future playground for himself, away from bitter, unappreciative monkeys.

Finally resting, sitting on top of his newly leased SUV conveyance, he noted the property's *For Sale* sign and asked John to make an inquiry. "Yes," said the real estate agent, "It is still available. Additionally, there are a couple of adjacent empty lots if you are interested in expanding. We have had a couple of interested parties who want to clear everything off and build high-density apartments, but I must say the market economics and population concentration around here are not quite ready for that grandiose kind of project." What the realtor did not say aloud was that Short Skiff Key did not draw tourists like the other coastal destinations; it was a hodgepodge pass-by village without distinction, without a tourist 'hook'; hence, businesses struggled to keep their doors open.

The price quoted, John asked if a counteroffer might be acceptable. Yes, responded the hustling realtor, himself starved for commissions. Tempered his eagerness "An offer I am sure will gain serious consideration."

John saw Roark's pleased expression and recent enjoyment of exploring the massive tree.

"Well?" queried John, "Are you seriously interested?"

Yet second thoughts festered in Roark, his sudden caution: "*What would I do with this property? Of course, I can raise the cash. Sell the commercial office I own in Santa Monica. Then, I won't need financing…but…?*"

John had no opinion but wanted to see his boss happy and out of his funk. "Any offer should have the standard clause to investigate problems developing this property. There must be a reason it has been sitting vacant for a couple of years. I have a gut feeling a lower counteroffer might move the sellers."

And that's what Roark did, through the realtor, not revealing who the buyer was. A 20-day due diligence option was gained for the property, pending a closing date to finalize the land purchase. The buying entity would be, under the appropriate name, 'Banyan Tree Enterprises,' which John had incorporated with the Florida Secretary of State. The incorporating lawyer became the business agent, keeping Roark's name out of the legal filings; Roark was the only shareholder.

A SURPRISE GUEST

"She's in a motel near here?!"

Roark was in a meeting with John and Orville discussing Herd Apartment gossip and brainstorming what he could do with this banyan tree property if he exercised the option and acquired it. Deadline two days hence. Did he want a new project? Become a developer? Or once the land is cleaned up and the buildings torn down, flip the vacant property for quick resale?

"You said to take care of her, and we did that," said Orville, not defensive but reminding the movie star that his direction had been obeyed.

John gave his support. "Although I have seen her only once, it seems Eliza, this orangutan, is quite intelligent."

"You said you saw her once?"

"Because of her captivity, terrible conditions, she has an intolerance to humans." Silent John was kind. A detestable hatred of humans would have been a more appropriate response from her. Teeth bared.

"And you had an ITSE installed?"

John affirmed. "When I incorporated Banyan Tree Enterprises, I listed 'educational institution' as one of its business descriptions. The local vet who services the Herd residents is ITSE license certified. Your Eliza did quite well. Recovering. No medical side effects."

Roark frowned. He did not like the applied affectation of 'your Eliza.' he needed to find her sanctuary, some other place, far away. To Orville, Roark inquired, still not knowing where all this was going and what his responsibility might be. "Is she learning English and understanding how human society acts?"

"Catching on quite quickly." The ITSE implants were not Frankenstein-esque, changing an animal into a human. Animals by nature have a series of physiological barriers that block conversion to homo sapiens capabilities. ITSE can short-circuit and reroute brain signals to create the animal that maintains all its hereditary DNA but develops an entirely new 'channel' to allow for certain human-like functions, as in speech and broader thought process patterns, to be built upon. Not a 'cartoon' talking animal, but intelligently cognizant. [See 'Appendix']

Within this implanted *clean slate*, a blank channel requires language and behavioral education. The ITSE Governing Committee offers a series of videos/CDs and online audio programs to accelerate the integration of basic Intelligent Animals into the human world. These are teaching aids on the English language and information on the human world, with subtle suggestions that newly processed IA ought to learn a great deal from humans. One presentation bluntly noting that Animals should consider humans more as their benefactors than as equals.

Orville, who had once gone through the program himself to become an Intelligent Animal, as did Roark, as did all IAs, now found the indoctrination pure propaganda brainwashing and told Roark as much. "She is learning quickly. I'm impressed; she's a smart one. Some of the government programming is now repulsive to me, so I have been giving my perspective, The Herd story, as an example of Animals thriving, not solely dependent upon human generosity."

Roark did not know if he liked Orville teaching an ITSE student a dogma that might be in contrast to the idea of Animals and humans working together, the Herd model, instead integrating into the human world as he had learned and risen within, which seemed to work fine for him. And now, this.

"But you put her at this motel? She can't stay there forever."

Silent John affirmed, "I agree. Once she has finished the courses, we need to find accommodation that will allow her to flourish." He and Orville exchanged glances, Roark not realizing once more he was being nudged towards a decision he did not wish to make.

So, a week later, Roark requested an appointment and visited Chairman Balfour's office at The Herd Apartments. He had thought long and hard, talked to John, then Orville, and finally decided on his approach.

After exchanging pleasantries, he got to the point: "I would like to rent that open apartment down from me. I have a cousin who is coming through town to visit."

"Well, we have short-term guest quarters for Animal visitors."

"She might be staying for a month or two, maybe longer. She wants me to take her around the State on an extended vacation I have the time to make day trips."

"That long of a stay? Our guest quarters are free for short stays, like a couple of days. We would probably have to charge you for anything longer." Chairman Balfour saw dollar signs. "Probably could do a six-month lease, half of your annual rate." The Chairman was pleased when Roark grumbled at the pricing but accepted with the throw-away line: "If she leaves early, I guess I can use the space for overflow storage of my Hollywood furniture and knick-knacks yet to arrive."

The Chairman was pleased, believing he had gained the advantage of this wealthy primate. A fun game of one-upmanship from this bird. As the conversation ended, he asked, "When will she arrive?"

"In about two weeks."

"And for our records, what is your cousin's name?"

Roark did not miss a beat. "Eliza. She is pleasant. Quite talented, an entertainer herself." Roark knew her name and had the Bill of Sale to prove ownership.

RoarUni Fact

Emperor penguins are the least common Antarctic penguins, with global population estimates of 265,500-278,500 breeding pairs. They are uniquely adapted to survive harsh conditions when temperatures drop to -50° C with winds up to 200 km/hr. Emperors have two layers of feathers, a good reserve of fat and proportionally smaller beaks and flippers than other penguins to prevent heat loss. They have leg feathers for further warmth. Male Emperor penguins will not eat up to four months; from the time they arrive at the colony to breed until the egg has hatched and the mother returns to feed. They lose almost half of their body weight during this time.

TAMING THE SAVAGE BEAST

Roark had no experience, ill-prepared to be a 'caregiver.' When he heard more about her living in a cage, he opposed the injustice; as an infant, he had been there. He did his part. He realized that in the same transaction, Oliver had assisted SOCA in buying the small troop of monkeys at the auction, and that he, Roark, promised SOCA (via Orville) to make a modest donation to provide them clean and comfortable housing. Roark accepted that his generosity would put these monkeys into the SOCA goal of the 'Back to Africa' program as a test and promotion. Roark had little faith in that pie-in-the-sky malarky, but it might earn him some points, so he went along and let Orville have a 'good chimpanzee' moment.

He accepted that he would directly sponsor one Animal, this fellow orangutan, into a better environment. Well, he had convinced himself that his actions had no doubt saved her life. This gave Roark satisfaction; the first step had been the rescue and her purchase, little knowing that these next steps—educational, and societal insertion—would be similar to using a ladder to climb a mountain.

Oblivious to his thinking was Eliza, the sold 'inventory,' now recovering.

* * *

Eliza woke up in a motel room, looking into the face of a chimpanzee. That chimp, from the auction. Her head hurt.

Confusion. All her emotions welled up, feeling where the pain came from, realizing she had stitches on the back of her head, and she began screeching until the chimpanzee smiled at her and said quietly, in English.

"Hello, Eliza. I'm Orville. Welcome to your new life."

Overwhelming, paralyzing shock stilled her when she recognized Orville speaking with his first word, "Hello," and encouraging her to try to repeat him. Her attempt at the word came out strained, along with the fearful revelation that she could mimic him and say human-speak—she could sense what the word implied. During her first few days in this new 'captivity,' she realized that this Animal was trying to help. That she had become this Intelligent Animal, no longer just an animal. She cried when she understood that her abuse had ended.

So began intense immersion with the training tapes and videos Orville had obtained. He had rented two rooms in a run-down motel and cleared out most of the furniture. After meeting with Roark, Orville's task was to get her to speak basic English and understand that she would be moved to a housing unit where Animals ruled themselves—where lions no longer ate primates, and that a penguin was the leader. First, she must learn simple rules to get by, emphasizing that she must stay within her apartment, away from other Herd Animals, until she had mastered English-speak and basic human customs.

One day, a week later, while studying with Orville and going through her learning programs on a computer screen, the motel room door opened, and she looked up to see the most gorgeous male orangutan she had ever met in person. Immediately, she knew he was Tapanuli, a rare breed. Eliza's later computer search discovered that among ITSE female orangutans, a Tapanuli was considered a remarkable conquest, even though mating with one was prohibited by human scientists who sought to preserve species purity. This, she could not understand. To her, not yet matured into the fertile stage, mating was mating. Sniff, and scratch the itch, so she later read on an internet soft porn site that pandered to ITSE's Animal urges.

"I am Roark," he said, and sat in one of the few chairs in the room. *Very Human*, she thought, noticing he dressed quite well, stylishly—like them, like humans.

"I am Eliza," she said in a slow conversational tone, blushing when he smiled at her. Then he turned to Orville.

"How is she doing?"

"I think she is capturing the concepts, thought to speech."

"Will she be ready? In, say, ten days? That's when I want to bring her to the Apartments."

"We need to improve her intensity, but I believe she can do it." Oliver smiled at Eliza.

Roark turned to her and said, in a paternal manner, "Eliza, I will now be here once a day for two hours. I will be responsible for teaching you various everyday expressions to understand and respond to questions you might be asked. I have brought you some new *How to Speak English* computer videos. Very basic—I don't want you sounding like a stiff robot."

Eliza had no idea what he was talking about, but it sounded good.

Roark's second, more critical job was an introduction to *good* humans. "I know you have been through a difficult life, and you have a bad opinion, rightfully so, of humans. I understand. But to be out of a cage, which you are now, you must learn how to live and relate to humans you might come in contact with." He then called out, and hearing his name, Silent John walked in. Eliza recoiled and snarled.

Roark shook his head. It was a more difficult situation than he had thought. Silent John was his only man-friend, and his clown mask was not the best representation of what a 'nice' human might look like.

"Eliza," explained Roark. "This is my friend, John. He wears a mask for his own reasons. Please give him the benefit of the doubt. I have asked him to work with you one day a week, looking at human situations on television and explaining them to you. If you wish to guard your freedom." He looked to her for a reaction. English-speaking gave Eliza an open world in which to process and express her thoughts, but she stayed silent, wary, and suspicious.

After Roark and John left, Orville did his best to convey what Roark had glibly voiced, knowing she did not understand but must see the intent behind it. From Orville's slow explanation, Eliza decided she would do what the 'gorgeous' male orangutan told her. You must trust your own kind, but at the same time, she wanted to learn so much more beyond this 'acting' required to be accepted by Animals who were strangers to her.

As the process became intense, and between them, her three 'teachers' had decided not to expose her to standard human television programming, including violence, current international news of wars, and even depressing human drama shows, that revealed human foibles and flaws. Such truth would come in time, hopefully not by direct experience.

RISKY INVESTMENT

In the rush to bring Eliza into The Herd, Roark found himself simultaneously dealing behind the scenes with the acquisition of the 'banyan tree' property.

He and John had learned that the property was prone to flooding in intense storms or water surges, even though it was two miles from the ocean. The swamp land near the banyan tree at the property line was environmentally protected, meaning it had been left untouched, but it was now filled with human trash and invasive weeds. Occasionally, a news story spoke of python sightings in the lagoon swamp. During the boa-python-constrictor hunting season, people waded through the property looking for elusive reptiles to collect cash bounties.

Next came the zoning issues. Although commercial zoning existed, any building permits would require the approval (i.e., participation) of the Short Skiff Key Town Council as they sought to direct what new businesses might replace the existing buildings where deterioration required demolition.

What amplified Roark's decision to purchase the property, which to others might have been trivial, was his learning that Florida had no law protecting banyan trees. For example, a banyan tree was removed in St. Petersburg because it did not fit the developer's purposes. Any request for banyan tree removal occurred easily with the support of sympathetic politicians. Destroy, build, tax. Banyan trees, which could live as long as 500 years, were iconic symbols of strength, resilience, and longevity in historical religions and philosophies. To those in India, these trees were symbols of home and family, and they might take care of a tree within their families for generations.

Roark could understand. He had found a tree that could be all those things to him. Save a tree and save an orangutan. *Short-term good deeds*, he told himself. This was just a lark, an emotional purchase, something to do, with Hollywood redux, his true goal. Okay, he would do something to keep himself busy. His memoir project was now shelved for the time being.

Taking the risk, he plunged; Roark became a Florida landowner.

* * *

No closed political meeting is ever secret.

The Short Skiff Key town leaders came together to meet the new owner of the abandoned commercial property to discuss ideas for future development, seeking to regenerate their moribund tax base. Tourists drove past the town with other resorts down the road in mind— Short Skiff Key seemed to be always in the middle between two points of destination.

The surprise, of course, was when the 'clown and the monkey' walked in, decked in business attire. They were more surprised when the clown passed out a short bio on Roark, which alerted them that this was indeed the mysterious celebrity they had heard had come to live among them. After being rebuffed by the management of The Herd for being engaged citizens, the politicians were wary of what this Animal was after, with the City Manager and the Mayor silently signaling each other that there may be some conditions they could place into any building permit. But they were surprised at Roark's opening statement.

"I am going to clean up the property. Whether I will build something new right away or put a fence around the property and let it sit for a couple of years depends on the mutual agreements we can reach. My stimulus to build something now versus what you call 'land-banking' my property."

At this time, Silent John handed them a memo on development points. The property owner was being proactive in his wish list.

- 70% of the property could be used by a non-profit. The remainder will be business-oriented. The politicians frowned that a portion of the tax base would be lost if a non-profit opened an office. Roark had merely thrown that in as a bargaining give-away in future negotiations.
- We will attempt to save the old Harris Funeral Home (a three-story Victorian-styled house, boarded up). If we do, we may seek Historical Preservation designation for tax credits.
- We would like mixed zoning that would allow up to 150 housing units.
- Five-year sales tax deferment on businesses and five-year abeyance of property taxes if new construction begins in the second year.
- No property or sales tax valuation increases for five years, or no greater than all other city current property tax adjustments after the fifth year.

Once the 'suggestions' were presented, Silent John spoke for the first time: "Let us take a lunch break and meet this afternoon and see if we can hammer out a mutual Use of Property Agreement."

Roark and John retired, leaving the city leaders dumbfounded. Were they being railroaded, or would the future development bring new taxes and tax-paying employees to this under-utilized property?

Resuming their meeting, the town fathers (and mothers) presented their counteroffer, with the building department manager pointing out that any new project still had to adhere to current building codes.

Roark let John take the lead in the negotiations.

"The building codes will be respected if a caveat amendment is included that 'there will be no untimely delay in gaining such permits subject to damage sanctions.'"

The town's position was that they felt the tax deferments were too long and sought to have shortened to three years, to which John agreed. Roark's team (a lawyer and architect, both Human, were waiting outside) felt any deferment was a bonus, so the acquiescence looked like the developer's (known as *Banyan Tree Enterprises*) had caved to the town's arguments.

The town politicians, seeking to regain the moral high ground and wishing to demonstrate to their constituents that they could make firm demands, sought an amendment that would require owners to begin construction within 12 months of signing the Agreement. John requested a minor modification that read: 'Temporary construction would be allowed employing pre-fabrication or removable tenting that might operate as businesses without zoning use required as for future permanent buildings.'

The town countered with a 'two-year limitation on temporary structures after construction commences.' Back and forth, the agreement was hammered into legalese.

The mayor asked the tricky question, 'What would be the use of the property?' Roark, as owner, answered: "We have not finalized usage, which may be determinant of the tenants we can bring in, and usage may be in steps and not all at once." The agreement thereby left the final use of the property open-ended.

The Mayor of Short Skiff Key made the final pitch, being conciliatory, talking about the area being a growing tourist destination, which was a slight political stretch of the truth. His request was firm, not a deal breaker, edging Roark into a difficult position.

"As we understand it," intoned the mayor, "you are a resident of The Herd Apartments. For the last year, we have asked them several times to consider participating in our Annual Founder's Regatta parade held in early December. The parade goes through our Gulf Boulevard to the Marina, ending with entertainment and ceremonies at the Gale Winns Cabaret. It always stimulates our tourist season. We hope that The Herd's participation will become an annual event, the perfect draw for visitors and fans of circus history. I can assure you, as a resident of The Herd, that the town will certainly look on this favorably and be even supporters of your project, whatever it might be, *if* The Herd, or in some way, you can persuade many of the residents to join us in becoming active boosters of Short Skiff Key."

They all looked to Roark. He knew he did not have the clout to make The Herd abandon their stringent philosophy of staying away from human influences. Yet after a few moments of contemplation, Roark realized that the banyan tree property had an importance—its purpose yet undefined—but an asset where any development would double or triple its value. He could then sell it, make a tidy profit, and move back West to La La Land. He saw the mayor's political posturing as neither an impediment nor a roadblock but a challenge. And he liked challenges. He only had to ensure the participation of a few members from The Herd. An elephant and a lion marching in the parade would probably satisfy the humans. Not insurmountable. Divide and conquer might just work. Roark responded honestly:

"I appreciate your confidence in my abilities to sway crowds. I have done so on the silver screen, although I cannot guarantee I can accomplish your goal. But if you keep this 'invitation' as an unspoken and non-binding request outside of our Use of Property Agreement, I will pledge the efforts of myself and my team to seek to bring as many Animals as possible to join your festivities."

The mayor smiled. During their luncheon break, he had learned more about Roark's fame as an Animal movie star. The mayor and town leaders jointly concluded that if anyone could create an Animal contingent for the parade, this Animal would be the one to do so.

"Agreed," said the mayor. "What do you need next from us?

"I have two of our team members outside, and I would like them to join us."

The attorney and architect entered. When introduced, it became apparent they were from high-powered Miami firms. The orangutan was savvier than they had initially assumed. Legal documents outlining the general boilerplate of the agreement were presented, blanks left open, subject to the agreed-upon negotiated points to be added. The mayor asked his secretary to invite the Town Attorney to join the meeting. The architect laid out a general land use and building design map, providing copies for the building department to initiate their review for underground utilities. The town leaders were impressed. If this design were built, it would be a draw—both for business and tourism, depending on the final occupants.

Roark still did not know what he would do with the property. On his team's advice, he maximized the building footprint, suggesting that buildings be no more than four stories and feature Southern Florida architectural design, with open spaces, greenery landscaping, and building codes to survive the strongest hurricane. A promising new addition to Short Skiff Key that the town leaders prayed would be constructed as envisioned, sooner rather than later.

Two days later, the building department and the town signed off on the agreement, which was to be kept secret until the building and remodeling permits were issued.

INTRODUCTION

"May I introduce my cousin, Eliza. My dear, this is the highly praised Executive Committee."

Eliza wore a quaint floor-length skirt and a bright, flowered blouse crowned with a summer hat (to hide her healing scar as her hair grew back). She replied quietly and politely, "Pleasure to meet you." Her response was spoken slowly, drawn out. As if shy, which she was.

Roark made individual introductions. They were all in the Committee's meeting room, a small group, so she would not be overwhelmed by every other resident hemming in to crowd her and cause a panic attack.

Hazel asked: "How do you like being in Florida?"

Eliza smiled and glanced at Orville, who stood on the outer rim of the crowd and flashed a few pre-planned, abbreviated hand signs.

"The rain in Flori-da is wonder-fa." Repeating part of her elocution exercises.

Skye flapped, inquiring, "I hear you are touring. Where is your first stop?"

A quick glance at Orville, and she responded, "The Everglades."

The Executive Committee smiled as one. They would have been disappointed if she had visited one of the several human amusement parks.

Chairman Balfour sought center stage for an important question: "And how do you like your apartment here in The Herd?"

Eliza required no coaxing from Oliver.

"I have never been so happy."

The chairman beamed.

She answered other questions without difficulty. Roark knew his 'cousin's' limitations. It had been grueling work teaching her how to enter Intelligent Animal society.

Very shortly, he begged off; his cousin was tired from her travels, and taking her by the hand, they made a quick tour of the committee members, she offering canned individual farewells. "I hope to see you again." "It was a pleasure to meet you." "Goodbye."

Back at her apartment, the three of them met John, who asked for a report.

"Were you happy?" Eliza asked Roark. She was particularly interested in his opinion.

"We were quite fortunate it came off." He saw her look at him with squinty eyes and added. "Yes, you were quite the actress.

"Well done."

Orville was ecstatic. "Excellent! You did it. By George, you did it!"

"Congratulations," said John. Eliza smiled at him. That smile to a human was a significant step in her transformation—to smile at the good humans.

John looked to Roark as if cueing his boss.

"Oh, yes," beamed Roark, "As a reward for your diligent studies, I, we, have a little surprise for you."

The next day, John drove Eliza and Roark to the strange site of wrecked human buildings and, behind them, the wonderous site of the banyan tree.

Like Roark, she fell in love with the tree, to swing, to pick at the leaves, to eat the figs. To discover a lost freedom she had nearly forgotten. Her mind was still skeptical of all those who had controlled her: *Who was this orangutan who could treat her so well? What was he after?*

She looked down and saw that Roark had a slight smile on his face. His expression was not only of sincere happiness for her, but more recognition that his little project of educating an animal into an Intelligent Animal seemed successful. *Perhaps*, he mused, *I could do this again, perhaps on a larger scale.*

* * *

Eliza's education did not end; in fact, she dove in, enthused to learn and read, absorbing everything. A routine was developed. Work hard for three days, and then take a day break to enjoy the languid weather in the banyan tree. Prior to her next visit, workers had surrounded the entire property on three sides with a high chain fence and signs that warned: 'No Trespassing.' They announced: 'Future Banyan Tree Enterprises Re-Development.' The back side of the property had the fencing on both sides set several yards into the swamp, forming an open horseshoe, with another sign on both sides saying, 'Beware of Alligators. ' There had never been any sightings of these reptiles, but the message did the trick as a strong deterrence. Who would take the chance to wander and wade into the swamp land?

DIALOGUES – WHO AM I?

Eliza's continuing education bore consequences, primarily curiosity sparked by her newly acquired knowledge.

One day, while they sat resting in the banyan tree, satisfied and at leisure, Roark was reading a script for a possible film, and Eliza was going through an elementary text—a picture book—her finger tracing the words. In Orville's contribution to teaching her to read English, he read her copies of the Association newsletter that he had written as editor. He showed her outside world news stories he thought might interest her and add to her knowledge of the Animal and Human societies she someday must confront.

"What will you build?"

Roark blinked up from his script. "What?"

"What is Banyan Tree Enterprises, and what will you build here? This tree must remain."

He accepted that she had opinions. "Of course, I initially bought this property to protect the banyan tree. Not the smartest investment, I must say." She looked at him in awe. *Buying all this land for one tree!*

He gave her a look, saw her eyes begging for information, and closed the script for the moment. It was not a script for him; it was another jungle plot. He was sick of jungles, too hot and buggy, though he had not been to a real one in five years—on the day of John's accident, a tragedy he sought to forget.

He gave speech to his thoughts. "As to what to build around the tree, I am not sure. Humans are giving me suggestions, but they are all commonplace. Nothing that will be a draw to attract revenues. We are located just a mile or so from the beach, so I must encourage tourists to consider this property. That will be expensive in advertising dollars. Or I could try to locate a bunch of doctors to rent a remodeled building for their clinic practice. Humans are big on seeking answers to all their woes, even the trivial."

She still did not have a complete comprehension of what he considered mere talking, as it was still complicated for her to digest. She posed her own thought: "You should have a place to teach us average animals to be smart animals, like the Circus Animals at The Herd."

"Eliza, you were never 'average.' I can tell you frankly that you have more inquisitiveness than most of those living in The Herd who are glued to televisions and their social media. Use this new knowledge we are teaching you personally as best we can, and you will succeed at whatever you do." He felt good in saying all this, a part of mentoring his *protégé*.

She saw only one impact in her life. "I think what you have done for me is remarkable. I am pleased."

Her comment was sincere. Roark thanked her and picked up another script submitted to him, again his part as a 'second banana.' Eliza's suggestion remained in his mind, more so when she leaned down from an upper branch, picked a bug from the top of his head, and ate it.

Another time, in the tree, she had doubts. Perhaps she had read too much about what was out there beyond what she could visibly see.

Eliza asked the lounging Roark: "What is my purpose here?"

"What do you mean?"

"You changed me. I can think more. I see the world differently. But I don't see who I am, this new me in this world."

For the first time, he looked at her, not as his project, but as the Animal he had aided into cognitive existence. His response required him to reflect, using his own experiences.

"Eliza, you and I have become fortunate. Humans do not see what they have done. Yes, we were given a new life. What is exciting is that it was placed in us not only to be more than we were, but also to have the advantage of being greater. We can now think, reason, and, most importantly, we can create.

"Humans just accept circumstances as they fall into place; they set comfortable patterns and repeat them. They can accept the trudge and drudge of an everyday existence since they believe they will live for a long time.

"Our lives compared to theirs are much shorter. Where, for them, days, weeks, and months can easily pass by without notice, so they let time slip away, but we must live for the moment. Time is precious to us, and we must strive to live a life of crowded hours.

"You, Eliza, are extraordinary. You have no limitations to be anything that would most excite you. Every day should be a blessing to excel at what might make you most happy."

"I can be better than humans?"

"That is not the goal. The objective is to be a better *you*. We all wait to see the talented Eliza."

She listened seriously, soaking it all in, not comprehending what was being delivered to her, but rather what it stirred in her deepest thoughts —whether she retained what Roark said: inspirational, yet wise. And Roark felt pleased with himself with this spurt of advice. *Yes, very profound of me, I should write my little speech down.* He did not yet contemplate that when speech is listened to, it may become 'educational' and on this special day, at this moment, his wisdom imparted had created a unique orangutan with values.

RoarUni Fact

A Robin Redbreast in a Cage
Puts all Heaven in a Rage.
A dove house fill'd with doves and pigeons
Shudders Hell thro' all its regions.
A Dog starv'd at his Master's Gate
Predicts the ruin of the State.
A Horse misus'd upon the Road
Calls to Heaven for Human blood.
Each outcry of the hunted Hare
A fiber from the Brain does tear.

—William Blake

INQUISITIVE

She was gaining a complete understanding of the language and its nuances and was now able to transcribe thoughts onto the computer and produce *writing*, and, just as importantly, view with a wary eye the culture of the Homo-sapiens society she would eventually face. For this rapid advancement, Roark and John rewarded her with an outing to enjoy quality beach time, Eliza's first at the sand and surf with John as their protector from any crowds.

As they settled in, Roark laughed at her timid approach to a wave, then her frolic, running in and out at the foaming waves, chortling without fear. Amazement at the child within.

Elza played with the sand, digging holes and burying shells in them. Roark and John discussed Association activities, analyzing various tenants, and which Animals they should approach and ask to participate in the parade, which was still nine months away. They were at a loss.

From her finger sand playing, Eliza casually commented, not looking at them.

"What do these Animals really want to do? That's what you should ask them. I have talked to a few. Most like watching television and playing outside in The Herd compound, but I think they are—what is the word—'bored'. No, not the word. 'Unsatisfied', is that the word?"

Roark regarded her and what she said, but John's question came first. "Should there be a challenge to the Association's current no human fraternization policies?"

Eliza thought abstractly, her hand trying to dig a cool sand depression to lie in, but seawater collapsed the sides. "They are past circus performers. Must that part of their lives be over?"

John mused on his distant past. "Performing made circus people and the Animals so alive."

Roark picked up on the thread, "Maybe some of them have other aspirations. Not to fight directly against the Rules & Regs, but to encourage other interests that might bring them greater happiness. Like a parade." He considered aloud his prior mantra. "Divide and conquer."

Later, the three of them sat under the *Shellfish* umbrella and had a picnic. Quiet in reflection or small talk of nothing in particular. Eliza mostly stared out to the Gulf, the expanse overwhelming her senses, an unstated feeling that there was a glorious power greater than her little self. One could call this an existential awakening, realizing that she existed but as a microcosm—a speck of sand on a crowded beach of like specks. What was her worth as a speck among specks? Again, revelations often come like a gentle wave to the shore, to either ebb and return or to absorb into the sand. Eliza, not yet spiritually awakened, merely absorbed her surroundings with deep breaths.

At the end of the day, as they exited the beach, Eliza spied an awful-looking scraggly human, dressed in shabby clothes, accompanying a dog which seemed more clean and groomed but with no hind legs. The man was removing the wagon's skids, used as prosthetic mover, replacing them with small wheels at the back, where the canine could pull the wagon more easily along the street, which was piled with discarded empty bottles and cans. Eliza stared. Humans and animals working together, she presumed—a concept not yet persuaded in her mind. Humans have only used animals, even Intelligent Animals, for their own selfish needs.

She refocused on the ending of a marvelous outing and being with Roark for an entire afternoon.

Eliza's eyes widened at what she viewed next, and she squealed, "Can I have an ice cream cone?"

THE MASTER AWAKENS

A week later, Eliza picked up a pamphlet and asked Orville, "What is this 'Back to Africa'?" He explained what SOCA was and their attempt at an experimental trip to Africa, taking a group of monkeys, those, in fact, from her previous Mississippi monkey farm, now closed and abandoned. It was hoped that this would be a trip of permanence and that the monkeys would enjoy returning to the wild.

Eliza thought about the idea but had no opinion on whether or not it was a good idea. Orville saw her pondering, "Would you like to interview the monkeys, if any return, and see what they discovered, and would they go back permanently? I think the majority might want to rebuild their ancestors' original animal habitats in the jungles."

Roark was not happy with Orville's indoctrination of Eliza and told him so. Orville responded strongly. "I did not ask her to go over there but to talk with those who return."

Roark huffed. "I would forbid her from ever going. She is totally unprepared. Both the human and Animal worlds have their own jungles to navigate. At this point, she would be mentally, if not physically, destroyed by either journey. It is up to us to prepare her for the human world; her first direct experience, being caged, was brutal. She must learn to see and try the positive opportunities."

"But Roark, you might own her, but you do not control her."

That caught the orangutan star off-balance. He had never thought of Eliza as chattel. His purchase was to free her. Save her. Nothing more. He had thought no more of this action. *Did she think he was her master, like a master over a slave*? The thought that she might think that and despise him was such an abhorrent possibility. He suddenly realized he had never given serious consideration to her feelings. What a louse he was—a self-centered hairy ape. He could admit when he had wronged.

* * *

That night, he knocked on her door.

Eliza engrossed, watching television—not mindless human programming but a National Geographic series on gorillas, their jungle habitat, daily living, hardships, and relationships.

"Am I bothering you?"

"No, not at all. Orville recorded these programs."

"Of course he did."

She turned off the TV with the remote. "Can I get you some fruit?"

"No, thank you. I can only stay a while. I am expecting a telephone call from the West Coast."

"I have not yet learned telephone etiquette. John said he would teach me. Also, credit card use."

"Credit cards are pretty dangerous." His humor fell flat against the expression of her base ignorance of credit and its ramifications.

"Could you teach me about credit cards when you think I am ready?"

He felt uncomfortable and reminded himself why he was there.

"Eliza, I want to give you this." He handed her a piece of paper, a notarized document.

"What is this?"

"It is a human legal document, your Bill of Sale. I paid to purchase you away from that horrible farm and this is my receipt. I have signed it over to you. Meaning into your ownership. The point is you are truly free; these are now your ownership papers. As I have said before, you are your own creature; all freedom is yours to use wisely. And understand, that is only what myself, John, and even Orville have tried to accomplish: to give you the tools to have the confidence to go out on your own eventually." He felt a pang at what he said, what this lame pep talk might imply, and paused before saying, "If that's what you want." He did not know what *he* wanted, but he hoped she understood that she was not ready to leave them and go back to someplace far away, like Africa.

Her eyes watered, so she couldn't read the document or even understand the big words in it. "Thank you." Almost a whisper. Then, she spoke another *thank you,* but in their private animal language.

There was a moment of silence, and then he cleared his throat and regained the stature of the strong male orangutan.

"So, as you wondered, let's make it tomorrow, and your next learning session will be on *banking*. We will go to a bank and open an account as well as a safety deposit box in which we will store the document I have just signed over to you. That is a valuable document no one can ever challenge. When we go to the bank, you will open a bank account and deposit a check from BT Enterprises. It is a consulting fee. Orville receives one for his teaching, and John receives a salary as my working administrative officer to the company."

"What is a 'consultant'?"

"Someone who gives good advice."

"I don't think I have done that."

Roark smiled. "Eliza, you speak ideas from the heart. New thoughts I need to analyze and I accept that from you. I appreciate this is common sense originality and thus possible merit. Consulting merit has value, and you get paid for this service."

"You should teach other animals like you did for me. You are so smart."

"Well, yes, that is something to consider. You have become very well educated."

"I have learned so much, so I talk too much. Is that consulting?"

Roark gave a genuine smile and answered, "Yes."

In a sudden move, a surprise to him, she jumped up and hugged him, skipped around the room, and jumped up on her fake wood perch. She became serious.

"How much do I get paid? What can I buy with the money? Can I get a credit card now?"

RoarUni Fact

"Be a good boy, remember; and be kind to animals and birds, and read all you can."

—Thomas Hardy, Jude the Obscure

DIALOGUES: WHAT GOD IS THE RIGHT ONE?

A week later, back in the banyan tree. Roark decided they should watch the sunset from the tree. The clouds in the sky produced a rainbow prism of purple hues as the sun dropped towards a green flash on the horizon. The mood set Eliza to ponder.

She asked her companion. “I have been reading online about humans and their religions. They have so many religions, and they have so many gods. Why not just one? I thought humans would all want to think the same way and have only one answer. I don’t understand. Should I accept a human god to be better in their world?”

Roark had come to expect these questions, which tested his own insight. In a way, it made him feel good that he might indeed have, from his own experiences, a talent for imparting wisdom.

“Ah, yes, I went through that same process early on. Does accepting gain acceptance? I don’t believe so. If you choose one of their religions, will you have chosen right or wrong? Perhaps you will come to realize that many other religions will hate or despise you for choosing what you believe is right. Why take on any belief that has discord attached?

"I cannot speak for other Animals, but personally, I believe we Animals must have our own spiritual guide. Look first at who we are and where we came from. Orangutans are 'of the forest.' This 'forest' is called Nature, all things that are trees, wind, and sun; here, our ancestors lived among fellow Animals of all kinds (he smiled), and sometimes we ate them or they ate us."

"This Nature is a god?"

"It is a living spirit. Not of human-built temples. Or in books with words to live by. And, so, if we are good primates, we must work for its continuance. Nature is fighting to survive like we do. It is being threatened every day by the human world. Where our people still live in trees, these trees are being torn down by humans to take tree oil and make cosmetics for human women."

"Then, to help Nature, Animals must stop humans?" He could see how her mind sought answers, her anger building, and he knew he was pushing her mind to think only one way. He did not like to see her torn and sought to reassure her.

"No. We must reassert *our* part in Nature. Help and improve Nature. Nature will fight back, reminding humans that their gods are not breathing ones. Take our tree—our banyan tree, for example. This tree cleans the air, it cools the Earth, it helps the soil to grow other trees, and it provides us shelter."

She accepted the logic. "I am going to protect it. I am helping a living spirit. That is what is right."

Eliza thought no more of religions. She only focused on what Roark had said, '*our* tree.' It put her in a happy mood, and in the growing shadows, she swung up into the branches, thinking of building a nest, thinking of ways to convince Roark to spend the night out here, in Nature, with her, in her nest.

Roark enjoyed the satisfaction after Eliza jumped away, peeling off in loping swings in happy, chatty laughter. His 'lecture' must have said the right things. He returned to translating his mental notes into his handheld tape recorder, recording snippets of idea fragments to formulate a plan initiated by Eliza on how to approach The Herd residents. He was putting the finishing touches on the strategy. Also, bouncing back and forth in his brain was another idea Eliza had proposed—educating animals. This past week, he had not picked up a script to review; his mind was instead concentrating on his local challenges.

RoarUni Fact

"You cannot share your life in a meaningful way with a dog, a cat, a rabbit, a rat, a bird, a horse, a pig, I don't care and not know that they have emotions similar to ours and that they have minds that can sometimes solve problems."

—Dr. Jane Goodall

COILING FEAR

Another evening in *their* tree, Eliza was nervous, jumping from branch to branch, swinging aimlessly. In a few days, the monkeys, if any, were to return from their trip to a pre-selected troop location in the Central African rainforest. Orville had set up a video conference call with the returnees, at least those who could speak ITSEE English. She informed Roark that several of the leading monkeys from the Anndwell Monkey Farm survivors knew sign language and that there might be a basic understanding Eliza could put into a tour report. She told Roark she was going to keep an open mind, and as part of her 'consulting,' she would have Orville help her create a report for discussion to see if Roark might actually underwrite a future 'return to nativism' among Intelligent Animals.

Tired from reading books all day and burdened with anxiety about the monkey interview meeting, Eliza found a large branch to stretch out on and think. Back to an earlier possibility. Had she forgotten how to build a nest? What materials should she use?

Tearing leaves and branches from *their* tree seemed like a crime against the Nature god.

A few minutes later, she called out to Roark.

"Roark, can you come here? Hurry, please. And come slowly."

To him, a strange request, with stress and anguish in her voice. Shrill. He stood, scanned the night and the branches for her, and, seeing the top of her head, slowly swung up to the branch above her. Perhaps her foot had been caught in a dangling root vine.

A large snake had Eliza in a coil draped tight around her foot, the reptile writhing, trying to better its grasp to cover her head in coils and strangle her.

Roark skipped his English and screamed primeval orangutan warnings at the snake before yelling in English: "What are you doing?! Turn her loose!"

The reticulated python, maybe a dozen feet long, raised its face to the interruption of its soon-to-be meal. "Hungry," was all the snake hissed.

Roark realized that neither a human entertainer nor a multi-reasoning animal faced them. Here, the threat was pure wild, a definite killer. He slowly stepped towards the snake, trying to recall a similar situation he had faced. Nearly ten years ago, he had wrestled a jungle snake, a giant special-effects latex reptile that had been 'doubled' for close-ups with the real thing, which had been heavily medicated. In this movie, *The Lost Jungle Found*, again, he saved the beautiful young human female, who was eventually enamored by the human adventurer. *Quick. Think snake. Think what snake needs.*

To the snake, he pounded his chest for attention and said succinctly and firmly. "Better food."

The snake relaxed only slightly. "Where? You?" It seemed the snake had picked up a few guttural words of speech, the voice more hiss than articulated.

"No, I will get. Promise. Animal to animal."

"Hungry."

"Wait." Roark pulled out his cell phone and hit the instant dial button. "John, have you gotten dinner yet?"

"Fast food line is long. Haven't placed an order yet."

"We were getting salads?"

"Yes. Want something else?"

"No, but besides our order, see if the restaurant has chicken or a fast-food place nearby that has chicken. I need a lot of buckets of chicken. And hurry. We are facing a true wild critter beast here."

John went serious. "I'll also bring a tire iron."

"But hide it. This guy can slither fast. And she has Eliza, not in a death grip yet, but we are debating the menu here."

"Snake. Got it."

To the snake, Roark said: "Food coming. You eat her, and I will eat you."

"No. Babies."

"Babies?"

"She's pregnant," Eliza's nervous analysis. "Eggs in the lower belly." Eliza remained frozen, afraid a coil would reach for her neck if she made any movement. "You need quiet speech to keep our friend from in-tree dining."

"You have humor," said Roark. "It's surfacing."

"At the wrong time. And that was not a joke."

He took the hint. To the snake whose back end was coiling for a deadly embrace of Eliza, he spoke seriously but gently. "This your home?"

"Yes."

"Is there no other food here?"

Hissing, the snake showed its open mouth, showing its reticulated fangs. "No. Water bad. Fish dead. Cat last dinner. Food here. Babies need."

Roark kept his mind working. "Food coming. Better dinner. Don't want to kill you. I have sharp teeth." He chomped in the dark, hoping the snake could see his incisors' intentions.

"Hungry," the only reply. The timing was getting worse—and shorter. Roark heard the car returning; the gate flung open, a rush of spinning gravel.

"Food here. Wait."

Roark jumped to a lower branch, and John threw up a tub of fried chicken.

Returning and without fanfare, he stuffed the opened container into the python's face.

Eliza jumped two branches higher as the snake uncoiled. Roak went to Eliza, who clung to him.

After a few minutes of catching their breath, they retreated from the tree to the top of the SUV. Nothing seemed safe anymore, tree or ground. Roark pointed upward. John advanced, weapon in hand.

Said Eliza, "Don't kill it. She's ready to drop eggs."

John, the former stuntman, looked to her, saw the expression, and took the second bucket of chicken. He climbed the tree and placed the bucket in the branches several yards from the python. On returning, he told the orangutans, "That is a Burmese python, guessing about 15 feet and maybe 150-180 pounds. Quite dangerous. Easily would've swallowed Eliza whole."

She moved closer to Roark, and he draped his arm around her.

John again retrieved his tire iron. "There's no permit needed to kill a python. They are invasive, overrunning the Everglades, and decimating local wildlife."

Eliza created a quandary with one word. "Babies."

John shrugged his shoulder, waving the tire iron. "Yep, lots of babies. Maybe 30, or even up to 100 new hungry slithering mouths. When grown, that number would make this swamp next to us uninhabitable and dangerous to Animals and humans alike on the land where your property is."

"Can't let that happen," Roark's harsh reality. He could not make his property unusable and thus unsaleable.

"You can't kill her," Eliza pleaded to Roark. "You of all Animals understand kindness to all Animals. Nature." Roark flinched. She had, in a way, 'humanized' him, or at least placed his 'celebrity' persona as a hero into play. He put it back on her.

"You are my consultant. What do you suggest, Miss Eliza?"

She, with quick analysis, gave the easiest solution. "Move her away from your property."

Reasonable. Roark replied as a devil's advocate. "But where? Into the Everglades might not be the best when the humans start hunting them for cash bounty. And the babies might not survive with other wild predators. Euthanasia might be a kind way of solving this problem."

"No. That is not you." He was surprised that she had defined his character even though he was not confident that he was so honorable. After all, he had lived in Hollywood and was an actor.

Eliza thinking.

"I have a place to take her. Quiet, away from humans. Plenty of fish." She purposefully overlooked telling him that the area was home to small animals like raccoons and opossums.

"Where, in this populace-crowded Florida?

She gave them both a snorting laugh.

"Mississippi. Anndwell Monkey Farm. No humans there now. No smart Animals there. Privacy."

"You are proposing what?" asked John. "A road trip?" Several months back, he and Orville had made the trek to the auction. He knew the route.

Roark had his solution. He now had to be the facilitating hero. He could be good at this.

ROAD TRIP

"Okay, Eliza gets to see Florida. John, rent a small trailer to put on our SUV. Then go to some market and buy, what, 50 pounds of raw beef, big chunks, not lean ground for this growing momma—a one-day, quickie trip up and an overnight leisurely trip back. Let's get our traveling clothes. And get going." He felt satisfied: the problem was now solved.

"You have to convince the snake," deadpanned John. "Maybe she won't leave home. Maybe she is in a maternity nesting mood."

With his newfound courage and hero status to Eliza, he thrust out his chest: "I will convince her." A random thought occurred to him. If he could motivate this ignorant wild animal to make the move, just maybe he could make inroads in changing the minds of the Animals at The Herd to his way of thinking. His thought suddenly took a wild turn. *I could probably educate Animals to be independent and work in the human world.* Reality prompted him to reflect on this possibility as a new challenge. *But could I make money off an idea no one had yet tried on a large scale?*

First things first, he grabbed the last bucket of chicken and jumped back into the tree, worrying Eliza and Silent John.

* * *

It was good that they brought flashlights with them. Miles and miles later, the SUV's headlights flashed on the fallen sign,

"Anndwell Animal Farm—Exotic Monkeys—Daily Show." The sign on the padlocked entry gate said otherwise: "Seized Property." A federal government sticker was posted, accompanied by a detailed legal notice. Another sign: "No Trespassing."

Roark went to the small trailer they had been pulling. John unlocked the back doors. They shone their flashlights on the snake, who, because of her simple wildlife habits, had never had a personal name until Eliza had corrected her when she rewarded the snake for not eating her. "I am going to call you 'Manasa,' a goddess of fertility."

Roark gave Eliza a quizzical look. "Where did that come from?"

"Internet."

Roark shined his light on the engorged snake. "How was the trip… Manasa.?"

"Shaking."

"You are here. This is your new home," said Eliza, using her flashlight to create a beam out of the trailer. "There is an island there for protection, where to have a family. Safe." Manasa slowly complied and slid out and stretched her full length. John gingerly moved back, glancing into the trailer to note that all the raw meat they'd placed in there had been devoured, and he could see a lump within the snake, still digesting.

The snake moved its head from side to side.

Eliza encouraged and pointed. "Your home is that way, under the gate."

Manasa turned to them and hissed words she had never before uttered, either in snake-speak or pidgin English. "Thank you." And the python slithered out of the beams of flashlights toward the darkened, empty grounds and the murky ponds within the abandoned monkey farm.

Eliza shuddered. This had been her home, her prison, for so long. She thought she would never return. And yet, this male orangutan, Roark, who everyone said was a famous entertainer, had saved her and helped bring her back to the mainstream of understanding and her new chance in this Intelligent Animal world. She was so grateful to him. *How can I show him my appreciation?*

RoarUni Fact

Elephants have a specific alarm call that means "human." Horses use facial expressions to communicate with each other. Researchers have identified 17 discrete facial movements. Young goats pick up accents from each other, joining humans, bats, and whales as mammals known to adjust their vocal sounds to fit into a new social group.

THE CLOWN'S STORY

The return trip to Short Skiff Key brought a few events of note.

While they drove straight through to drop off their 'guest' at the monkey farm, they headed back to The Herd Apartments more leisurely and stopped overnight in Tallahassee, Florida. The following day, they arose early and visited the expansive Maclay State Gardens, a public park where everyone could exercise. Trees included bald cypress, hickory, dogwood, and many other varieties. The flower garden plantings were centralized around azaleas and camellias with designs of rhododendron, gardenia, ginger, jasmine, and wisteria, providing a palette of flower choices. John stretched his legs as Roark headed to the trees, and Eliza sniffed the flowers. And when no human was looking, she had a little snack, chomping off the most delicious petals and leaves.

Eliza later returned to where John sat on a bench reading a paperback novel on the young Marquis de La Fayette, *Lafayette, Courtier to Crown Fugitive*. He explained to her as she rested near him that Maclay State Park was originally part of a land grant given to Lafayette both for his loans to the nascent government during the Revolution and thirty years later as Congress's response to help Lafayette after he lost his fortune during the French Revolution. This recitation of history went over her head, and she merely nodded. After a few quiet minutes, watching Roark roam happily, climbing, swinging from branches, and investigating with his own leaf-munching, Eliza spoke to John, interrupting his page-turning.

"Tell me the story of your face. Or do too many bother you with that question?" Eliza had yet to learn the art of tact. What she wondered about, she questioned.

John looked at her and saw no malicious intent.

"Few ask. Most are intimidated. A mask is a great defense mechanism."

Moments of silent reflection, before John began his story, not a memory he enjoyed reliving. To him, Eliza presented herself as the curious innocent.

"This is between us. No one else." She agreed. "I worked at being a stunt man, hired during the filming of the movie, '*Tarzan's Forbidden Love.*' R-rated if you know what that means?" She did not, but would look it up. "The movie's outdoor scenes were filmed in Africa. Among many other bit actors, I participated in a battle scene at a river that ran through a gorge cut between cliffs. Roark played the orangutan friend to the hero mercenary. The human hero part included fighting down along the river, and I, along with a group of stuntmen— portrayed as fierce African warriors—were directed to fire our rifles from the top of cliffs on both sides of the river. Roark's role in that sequence showed him running through the jungle, a rescuer, savior of the day, and for him to rush up behind me, I, the African warrior chief, shooting my rifle, and Roark would push me off the cliff."

"That must have been so dangerous for both of you." Eliza voiced concern.

"Not so much, except this time. Stunt people pride themselves on extreme safety measures. Below me, they had an inflatable mat I would fall onto. I had several practice falls, and everything went fine. Roark, the actor pushing me, had the vine he would hold onto and a wire line attached to his back. He would swing out behind me, push, then swing back safely. The stunt came off well-planned, and all went perfectly in execution, except ten seconds after my fall. As I lay there on the mat after a target-on 'death fall,' the cliff face suddenly collapsed right on top of me. I was buried under dirt and rock. The stunt team got to me quickly, digging to uncover me; the emergency team behind them for the rush to the local hospital, and by the time I was in emergency, Roark appeared, totally devastated. He blamed himself, though there was no fault assigned to him. An Act of Nature, as they say. Bad Karma, as others consoled." Eliza believed that the god Nature could be unforgiving if proper reverence were not given.

John continued. "I was a mess. The local doctors wanted to operate there and then. A tricky procedure, but Roark stepped in, took charge, and had me helicoptered out and flown to a better operating room in Nairobi. A critical operation performed to try and reattach facial muscles, one that would never make me a leading man." He removed his mask and turned to her.

She gasped. This human, indeed, had to wear a mask among his species.

He saw her recoil and understood her horror, as did all who had seen his reconstructed face.

"Plastic surgery did not reclaim my looks; it made me look like a zombie non-human. My worst long-term injury is my crushed neck and a destroyed larynx." He pointed to his throat and the white plastic wrap around his neck. "Most people with my condition will use a hand-held device called an 'electrolarynx' placed against the throat, which will produce a raspy conversation. People accept that handicap. Roark went a step further, researching and paying for the latest technology—a square of high-tech node mesh, silicon paper thin, accomplishing the same result but with better voice clarity. I will use some big words you won't understand; I barely do. This device—" he pointed to the small square on his neck 'is 'Magnetomechanical Coupling between Magnetic Induction layers.' What you see produces my speaking words."

"But years later, why do you work for him?" A harsh, bare question to him, more so, she meant: *Why does a human take orders from an Animal?*

He replaced his mask. Silent John looked up to see Roark, satisfied with his tree play, jump to the ground and begin a 'John Wayne' type ramble back to them, doing occasional somersaults in the grass. The male orangutan was healthy and in a good mood.

John sought his words carefully in response to Eliza.

"It may be to some that he has remorseful guilt about my accident, which again was not his fault. It was my choice to become his employee. Before, I saw him as an Animal actor, but following my 'incident' and multiple operations (he supplemented my insurance shortfall). During a lengthy rehabilitation and recovery, he was there, supportive at my bedside, not just financially.

My epiphany - that means a spiritual awakening - led me to discover a creature, part animalistic awareness, part humanity, and if human, he would be called the New Man and admired. If, as a mythological semi-religious animal icon, he would have been deified as the one dispensing insight and guidance. The Wise Animal Guru. What I see in him is a leadership presence that can bridge both species. Someone who may just be greater than the *goodness* parts of either Animal or human."

John paused and looked at his boss, who was approaching them. Roark was chasing fluttering butterflies, waving his loping hands among them, not trying to catch them.

"He is—we all are—Animals. He has his shortcomings, perhaps too hard on himself, and an attitude that when he is wronged, he seeks redress, even to the point of being obsessive. But above all that, he just has a 'good heart.' And in this world dominated by humans, he needs human support to manage the entanglements. He struggles with the challenges our human systems face due to the handicaps faced by Intelligent Animals who seek equal consideration, this parity where all are fairly treated. Better than my past jobs, which I am unable to perform one hundred percent, I am a useful crutch or a right-hand extension to his needs. I have come to accept this job responsibility quite seriously. He is worth the service I provide. Strange as it might seem, I believe, in time, he has some kind of destiny. Whatever it might be, I want to go along for the ride."

"That is saying a lot about one creature, not human." *And what was this 'destiny'?* she wondered. So much to learn and understand.

Silent John smiled as best he could.

"Beyond his personal goals, he is a very caring orangutan to others. You know he is a great supporter of your future."

Eliza had not processed all that she saw of Roark's actions, even those towards her. Wasn't he just helpful? Was there more to his attentions? If so, he did not brazenly demonstrate them. But then, in the orangutan world, females were the pursuers. But she had no idea how to do that or if she should. She didn't really think she was in that sort of mood, *hormones,* the humans called it. What if he rejects her advances? That does happen. Then what?

Roark joined them.

"Are we ready to get back on the road?" He turned to Eliza., "Don't you have a conference call tomorrow with some wild monkeys?"

THE MONKEY TALE

Eliza and Orville sat in the small office of The Heard's newsletter/ communication center on a group video conference call. Those on the computer screen included a group of chattering wild monkeys (formerly of the closed monkey farm), overseen now by a human representative of SOCA, the one called Harold and on another screen the president of SOCA, Mrs. Meryl Humphries, a socialite and a former elected Congresswoman, one of the reasons that the non-profit had so successfully lobbied Congress for their Save Circus Animals legislative bill.

Orville introduced himself, and then Eliza, as representative for Roark, the movie star and the monkey benefactor, and a resident of The Herd, the first SOCA-endorsed apartments for ex-Circus Animals.

Orville asked the anticipated question: "How did your trip go?"

The screeching resumed. The leader monkey chattered while another monkey behind the leader gave quick hand signals, 'Disaster. Failure.' This message Orville wrote on a yellow pad so Eliza could read.

"What did your monkey friend say?" inquired SOCA rep Harold, who was with the monkeys but on a separate screen. Orville gave his interpretation to mollify the human. "Interesting. The monkeys incarcerated at the same tourist monkey farm as Eliza have a minimal understanding of English, at least, and are not as linguistically proficient as Eliza now is under Roark's and Orville's tutelage.

SOCA president, Mrs. Humphries, admitted, "We feel we could have better handled the tour and the opportunity for our 'wards' to easily acclimate to the jungle environment and their fusion into the existing monkey colonies. I don't think it's anyone's fault. Perhaps a more investigative approach and a new game plan to accomplish SOCA's end goals."

"I would like to hear directly from the monkeys themselves," said Eliza, trying to voice politeness.

The human Harold, who had accompanied the monkeys to the Central African country's rainforest belt and visited their large wildlife animal preserve, started to speak, but Eliza interjected, "The monkeys only, please."

The leader monkey attempted to respond in halting English, with his monkey friend crowding into the video frame to the side, surreptitiously signing.

"Closed travel," said the monkey leader, while Orville wrote, 'Cages,' reading the hand signing.

Another pause, and the leader chattered out in pidgin English. "Jungle monkeys."

Orville translated the secret signing and wrote: "No humans let the jungle monkeys know the Monkey Farm monkeys were coming." Eliza understood—all the travel plans were made by humans to humans, as usual.

Orville asked, "Was this jungle monkey colony safe and secure?"

The leader's reply consisted of one word: "Photos." Private sign language from the other monkey: 'Tourists. Too close.'

Eliza questioned: "Did any monkeys stay?"

The response from the SOCA human representative: "Two monkeys stayed."

The leader monkey spoke the English word that he knew. "Kill."

The signing came quickly. 'Humans killed. Food. Leopard killed. Food.'

By some glitch, the computer conferencing call with the monkeys went dark and disconnected.

SOCA Humphries replaced the questioning silence with her thoughts. "We will work to improve our program." Eliza could spot when a human spoke down to Animals. "We want the support of The Herd as we continue our *Back to Africa* plans. This is the early frontier of a delicate political situation, and we will get it right. Naturally, we look forward to hearing from you both and Mr. Roark on any ideas or thoughts."

Orville responded, "Yes, we want to help. Perhaps the next trip will be more successful."

The ex-Congresswoman looked at Eliza. "I did not notice you on the list of The Herd C&B membership?" Orville wrote a snarky scribble for Eliza to glance at. 'Her Animal list.'

Eliza spoke very clear English, maybe with a little southern Mississippi drawl, barely noticeable. "I am the cousin of movie star Roark, just visiting. But I wish your organization well."

"And how is Mr. Roark doing at The Herd?"

"Everyone seems to like him," Orville answered. Eliza thought to herself, '*And so do I,*' wishing to clarify her muddled feelings better, comparing and balancing her desires with these SOCA goals of resettling animals. Did she want to live permanently at The Herd? Could she? Or would she take her chances in Africa or Southeast Asia? *Where is my final home to be?*

SOCA president Humphries gave her a dismissive smile again and disconnected.

ELIZA'S OPINION

The next night, she and Orville presented a verbal report to Roark with John in the background, listening, and preparing light snacks of cut mangoes and honey-drizzled ants.

Eliza, not Orville, offered her interpretation, telling what she heard from both monkeys and SOCA reps intertwined with the Anndwell Monkey Farm experience the monkeys had faced. Roark showed interest since he donated funds for Eliza and helped the monkeys after the Fed auction sale. However, he quickly ceded control of the monkeys to SOCA, which pledged to provide them with a new home outside of the country and would take care of all the details. Eliza's report suggested that it was not the case.

Eliza summarized: "The trip was a disaster. SOCA did not even select the right environmental home for the monkeys. There were 19 monkeys at the start. They never realized that most of the monkeys saved from the Farm were brown Capuchin and woolly spider monkeys from Central America, not Africa."

Oliver added, "These monkeys were totally unprepared to interact with the resident monkeys already in their jungle habitat."

Eliza continued, stating that the ex-Farm monkeys, after seeing the troop colony and talking to them, discovered none of them were even distant cousins and had nothing in common. They felt uncomfortable and did not want to stay. They wanted a secure jungle they could relate to and even suggested that they might prefer a nice zoo or preserve in the human world.

Orville made his observation, shaking his head. "But we need to keep in mind these animals are not zoo-acclimated or ITSE entertainer animals but basically wild, and yes, several are mentally diminished because of their mistreatment."

Eliza looked to Roark. "Personally, I don't have faith in SOCA to fairly represent the rights of animals. The wild animals of zoos, even any intelligent Animal entertainers, who want to try 'back to nature' need some sort of pre-education, what you call 'seminars', to make the correct final decision and learn the safest transition if they make the move."

Before this meeting, Roark had grown tolerant of Eliza's opinions spouting from Orville's influence, but now he was unsure. He reviewed what she had just said in his mind, and the word 'pre-education' stood out as significant. Was this intuitive original thinking from Eliza herself?

Orville, back in pitch mode, said to Roark. "If you could assist or give advice, coordinate placing them, SOCA and other humans might underwrite the financing of a complete package, education, and resettlement back to the wild."

Orville's statement: *Humans financing the education of animals* struck Roark as a missing piece of his mind puzzle.

Not realizing she was part of someone else's call to action (Orville's), Eliza bubbled, "Oh, that would be wonderful. The Banyan Tree property would be a perfect place for those poor, miserable monkeys. And then teach them how to live open and free."

Roark did not want other primates in his banyan tree, Eliza being the exception.

"Thank you, both of you," smiled Roark. "Well presented." He nibbled from the bowl of fruit. "Let me think on this." He wasn't dismissing their reporting. Actually, his thought processes over the last week or so had been percolating fragmented ideas into a cohesive, if somewhat jellied, concoction.

"I am dealing with quite a bit. Deciding on what to build on the Banyan Tree property, for one. Also, I must find a strategy to persuade The Herd to march in the annual Founder's Regatta parade. And there are my Hollywood plans that I have pushed to the side. That is still my highest priority. Dealing with this 'Back to Africa' movement, though it seems to be a benevolent cause, seems too much to add to my 'To Do Now' list.' Why should I?" He looked to his 'team' for honest comments without expecting an enlightened and firm answer.

"You have a big heart," said Eliza.

Silent John, in the kitchen, doing dishes, turned a glance at her.

She gave her new human friend a lopsided, funny face smile.

RoarUni Fact

"Each species is a masterpiece; a creation assembled with extreme care and genius."

—Edward O. Wilson

JUNK BECOMES TREASURE

One night later, Roark heard a loud crash in his apartment, in John's bedroom. Almost asleep, he thought the worst: some disaster, walls collapsing on John; if so, it would be mentally catastrophic for them both.

In his bedroom, John was picking up fallen papers, folders, and collapsed cardboard boxes.

A frustrated grunt to Roark.

"I put too much paperwork on the desk, and your grandmother's boxes collapsed inward, and the tabletop buckled." Greatly relieved that there was no physical disaster, Roark and John began to put everything aside, using new storage boxes as legs for the wood-plank desk to be rebalanced tomorrow.

Roark sat on John's bed and rifled through one of Grandmother Mercedes's collapsed boxes. He had not paid any attention to them, all taped boxes, pushed aside and out of his mind. Someday, he would have to cull them, keep interesting items, and throw away the rest as a granny orangutan's hoarded junk. Her papers, memorabilia, personal photos, and newspaper clippings were a testament to her circus days of performing—of her life. *A hard life, but was it rewarding*? wondered Roark.

After they had viewed the first box, with various piles already set aside, Roark said to John. "Could you sleep on the couch tonight? I want to look through my grandmother's history and what she kept."

"No, I will stay here and help you sort through them. Two are better than one."

By morning, exhausted, Roark was spent. John crashed first, asleep on the couch, and when Roark's man finally stirred, Roark, holding in his fists papers from the boxes, merely said, "There is a story here, one to be told, one that needs to be told."

In her personal papers and keepsakes, Roark had seen beyond his own insular film world, his career put on hold. Now, he saw a possible direction and strategy he could control to orchestrate his comeback. Through someone else's story. More than that. It would not be his original Hollywood thinking, marked by deals and subservience.

To take a new risk, Roark had to blend creativity with industriousness. He found himself putting the previously suggested concept of 'education' into his thinking. And so, multiple ideas found cohesion. And a realization hit him: he could multitask it all together. Two aphorisms came to mind: *A solution exists from collective evidence.* And, *outside influence, late to consideration, carries the most weight.*

* * *

The lightbulb clicking in his skull only took two days to brighten. And, in the late evening, at The Herd, John saw his boss do his orangutan happy jumping: "I believe I can solve everything and save the day. Go and rouse Eliza and Orville. We have work to do."

PONTIFICATING THE IDEA

I woke up one day wondering if I was more of a teacher than entertainer. Or maybe one and the same.

– from *Roark, the First Memoir*

Coalescing his jangled thinking was Roark's *Plan of Action,* which, over many iterations, would evolve into a working memorandum entitled ***Animal and Human Rights are Equal Rights***—general in the beginning, with a lack of specifics, which allowed for shifting strategic changes as warranted. Much later, four to five years down the road, others, motivated Animals and sympathetic humans came to support the fleshed-out concept, maneuvered Roark's thesis-turned-manifesto and into a call for political mobilization, and with the usual requirement of causes, the abbreviated cause became the *AERP*, the **Animal Equal Rights Party** in which Roark never played an overt role though he benefitted in the end. Political opponents in the future would ridicule them, calling the grassroots effort 'inconsequential hyperbole'. Even idealist fringe activists outside the AERP membership would demean and denounce the business-centric and non-combative strategies that Roark embraced, which he embodied as did pioneers before him. Steady progress was not fast enough for the radicals, with all actions on the table as acceptable to gain their goal. But all these reactions were far into the future.

Indeed, in the germination of the idea, the end product of a future national movement was in no way Roark's initial direction. He focused solely on the for-profit side outlined in his initial *Plan of Action,* which Banyan Tree (BT) Enterprises would begin implementing.

His first shrewd decision was to promote his team and increase their salaries. They would soon discover how much detail would be involved in their new job responsibilities.

In the early stages, and in condensing this new strategy into action goals, he had to emphasize utmost security, not to let any loose paperwork fall into the wrong hands, specifically the outside media and the inside gossip busybodies at The Herd.

Eliza, Oliver, and John, during Roark's evening oral presentation, collectively looked at each other and realized something momentous was happening. On a less lofty scale, but eventual historical comparisons held the *Action Plan* as a modern Magna Carta or Roark channeling Shakespeare's St. Crispin's Day speech. Or had Roark thought in terms of a film's best challenging orations? President Whitmore in *Independence Day*, *Braveheart* (William Wallace instilling bravery in his fated army), or Sparta's *300.*

Opportunity towards Greatness presentation by Roark, the orangutan movie star.

"We, you and I, will change society's way of thinking. We few will be the crusaders on an adventure of future achievement for the Animal and human world. Our platform and our cause will be enshrined as *Animal and Human Rights are Equal Rights.* This won't be an easy trek; any attempt will be epic. In our initial foray down this highway, we will seek to motivate others to carry on what I believe is the mission to overcome future challenges of IAs and raise high the torch of species unity. No doubt, we will face the hatred and prejudice of those who don't believe Animals can find success in the human world or those who can only accept that all humans must be evil. It is the middle ground we need to claim as our own and hold firm. Equal Rights!

"That is my overview."

Dazed yet pumped, the three listeners (disciples?) took in all he asked of them and saw themselves as banner carriers and 'first responder' implementers, until Eliza, as usual, asked the nut to the spiel: "What's this mean?"

Simple to his vision: "I intend to start a university for Animals."

* * *

And so, his *Plan of Action* was launched. Again, one is reminded that at this time in society, the ITSE invention had helped Animals assist humans in health care or entertainment. What was original and game-changing at this moment: there had never been a 'system' of Animals educating other Animals for the specific goal of working in the human world, giving them the advantage to work separately and compete equally, and by doing so, the Intelligent Animals could succeed, gaining goals they set. An understandable concept, but many humans before Roark's Plan came into existence could not grasp an animal educational institution, believing it was not to their advantage, and Animals themselves had never before envisioned that special education could be invaluable for them. Roark, and then his team saw the possibilities.

Roark would show, by action, not preaching, that humans and Animals were equal in a joint societal community. Roark might not have seen the beginning landscape as a revolutionary earthquake, for his cautious mindset initially sought narrow first steps.

So said his preamble: *Education* is the first immovable pillar of equal rights: those who want to be educated deserve opportunities, which in turn lead to equality. Politicians look to the future yet seldom act, while those visionaries, more practical, look into themselves and roll up their sleeves. That might be termed 'revolutionary', but not the word Roark wanted bantered around to be tainted and debased by any human perception.

Roark passed out assignments that were possible now in the current.

"Orville, you are a journalist, the newsletter editor, a writer with the talent to create a strong and compelling story. I would like you to be our Manager of Literary Production. I want you to write the biography of my grandmother, Mercedes.

"When you are not working on the Heard newsletter, you will work from my apartment. You will collect and outline her life story using these boxed career items and identify one of the Animals within The Herd, one who seems restless and wants a challenge to be your researcher. There must be other background materials that both you and your employee can gather. The C&B Circus will be a major part of the story, so you will interview residents of The Herd, transcribing their recollections, not only of Mercedes but also of the life and times of other Herd residents and their circus days. Even track down former C&B former human employees. Look for compelling anecdotes and private stories.

"During these interviews here at the Herd, I want you to quietly probe the residents individually: what are their hopes and dreams? Ask them hypothetically: 'If they had an opportunity to take on a job that would give them satisfaction, what would that be?'" He was parroting Eliza's questioning from the day on the beach.

"So, Orville, would you be willing to undertake this Manager of Literary Production position? I must tell you there will be other side jobs as we progress, like public relations and social media outreach."

Orville had been looking for stimulation and enthusiastically responded, "This sounds exciting." Roark smiled as the first thread of the intricate tapestry he was weaving spooled onto his private loom.

Roark continued, his enthusiasm for new challenges invigorating him.

"Let me expand on my project.

"At the Banyan Tree property site, I am going to start an educational institution. More than just a school; for us all I want to achieve dignity, a University has the reach of respectability. So, I'm going to call the institution, *Roar Animal University.* Its charter will be multi-dimensional. I am going to enroll animal students and educate them to become Intelligent Animals. They will learn English and how to cope in the human world. They will be taught the rudimentary history of their forebears and how their current lesser animal brethren are living in the jungles and forests. For those who are interested, I will allow them to decide if they would like to return to the wild. And I think I will make a test case out of those still unsettled monkeys from Anndwell Monkey Farm."

Eliza and Orville looked at him. Amazed. This was their answer to overcome the past failure of SOCA's plans, perhaps an ability to realize the true mission of animal relocation. Roark did not slow down, seeking to generate more enthusiasm among his core group.

"Per my agreement with Short Skiff Key, I will build new buildings or remodel the old ones into small student-run businesses that will teach Intelligent Animals, past and new ITSE Animals, to learn trade jobs in the human world. Those who don't return to their ancestral homelands will learn how to integrate into the human world, and humans will see the benefit of Intelligent Animals among them."

Eliza, Oliver, and John realized the magnitude of Roark's proposed undertaking. If accomplished, this would not only be earth-shattering but a realignment of society on Earth. *Equal Rights*, indeed. *Transformative anarchy*, Oliver said but only to himself.

John had to ask, a little worried for his boss, "How will you afford to start this University?"

Roark smiled the smile of the wily.

"Like any smart Animal, use the funds of supportive human benefactors. Of course, to seed this university as a start-up, I will have to liquidate several of my California real estate holdings. But I will keep my San Gabriel house and rent it out until I return."

Eliza started to look more closely at what he was saying. She did not like the thought of any dependence on human generosity. But more so, she was startled that Roark talked about having a place to live someday, far away.

Roark turned to Eliza. "In this new University concept, I will be the Chancellor. One of my primary functions will be to oversee the education and business side of educating animals into Animals with a capital 'A.' If you agree, I would like you to run the program for Animal resettlement if, in the end, they opt to return. It will be far different from what SOCA has in mind since it will be Animal-led. This will not be conversion therapy, going the opposite of capital 'A' as in an Intelligent Animal going back into a lower case of a wild animal, but solely up to the creature, their choice: intelligence or the jungle. Or both.

"And, getting back to financing this project through BT Enterprises, there will be side businesses that will support our goals to finance the University's goal.

"Are you all ready to step into this Animal New World?"

Roark was somewhat surprised, but not deterred, when Eliza said, "I would like to think about this. It is such a meaningful gesture to be included in the scope, as you've told us. I do want to help with this Animal relocation project. I know we can do better than SOCA. I just want to be sure of my feelings before saying yes."

Orville patted her shoulder. And John agreed, "You are very bright. Whatever you undertake, you will learn the job thoroughly and make it work."

Roark was a little miffed that he did not have everyone ready to raise his banner and seek the summit. Yes, he could understand her reluctance. He had pulled her from a dark place and opened her eyes to her potential as an Intelligent Animal. Now, the world was open to her choices. And he knew she still harbored distrust of humans. "Take your time. I will accept whatever decision you make."

Having set his mind to this *scheme*, if that was an appropriate definition; then, hustle, not hesitation, became his internal motivation. The return to Hollywood would happen, but not as soon as expected. Roark rationalized: They can wait.

As to group commitment, all Animal eyes turned to Silent John.

"Roark is my boss, and he's already asked me to serve as Vice President of Operations for BT Enterprises and oversee the construction of the University buildings.

"My prime task will be the handling of our projects between us and the outside human world. As I understand Roark's new *Action Plan,* there will always be two distinct groups: Animals and humans. They are separate, but for the benefit of all, we must work together. I can see that time coming."

Roark nodded his head to emphasize John's supporting words. He sought to lay out his philosophy further.

"One of my underlying directions, which you won't hear me say in public, is that for our needs, I don't want any human intervention that might gain power over us. Yes, I will have to accept human money, whether government grants or corporate contributions, because my goal is to solve Animal problems to further our success. What I want is Animal freedom, and I believe this first means financial freedom. I am willing to begin here in Short Skiff Key. To start small and careful, guard our resources, nurture just a few voices. Where it goes from there, our success will determine."

Eliza saw herself as more willing to help others without seeking remuneration. Still, she could see that money (which she was now earning) was essential in supporting causes that would be beneficial to Animals. She considered Roark's *Plan of Action* as it addressed her blossoming beliefs, which held caveats. *Help animals, all animals. I can use Roark's Equal Rights project to accomplish that goal. A successful resettlement program is first. Equal rights for all animals must follow.*

IMPLEMENTATION

Orville, the writer, living off the government's stipend for his housing and food expenses, had never really accepted that this easy life had limitations. He could partially see Roark's point of view. The orangutan had come from nothing, made something of himself, and depended on his talent. As an ex-circus chimpanzee Orville lived without repercussions or concern for money; first, from the communal bondage of circus life now ended; then, second, a shift in his daily existence through the generosity of the government, which someday would likewise end with 8 years left on the government stipends. He wanted to ignore this future reality, but he could see it coming. To continue his survival and enjoy comfort, he must be paid for real work. Yes, he knew he had to find a real job, using a financial base to help others. Here was such a chance: this story of Mercedes, Roark's grandmother, must be written with sensitivity to elevate Animal ethos and redefine the word 'humanity' as belonging to all species—yes, this direction would judge his own worth.

The four of them were threads in a tapestry now being woven. In another analogy, drip and drips can preclude a flood.

* * *

Roark walked the inside fence perimeter, not within the Monkey Garden, but along a grassy open walkway where the giraffes exercised and past the muddy ponds where the elephants wallowed and sunned themselves. He ended up near the aviary rookery where Skye, the brown eagle, came out to preen, then fly up and away as part of the bird's daily soaring routine.

As Skye returned to his perch, Roark walked up and made a seemingly innocent remark.

"What do you see on your daily flights?"

Skye eyed the orangutan. He held no bad opinion of this new resident, so he responded, "I cruise the Short Skiff Key area but stay over residential homes. Any bird might run a risk flying out into the Glades, where human hunters might take a potshot."

Roark could understand that fear and see what set Skye's feelings against the humans, which made him the right board director asset to Chairman Balfour's minimal human contact position.

Roark readied to throw out a 'drip.'

"I wonder why you don't go into real estate. I heard you were the one to fly over this Kure Steel Fabricators site and help identify it as the perfect place for The Herd."

Skye chirped a dismissal. "How could a bird be that? A real estate agent?"

"Nothing's impossible, is it?" Roark still feigning nonchalance. "With technology today, you could mount a miniature head camera to take aerial photos of a property, then swoop down to video the internal rooms. I bet a real estate company would take you on in a minute as an associate, and then, with experience, you could become a full agent." He thought he had the closing hook. "You can give verbal comments to prospective buyers, which drones can't do. A strong marketing tool. Just a wild thought I had. Have a good day."

The following day, a book was delivered to Skye's rookery: '*Florida Real Estate License Test Primer.*'

* * *

Drip, drip.

Orville saw the lioness Sekhmet in the common area. She was watching her fellow felines, Calypso, Calliope, and Clio, imitate and perform a modern dance routine they had seen on television. Their mimicry was spot on, and Sekhmet was impressed that their talent was fresh, even if it was only for internal Herd audiences.

Orville spoke as Sekhmet watched the ongoing dance.

"Did you see where there is a public hearing at the Town Council about a new school crossing walk for the human children, down on Ocean Boulevard? That's only three blocks away from us."

The lioness did not look at the chimpanzee but nodded her head. "I did see that on the local net news."

"You know, we should send a representative. Human safety is reflected in our neighborhood. You know you would make a terrific spokesperson for us."

"They don't want to hear from an Animal."

"Neighborhood safety is always important. Don't you think they would listen to you if you showed up and smiled with your pretty teeth?"

Sekhmet looked at him to see that his smile held humor, which caused her to think about what he was saying. Politics interested her, the art of debate, and standing up for one's beliefs.

"Do you really think I would have any sway?"

"Definitely. I would even cover it for *The Heard*. Maybe make sure the local Skiff *News* interviews you. I will get you more details, so you're prepared. The Herd needs a public voice representing us."

"I will think on it."

The Three Cool Cats, as they called themselves, finished their routine, and the scattered applause from the few viewing Animals gave the female lions pure satisfaction that they still had 'it.'

RoarUni Facts

A type of lemur monkey which communicates in rhythmic song, has given scientists an insight into how humans evolved to create music. The researchers found that the lemurs had consistent rhythmic patterns or beats in their communications, much like music. Indris lemurs, along with humans, have the highest number of vocal rhythms in the animal kingdom, surpassing songbirds and other mammals. The findings highlight the evolutionary roots of musical rhythm, demonstrating that the foundational elements of human music can be traced back to early primate communication systems.

OUTSIDE AWARENESS

Silent John and the BT Enterprises architect appeared at the Short Skiff Key Building Department, filed several copies of the development building plans, and paid the appropriate fees.

The property would be developed in the first phase by remodeling the shuttered Harris Funeral Home into the administration building for the newly proposed Roar Animal University, the name first seen on the renderings. Construction of the actual University central education building would begin in about four months. A sub-permit had been filed to allow temporary tent(s) to house classrooms, and an application for accreditation had been filed with the State of Florida Department of Education. Another form filed with the appropriate government agency committee towards licensing permits of multiple ITSE devices for 'educational, entertainment, and public service Animals.' A final blanket grant request was prepared to be sent to pro-animal groups to assist in financing University operations and setting up scholarship resources to cover student costs. Roark knew he would have to establish a fundraising office for this undertaking, as he was in the process of liquidating most of his assets to launch this educational program and break ground for classrooms. Regarding the University design, the most dilapidated and abandoned buildings would be demolished, and remodeling plans were in place to create the first of several small pop-up businesses facing the main road in front of the property.

There would be room for expansion if the planned businesses were successful. One such business would be a training restaurant, totally run by Animals.

In these design plans, the banyan tree would be the center of the open space, featuring a small circular garden and a reflection walkway called Mercedes Garden. BT Enterprises filed for a permit to clean up the back brackish swamp, seeking Federal EPA grants, which included building several pier structures for student ecosystem studies.

Demolition permits were approved within a week, and a human construction crew immediately began dismantling several shuttered buildings, while starting with the Roar administrative building remodel on the former Harris Funeral Home site.

A posted sign outside the gated land announced, "***Future Home of Roar Animal University.***

* * *

Chairman Balfour, not angry but concerned, spoke to Larry, the lion.

"What is this University for Animals?"

"I have no idea," replied Larry. "I assume it will be like an animal preserve, or a tourist attraction with animals in school-like viewing cages. I really don't know."

"You haven't heard if any of our Animal residents are involved in this 'school'?

"No, I don't think so."

"Well, keep your eyes on this. The Herd has a reputation. I don't want some tourist trap zoo to take away from what we have so far accomplished by maintaining our integrity as the correct public perception."

* * *

Drip, drip.

Roark and Eliza sat before his computer and initiated a video call with Mrs. Humphries, president of SOCA. Eliza made the introduction, and Mrs. Humphries, whether her admiration was genuine or not, fawned over Roark by telling him that she had recently watched the movie *Every Which Way But Loose* on late-night cable TV and found his role 'delightful.' Roark merely nodded, not revealing that the role was played by another orangutan actor, Manis, who played the character Clyde in the movie starring human actor Clint Eastwood. Roark had not yet been born.

After further pleasantries, Mrs. Humphries delicately asked the nature of the call, allowing Roark to begin another 'drip' of his *Action Plan*, from rivulet to creek to stream to rushing river of Animal attainment.

"Mrs. Humphries, I have noted that your inaugural reintroduction of animals to the wild was not a complete success. I believe I have a solution. From my Hollywood experiences, I have observed that animals that wish to return to the wild still need a basic introductory course on how to do so—a survival manual, so to speak—which will give them added support in grassland, jungle, or rainforest survival. At the same time, education on interacting with humans would give them an advantage in dealing with unforeseen challenges that might interfere with their reintroduction to the wild. Certainly, we both would not want them to return to inhumane conditions. A fallback alternative is required to match the good deeds that SOCA has so far accomplished. But from an Animal perspective."

Roark went silent, awaiting a response.

"You speak quite articulately, Mr. Roark."

"Roark, just Roark."

The head of SOCA gave that smile that so concerned Eliza. "Roark, I see that you have given our situation and our goals deep consideration. I agree with your outline. SOCA now realizes that just dumping our beloved animals into unprepared situations would not be positive; let alone any possible negative publicity would prevent other animals from considering transferring to a simpler natural existence, one with comfort."

Roark, to himself, still thought this return to nativism was a pipe dream among do-gooders. He could use this altruism for his more comprehensive *Action Plan*.

Eliza sat quietly listening, forming no opinion, just observing what SOCA might agree to, and a little mystified as to why Roark would want to partner with SOCA. He had privately chastised SOCA, saying that Animal freedom of choice had been damaged by passing the original SOCA law, forcing ex-circus animals into unemployment. She thought she saw his real fear: what if SOCA turns on animal movie stars next and lets this Artificial Intelligence digitization, whatever that is, replace real-life acting Animals? It did not bother her, as she saw his worry would reinforce her resettlement project as an answer to Animal's search for open freedom, away from human rule.

"What do you propose?" Mrs. Humphries asked Roark. She was cautious and reluctant, not having dealt directly with an Intelligent Animal, accepting he was a special breed, not a mere circus performer. His success in films gave him the credentials to speak and be listened to. And he did.

"Simply, let select Animals carry your burden and let SOCA take all credit, and in doing so, perhaps generate funds for other projects you might wish to undertake.

"Let me elaborate. SOCA will handle the public relations to identify animals who would like to be educated. You will send us the names and locations of interested parties, and we will interview them and select those who meet the standards of knowing what they must do to assimilate. One example is to learn English. We find that an international language with humans would benefit all communication and work best in the Animal world.

"Further, I believe SOCA would retain its expertise as the fundraising connection among humans to support these goals. The monies raised would pay for a reasonable tuition at an animal school that we have started to develop here in Florida. Of course, SOCA retains a fee for funds raised. For those animals that graduate from the courses offered, if they choose, we will coordinate their return to their ancestral native homelands.

Mrs. Humphries interjected.

"But what if the animals go to the jungle, don't like the circumstances, and wish to return? We can't be burdened with the overhead of housing and maintaining the returnees."

"Very understandable. Why don't you leave that to our Animals? We will create a job placement board, hopefully within the human and Animal worlds. That will be our responsibility. From our perspective, we do not wish to return animals to bad situations, which I believe your organization's charter likewise opposes. We would only offer comfortable habitats in this country."

"Very true indeed. No harm to Animals."

"Agreed."

"All sounds possible," Mrs. Humphries mentally envisioned the nuances of the contract. "Since what you are talking about does not seem to be a financial drain on us."

"Just maintain a strong and constant fundraising program. Your SOCA has had quite a successful past. I am sure this new 'Back to Africa' or wherever, can generate new contributors."

"How do we proceed so that we can see the written points of your proposal?"

"My lawyer will call your lawyer."

"Sounds promising." And the video meeting ended.

Eliza squished her face..

"What?" asked Roark.

"It all sounds fantastic. Can you do it?"

"I can start the melon rolling, so to speak. However, any new endeavor never looks like the original idea in the final proposal. It's metamorphic."—he looked to her. "Our goal is that a caterpillar becomes a butterfly."

"And juicy caterpillars taste good," smiled Eliza. "But how can you afford or take so much time to undertake this benevolent saving of Animals? Aren't you going back to make more movies?" That was her worry. He was a friend, and she could count her only friends on three fingers.

Roark replied, realizing they were having a serious discussion. "I have put my career into a short-term hiatus—a pause. I'm not focused on it for the time being. I have two more years before I can return to acting in the movie industry. But Eliza, please realize my drive is not 100% benevolent. I want to judge my success by the happiness of Animals and, yes, by profit if this University and land development are to be successful. I have limited funds and have been liquidating—selling-- my real estate in California. I am taking a great risk."

She did not mean to say this critically, but said, "You sound like one of those humans on television who always tells people how good it could be and then sells them a used car or a loan on their insurance policy."

He laughed. "We must work with humans but be wary of their agendas."

"I hope we don't have to work with humans," Eliza replied, recalling her past tribulations, but then thought of Silent John. "Good humans are okay if they work for our goals, not the other way around."

Roark accepted the consequences of a female orangutan becoming set in her beliefs; he just had not been around any. *I guess there must be a compromise in non-divergent discourse.* "If you are part of this, you will face jealousy from those animals and humans who believe that what you achieve should, in part, belong to them. Beware of the underachievers. They would destroy our vision just for cruel spite."

"But this seems like a great cause."

"We shall see." His reply startled Eliza.

"It won't be?"

"With you involved, with your honesty, I am sure those against us will fail."

"I don't want your Equal Rights to fail." She did not say his *Action Plan.* She had interpreted all that he had been saying but extrapolated it into a meaning that it applied to *all* animals, big 'A' or small 'a.' The end goal. "I have decided I will help with this first step, placing animals in a new, safe country, in their homelands."

Tepid reluctance on her part was not the enthusiasm he had hoped for. He enjoyed having her around. More of a commitment, he thought, would be some sign that she might immerse herself in the project—his project—to be at his side.

Too soon, Eliza would become wholly cognizant of the truth: that significant change more often than not is born in chaos.

And back to the drip analogy: ravishing floods spring from innocent rivulets.

RoarUni Fact

Zebras communicate using various vocalizations, including barks, snorts, and high-pitched squeals, as well as complex facial expressions and ear postures. No two zebras have the exact same black-and-white stripe pattern; a group of zebras is called a "dazzle," and their stripes serve multiple purposes from deterring flies to cooling. Underneath all that striped fur, a zebra's skin is black. Like horses, zebras can enter a light sleep while standing up. Aggressive towards humans, they've never been bred into domesticity.

ADVANCING THE PLAN

During the next several months, the *Action Plan* remained in underground organizational mode, featuring stealth forays and below-the-radar actions.

Orville and Roark pored over the discovered boxed trove of documents and photos, creating an outline of Mercedes's life. As Orville began to put words into sentences crowded into paragraphs, a bittersweet true story began to unfold—one that exemplified what almost all animals lived through in their captivity within the human world structure of dominance.

What benefited Orville's assignment was that Mercedes had kept a diary. Once, before television, if it can be believed, diaries had been the source record of how humans thought and expressed emotions when their cultural mores prevented them from publicly voicing their heartfelt honesty. A diary published back then offered a personal intra-social media calendar, broadening behind-the-scenes history or scandalizing news with juicy gossip about yet-unknown liaisons of the high and mighty. It has been said that a diary is best positioned when published posthumously, when the diarist is mortally absent from criticism or defamation lawsuits.

In her C&B Circus life, Mercedes had plenty of downtime between shows to reflect on her upbringing and career, how she survived diseases that weakened her heart, and her family torn from her and scattered across the country. Orville often had to stop his reading of her scrawled penmanship to dab at his eyes.

In his interview with Sekhmet concerning her remembrances of Mercedes, Orville said, "Oh, by the way, the Short Skiff Key Town Council at their next meeting wants to visit with local neighborhoods to gain support in their 'Best Florida Small City' competition. Since you've attended several meetings, I think it's important that you sit up and say something nice so we Animals, through you, are seen as good citizens."

DRIP, DRIP

Roark leaned over the short fence enclosure at The Herd daycare center. When PennyRae, one of the elephants helping with the young animals noticed him, she trundled over to see what he might want.

Admiringly, he said as she approached, "You and Sebayet (the female camel) take marvelous care of all the babies. Do I see some of our troubled friends from the Petting Zoo alumni?"

Accepting the compliment, PennyRae flipped her trunk towards the menagerie. "Once a week, we combine the petting zoo members and the daycare youngsters. Both groups can learn from each other. The frolics of the young bring back a tenderness that those traumatized in the past petting zoo incidents can find comfort and calmness. The young come to understand our 'herd' co-living. It is a win-win."

"At what age do you begin to teach the young ones the English language?" Roark sought to define the age range for accepting students to his new university. He thought he might start with a class number of 25, cautious to test a never-before-used curriculum.

PennyRae well thought of in being an 'information provider'. "It is important that they grow from birth, learning their own language. Once they are weaned, we schedule the operation for the *ITSE* insertion. Soon after that, we can judge if the brain stimulation is working, and then we can begin basic vocal chord exercises and English word associations with what they know of their environment, like 'food, rain, sun, sleep.'"

"What about learning the Rules and Regs of The Herd Association?"

She snorted a laugh. "Oh, we don't do that. Chairman Balfour has set up a lecture once they have reached the phase of grasping more complex human language and thought formation."

At this point, a small elephant ran up and started nuzzling PennyRae.

"Yours?" Roark noted their love and affection—apparently, mother and child.

"Yes, and a handful. Huntington is quite the proud father."

Roark concurred. "A family is central to the happiness of any herd." A quick pang, realizing he had no family nor one on the horizon. He let any expansion on this thought lie fallow as Sebayet approached to see what gossip this recluse movie star might generate.

Roark said, "I was just saying that you two make excellent teachers. You should be out in the world with your skills. I think I've heard of teaching positions available at this Animal university soon opening." And, he let that silent 'drip' ease into their discussion.

FEW GOOD CHOICES

Orville took a break from his bio writing and visited the Monkey Garden to talk to Edgar, the designated leader of The Herd primate troop. Orville wasn't a fan—Edgar was a bully and took food from the weak. With the leftover stipend from the government to all the Animals at The Herd, Edgar received a percentage of monkey dollars as the 'boss,' supposedly offering protection, security, and power in representing a monkey voting bloc's impact in The Herd decision-making. To that end, the Monkey Garden became the nicest housing facility that someone else's money could buy and decorate. But Orville knew that Edgar could provide assistance for the right price, and Roark had not yet built his staff, so he must rely, temporarily, on whomever he could scrounge up to kick off his first resettlement project.

"What do you want?" snapped Edgar. His face bore old fight scars, and from back in the day, the circus had filed down his sharp front teeth to prevent his biting everyone he did not like or who got in his way. That did not stop his mean streak.

"I met someone looking to hire some smart monkeys who are bored."

"We got no one here, Orv, who is remotely like that." Orville had only to glance at the trees to see that most of the tree swingers were not really into swinging but were watching television.

"Maybe. I wondered if four or so wanted a little excitement and to make some money on the side. But you know the Chairman doesn't like to see anyone in this compound working for themselves, especially away from the grounds." Orville knew which buttons to push when it came to Herd politics.

Edgar held his silence. He did not necessarily disagree but knew his group's work on any side jobs had to be an under-the-table transaction, with his approval and his cut.

"What's the job, just if someone is interested?"

"Baby-sitting gig." Sometimes, the old C&B Circus slang slipped in. "A group of regular common monkeys have been rescued from a crappy baby-making farm, and a group of good-hearted humans want to send them home, meaning outside the country."

"Set them down on a tree somewhere and say, 'Look what we did.' And what? A bunch of us have to keep the dumbasses in line? Play the tough bulls?"

"Yeah, call it that if you want, but look at it. What's the word the humans use, 'chap.e.roning'? Free travel to sit on them until they meet up with their kind in the jungle or out on the Serengeti range. Not quite sure yet. Travel accommodation has your group in economy class, and those you are in charge of will travel in nice, secure accommodations."

Edgar didn't need to know, and Orville kept to himself, that if the resettlement monkeys saw only humans taking them, they would fear a repeat of their first lousy trip, where two of their kind were killed.

"And humans are running this show?"

"Not quite. There is only one human for each trip to handle human issues, such as Customs, and avoid quarantine screwups. But there are some key Animals in charge. I can't say more. The problem is, can you find four of you who can ditch the Garden for about a week and not get fined by the Executive Committee?"

"A trip out of these Apartments. A vacation of sorts." Edgar thought he might consider running the show. However, he grunted a response of derision. "Chairman Balfour has no real control. A few of us go missing for a couple of weeks, so what? They never perform a head count."

Edgar found the offer intriguing and began figuring out a travel team that could be trusted and would follow only his orders. "I could make it happen if the price is right. No fruit. I want cash up front. I got a 401K to feed."

Orville did not like 'scary' Edgar.

RoarUni Fact

The term, "Survival of the fittest," was actually first used by English philosopher Herbert Spencer in his 1864 "Principles of Biology" to connect his economic and sociological theories with Charles Darwin's biological concepts. Darwin first adopted the phrase in his fifth edition of "The Origin of Species," published in 1869, giving credit to Spenser for the term.

EVER-CHANGING IDEAS

A good plan is open to constant modification. Roark wanted a test case using the SOCA contract to prove the concept of his fledgling Roar University and to understand if a good deed could also be a money earner.

And, just starting out, he did not have a large cadre of Animals who would be impressed with his novel ideas. Here, to quickly get his program launched, money talked; thus, Edgar and his cohorts were signed up. Roark envisioned a three-pronged jumpstart to his operations: (1) seeing if the SOCA program of re-inserting animals back into the wild would work; (2) through a vetting process of animal applications define those with traits towards intelligence who might work better if they stayed within the country and the University would, by education, turn them into ITSE Animals with skills to work among humans; and (3) provide a profit source for BT Enterprises with the animal relocations and the University start-up and hopefully new subsidiary operations he was considering: (a) an adjacent student-run training restaurant; (b) an employment agency for ITSE Animal job placement; and (c) a travel agency to have generous humans who believe in animal kindness pay for those animals wishing to return to the wild plus special tours to exotic places for those Intelligent Animals who had the freedom and would pay money to see the world. Go as tourists and return safely, unstuffed, and not wall mounted.

In the big picture, Roark did not confide all his ideas with his team; many creative thoughts were still germinating. Oliver focused on writing. Silent John oversaw the first phase of construction for the University site, including demolition, grading, gutting, and remodeling.

And Eliza, sweet Eliza.

Roark thought fondly of her progress as one of the smarter ITSE Animals he had met. She voraciously devoured audiobooks, constantly in learning mode. The world of knowledge became an addiction. Her rapid development into an Intelligent Animal, one of his successes, spurred him to think about discovering a hundred or more future Intelligent Animals (IAs) who could help run his side businesses and improve Animal life—a win-win situation.

Roark, optimistic but forearmed, had been through the grind of Hollywood. He saw the gritty side of stardom, the rise and fall of hopes. He, the dark realist, while Eliza was plainly happy talking about a fluffy world where all animals could return to their ancestral homeland—a kind of reverse *Roots*.

Thus, without much encouragement, Eliza began her first responsibility, taking former comrades (survivors) from Anndwell Animal Farm, the monkeys, and preparing them for the return trip. This time, they would be better prepared and under the co-sponsorship of SOCA and Roar University, the latter to serve as the educational center of re-entry training. But there was more to this beneath the surface within Roark's operational setup.

TESTING #101

The first wild monkey orientation was held in a circus-like tent on the future University grounds on the Banyan Tree property.

Since these Anndwell monkeys had been mistreated and were not ITSE Animals, for their protection and that of the general public, they were contained in a secure compound under a large netting bubble, which Eliza entered to conduct 'examinations of their abilities to cope in the wild.' Based on these test results, each monkey would be separated according to its species and the location to which it would be returned: Group A—twelve Capuchin and woolly spider monkeys to Central America, and Group B—five Vervet monkeys to South Africa.

In private sessions, the groups were divided into individuals, and each was asked personal questions about their background in monkey-speak or sign language. Were any of them 'natural' (taken from their homes), or were they bred at Anndwell Animal Farm? Then, they were asked a series of questions: Did they know how to cope in the wild? What food would they be searching for? If they encountered indigenous monkey troops, how would they greet them, visit, and interact with them? Would the locals take them into their group permanently? In the wild, current inter-family mating between small troop members could raise genetic issues, so it was hoped that this new insertion of 'distant cousins' would improve the next generation's health.

Eliza wondered about the end purpose of the questions she was told to ask. Certain questions seemed to have nothing to do with making the trip and insertion; instead, they sought responses on various subjects, including psychological prying, problem-solving, IQ testing, and even their feelings about humans. Eliza questioned Roark about what this testing was designed to accomplish.

He would be patient with her. "You want to return all these monkeys to their natural environment, correct?"

"Yes, freedom away from humans, in their own domain, among their own kind."

He walked with her to the base of the banyan tree, gazing at the branches and the tree's foliage, teasing him to swing away into joy now absent from his new daily burdens. He'd had no 'tree escapism' and missed those lost moments, especially with Eliza.

"But if it is freedom you give them, what happens if one, two, or several monkeys don't want that type of freedom but would rather live in or around the human world? They may come to see a better place here than over there, which is their *Equal Right.* The right to have freedom as we suppose they want, or do we give them the right of free choice to do anything they want to do? Then, will we only be the educators and providers to see if their choices have the minimum chance of thriving?"

Eliza paused. Roark did have a point. All animals could be free, but it had to be their choice. But in her mind, she felt that once they were taught how to live in the wild, they would make that the correct choice. But then....

"But if some of these monkeys choose to come back here, what do we do with them?"

"A good question. This is the paradox, which means one choice offers another choice, but which is the right choice?

The University, I hope, will be a teaching institution that educates those who wish either to return to the jungle or forests or stay and enter the human world, hopefully on an equal basis to humans in some form. I believe we have a dual purpose. But here is another dilemma you must consider:

"Wherever our 'students' go, we must educate them to make the right decisions in their lives. When our education ends, they are on their own. To achieve this, we ought to 'graduate' smart and intelligent animals who themselves will make the choice. Those that stay can be rewarded during their educational period with ITSE implants and learn how to utilise their thinking mind to survive. Those deciding to go back to the jungle, must learn jungle skills.

"And here comes another question for you—what if an animal cannot learn, has neither the desire nor willingness to learn jungle or civilization, perhaps has a brain impairment, or is just lazy? Do we let a zoo or the government take care of them?

"By using these tests, you and your teachers will have discovered any shortcomings on the front end of admission before they enter our university system. Tell me, Eliza, what do we do with the unteachable, those who will or wish to remain ignorant? It is a fact that ignorance, either in the jungle or in civilization, is a weakness, and in the end, may be fatal, or perhaps they will mimic the worst habits of humans. I don't want to see that, but what is to be done with the weak, ignorant, or even evil? And is it our responsibility?"

Eliza, shaken, had no solution. She felt Roark, trapped in this 'paradox,' had not yet decided. Without trying to understand everything or the possible impacts, Eliza fell back on a core belief that no animal should be left behind if education were possible.

So, she affirmed, "We must educate them all and take our chance that they will be good citizens or strong family unit members."

He could have ridiculed her naivety, but he did not. "A noble quest, but we might not have the capacity or financial position to take everyone into our university, and the human world has put limitations on the use of ITSE. Thus, we will have limitations when offering our miracle of teaching.

"But it is not available for all creatures, nor free to all who want it. There is a production limitation and a monetary limitation, so there must be a classification system to select those who can best adapt as Intelligent Animals. The beginning is the first step, not the final leap. Success will build more success. If you see this as some crusade, you must first support education, which you and I are doing. As the door openers, we must enter carefully and watch for pitfalls and traps."

She responded: "I still don't understand, Roark. What do you really want to do? I see the good you are trying to bring to the unfortunate, but now you tell me that this selection process is going to, as you say, limit those we help." Sadness creased her face. Should she cry or get mad? She reiterated her mantra: "All animals must have rights, Equal Rights."

"Yes, let's hope so, but someday."

Roark pointed to the construction underway. "Well, I think we both agree that this is the place to begin such work. No one else is doing something like this with Animals in charge. You will be a teacher and a guide. An honorable profession worthy of your talents. And, as I've said, we shall see what happens."

"And again, I ask, what do you think will happen?"

"I am not sure. Unlike you, who is looking for a brighter day, I believe the world is hard. There is a human saying, 'Only the strong survive.' We must accept that we're in a human-dominated world. We can hide in the jungle, but they might come for us. Any thought that the world will ever be ruled by primates, a world dominated and controlled by apes, gorillas, or we orangutans, is only a figment in the imagination of movies."

Roark dug deep. "Yes, I could someday see the integration of both species working side by side. In my career, I have been there." A sadness came over him. "But only in a limited capacity and not always under my control. I have had ups and downs, successes and failures. My grandmother Mercedes struggled with great strength. And I believe she persevered and prevailed. Eliza, you and I are not on different paths, but maybe on two roads side by side, going somewhere important: the education of Animals. Educating them to be intelligent is critical."

She could not find any of his logic restricting her tomorrow or a week from tomorrow, and reached for his hand. "I look forward to seeing what you discover in your *Plan of Action*. I will prepare *my students* for the trip back to their historic homeland. First step."

Roark felt much better with this hand-in-hand gesture. He hoped she saw he was unburdening himself, not trying to lecture her into accepting his positions. He was rewarded with a smile from her, and she said, "So, at this new University you are trying to open, what are we going to call our Animal students when we've educated them and you 'graduate' them?"—she gave her teeth/lip laugh—"and they are able to go into the jungle, live away from human civilization, become free animals, live off the bountiful nature around them, and are happy?"

"I think the humans once called them 'hippies.' They are a vanishing species, I'm told."

A NEW EMPLOYEE

Anticipated circumstances and expected deadlines never coincide.

The following month, Roark found himself multi-tasking, juggling, and re-prioritizing.

Orville brought him a new hire, a fellow chimpanzee.

"This is Gort. He is an IA (Intelligent Animal). Originally from the Beppo Family Circus, which shut down due to SOCA. He was bought by Western Tech College as their mascot, but he really became their 'lab rat.' Gort specializes in computer software programming. He told me that they reprogrammed his ITSE. Maybe 'over-programmed' is the better word. They taught him special computer systems, including hacking expertise. When he thought he knew everything, he went 'vegetable' on them. He says he faked it. And when he overheard they might put him down, he skipped out. He heard about the Animals-only Herd commune, which led him to discover me, and considering his talents, I thought you could use him best, especially this one database he created."

"And what's that?" Roark fiddling with papers on his desk, his mind drifting while one eye looked at the small chimpanzee, looking nervous and too young.

"Gort here has created a database of all listed IA circus animals in the country and where they are now."

"He did what, and how?" Roark was now suitably attentive.

"You, he, and I are probably the only animals who will know that the ITSE Committee worried about the usage, misuse, or liability breakdowns have programmed a microscopic tracking device into their computer chip brain implant. They know where *we all are* right at this minute. And Gort hacked their system bank and planted what he says is a 'back door.' Don't ask. He can go visiting anytime. I don't yet know how we can use it, but that alone validates his credentials."

"Interesting." Roark impressed. Years ago, he appeared in an hour-long dramatic television limited series, a remake of *Dr. Jekyll and Mr. Hyde*, which had an interesting plot twist where he played a circus animal turned by chemicals into a mad killer human. It won an Emmy…for the human actor.

"What other computer whiz stuff do you know, Gort?" Roark could use a computer nerd.

Gort spoke rapidly. "CGI-HTML-JAVA-C++,Cuneiform-Fortran-Prolog-Wolfram-SQL-COBOL-BASIC-HyperTalk-Python-Eiffel-ABAP-Grasshopper-and-ToonTalk."

Explained Orville, "He's a little high-strung. All the time."

Roark needed expertise, eccentric genius allowable, but not the Dr. Frankenstein demented.

"Let's start him off with something easy, like setting up our university computer system. Nothing elaborate." Roark gravely considered his own ITSE implant. "Could Gort disconnect the tracking system on an Intelligent Animal and have the ITSE still function?"

Gort babbled out a reply, and Orville had to translate.

He said, "No, if the transmitter stops working, the brain-computer assumes the carrier's death, and ITSE shuts down."

Roark horrified. "Can the ITSE people remotely shut down the computer-brain device in all of us, or a group or Animal, specifically targeted? And leave us alive but non-speaking/thinking animals?"

Gort said, "No." Then babbled on again.

"He says," Orville tried to follow. "He found nothing; he believes they were worried about a huge liability if there was a systems-wide malfunction that destroyed multiple assets. The Animal dies, and the computer dies. Or, I guess, if a computer malfunctions or this 10-year warranty I've heard about expires, you become a normal animal without speech-thought until a new operation puts in a replacement."

Relieved somewhat, Roark smiled at the chimp IA, whose mind floated somewhere to the tenth power.

"Welcome to the University, Gort. We have temporary staff headquarters set up, so we'll put you there. Make a list of the equipment you will need. First things first—we will need phones, laptops, and lab computers for teachers and students."

Gort smiled, realizing he could use his over-stimulated brain capacity to be genuinely creative for the Animal world, all of them, everyone, maybe. Like Roark, he was a dreamer, thinking not only on many levels but in several dimensions. Hyper-crazy a fair description.

WRITING ON THE WALL

Another day, another interruption.

Silent John entered the temporary office tent. "You gotta minute?"

Roark didn't, but he followed John outside into the light, drizzling rain from a single grey cloud surrounded by sunshine. Concentrating on his pile of tasks, he had not even registered that the noise on the tent top where he worked was the patter of rain.

John led Roark through the construction site, past the demolition debris, to the street.

Against the outer wall facing the street, Roark saw the defacement.

"*Humans Rule, Animals Serve*," and "*Humans First + Only*."

Roark shrugged at the eventuality of fatalism as much as the crime. "Cowards of free universal expression. I expected blowback, so it's not unexpected."

"I'll get it cleaned up," said John, disgusted. *Hate is hate.* He had been targeted during recent times for what might be inferred behind a mask.

"We have a chimpanzee wizard around here somewhere plugging wires into gizmos. Ask him to create a security system for us, with motion sensors, cameras, and all the bells and whistles. And please, don't start a conversation with him," Roark warned.

"We may want to consider hiring a security team. Protect your property from the rowdies." John did not want to see Roark's ambitious *Action Plan* program blighted by ignorant, fearful hooligans.

Roark mulled this hiccup to his quest.

"We can't hire security guards with guns. If a human were shot, the newspapers would destroy our educational approach to Animal-human relations, which, to me, will always be non-violent. Period. So my answer is 'no'—non-lethal equipment only. And, okday, let's draft our own security employees into teams, one Animal for every human. And no gorillas. Sadly, they have a bad reputation because of the movies. I suppose I'll have to amend my imaginary IA rules of living, of surviving; let's see, how about this for a slogan? *'Protecting Animal Rights Guarantees Human Integrity.'* Something like that, if the anti-Intelligent Animal foes will listen at all."

* * *

The Town Building Department inspectors were impressed and found little to criticize or require change orders to justify their jobs. The University's architects and engineers had the main building structure conform to all the latest codes, including those capable of withstanding a Category 5 hurricane. The Harris Funeral Home was remodeled into the new administration building, with a new name, *Animal Roar Center,* also known as the *ARC* building.

* * *

The dark-tinted passenger window edged down as the van drove slowly by the University building site. Chairman Balfour gazed out, appraising, not knowing what this building activity meant; was it some sort of scam or a minimal school for teaching animals basic demeaning 'tricks'? Is it a threat to the peace of the neighborhood and The Herd? "Okay, I've seen enough, which is not much to see." He did spot two untrained lowbrow monkeys scampering about, being chased by a human construction worker.

Non-intelligent animals would be no threat to his apartment dwellers. Probably some sort of tourist attraction, he decided. What he feared most was any internal challenge to the Association's privacy standards, which might compromise the rules governing human intervention at The Herd Apartments. He could boast a high-caliber membership, and as the leader, Balfour breathed determination to keep away any looky-loos who'd want to treat them like some tawdry zoo exhibition. "And, Benny," he said to the bear at the driver's wheel. "Don't be too heavy with your paw. Within the speed limit is the example we must set. To go unnoticed."

But for Benny, the bear's paw was too heavy, and the van lurched with a squeal before regaining an acceptable and correct speed back to The Herd complex and the walled security of home.

PETRA JOINS THE TEAM

Eliza had been busy. Her indoctrination program consisted of nineteen monkeys enrolled. Roark and Eliza reviewed the test results, with Roark making the final designations. Two woolly spider monkeys and one Capuchin monkey had tested high on the IQ exam part, and, after a confidential visit with Roark, all three had decided not to be relocated and would stay at the University and enroll in classes towards an IA degree.

Four of the Capuchin monkeys had tested borderline mental issues, prone to nervous outbreaks and violent streaks. Roark did not want them to be put in a new reconstituted troop and thrown in with any other monkeys they might encounter. But he could not answer Eliza's question of where the four would go if they were left behind. Roark did not want them to stay here as disrupters in the University, and he had no quick solution as to where else they might be sent or adopted by whom. So, he relented, rationalizing and mumbling, "Being in the wild works for those who are wild-acting."

They both agreed that the Central American trip would come first as it consisted of the largest group: eleven monkeys, currently composed of four woolly spider monkeys and seven Capuchins (two of whom were the unruly). The five Vervet monkeys destined for South Africa would travel later. All five of the Vervets seemed acceptable as they were told their home would be in a sanctuary, overseen by 'kind' humans, and they would not be placed directly into the wild; the fact being that their historic territories had disappeared due to human expansionary developments, and no Vervets were known to live unprotected in the wild. Two of the failed tested monkeys went this direction.

For all of those eventually being released, as part of easing them towards their new location, Eliza brought in a human zoologist to explain the environment where they would settle. Accepting a human's word did not go over well for those who had lived under poor conditions, all of them survivors of the Anndwell Animal Farm. Probably, the four mentally disturbed monkeys' behavior was caused by direct mistreatment that created an uncomfortable situation when monkeys screamed in unity and spat their dislike.

Eliza found a Capuchin who had been born in the wild in Central America but had lived in the State of Georgia with a teenager in his cramped bedroom for the past two years. The human kid, now off to college, had run a 'for-sale' advertisement in a local newspaper, and Eliza, with Roark's approval, had purchased the monkey (on behalf of the University, ownership to be held in trust). Eliza, in turn, paid the Capuchin, a non-ITSE female called Petra, her document-listed name, a speaking stipend on the condition that Petra would talk positively about her experience living in the Central American jungle and not mention anything about how hunter-collectors had trapped and caged her, nor the long torturous trip, including multiple hand-offs into this country, to be animal brokered to a pet shop. Every foreign-born primate had similar stories of how they arrived here, and they were not pleasant memories.

During this session, the Central American bound monkeys listened to Petra's animal-speak stories of the wild, gained confidence that this new home should not be so bad, and, more importantly, they would be free to roam around with other troops of their own species—the Capuchins with Family *Cebidae* and the woolly spider monkeys with Family *Atelidae*.

Surprisingly, Petra, the newly acquired Capuchin 'guest speaker,' chose not to accompany the other Capuchins back to her homeland and rejoin her lost colony family. Nor be sent to a zoo or wildlife sanctuary. Instead, Roark and eventually Eliza accepted Petra's decision and agreed to keep her on the premises as one of Eliza's speakers and as an assistant on other anticipated animal reparations. For that service, she would be placed on the priority list for an ITSE implant if and when the expected first lot of fifty educational ITSE devices for which the university had applied were granted.

To that end, a local neurologist and brain specialist was vetted and certified by ITSE to perform these operations. Part of the fine print on the ITSE applications stipulated that the insertion devices would not be sent until the University (Roark) designated which species would receive the 'gift,' as each device required synchronization of the computer chip and brain implant, calibrated to each specific animal species—kangaroo throats and brains were a long way from those of birds.

The most compatible for the implants, scientifically, was, of course, primates, whose similarities were so close to homo sapiens that the computerized insert into the brain and the vocal chord chip implant allowed primates to become the best conversationalists and spatial thinkers. By Animal standards, Roark was an orator and linguist compared to the English speech patterns of elephants or zebras.

* * *

As such, like the Test, an application for the University was required by all who were interested in becoming students. In the *Action Plan,* several levels of consideration were outlined: the *IAs* who could already speak English and wanted to improve themselves for a vocation in the human world, or work for Roark as employees of the University, perhaps as outreach to gain new recruits. Then, the *non-IAs*, divided by the Test into possibly intelligent candidates and put on a waiting list for a future ITSE. And the failed, *non-processed applicants*, who would remain at the bottom of the new Animal pecking order, hoping for fortuitous luck in the far distant future by being the million-to-one lottery winner. And finally, *the non-entities*, the common, unaffected, domesticated animals, who did not fill out the Application and couldn't care less about anything except food, sleep, and, when directed or by stimulus, procreation.

For the most part, there was widespread unhappiness among those with ambition or a belief in their abilities who applied but received no acceptance.

Thus, without desiring it, Roark, under his plan, became a 'demi-god' by which animals were to be only blessed with human communication by his approval. To some, the limitations imposed by device regulations that were not accepted in the first class complained that the new University Chancellor acted like a manipulative tyrant, rather than a considerate benefactor.

Indirectly, this created a caste system. ITSE IA versus the animals waiting and hoping for an ITSE device and at the bottom those uninterested animals (small 'a') who accepted the status quo of just being a farmyard animal or in the wild with no urge to be like a human.

The quandary of technological choice now existed where right could be wrong and wrong seemed right.

TOWARDS A NEW HOME

The day of embarkation arrived. The bus started the loading process to go to the local airport and the privately leased turboprop. (SOCA would pick up this expenditure to gain publicity.)

Each monkey had a seat on the bus. A to-go bag of munchies would be supplied. The planned 'cage' at the back of the aircraft, set up more as a separation barrier of wire mesh, would look tolerable, and the flight would be short.

The SOCA human, Harold (from the monkey farm auction), would accompany the travelers but would sit apart. He would handle any difficulties with human bureaucracies. Edgar and three of his monkeys accompanied the travelers, dressed in casual human attire, while the wild monkeys wore no clothes to distinguish them from those being transplanted. Petra agreed to go along, having been coached by Eliza to be the coordinator when they arrived at the drop-off jungle location and established a day work camp for insertion. Petra would act as an intermediary when meeting any new feral troops of natural wild monkeys.

Petra warily eyed Edgar and his bunch since they were all males. He likewise gave her a hard stare, more lascivious, undressing Petra and her loose-fitting garb. Eliza saw the interchange and told Petra, "Orville has put Edgar and his cadre on notice that there will be, pardon the pun, no monkey business, or they won't get paid, and any future deals will be null and void."

"I can take care of myself. Maybe not four of them all at once."

"I'll tell Harold to keep an eye out if they start to get rambunctious." (Recently, John had given her a grammar book devoted to more colorful, expressive words.)

She did not quite comprehend that when imprisoned at Anndwell Animal Farm, Eliza had been in a separate cage with no socializing, so she had little personal experience of what might happen when monkeys ended up on the same bus, plane, or in close proximity in the jungle. Her learning curve was still curving—she was as blind as the virtuous idealists sometimes are.

Edgar was ready to board the bus when he noted Eliza, then saw Roark back on the steps of a building within the University grounds.

"What is that show-off actor doing here?" Edgar's deal and employment had gone through Orville.

Eliza, blithely innocent, replied, 'We are coordinators. I want to see all willing animals returned to their native homes." She remembered Roark's doubtfulness and added, "If they so choose."

"I don't report to no stinkin' orange baboon," snarled Edgar, pointing at Roark.

Affronted by his venom, Eliza collected herself and responded harshly. "You will take orders from me and Orville," she lied, partially. "Please get on the bus. You have a group of anxious monkeys to keep in control."

"For the money, we will do that." Edgar's meanness shot from his eyes before he turned, entering the bus and shouting at the agitated monkeys. They knew a threat when they heard one, and the bus quieted, the door closed, and the adventure toward a new life commenced.

Eliza sensed trouble might be ahead. She understood Orville's push to hire the IA monkeys and had noted Roark's reluctance before caving to the necessity. Help from whatever quarter at the start was critical and essential. Were the IA Capuchins going to be mere handlers or more prison guards? She wished she had done her own background check on Edgar and his circus days. She felt a responsibility for her wild monkey students, feeling the urge to chase the bus and jump aboard.

She walked to where Roark stood, believing that perhaps he wished the bus would hustle out of sight, down the street to the Short Skiff Key regional airport.

"My understanding," she said. "There is a ten-day adjustment period in their new surroundings, then another SOCA rep goes down and brings back Petra, Harold, Edgar, and his group, and any unsatisfied monkeys who want to return, of which I hope there will be none."

"That's our agreement with SOCA. They will issue a press release when the plane returns. Our responsibility ended when that bus headed out. As far as I can see, your education syllabus,"—she looked quizzically at him, and he simplified his comment; "I mean, the curriculum—you educating them about jungle survival, and Edgar and Petra getting them settled—is the completion of our contract arrangement."

Eliza surprised him, saying, "I am going down there in ten days. I need Gort to prepare a hurried passport for me."

"What? Your job is done."

"No, as you said, with the return trip and the monkeys left behind, *then* it is complete. I want to ensure it goes right and see them settled and happy. My trip will allow me to set our procedure guidelines for the next animal relocation."

Roark didn't know how to react. He wanted to shout at her, dissuade her. Her being on the scene not necessary. Away from the University, from him.

He tried to dissuade her.

"SOCA will send another employee to coordinate with Harold, a human experienced with animal rescue. Petra, I have found, has a strong personality and can help with animal readjustment, and Edgar and his goons can fend off any angry monkeys who think our clients are staking a claim to their territory."

"I am determined to see my hard work and the program's success firsthand. Please, make it happen." He glared at her obstinacy, then both walked away, upset, in separate directions. Had he not been so overwhelmed with the University project, he might have easily supported her by going along with her, for *his* peace of mind.

For the next nine days, Roark and Eliza seldom spoke, except with cool cordiality, both set in their stubbornness. Roark had to concede that the reintroduction of animals to their former ancestral habitat became Eliza's pride and joy. The first success would validate not only the program but also give her the confidence to do more for animals.

From her perspective, she only saw Roark as *the* boss, not understanding that his internal fuming might be because he cared for her. She did not understand the feelings of male orangutans. Males will show indifference, and if coy, the female will usually force the issue.

Eliza had come to accept that an acquaintanceship existed between them, a working relationship, perhaps more than a friendship, which could develop into something more if she overcame her hesitancy and acted amorous. But he was a big star, and she was half intimidated by his aura and rumors about his lifestyle. He probably enjoyed, she presumed, his pick of female orangutans, and a harem fan club must await his return to Rodeo Drive in this place called Hollywood, where all the human stars talked to only each other, ate great food, and fornicated a lot.

But she had to go; she was determined to see this Great Experiment, driven by a passion for helping unfortunate animals, and that day came with the arrival of the assigned SOCA representative, a human named Jill.

Roark self-agitated. Jill, a pre-med vet, showed up lugging a weathered backpack, and before her arrival, certainly at the airport, bought herself a 'Save the Manatee' tee shirt. Roark dismissed her as a grain-eater and *Save Our World* zealot, no doubt a feminist refugee from the unscrupulous human male hierarchy.

Jill and Eliza did not bond, though they quickly reached a common understanding that saving all animals from human pollution must be the only and immediate answer to the continuation of all life on the planet. As for Eliza, her beliefs had matured quickly to hard-core 'animals must be free.' Jill ranted her mantras in supportive agreement. Roark dismissed the human woman's radical causes as 'here today, another cause tomorrow.' Animal reparations were Jill's latest cause célèbre moment. She probably had a dozen T-shirts bearing every captioned slogan starting with the word 'Free' and various other phrases.

Roark watched both 'do-gooders' leave side by side in upbeat excitement. Eliza looked back at him with a brief, hesitant smile. He had wished her a safe journey and had given her a 'Goodbye, come home soon' wave. His gesture hid sadness, a genuine longing manifesting. Their separate positions on what was the priority to each and the opportunity to part as very close friends instead produced a stress fracture. When she returned, he would make amends for his stubborn conduct. He turned, entered the ARC building, and compartmentalized his feelings, then faced the new challenges that happened immediately.

THE RISE OF BUREAUCRACY

In the week preceding and the days immediately following Eliza's departure, Roark found himself in the interview and hiring mode, seeking employees for BT Enterprises and Roar Animal University. The burden of selecting the 'right' animals fell mostly to his intuition about his past experiences, knowing what he sought, seeking a balance of harmony and opportunity through a selective process, part mystical and part gut-feel.

Newspaper advertisements circulated throughout Florida, in social and print media, seeking: "Human and Animal Teachers for Roar University." Another separate posting was announced: "Open Enrollment for Animal Students," which stated that both Intelligent Animals (ITSE) and general animals are eligible to apply, subject to testing requirements. The battery of tests that Eliza felt discriminated against all animals, Roark saw as a requirement to limit the initial student population, as he was restrained by his capital funding ceiling.

Never ultra-wealthy, Roark's real estate portfolio had diminished to near zero, having sold off his West Coast land and buildings, as did the bulk of his lawsuit settlement, to fund this 'roll-of-the-dice' project, primarily the initial capital construction costs. All that remained was his house in the mountain foothills, his last holding, rented out for income. The lease was to expire in two years when he planned to return. The University was only a short-term-but expensive-project to keep his creative juices flowing.

To regain his spent capital, at least to cover operating costs, tuition income for the University could come from any receptive affluent IAs enrolling as students, but there were few. If they were already wealthy, why did they need an 'education'? However, the fundraising efforts of SOCA and other benevolent pro-animal organizations agreed to establish scholarships and grants to help cover basic tuition expenses. The business plan budget meant hand-to-mouth survival, in the first year, when the University would pocket little coin for future expansion. Ironically, Roark himself could live comfortably off his royalties from merchandise sales featuring his likeness, such as *Mad Monkeys* action toys.

His public announcements of a university for animals opening worked too well, and a large number of applications were filed for enrollment. The conditions all aligned: many animals sought to improve themselves and seek advancement in the human world. Sadly, those turned away received a vague promise of being placed on the waitlist for the next semester's admissions. Roark faced frustration that many applicants he discovered through the testing process had real promise, but what to do with them? He did not want to see them drift back into human servitude. Brainstorming brought little satisfaction.

If the University could continue to break even into the next year and beyond, it held hope that a Preparation (Prep) School might be formed for the animals on the Wait List to give them a foundation to help eventually meet the University enrollment standards. And Roark needed to increase the ITSE implant quotas to match student demand. The university's first class now consisted of 125 students, more than 35 percent of whom would require an ITSE implant.

What Roark did not realize until much later, and could only laugh at, was that in a sense, analogous to the point, he had made himself a Producer-Director to a great Production, and these casting calls, the auditions, the testing would, if wisely handled, set the University's reputation by graduating an eventual field of qualified Intelligent Animals. At this moment in the initial founding, his decisions were a matter of chance or a guesstimate of what the appropriate direction might be. More often than not, Roark saw something unstated called that dread word 'potential' in an animal when perhaps they did not see it in themselves, or even when the Tests did not reveal a great 'star' student hidden beneath shyness and awkwardness. Roark put faith in his judgment; humans called this Leadership.

SECURITY

The usual staffing issues occurred in finding qualified 'professors', and a wider net was flung out nationwide to entice Animal and human educators to become a part of this historic 'experiment'.

More serious dissension arose regarding the hiring of security. Roark, wanting to hold down costs, suggested a basic security package of maybe two hires to patrol the campus and ward off the curious or troublemakers. Silent John sought a full SWAT team, believing Roark's fame might unleash serious threats when the public got wind of his new venture. Finally, they compromised on a security team capable of performing multiple functions.

Security team candidates boasted past credentials and merit, with Gort doing invasive background checks (hacking previous employer personnel files). Silent John, who was deep in his tasks overseeing the University buildings under construction, could no longer continue to be the human watchdog, the administrative assistant Roark depended on. Security was deemed imperative since the cost of doing business in the limelight began to see a trickle of threatening letters, anonymous hate calls, and virulent emails, and Roark no longer had a studio security team for buffer protection.

Again, balance. The final choices made were:

JS (short for 'Just Smith'), an Army military policewoman with short blond hair and martial arts skills. She would give a class on Animal personal safety and protection.

Cooper, Navy, demolitions/explosives expert, with multiple tattoos of heavy metal bands. Not to teach students how to blow things up, but interestingly, he would become the University's popular human musical culture instructor. Adept at guitar and piano. A University choir seemed possible if the student population were to increase.

Rammie (Ramirez), a second-generation Cuban, Special Forces field combat medic, would fill in nicely as a substitute teacher in the Public Health Department. Animals were encouraged to care for their own basic exercise and vitamin regimen.

Jackson, an Orlando police officer, a bald black man who had retired from the Intelligence Division. Roark liked his resume, and that Jackson had also been in charge of event logistics for celebrity and political guest visits to the State Capitol. He was assigned to Gort in the Tech Department, both mutually enthused about a database of potential threat groups.

On the Intelligent Animal side, security brought out fewer choices.

Murray, falcon, and former college mascot. The college's football team had such a lousy season that the administration cut back on costs, and Murray was unceremoniously laid off. His talent would be aerial surveillance. And if ever in a fight, he demonstrated he could quickly attach 'metal-extended claws' and presto-- avian brass knuckles.

Zing, short for Nzinga, a German Shepherd mix, female, Army K-9 Corps, prematurely retired because of a bullet wound in combat. Regarding skills, she growled with full canines bared during her interview and was hired immediately.

Mildred, a small donkey. While she did not meet the qualifications they were seeking, Roark made a heartfelt decision. Mildred somehow had 'escaped' from The Herd Apartments, a talent in itself. She had been part of the troubled Animals within the Petting Zoo confines, highly strung out with a phobia of small children touching her. She was put in charge of carrying supply equipment and field support if required. Roark allowed her to stay on the University property, giving her the responsibility of patrolling the swamp area that encroached on the back of the property. Although shy, she demonstrated lightning-fast kick-hoof moves that even impressed the human team members, who were skilled in the Oriental arts of kung fu and kickboxing.

To maintain balance, Roark assigned a human and an Animal to patrol the outer perimeter on rotation. This demonstrated to the public that human and Animal cooperation was possible and encouraged team bonding to foster unity.

THE TEAM ASSEMBLES

Whenever there was no apparent crisis at the University site, Roark spent evenings at his Herd apartment residence. Here, he mainly worked on editing and tightening Orville's draft of his grandmother's story. Like Orville, he found the narrative compelling and moving: an idyllic childhood in Sumatra, captured by local animal hunters, sold to traders, shipped to this country, exchanged through various circuses, eventually finding her way to the C&B Circus and an ITSE. A harsh journey of abuse and brutal training, since orangutans never took to instructions as quickly as monkeys could learn simple tricks. Finally, more of a spectacle at the C&B, limited to a routine with clowns. Mercedes recounted and wrote about her circus days—the good stories at C&B—and recorded incidents of ill treatment of animals in other circuses. Finally, the SOCA law was passed, and Mercedes, a formidable leader along with Balfour, made the move and set up a comfortable life at The Herd, where ex-circus Animals could find refuge from the anxieties and uncertainty in the human world, only to face heart disease at the moment of her personal triumph.

Reading the third draft, the working title, 'Mercedes of the Orangutans—Her Story,' Roark mused aloud, "This would make a great documentary film." Always thinking outside the box, while Orville focused on his writing, Roark saw an idea, and his mind generated a plethora of configurations, analyzing, discarding mistakes, and retooling into the art of creativity, where one knows without a doubt the answer has to be behind Door #3.

"I think I will call a few of my entertainment friends." Roark's settlement with Hollywood producers stipulated that he did not star in any films, television, or commercials bearing his likeness. Nowhere in the agreement did it forbid him from *producing*. This 'documentary' idea was added to his 'to-do' list—a long list of ideas in perpetual germination.

A knock at his door. He and Orville exchanged glances. Hardly anyone these days paid a visit this late at night. Resident interest in his celebrity had waned as he seldom now wandered the Herd compound unless to exit and head over to his new educational project several miles away.

An elephant and a camel faced him. He stepped outside. Because of their size, neither of his visitors would be able to enter his apartment.

Said Pennyrae, the elephant, "We hear you are starting a school for Animals?"

Roark had kept a low profile, avoiding controversy, but denial was not his style—the smart ones were discovering who was behind this 'school' in Short Skiff Key.

"Yes, we are going to educate Animals such as yourselves on how better to use the tools within the human world, and on a limited basis, we will educate animals who gain ITSE how to speak and employ the English language, then move them into Intelligent Animal classes." He wanted to speak succinctly so as not to start rumors about his objectives. "My desire is only to help Animals achieve." That sentence best established his overall vision.

But what did they want?

"We want to be teachers," said Pennyrae, and Sebayet, the camel, nodded.

"But you have your daycare. And Balfour and the Executive Committee discourage Herd Animals from undertaking outside work." This situation would definitely lead to a collision with Herd-implied rules.

"We thought it over. We can ask one of the Herd vans to drop us off at a nearby park and walk over to your school. Then they'll pick us up back at the park."

Sebayet offered, "Some days, we can tell the gate guard we are going to start a physical walking club. The Herd doesn't pay too much attention to everyone's whereabouts. We've got it all figured out."

"Besides," added PennyRae, "our children are in the daycare program. Sebayet and I feel it is time for them and us to have a little space. Let them have more play time with other young animals and listen to other adults than their parents."

"But how about the Petting Zoo animals; don't they still need supervision?"

"We have asked the tapirs, Elizabeth and Darcey, to step in. They are the perfect docile type to calm the group's nervousness. The human veterinarian has agreed that we can administer a daily dose of anti-anxiety medicine to the Petting Zoo patients. They'll be fine. The Herd is as calm and boring as one can find in all of Florida."

Sebayet said in a hushed voice. "Besides, we don't want to be in charge, and around when Balfour learns the donkey in the Petting Zoo, Mildred, has wandered off to who knows where.

'That will cause a ruckus when it's discovered."

Roark could not turn down the gift of a volunteering elephant and camel. As IAs and ex-circus Animals, they were perfect for what he sought as educators.

"If it all works out, welcome to Roar University. See Silent John at our building site tomorrow. He's in what we call the ARC Building."

* * *

Silent John found himself overwhelmed, but he bore up and kept moving from one building site to another. Hard hat on, he had finished walking the grounds with the human construction manager. Both, with little rest, were going through check-off lists, subtracting and adding. Roark just texted him about several new teachers he wanted to be vetted and would send over resumes for him and Gort to check references. This morning, he supervised the workers as they set up temporary tent housing for the security team.

And another challenge. More and more animals wanted to reside at the University, a trend against living among humans, so the designs of a new dormitory required review with the project architect.

Silent John took a deep breath, frazzled, when he saw a young woman standing near Roark's banyan tree, looking up at its dangling canopy. He thought he saw the awe and wonderment of nature in her smile. *Did she glow?*

Walking over. "Can I help you?" She did appear lost, and she stood in an active construction zone.

"I would hope so," she replied. "My name is Nebbie. I am interested in applying for a job with your organization, which I hear will be an animal teaching institution."

"That's right." He immediately received a cellphone call, momentarily excused himself—one of those supposed crises the person calling could've dealt with. Half a minute later, he returned to her and found that her smile had transferred to him.

"You're a busy man."

"A drowning man is a better description." After the casual greeting, he focused on her. Nebbie had a coif of frizzy hair and wore glasses, not that he was judging. Neither a cheerleader nor a glamorous model type, but her facial features, to John, defined an attractiveness, an expression of pixie perkiness, bearing a mischievous smile. Then, for a moment Silent John went silent. He saw that she had a prosthetic arm and then, with a glance, noticed that her leg was also artificial, hidden by the pantsuit she wore. She saw he noticed this in his quick appraisal, but her smile remained. He assumed she had noted his mask. He parried his thoughts with a question:

"Any experience working with Animals?"

"If you count birds and fish, yes. My first job out of college was with a well-known aquarium after graduating with a degree in marine ecology. I fed penguins and gave lectures. They had a killer whale, but when they put him in an experimental ITSE, all the whale wanted to do, instead of his show, complained to the audience about how much he wanted to return to the open ocean. Animal activists protested, and tourist visits dropped. I was laid off. For the last few years, I've been working at the Oceanographic Coastal Center on the Atlantic side on Hutchison Island, between Fort Pierce and Jupiter. Eco-oriented, I worked with sea turtle preservation. They are non-ITSE. Again, I gave lectures and wrote a lot of press releases and marketing newsletters."

"And now, why here?"

Her answer showed thought.

"I'm an anomaly regarding human perfection, of what is expected in the career world. Not ignored, always noticed. You noticed my arm and leg. That's expected. Short story: auto accident, drunk driver. Sometimes, I find myself in awkward situations. Animals have no comprehension when judging the abilities of those with—she made air quotations—'defects.' A place trying to help Animals aligns with my own beliefs, and a place, as I now discover, has a man who wears a mask and seems to be in charge of the human side. That impresses me that there might be a place for me?"

That smile again. Silent John noted that she had been talking to him, neither fearful nor repulsed by his hidden appearance. She saw him as one of *her* kind. He returned her smile.

"Forget teaching. You said you handled marketing in your most recent position. How would you like to be in University Administration, as Assistant to the Chancellor, who is a very outstanding orangutan?" He laughed aloud at the truism. "We both require a superhero to hurl away our burdens."

"I'm John." He extended his hand.

"And I'm 'Nebula.' Friends call me Nebbie." They shook, and the offer was tentatively accepted, subject to a personal tour and final okay from the Boss.

CRISIS

Roark's cell phone woke him at 12:30 am.

SOCA President Hutchinson. "There's been an incident."

Roark was wide awake, his stomach tightening. *He knew. He knew.*

She continued, "I have Harold, our rep, on the phone with me. He just returned from Costa Rica and our base on the Osa Peninsula."

Harold, on the call, was definitely in a state and rushed out his story.

"For the last two hours, I have been expecting a call from Jill, who, with your Eliza, flew down to assess the project. It was just a normal check-in phone call. She was supposed to fly home this morning. I didn't hear from her until an hour ago. She's in a hospital in San José. After I left, she was attacked by humans and beaten. She was sedated and couldn't speak. I talked mostly with a doctor there."

Roark spoke through clenched teeth, "And our people, Eliza and Petra?"

President Hutchinson replied somberly, "Both are missing."

Harold jumped back in. "When Jill and Eliza flew in. I assume Petra met them, and they all went off to see where our program was situated and what we had set up. I was very pleased with the progress in setting up their new home."

Roark was distressed. Eliza missing? He scurried to the living room and pounded on Silent John's door. When a sleepy-eyed John showed his face, his mask off, Roark could only blurt out, "Eliza's disappeared."

He turned back to his phone. "And what about The Herd monkeys we sent along to watch over everybody? Are they still there? Can I call them? I need all the facts."

Harold hesitated but replied, "No, I thought you knew.

They flew back with me yesterday. Said their job was finished, and everyone was happy. And we were. Of course, they had a few injuries and wanted to get back to the vets in this country."

Roark put his cell on speakerphone so John could listen in.

"Injuries? How? The attack came after you left?"

"Some sort of altercation, monkey to monkey. I don't know the details. It was mentioned to me just before I left. One monkey had a broken leg, and another was stabbed in the shoulder."

"Stabbed?" Roark felt himself hyperventilating with confusion and worry.

"Don't know the details. They weren't mentioned to me."

Roark angrily interpreted whatever had happened as either Eliza and all the monkeys not wanting to inform a human, or a human couldn't care less if monkeys decided to fight it out. But what monkeys fought Edgar's team? Roark covered the phone and spoke to John. He had to do something.

"We need to gather our forces. Get hold of your new hire, this Nebbie. Find Gort and have him rouse the Security Team. Meeting in an hour in the ARC Building."

At this point, President Hutchinson got to what she considered most serious, other than her employee being attacked.

"I hate to say this, Roark, but SOCA can't have bad publicity, and this is our second attempt at this program. Something must be done to keep a lid on this before the press finds out."

Roark seethed. Of course, a non-profit's priorities are dependent on the public's goodwill and risking those deep financial pockets. He covered the phone again and cursed in orangutan-speak. Then, he responded, not coolly, but with a measured response.

"Mrs. Hutchinson, we will not contact local authorities. We will send a team down there immediately to find out what happened, retrieve our employees, and bring your rep Jill home. And believe me, no news will get out from us. We will put a lid on it all. And if we come back and there are no press leaks, I expect your organization will issue a positive press release on SOCA's animal relocation and your continued partnership with the Roar Animal University."

He damned himself; he still needed SOCA to raise funds to underwrite University students. *Invisible chains. Never free at last, never free at last.*

RoarUni Fact

"The more I learn about people, the more I like my dog."
–Charles de Gaulle

RAPID RESPONSE

Upon her arrival with Jill, Eliza was surprised to see Harold, the SOCA rep, at the San José Airport, ready to make a return trip. It had been her understanding that he would meet her at the day camp and deliver his report on the monkeys' release.

In a hurried conversation, he provided an update: everything had gone well. According to Harold, the woolly spider monkeys were released without difficulty. They scampered off to their new home carrying small backpacks filled with basic survival medical supplies and a few emergency food supplies, which were easily accessible. No complaints. Next came the Capuchin release at the base camp. That, too, went well.

His reason for leaving early instead of showing them around the camp seemed vague. Petra would do that, he explained. His excuse was that Edgar and his monkeys wanted to return to The Herd to take care of some injuries sustained in the jungle. He said no more, and the monkeys were already moving to a commercial airline departure gate, now boarding.

It all seemed strange—the rush and the abbreviated report. Harold seemed to be glad that his tasks were completed. She made a note that the next relocation would require in-depth reports from all those working on the ground.

Eliza found Jill in a store, shopping for a new, locally designed T-shirt, oblivious to the conversation Eliza had just had with

Harold, Jill's SOCA counterpart. A lack of human communication within SOCA worried her.

The bumpy dirt track led into the Parque Nacional Corcovado, the most remote of the Costa Rica rainforest jungles, situated on the Osa Peninsula at the Golfo Dulce. From Eliza and Jill's San José airport arrival, it was a six-hour drive to the Playa Osa Lodge near Puerto Jiménez, their night accommodations, then the next morning, an hour's drive into the Parque to the day camp SOCA used as their monkey observation post and where Harold and Petra had turned the Capuchins loose.

Eliza found the jungle foliage exciting, the trees filled with birds, especially the abundance of Scarlet Macaws. She spied a sloth hanging, just hanging. It seemed like paradise until she reached the camp.

* * *

One hour later, on the main floor of the ARC Building, Roark laid out the few circumstances of what had happened and what he intended to do about it. But he knew very little.

There was to be no discussion. These were commands, and the experts gathered could figure out the details. He didn't hesitate and simply rattled off his list of actions required.

"John, you, Gort, and you are—yes, Nebbie. Welcome aboard, by the way. You three will be the command center here and take care of University business until I return."

"You're going?" Nebbie was surprised. She did not expect an Animal movie star to suddenly morph into an orangutan warrior—less surprise, perhaps, more a reflection of insight into her new employer.

"We take care of our own."

Roark turned to his tech nerd.

"Gort, the other day, we talked about how you could do your magic." His comment was purposely obtuse. The other assembled IAs did not need to know they could be tracked through their ITSE implants. Only Gort knew how and keeping the secret had value.

"I've rented a medium-sized jet. Wheels-up in two hours. I am taking the entire Security Team. If anyone has a problem working with me out of the country, let me know now. But one way or the other, we are going to find our lost people, find out what happened."

The Security Team looked at each other. The designated group leader, J-S, said, "Whatever went down could have happened here. It's in our job description."

Mildred, the donkey, a little nervous, just had to confirm, "And there's room for me?"

For the first time in this early morning hour, Roark smiled kindly. *Animal access* must always be a requirement in any future undertaking. "Yes, some seats will be removed, and there'll even be room to sleep for an hour or so." He did not tell them how much this jet jaunt would cost, but it didn't matter. Eliza faced dire peril. He turned serious again.

"I will make one change to your job description, but only in this particular set of circumstances. I don't know who or what we're facing. The fact that Jill was attacked means we are dealing with violent people. If it can be accomplished without direct engagement, you do it with sleepy darts, stun guns, or bean bag projectiles. If you can take the bad guys down, do so. But I want you all to be prepared to consider lethal force if you are facing lethal force. This is not the direction I wanted to go, but I won't put you in danger. I now suspect, but I'm only guessing, that this could be an Animal kidnapping. Unless Eliza and Petra escaped into the jungle, which I fervently hope is the case. If they are hostages, keep their safety in mind. No heroics. Just professionalism."

"We will be ready," J-S affirmed. Even Mildred felt a little better, but only slightly. She had team members who would have her back.

* * *

Eliza could hear the Capuchins deep in the jungle, the cries of monkeys at play. Petra was there to meet them. Since Petra was non-ITSE, Jill soon wandered off towards the sounds of the primates to observe.

In basic Capuchin dialect, which Eliza had learned the basics of, she asked Petra if the insertion reached the success parameters. Petra nodded and said yes. Eliza could not help but note the gauze bandage on her upper thigh. She had to ask the more difficult question. "How did Edgar and his crew work out?"

Petra took a deep breath, then exploded in anger; she let it all out. Edgar and his Herd bullies (because that's what they were) handled the Capuchins harshly on the flight down and got them to the base camp before Harold and Petra had to step in and calm everyone down before the release procedure could occur. The Capuchins were quite upset and more than happy to run off into the jungle, seeking high trees and exploring.

After two days, Edgar and his followers, who were responsible for spending the nights guarding the base camp, abruptly left after telling Harold their contract was over. They returned four days later to the day camp, awaiting to go home. Then, last night, they came back from a nearby village, drunk. And three of the monkeys, after Edgar passed out, attempted to molest Petra. It did not go well for the monkeys as they were former Circus animals, not jungle-smart like Petra.

The next morning, they all harassed Harold and demanded that they go with him, leave now, and not wait at the camp to meet whoever arrived to assess the project's success. Two of them required medical attention. Edgar had a hangover.

By late afternoon, most of the base camp had been packed up. Eliza and Jill, with Petra's input, sat making notes for their SOCA wrap report. The Capuchins in the trees suddenly screeched a warning. And humans came out of the under-foliage, armed with rifles… and nets.

RoarUni Fact

Owls don't have eyeballs. They have eye tubes. Barn owls eat their prey—like mice and small birds—without chewing. Later, they regurgitate indigestible parts like bones and fur in neat little pellets.

BOOTS ON THE GROUND

Jill looked like an Egyptian mummy, head and arms bandaged, one eye swollen shut, broken leg elevated. At first, her attending physician and a nurse refused to let Roark's group see her. They knew about English-speaking IAs but had not expected an orangutan, who looked menacing and was here to visit her and take her home. In the meeting were J-S, who came in with a sidearm revolver, and Zing, who snarled at the medical staff at the doctor's opposition.

Jill, with the commotion, opened her one eye. Weakly, she asked the nurse for some water and received a glass with a straw. Roark questioned her gently. It would not be mentioned that she had been sexually assaulted, as the attending physicians informed them. That horror was no doubt deeply buried in her memory of the attack.

"We flew in," she began. "Harold met us and said everything was successful. He provided a map and directions and told us that Petra would meet us at the base camp and take us to the settled monkeys."

Roark had to ask, knowing this was a delicate question.

"How did Edgar and his group act? And why did they return with Harold? Weren't they supposed to come back with you, Eliza, and Petra?"

Darkness in her eye, her bandaged face trying to frown.

"A fuckin' mess. I don't know too much. They got all the new colony monkeys through the trip down here with no problems."

She took another sip of water. "They got them to the site where they would have a new home. Edgar told Eliza that their job was done. Then they went, what do you call it—rogue? Off reservation. They took off for a couple of days, then returned for one day and night. I was more or less concentrating on ensuring all the monkeys we were leaving behind were adjusted. I'm not sure what happened the night before Harold left; he just called me from the airport saying Edgar and his monkeys were going back early, and two of them had to see a doctor. That's all I know."

Roark went for the heart of the story. "What happened next?"

Jill hesitated, took another sip of water before she continued, saying very haltingly, "We had the day to make sure that what Harold reported as being a success was so, then Eliza and I would write up our report for you and SOCA. Harold, with Edgar and his bullies, left that morning. I didn't see them in San José. Eliza said she did. Around 4 pm, as we were packing up, a group of bad motherfuckers walked into a clearing where we had finished breaking down our field base.

"How many?" interjected J-S, looking for facts, her voice gentle in contrast to the woman's hard-weathered features.

"About five. It happened so quickly. And they had rifles." She glanced at J-S's side holster. "I didn't see any revolvers, but they were scary-looking. Eliza knew right away what they were. Kidnappers." She paused, her voice cracked, and they had to wait as her tears subsided and she regained her voice. Zing, the K-9 protector, usually growling and mean, went over and put her head on Jill's lap, while Jill stroked her with her free hand, finding minimal comfort.

Jill focused more on the horror.

"They were kidnappers, but not for me." That said it all. She spoke more quietly. "Eliza jumped to the trees and screamed at the monkey troop, who seemed frozen, and then they all scattered. Petra attacked one man, scratched and bit him, and then rushed away when another one shot at her. That scared me to death. And I tried to run…" Again, her voice trailed off. "That's all I remember." Forced forgetfulness. "Our driver, who came to take us back to the lodge, found me—no sign of Eliza or Petra. A few monkeys returned and tried to say something, but I didn't understand, and then they went away. I guess far back into the jungle. Away from humans." Jill closed her eyes, and exhaustion took her into sleep. They all hoped she could find a better world in her dreams, but they didn't see how that would be possible.

Roark gave directions to the medical staff, who were likewise upset that such violence had savaged a foreign guest who had arrived only with the best intentions. Roark informed them that they would return in the next few days and requested that the doctors have her ready for air transport. They would return her to her family and friends.

PRISONER

The bouncing of the truck jostled Eliza into queasy wakefulness. Where was she? The last thing she remembered, her dazed mind becoming more coherent, was swinging in the trees as the monkey troop scattered into the foliage, screaming in terror. The prick of a dart in her butt. Her fall. Human hands on her.

Another bounce across the road ruts, and her eyes opened to a drastic situation.

She was in a cage! In the bed of a truck traveling.

Somewhere. As she moved, her body felt bruises and pain, no doubt from her tumble to the jungle floor. Where was Petra? She recalled seeing the monkey flinging small rocks at the attackers, but then Eliza turned and scampered to save the monkeys. She thought of them, how traumatized they would be—their saviors replaced by bad humans.

Roark. His image flashed over her dazed mind. Would she ever see him again? Where were they taking her? Her thoughts brought the fear that she might be a meal for hungry hunters.

The truck came to a stop, the tarp pulled back, and rough, snarling humans looked in at their prize. One poked her with a long pole. She jerked upright and crowded back in her confinement, trapped. He kept poking—for what—to anger her, to torment.

One of her captors spoke Spanish to another man dressed in much finer clothes than those who had caged her. Money exchanged hands.

The 'businessman' looked at his purchase and spoke to her.

"You will bring a high price where you are being sent, pretty one." His English broken, with a Spanish lilt she had never heard. The tarp dropped her back into darkness, then the truck jerked forward, rattled for a while, and then onto a paved road. To where? Then, it hit her. The assumed buyer had spoken English to her! How did they know she spoke English? Were they being spied on from their arrival, the hotel they stayed at, or the day camp they worked at? Confusion dimmed her unknown prospects. She would be taken away from all she had known, from her hopes of helping others, away from the University, and from Roark.

This captivity bore the anger of her helplessness, and hatred jumbled her thoughts and multiplied. Festered. Over and over. *I hate humans. I hate humans. I hate all humans.* Another realization tore her apart. The University may be for Animals, but humans would be everywhere as teachers, construction workers, and security personnel. *Who could be trusted?* The University had human affiliates, partnerships, and supporters, such as SOCA and other pro-animal nonprofits. *But who really wanted Animals to be safe?*

* * *

The rescue team regrouped and headed out in two trucks from the hospital, traveling south before stopping. On their earlier arrival, Gort contacted Roark and provided him with a phone app that tracked Eliza's location. He did not know where or how to find Petra. She was not ITSE.

The Security Team said nothing but were impressed that Eliza could be located, Gort conveying that Eliza was still alive and on the move. What that meant, they did not know. Was she on her own or being carried off? Gort informed them, if you could understand his fast-speak, that the speed of her travel suggested she was in a vehicle, which validated the idea that she had been caught and was being transported. Roark felt somewhat assured but did not tell those with him that if she had been slain in the attack, the ITSE would cease to function.

A hard decision to make. The way the kidnapper's vehicle seemed to be heading, movement indicated travel heading north from the Parque Nacional Corcovado and the day camp, coming back, Roark had to guess, back to the city of San José, probably to the airport and embarkation to somewhere distant, and she might be lost forever. Roark found this thought unimaginable.

The proposed 'ambush' was to stop the kidnappers somewhere along Highway 2 before they reached the city and the airport.

That was not to happen.

"They've turned towards the west coast highways."

J-S grabbed a country map. "They must be going to a port, taking a ship out. Maybe a seaplane. At the San José airport, permits and Customs might stop them. This will be an illegal extraction. Smuggling."

They studied the map—two ports, both close to each other; a close race when the final direction was detected. And to make the wrong choice was for Roark, unthinkable. Puntarenas or Caldera?

EVIL IS AS EVIL DOES

Chairman Balfour looked up from his desk. He didn't need interruptions, especially from the monkey. However, Edgar ruled over the Monkey Garden troop, and apartment politics and alliances were essential for the penguin to maintain a solid show of unity.

"Edgar," Balfour said politely. "Haven't seen you around this last week?"

"Been staying in the Garden, watching some TV."

"Well, what can I do for you?"

"Balfour, I know you run a tight ship around here, but I thought you might want to know some unsettling information that concerns me and my fellow buddies." Edgar gave off a sympathetic smile.

"About what? If it was the cable glitch on the TV system last week, that was quickly fixed. Everyone is happy now."

"You know about this school they are opening here in town."

Balfour gave Edgar a serious look.

"Yes, I do, but it does not concern The Herd."

"Well, you might not know it, but an Animal is behind it all. Roark, the orangutan."

Balfour's surprise turned to anger.

"He has no right. He is a registered resident of The Herd Apartments. There are the Rules and Regs."

"Guess he doesn't think they apply to him. But that's not the worst. A few of our Animals here, so I've heard, are talking about working there. Doing what, I couldn't guess."

"Our Animals? Preposterous. We have built an exclusive and private community here. Everyone is enjoying the amenities away from the human world. I've got it on good authority that we are the only human-free housing in the country."

"Just telling you what I heard. You should probably do something about it. It's a disgrace to all of us Intelligent Animals. Who needs an education? Everything we need is on TV or the computer."

"Of course, I totally agree." Balfour pondered the disquieting news. "I wonder if Roark's cousin is part of this so-called University. Maybe she was the instigator, and her feminine wiles seduced him to this behavior?"

Edgar gave his lopsided smile, his etched scar like a furrowing canyon.

"Oh, I don't think you have to worry about her. I hear she's long gone."

THE RESCUE

Eliza felt the truck stop. She heard human voices. A strange language being spoken. Not English. Then, that smell, like on her beach visits--the ocean: fear and foreboding enveloped her. The tarp pulled back, and a forklift engine sputtered, moving towards her, ready to remove the cage and her inside.

* * *

A block away, crouched behind their trucks against the side of a warehouse, the University Security Team, plus their boss, surveyed the dockside facilities to spy on what they were up against. High above Murray, the falcon circled the truck, watching a medium-sized cargo ship make its way to the pier and dock.

A surprise.

"Chinese freighter." Came the intel observation.

J-S had her opinion. "Communist Chinese in Central America. They're everywhere these days, like ticks under the skin. Infecting."

"But why kidnap Eliza?" asked Rammie. "For a zoo back home?"

Roark knew. He understood the ITSE technology.

"They're after her ITSE implant. They're probably spending billions of yuan trying to create an ITSE that speaks Chinese. It's

ANGUISH, NOT RELIEF

Groggy and with the expected headache, Eliza rolled over to see Roark staring at her. She took in her surroundings: a first-class hotel room with twin beds and Roark sitting on the other bed. He had been reading. Probably up all night watching over her.

He brought her a glass of water. She slurped it all down with a raspy thirst.

"Take it easy. Until the drugs they gave you wear off totally, my crew is telling me not to feed you; let your stomach settle."

All memories flooded back. She rushed to sit up, but her head clanged like a temple bell, and she dropped prone on the bed. Stressed, she had to ask, "What about Jill and Petra? And the Capuchins we are leaving behind?"

He sought simplicity as if it would ease the pain. "Jill is in the hospital. She was beaten and will recover." He did not say, 'But maybe not mentally'.

"Of Petra, we have no word; the same is true for the monkeys. I'm sending some of my new Security men out to your base camp to see what can be found."

She blanched at his comment.

"You have human men working for you?" Her tone went beyond defensive to bitterness.

"A mixture: four qualified humans, three Animals." He stressed, "They saved you; I just directed the mayhem that broke you out."

"Roark, I don't want to go home with any humans, especially if they are armed." She used her 'adamant' voice, though weak from her ordeal. He let it pass and would deal with all issues later, when she recovered, including her senses.

"More rest will help you. I will stay here. I will order breakfast in a couple of hours, then I'll meet with my team and plan our extraction, and hopefully bring Jill and Petra home."

She watched him turn out the lights and lie down. In the dark, in the silence, she finally said quietly. "You saved me, Roark. It was *you* who came to find me."

In the early morning hours, Eliza awoke feeling much better. She crawled over to Roark's bed and gently aroused him sexually awake. Among orangutans and no other primates, they believed in gentle, teasing foreplay, a little gross by human standards. Roark said nothing as the males usually did, and she led the love-making, less grunting and rutting, more an ease of friction that excited them both. Eliza would not tell him that the excitement of the jungle attack by the kidnappers, her abject fear of death, realizing all things she had been desiring would be lost, plus the intense road vibration in the back of the truck, had stimulated her into heat, her first time. Roark made no complaints.

They said little, except she reiterated her awakened aversion to humans.

Roark and Eliza flew back together on a small chartered private plane. She held his hand for nearly the entire flight, not looking at any of the human crew and fighting panic attacks when they got too close. Left behind in Costa Rica, the Security Team remained, delegated to scout the crime scene, search for Petra, check on the monkeys, and bring Jill back with them in a few days. Roark wanted all relevant facts on the attack, though he already knew he would give a sanitized report to SOCA to appease their

PR mindset: 'Everything was a total success. Time to place more animals who want to migrate to their ancestral home.'

When he escorted her back to The Herd Apartments, her demeanor changed, becoming brusque and curt.

"I am sorry, Roark. I can't deal with this anymore. The evil of humans, and that you are trying to work with them! No more! Leave me alone, please." And Eliza disappeared into her apartment, incommunicado.

Roark was unprepared for the shock transformation in Eliza. She repudiated everything he was trying to accomplish with the University. It seemed she never wanted to see him again , her cold silence he interpreted as derision, that he as an Animal had given in, co-opted to work for humans. Her embrace of anti-humanism, which he could well understand by her ordeal, he soon heard about, drove her into Animal-only philosophies, and the extremist wing claimed her soul.

In the following days and weeks Roark felt hurt. He could not believe the only sex they had enjoyed might not have been passionate copulation but a harsh, brutal purging, refocusing her goals. As an Intelligent Animal, he had to accept her new journey did not include him. Hurt became betrayal, then self-doubt. Was he in the wrong?

In Roark's confusion and sadness of loss, he turned to his internal constitution embracing his only introspective option—which he hated to accept-- was to harden himself. His goals he repeated over and over were not wrong; he became reaffirmed and immovable, with his foremost priority being the opening of Roar Animal University, his 'true baby', his erstwhile challenge, he turned to face all tribulations that followed, including her spite.

AFTERMATH REPORT

The University would not be like those in the human world, with four years of wandering toward a Bachelor of Arts degree. Roar Uni, as it was known to the students, offered intensive educational courses that allowed a degree to be achieved in just 10 months. Specialty vocational training would typically follow as add-ons for an additional six months.

Those IAs who were students had the choice of living on campus in completed dorm rooms or a few Animal-only apartments off campus, many of which had a mini-configuration similar to the Herd Apartment living units, to accommodate small and large Animals.

As mentioned, the first inaugural class of IAs was closed for admissions with 125 students. They were a veritable composite of all varieties of animals, the majority ex-circus Animals from other closed circuses who had yet to define their future and saw education as a means to further their chances.

It should be noted that the University was inundated with applications indirectly submitted from humans seeking a place for unwanted animals or non-profits that ran overcrowded animal shelters. A second tier of qualifications had to be imposed to better identify those animals who genuinely wanted to improve themselves and to deter human organizations from animal dumping.

One of the animals chosen to receive an ITSE implant was Petra, the Capuchin monkey, found alive in Central America.

Four days after Roark and Eliza returned, the Security Team arrived, and J-S and Cooper submitted a written report of their findings to Roark, offering him a shorter verbal report.

> *We arrived at the site of the SOCA day camp at approximately 1300 hours. The camp had been ransacked, and its valuables, including food and equipment, seemed to have been hauled away. We found one dead monkey, which appeared to be a Capuchin but was determined not to be the facilitator for the troop insertion, the Capuchin named Petra. The monkey had been shot in the chest. Per your direction, we retrieved the body and, upon our return, delivered it to Gort for autopsy/study.*
>
> *During our inspection of the camp, we decided to send a team into the jungle to assess whether the surviving monkeys were safe and had not been further attacked or kidnapped—Murray, for aerial surveillance, and Zing, our K-9, for ground investigation and tracking. Based on your conversations with the rescued Eliza, we were concerned that the monkeys might be shy of humans.*
>
> *After an hour's search, the monkey troop was discovered in a valley, protected by a small stream on one side and steep mountainous terrain on the other. At the same time, the team found Petra among them. She had been wounded in the thigh, which we later found was not severe, and was triaged. Petra had been instrumental in moving the monkey troop away from the human attackers and keeping them calm. In our estimation, the monkeys appeared to be settled at their new location as they had found numerous food sources. The monkeys told us*

(through Petra) that none of them wished to re-enter the human world.

Petra did wish to return, so we transported her to the hospital to have her wound medically treated. At the same time, we gathered up Jill, the SOCA rep, and made the return trip. Jill is with her family and under the care of her own doctor. We recommended counseling for her.

During our further investigation, including careful interviews with Jill and, later, upon our return with Petra, plus Jefferson's quick interrogation of one of the kidnappers at the Port of Caldera, we can make these observations, which we all find disturbing.

The attack on the SOCA camp was premeditated and planned with the sole purpose of kidnapping Eliza, the orangutan. The dead monkey and Jill's attack, as horrible as they were, were merely collateral damage.

From what we gather, the attack was instigated by a small group of four Capuchin monkeys, all of whom were IA. The kidnappers paid the primate leader a finder's fee for the information and location of this prize. The interrogated kidnapper said they had contacts with Chinese in the area who would pay a great deal for the delivery of an ITSE primate unharmed. What they would do with her was left unsaid.

It is our opinion that the guilty IA monkeys were the Capuchins, all four from The Herd Apartments, who had been tasked with providing trip protection. Petra told us that the monkeys had returned the night before the attack, and three of them, under alcoholic influence, sought to molest her. She fought them off, stabbing two of them before fleeing into the trees. Edgar had passed out and did not participate. The monkeys and Harold the SOCA, rep left the next morning, the day of the human attack, probably to establish an alibi. Petra witnessed the attackers killing one of the wild monkeys and then targeting Eliza with a dart gun, then tying her to a pole for transportation. Petra followed them to a truck, where they placed Eliza in a cage. Petra was away from the camp when two of the kidnappers turned from looting to attack and rape Jill. Upon Petra's return, the SOCA-hired driver discovered Jill and took her to the closest town, and other local officials quickly transported her to the San José hospital.

Petra then went to ensure the monkey troop was safe, found them excitable, gathered them, and took them further into the jungle to a place as inaccessible as possible to humans, where our two-Animal team discovered her. In our opinion, Petra is the heroine during this sad event.

We could have spent several more days tracking down the stolen equipment and try to identify Jill's attackers and Eliza's kidnappers, but we decided to return as soon as possible, as our primary mission is to protect the University and its property. We leave any action against 'Scarface' Edgar and his culpable primates to your discretion.

Respectfully submitted, Roar Animal University Security

* * *

Roark did nothing with the report. He saw no value or advantage in making it public. It would have undermined the SOCA mission and also harmed The Herd residents if he had done so, and he did not believe he would have the support of the

Executive Committee in Edgar's condemnation. If he showed it to Eliza, what would that do? Confuse her more, add distrust of traitorous Animals. No, Roar decided against opening this can of depravity. Just stay clear of Edgar.

He turned to Petra's bravery and put her at the top of the list to receive the next ITSE. She, in turn, became one of his most loyal and supportive employees. Not on par as Eliza, but of equal respect and value.

RoarUni Fact

Charles Darwin (1809-1882) waited more than 20 years to publish his groundbreaking theory on evolution. Darwin's five-year voyage around the world on HMS Beagle, which ended in 1836, provided him with invaluable research that contributed to the development of his theory of evolution and natural selection. Concerned, however, about the public and ecclesiastical acceptance of his deeply radical idea, he did not present his theory on evolution until 1858 when he made a joint announcement with British naturalist Alfred Russel Wallace, who was about to go public with a similar concept to Darwin's. The next year, Darwin published his seminal work, "The Origin of Species by Means of Natural Selection or the Preservation of Favoured Races in the Struggle for Life."

ESTRANGEMENT

In the founding of the University, all state and federal regulations were efficiently applied in the name of *Roar University*, subtitled in the small print as *Roar University for Animals.*

The misdirection to avoid unwanted publicity and any prejudices at the outset of the inaugural launch is crucial for gaining essential certifications. It worked. The most important was the approval from the ITSE Governing Committee, which approved Roar University's application as an 'educational research' institution, therefore entitled to ITSE devices when specifically applied for.

Soon after, the University applied for 50 ITSE devices, and the Committee assumed the University had an extensive animal research laboratory to benefit humans, so there was no hesitation in issuing the Animal-specific ITSEs. However, the bureaucratic subcommittee validating the requests became curious that the research included various equestrian breeds, birds, a rhinoceros, three giraffes, two llamas, a Florida panther, a herd of Rocky Mountain big horn sheep, a Hollywood-trained grizzly bear (whose owners had denied him an implant), and ten primates of differing varieties. To Roark's plan, diversity mattered with a single purpose: to improve Animals, financially and culturally, by embedding self-confidence in all.

He missed having Eliza involved at the University launch.

* * *

On her return, Eliza saw very little of Roark at The Herd. And only from a distance. He had looked in on her the morning of her return, but she did not unlock her door, and he went away. She followed his departure with a letter to him, one of resignation.

"I can no longer work on your University project as it supports the concept of integration within the human world."

She signed her name, over drying tear drops on the paper. Whether falling from anger or remorse, was never discussed.

Her prejudices against humans, all humans, had stewed in rancid juices of what happened to her, what humans did to humans as they did to Jill. She could not even visit Jill and did not ask about her recovery. Hatred never has a clear vision. This inner turmoil led her to realize that her only recourse was to remove herself from human pollution. Ironically, the best place to achieve such withdrawal was at The Herd, whose Rules & Regulations were a bible to such anti-human contact.

Instead of using Roark as a stalwart support as he had been, she turned to Orville. She could not be dependent on Roark's financial support. She had to create her own resources and find her own apartment.

Orville provided the sympathy, bringing her calm only because he remembered the innocence Eliza had first shown him. Like many Animals, he could see how easy it might be, especially after a traumatic impact, for an Animal to despise humans and their society.

Orville found Eliza a smaller Herd housing unit far from Roark's apartment and the Monkey Garden. Knowing she needed an income, he put her on The Heard staff and taught her writing style, syntax, and construction of thoughts in his spare time. It finally occurred to Eliza that she needed better skills in English writing to effectively communicate her strong opinions; that Animals must educate themselves to stand on their own (Roark's position on this point), but also that Animals, if independent, need not live within the human world (The Herd model).

It was during this time, post-ITSE invention, that some of the more radical Intelligent Animals sought to establish wilderness communes or back-to-homeland nativism, but these usually failed without substantial financial resources (like SOCA). As they espoused, if Animals touched the human world, they were not Animals. Only purists must refrain contact. Hypocrisy ran rampant among radical Animal dogma. To define Animal-human separation versus the overlaps of black being black and white being white was impossible. This was the turmoil Eliza thrust herself into as she sought to clarify her core beliefs.

When she wrote an occasional op-ed piece for The Heard, her tone was in total support of Animal-human separation, a position Chairman Balfour enunciated as much as his lectern allowed. He became an indirect fan, and in time, so did the Executive Committee. Through her writings, Eliza became an accepted resident of The Herd.

As she avoided Roark, her mind could not erase him. A part of her understood the various situations that he faced with the new administration of his University, and seldom did she see him arrive to stay at his apartment (he had a sleeping couch at the University in the refurbished ARC Building).

Her deeper feelings were conflicted. She had driven him away, which was her guilt to bear, but she was angry that he had made no effort to establish any relationship with her. She considered this negligence on his part. She could not reconcile that her hatred for humans had destroyed a relationship with someone she believed also bore the true spirit of the 'all-powerful magnificent beast.'

Distancing from a promising relationship cuts both ways. Roark also felt the pain. He disagreed but respected Eliza's decision; as said before, he excelled at compartmentalizing his feelings. Was this to be construed as a personality fault or lauded as taking the high road of chivalry?

He turned his mind and actions to those events he could control.

ROAR UNI RAH-RAH

The start-up of any business is overwhelming. Founding a university is like launching a space exploration vehicle. The rocket going up is visible, but the unseen workers on the ground, engineers and techs that made it happen don't even become footnotes in history.

In late summer, Roar Animal University opened to great excitement, and a few empirical and historical events should be documented.

The teaching staff was fully on board—an equal mix of humans and Animals. A week of orientation helped build an understanding of purpose, with an interesting side effect that caught Roark totally off guard.

University spirit, good old rah-rah.

Students began calling the University *Roar Uni.* The vote on a team mascot would be held near the end of the term. As this was an Animal University where an Animal ought to be chosen, there was concern that one Animal's selection would offend another group, given the diverse range of animals in attendance. Having a human mascot was not a suitable representation for an Animal University and might even be interpreted as demeaning to humans. So far, the candidates were a Centaur, half-human, half-horse; Dracotaur, half-human, half-dragon; and Minotaur, half-bull, half-human. These were perfect for a sports team that the University could not field with its student population, as it should be, since elephants and bears on the offensive and defensive line would deter opposing schools from playing football against them. The mascot vote might have gone to a more cerebral candidate, such as the Phoenix, with the implication left vague and open to interpretation.

In the end, compromise won the day. The University coat of arms featured a Dracotaur facing a Minotaur in a classic Greek pose of two combatants ready for a wrestling match. Though the Animals might seem to have human mannerisms ready for the struggle, in design, both creatures were all Animal—fierce and powerful. Two mythical beasts are depicted on the shield with the University's name prominently displayed. Usually overlooked is the motto at the bottom, the Latin inscription, '*Ipsa scientia potestas est*.' Translated: *Knowledge itself is power*—a prophetic culture and ethos *in situ*.

Several club activities emerged, and Roark directed their formation to further support student progress. With ITSE implants, the Oration & Debate Club honed analytical and extemporaneous skills. A Computer Club had Gort as a faculty sponsor.

Near graduation in the first year, a new fraternal club devoted to Animal Career Pairing was formed by the Administration's Placement Office. Because of their anatomy, Animals cannot duplicate all human ranges of motion. Yes, they could think and compute on parity, but using human equipment, devices, and even opening doors might pose a challenge for those with handicaps. Animal Career Pairing, also known as *Pairs*, matched Animals so that both could apply for the same job, and then the two Animals could perform the function of a human. Novel and controversial in the real world, this system gained some traction in the workforce. Roar Uni is noted as the first to develop this program.

It would be remiss not to mention another surprise spin-off of University loyalty fervor: merchandising. Roark, himself a caricature on *Mad Monkey* products, should have been prepared for the demand, and a rush ensued to open an online store where all kinds of Roar Uni logo paraphernalia were made available to students, and soon an avalanche of demand from the public followed.

With this great interest from the curious public, the brand soared in sales as the hot marketing item of the year, outstripping production and fostering foreign knock-offs, which, in turn, required lawyers to earn their pay with desist letters of litigious threats. Behind the scenes, the royalties were split between BT Enterprises, 100% owned by Roark, and the University's scholarship fund to cover student costs. This lowered the University's operating expenses, which would benefit Roark if the University earned a profit since Roar Uni was a privately owned corporation and not a public state educational facility.

Chancellor Roark's thinking worked on two levels: project profitability and student satisfaction with the product, as evidenced by the graduation of students with career capabilities. Unusual for a university program, a student-run teaching restaurant on the street right outside the campus is open to the public. Interested students could learn all aspects of food preparation, including roles such as chef and server. The two most favored courses were bartending and opening/managing a restaurant (or food truck).

Within a week of the restaurant opening, humans and Animals crowded the restaurant. Although there were mixed reviews—students were, after all, learning on the job—the overall opinions were supportive, and repeat business followed.

RoarUni Fact

Roosters prevent themselves from going deaf due to their own loud crowing by tilting their head backs when they crow which covers their ear canal completely, serving as a built-in ear-plug.

CRITICAL HUNTERS

As expected, word of Roar Animal University's existence became suddenly universally known outside of Short Skiff Key. The clickbait media were the first to descend, with their own form of animalistic hunger. Also, the story became more of a hot scoop, celebrity-driven, when journalists discovered that the Chancellor of the new University was none other than the famed movie actor Roark, who had disappeared from the notoriety scene of Hollywood to reappear as a Florida educator. Storylines and headlines abounded.

Star Starts to Roar (with a recap of all his earlier controversial legal issues)

Roar(k) University to Teach Students Acting (False)

Animal University Seeks Parity with Human Colleges (Partly true, but wrong track)

Lone Orangutans Desire Educated Mates (gossip mag slant, the worst story by far)

Such headlines as these are loosely interpreted into pre-established beliefs of readers.

* * *

Florida State Senator Wilford Mumford scrolled through various news stories while hunched down in a duck blind in Texas Hill Country, the paying guest of the owner of the 10,000-acre

Safari Ranch, an exotic animal hunting experience, located near the town of Pride Rock. He turned to his companion host sitting next to him, the man staring at the skies, blow vooting on his mallard double reed duck call, drawing in their quarries. Senator Mumford read off the headline text announcing an animal school being started in his own state, goddammit.

'Here they come," loudly whispered his host, and both men blasted away with their custom designed Mossberg Pro Waterfowl shotguns. Ducks fell flapping lifeless; colorful banded mallards, pink-heads, pochards. Not wild flights in migration but ranch-raised rare species, guaranteed bagging set forth in the marketing brochure. The ducks, had been caged released and harried and driven by the staff game beaters with blasting air horns, set off only two miles from the killing zone, flying to escape, flying directly into their pre-paid doom.

That night, all guests satisfied with their kills, and with hard Bourbon in hand, among fellow tourist-packaged big game hunters, Florida State Senator Mumford railed against ITSE and the rise of Animals seeking to be equal to humans, against God's will for the survival of the fittest. Man is the most advanced of all animals, and rightfully deserved to be at the top of the food chain, extolled the Senator, at ease in the ranch's comfort wood- carved living room-social bar, surrounded by the wall art of mounted trophies culled from the Safari Ranch's exotic inventory: Black Wildebeest, Arabian Oryx, White Buffalo, even kangaroo, zebra, ostrich. Peering down on the revelers were other taxidermy examples of regional white tail deer, javelina and sagebrush turkeys. On one wall, silently featured, suggestive of African trip opportunities, the head of a cheetah, a stunning impala gazelle, and at the bar, an elephant foot wastepaper basket. A male lion head and skin rug offered décor before the fireplace.

All nodded in agreement to the Senator's pontification and his concluding rant: 'Someone should stop them." Charlie, the twentyish heir to Safari Ranch, listened intently to wise men recounting great hunting stories, and accepting the Senator's intense monologue that this man representing the people knew what he was talking about. Hunting and wildlife asset management was Charlie's life, and what was said seemed a threat to his livelihood, that if a cause to educate animals succeeded; the next cause might be to shut down his business. A fleeting idea passed through Charlie's brain: too bad an educated Intelligent Animal as they were described could not be packaged as an actual hunt: becoming *the most dangerous game* challenge. But at this time his mind came back to reality of the imbibing gathering before him. Still, he rubbed his arm, patting the tattoo on his upper arm, featuring him with rifle in hand, a foot on the water buffalo slain on the ranch. Awed by the distinguished ranch guest, Charlie refilled State Senator Mumford's empty glass.

GOING HER OWN WAY

Far back at Short Skiff Key, Eliza likewise read these journalistic droppings online about Chancellor Roark, the most concerning to her of 'orangutans desiring educated mates'. She did not really understand that emotion except to believe that gold diggers, floozies, and harlots would now accost Roark (yes, those were her snide thoughts as she searched online for appropriate reprobate names). She was not far off the mark, not that the descriptive definitions were accurate, but the student applications in the second year did include several female orangutans seeking admission.

The Heard newsletter did not report the story on the University's existence. Orville walked a fine line in his relationship with Roark, having completed the final draft of '*The Orangutan Called Mercedes—Her Story*" and his support of the SOCA mission, the first animal insertions highly publicized as successful. Orville knew this was not true, hearing the inside truth from Eliza, but felt the cause deemed more important than detailing a few 'mishaps.'

Chairman Balfour read the local *Short Skiff News*. The University's grand opening upset him since The Herd Apartment complex was mentioned several times in news stories, usually as a throwaway footnote, such as *Ex-circus Animals live nearby in Animal Only hibernation*. Mulling over what to do with the usurper Roark, he penned a guest op-ed in The Heard decrying this 'school' as bad for Animals.

In his expository outburst, he stated in part, *"There is no doubt that educating these animals to work and live among humans, and encouraging them to do so, will again re-establish human dominance in mastering animals to be subservient to evil wills and harsh treatment as we so often witnessed in our circus lives."* He made his opinion known to the residents. To the contrary, an anonymous one-sentence letter to the editor that Orville received could not be printed without Balfour's ire. Nevertheless, the message gained wide circulation among the residents, supposedly by the anonymous letter-writer. *"I liked my years with the C&B Circus."* Not widely known yet, but five Herd residents worked at the University, primarily in teaching or maintenance positions.

During this publicity hype benefiting the University, Eliza neither spoke nor wrote on this subject, a valid storyline for the serious primate turned newspaper reporter. Instead, she continued to write tidbit articles of Herd interest among the residents, such as births, deaths, exercise class schedules, and reviews of Animal Only television programming.

Over time, her writing expanded when she was asked to write an article after interviewing a group of IA zoo elephants who had requested a radical human-animal rights legal organization to represent them in court to be granted full legal rights, including, and especially, the right to vote, which humans enjoyed. Her article gained great praise from both elephant litigants and the human legal animal rights group. The elephants lost when a judge dismissed the defendant's petition, which set forth that 'rights are part of nature and therefore one right is that of representation to all legislative decisions which might affect them.' The judge's position was that any right to vote must be sanctioned by an official legislative body, not by court interference in such determinations.

Without publicly acknowledging her hardline position of 'no humans are good for animals,' her growing journalistic advocacy gained recognition from pro-animal groups run by humans. Eliza created a rationale to soothe her contrarian conflict: if she communicated with any humans, it must be online, not by direct contact. She would not be untrue to her beliefs, and, in demand, she began to write more articles for publications of those human animal rights groups that supported full rights and animal welfare protection for all creatures.

In slow acceptance, another tenet fell by the wayside. To gain equal rights, she had to convince humans. She did not like having to bend, but Eliza could not have only animals supporting her outspoken political position—she had to motivate humans to agree with her way of thinking. She needed them to change the legislation, and that meant doing so through the ballot box.

Her articles gained a following as her online research and editorial feature writing improved. She learned and imitated the word 'influencer' and found a revenue source for anyone who would buy her online newsletter, which Orville helped her create.

Drawn to various causes in the Animal rights battles, Eliza required more investigative analysis, which led her to start taking online night classes in law to learn to speak human legalese and lend more weight to her opinions. She noted, then researched, and realized that no Animal Rights lawyers were Animals. *No surprise,* she mused. *And who could better understand Animal feelings and psyche than an Intelligent Animal...like myself?*

In apartment newsletter reporter coverage, she was drawn back to one news story for The Heard that she did not want to cover without being prejudiced. Sparse in details, her opening sentence of the news item said it all. "Five primates, including Troop Leader Edgar, go missing from the Herd's Monkey Garden."

Chairman Balfour, who had the last word, killed the story. He could not afford for other Animals to believe a better life existed beyond the gates of The Herd.

RoarUni Fact

White rhinos use communal dung piles as a sort of "community bulletin board" to leave messages about health, mating status, or territory.

THE DEAL MAKER

For Roark, fortuitous luck stumbled through the door when he least expected it. Administrative details of start-up management had whipsawed through his mind in recent months. Even disciplinary matters used up his time. Not serious, but a monkey who thought graffiti around Short Skiff Key would spark his muse to artistic recognition had to be redirected to an online art course. Another time, one of the elephant students sprayed water over the campus wall on unsuspecting customers going to the student-managed restaurant, who could not fathom why there was rain with no clouds in the sky. The culprit faced a first-count reprimand; two more incidents or infractions could lead to expulsion. The elephant apologized, and his attitude adjusted to believe that his talent for nozzle spraying could be used better as a landscaper if he graduated with studies as an arboriculturist. His grades showed improvement.

"You have a long-distance call from a Mr. Leibowitz," came a shout from Nebbie, his secretary and administrative assistant in the outer office. "He said you would take his call."

A voice from the past. His had agent felt let down when Roark settled his lawsuit against the producers who allegedly

'stolen' his image, and when Roark decided to abandon (he had to, according to the settlement) and not make any more films for five years, with two years remaining. Samuel 'Sammie' Leibowitz held no bitterness and merely went on to other clients.

Sammie, to his agent credo, retained his mercenary ways, not so out-of-pocket as he still had a contractual small agent commission on all future *'Mad Monkeys of the Universe'* sequels.

Sammie, as always, was direct. "I saw in *Variety* and the trades that you're a teacher or something. It's a few years off for you, but we could develop a script for a comeback." He was aware of Roark's determination to have all the entertainment world cheer his return to new glory.

Roark smiled at the patter. He knew Leibowitz saw his only primate client's career as kaput, and he was being what? Gracious snobbery or perhaps fishing—for what? An actual comeback, or just a chat about old times? Roark's mind flickered. Leibowitz had risen the stardom ladder with Roark and gained significant commission revenue on the ride up. Just maybe....

"Sammy, I might have a property in mind. It has *potential* [a very dangerous word]. But I'm not going to shmooze you."

"You're locked out of films for another couple of years. How are you going to get around that?"

"This won't be a blockbuster for you, but it may fit a strategy for a bigger project when I return." That was still his mantra: return to Number One among Animals and, in a new twist, among humans, show them all. Standing from a distance, you would see the parallels in his comeback, the similarity in his attempt at making the University a success, as one of those progressions of 'I told you so.'

"But I need a few things on this concept project, and the talent I might need is you. I know your agency represents authors,

and I have a final book draft for you. But, and take a deep breath, I see this as a documentary if it were worked up as a script spec. And I won't be the star; I will be the producer. I will let you shop around a 'First Look' deal without mentioning my name.

Our lawyer friend says my hands-tied settlement is limited to starring roles only, but not behind-the-scenes directing or running production."

"Roark, babe, I don't know if I can sell the deal or financing unless it's a big name on the marquee."

"I might finance the entire production." That got Sammy to pause for several seconds. A concept pre-banked is a strong sell to a production company and a distributor. Roark did not have the funds; he was tapped out, his capital buried in the University. His bluff was to set the hook for a company to be 'intrigued' and negotiations put in play. He knew the industry and would not walk in the front door like all the other wannabes. He would arrive, doors flung open, with a well-written and marketable product, *"The Orangutan Called Mercedes, Her Story."* A book already published with good notices and reasonable sales always jumpstarts the Hollywood talk.

"Well…" Sammy's who-do-I-know-and-what's-in-it-for-me brain cells began percolating. Roark jumped in.

"Well, I won't rush my idea too fast. Let's work on getting this manuscript published by a reputable NYC publishing house. Do that simple thing for me, Sammy, for old time's sake. Let's see where it runs."

"Send me a copy of the manuscript."

"That I will do, but all hush-hush. My name on this will come out soon enough. The timing must be right." After further niceties and slamming bad movies in productions by lousy directors, they rang off.

"Nebbie, I need you to get hold of Orville. Tell him I need the Mercedes final draft, and can you coordinate with him to make about five bound copies for me? And, Nebbie, I have an address for one copy to go out by express mail."

Roark, in his plan for the *Mercedes Story*, had studied the publishing industry of the day. He could have self-published Mercedes's story, but the market was weak due to saturation by everyone and their aunt knocking out supposed great biographical tomes destined to be best-sellers. Not to be. Over two million self-published books last year. Roark knew he had to go the agent route and use a Hollywood agent to ask a New York publisher to read this template—*a sob story about a female heroine achieving final happiness, and which was about a circus Animal*—would have a better than even chance when the Roark name became attached.

* * *

Petra had an appointment with Roark later in the week. Her ITSE English tied to her thoughts via a rushed program, now met human-based conversation parameters even above average. Her desire to work for him generated positive vibes, but her strong and forceful personality ultimately influenced his decision about her placement at the University. She would take over Eliza's position in running the renamed SOCA mission, 'Back to the Future.'

As example, a traveling group consisting of a Texas ex-circus pride of lions had been stranded in Oregon when their circus closed. After a year of uncertainty and hopes dashed, they had not found the perfect resettlement in this country and opted for a return to an open space reserve park in Africa. The testing of the six lions and lionesses revealed that only one lion was willing to stay and attend the University. The male lion, named Keith, had issues that were not insurmountable. As the youngest lion in the pride, he did not see himself replacing the current dominant male leader anytime soon; to Keith, the depressing fact was that he had lost his challenge to pride leadership two years in a row. Roark had this young male lion undergo a different battery of tests based on 'What do you want to do in life?' When applied to a computerized matrix algorithm, the response bore cross-sectional match points. *Sales.*

Roark did not want the University to be all things to all creatures. He did not have the financial resources to enlarge departmental curriculum to everyone's whim of career choice. On the other hand, sales could be expansive enough to act as a catch-all umbrella. His talk with Petra gave him a focus on overlapping disciplines, hence the creation of the on-campus *Roar Travel Center*, which Keith, the young Texas lion, would run—and refreshed with new ambition, did so with hustler aplomb. In a video call with two North American bison, he raved, "The Oder Delta between Germany and Poland would be the most wonderful two-week vacation, with plenty of roaming room and fellow European bison to discuss the best grazing locations."

A call center was developed. ITSE students learning English and IAs seeking extra income could work part-time speaking from a prepared text, pitching numerous trip packages tailored to individual species, offering getaways away from human camera-clicking tourists. The war room pitch telephoning nationwide did not suggest 'a return to your roots forever', instead selling trip packages to exotic locations. And just in case the Animal tourists saw on their travels a special place they might like to settle, they were sold a 'Settlement Package' and moved into Petra's Relocation Program. The tourists-future-settlers could apply for grants under the SOCA 'Back to the Future' partnership funding.

For the University, a profit center, Animal-staffed and managed.

POLITICS AND DANCING

Several months passed, the University hummed, teachers taught, and students gained confidence that a world of opportunities might exist for them. Roark worked with outside consultants to develop a Career Center (and Employment Agency), defining how a graduate of Roar Uni could create a resume with no past job experience, seek employment, handle an interview in person or online, and make the best impression, then hold the job offered by imbued strong work ethics and against intra-office politics—a online correspondence course in itself.

Optimism came from a slew of employers, both locally and nationally, willing to take a chance on those supportive of Animals seeking personal achievement and hard-pressed employers who had defined that there was a slot in a production line where Animals might fit in. Roark had to guard against unscrupulous employers who sought to hire at lower salaries than human wages. Job equality meant wage parity, and many employers went away thwarted. Roark did not personally initiate this policy; it came by happenstance, and he supported it as good business practice, reflecting his attitude of fairness. Within the University community, teachers and students saw his stand as a bulwark, an example of his leadership in protecting their interests. A reputation for this fair-mindedness added stature, enhancing Roark's public persona.

* * *

The Mayor of Short Skiff Key came to visit and took the campus and classroom tour. When it ended, he praised the virtues of Animal education in a politically astute manner. To the town, the University surprised everyone by delivering a tax revenue windfall from the curious tourists who stayed overnight and spent their dollars. In a private conversation between the Mayor and Chancellor, the hanging chad of choice came to the forefront.

"Our Founding Day Regatta is next month. As much as we are ecstatic about what you have done with this educational program, it would further cement our tourist resurgence if we could get Animals from The Herd to participate in the Short Skiff Key Parade. Most businesses and shops will be represented with sponsored business floats. As I pitched to Chairman Balfour and you, having ex-circus Animals as prominent participants would draw publicity to our town, increasing tourism."

Roark remembered his promise. Opening the University had moved this to-do item into forgetfulness; his and Orville's subtle encouragement to Herd residents seemed not to have excited the Animals, who seemed satisfied with changing television channels. He did feel bad that he had let down the Mayor and Town Council. Perhaps there was a halfway answer until he could give the problem his full concentration.

"Mayor, I am having the same frustration as you on seeking Herd resident volunteers to be in your glorious historic pageant. If they don't want to participate and you and I can't convince them, I see no hope. But what if, and even better, on such short notice, the University sponsors one of your floats? Our students and teachers will decorate it, and you will have Animals excited to be part of the festivities. Our participation might galvanize the Herd into their involvement."

The Mayor went away half-satisfied. He had Animals involved so that he could satisfy constituency pressure, and the University was front and center in the national media at the moment for its uniqueness. He called the town's communication director to initiate a press release on the new parade participants. That should draw a larger crowd to the Founder's Day event.

Roark knew if he had focused more energy on activating The Herd to support the community, he might have made inroads and gained volunteers. With everything he had going, he resorted to his drip-drip method. A drip this year, a trickle next, and so forth. Over the last months, he and Orville had left many such drips of encouragement among Herd residents. His analogy needed some actual moisture.

* * *

"That is the most amazing dance routine I have seen," Roark praised the three lionesses, The Cool Cats, at the conclusion of one of their practice sessions in the Herd Common Room. It was late at night, and he was returning from the University and going directly to a deserved slumber. The three lionesses were coming down from a sweaty set of gyrating moves similar, as Roark recalled, to several award-winning motion pictures featuring the dance routines of Bob Fosse, classic jazz interpretation.

"I have told you this before: the public needs to see you all perform."

Cleo, wiping her face with a towel, replied, "No one would want to see us do our old act. We are rusty."

"Old? Nonsense. I have been watching you. These routines are entirely new and refreshingly different. No circus tripe about them. They're more Broadway, and I should know."

They looked at each other, nodding. They had improved for the last two years, becoming more artistically smooth, with individually woven steps, leaps, and glides between each other, an intricate tableau of feline symmetry.

"No. We have given our word, as have all of us, that we are out of the business. Out of the limelight of humans."

Roark gave one of his best 'pondering' moments that brought questioning stares from them.

"You know, I have been asked to help plan the Short Skiff Key Founder's Day (he had not). I discovered that the Gail Winns Cabaret at the Marina is hosting a stage show featuring local talent. I am sure they would want to showcase your act. In fact, I can make that happen (yes, he had already talked to the Cabaret management, and they were intrigued).

"The Chairman would never allow us to exhibit ourselves like that."

"With such talent, he does not understand your gift as entertainers as I do. And this won't be publicized, so that no one can interfere. The way I see it: the parade ends at the marina, where sailboats and motorboats cruise around, festooned with banners and ribbons. Then the citizens have a cookout and attend the show. The crowd is ready-made. In fact, I will see if I can ask a few University students and faculty to attend. We'll secure a few seats to be your applauding fans, so you're not facing a crowd of humans. No one at The Herd would deny your recognition among an Animal and human audience.

Glances went between the three, considering but hesitating.

"Let's keep this among the four of us. Let me work out the details. You'll just have to show up and perform maybe two dance sets. You want to dazzle them and leave the audience wanting more. Beyond this event, there might be other places to perform. I'll call you in a couple of days to get your response. Good night."

* * *

From across the common area, Eliza watched the four Animals in a quiet conversation she could not hear. Roark looked tired. Still, he had that mystique about him she had first admired. He seldom talked to Herd residents except to exchange quick pleasantries as he went and returned from his day job of running the University. Was he up to something? She could be an investigative reporter and spy but had to study for an upcoming law course exam. And equally important, in a week, the National Animal Rights Legal Group (NARL) wanted a video conference call with her. Face-to-face. They had asked her to be their legal research intern on a suit they were about to file in Federal court seeking voting rights for IAs. Eliza had lobbied the group for all rights for all animals. Their response: they sought only to get their foot-paw-hoof in the door—one step at a time. This approach bothered Eliza. The Activist Group seemed to march to the same slow cadence as Roark had preached to her. Her lofty visions, *Action Now—To the barricades!* always seemed to be pushed aside by those preaching prudent waddling versus thoroughbred strides.

Seeing Roark made her inside ache. If only he could see what was most important to Animals. Total freedom. From humans.

THE BREAK-IN

The Annual Founder's Day Regatta in Short Skiff Key represented the best in community neighborly spirit. National and state flags flew along the main parade route. Colorful bunting draped buildings and streetlamps. Stores were decorated, and window signs detailed all the events that citizens and arriving tourists could enjoy throughout the day, from the street parade to the regatta on the water, to the cookout featuring Western Florida multi-ethnic cuisines, to locally brewed artisanal beers, to the finale show at the Gail Winns Cabaret.

An antique fire truck led the parade, and the local high school band played a mix of John Phillip Sousa and Broadway musical hits. Floats included assorted car dealerships and insurance agencies, the city of Short Skiff Key, the Chamber of Commerce, various fraternal organizations, and several open classic cars with area politicians and their smiling families waving.

And bringing up the parade's end, as the final float, the entry from the Roar Animal University. Made of local flowers, palmetto leaves, and colored tissue paper, the truck-bed float had been transformed into a gigantic open book with words written on the pages—on one side: *Education for a Better Tomorrow*, showing a group of Animal students in deep study. On the other page, the words, *Teachers Spread Humanity*. And in front of that page were four teachers and professors, two Animal and two

Human instructors, waving with buoyant grins—a very balanced presentation.

The passing float garnered loud cheers and clapping, more than the car dealership float featuring an EV car with side door placards: '15% discount this weekend only.'

Again, Roar Uni found itself in the national media. Not only was their parade float featured, but indirectly due to the debut of the *Three Cool Cats* at the Gail Winn Cabaret, wrote one online newspaper, whose reporter had videoed the performance.

"*The dancing captured the festival's essence of good bonhomie of talented animals paying homage to the town they live in. Their act brought back feel-good memories when my mother and father would take me to see the circus under the Big Top.*"

From the back of the cabaret, Roark enjoyed the dancers caught up in the theatrical atmosphere of putting on a show, basking in the glow as they took their bows. The triumph of the evening for the ex-circus entertainers brought out nostalgia for his stifled career.

His phone, on silent, vibrated with an incoming message.

"We've been robbed." Silent John texted.

* * *

Roark entered the room they called the Lab; here lay Gort's domain. Those waiting for their boss included Silent John with Nebbie (Roark's AA), Gort, and three Security Team members with J-S as leader, Jefferson as investigation liaison, and Zing representing the Animals and excelling in olfactory clue-hunting.

"What's missing?" Roark to the point.

Jefferson briefly told him of the break-in. "Entered through a second-floor window in the corridor, but no ransacking of the Admin offices on this floor; nothing as far as we can tell has been taken. Strange though. All the locks upstairs are pre-remodeling, antique, easy to pick."

"On my list to upgrade," groused an upset Gort. "We did put key biometric locks on the downstairs doors." He communicated the blunt truth of his devastation that he had failed. Everyone noted the trauma had slowed down his speech, as he rambled on dolefully.

Jefferson stepped in to mollify Gort's anguish. "It was a targeted break-in: the cabinets with the ITSE devices were broken into. Four were stolen."

"Just four devices?" Silent John wondered. "No other devices? They are worth a fortune on the black market."

"The four are programmed only for primates." Gort had double-checked his inventory.

"We have security," added Nebbie, "I turn the alarm on every night if I'm the last one out."

"Perimeter and downstairs with the latest detection. Motion sensors. Doors and windows monitored," affirmed Jefferson. "And we regularly check that systems are working."

Gort couldn't contain himself any longer. A weak smile spread over his face.

"I do have them on video."

"What?" Surprise from Roark and the others.

"They did not walk in. They swung in. Above the sensors. They're Animals."

They crowded around as Gort ran the digital card he had retrieved from his computer. They all saw a night vision optic, grainy and yellow-green —not regular cameras—of the Lab

Research office, where they now stood. Empty for the moment, then there was movement. The outer door opened, not at the bottom but at the top of the door; two figures like acrobats, as Gort pointed out, 'swung' into the room to the top of a series of file cabinets.

"Monkeys," growled Zing.

The lithe burglars with Cirque du Soleil-like flexibility seemed to know what they were doing and where they were going. Over to a closet door. Upside down, the lock successfully clicked, and the door opened.

"All our planned ITSE implants, I had moved two days ago to a better cold storage facility off the break room, where I keep the 'body.'"

"Body?" Nebbie asked, not understanding.

Roark filled in. "We have a deceased monkey on the premises. Gort performed an autopsy. Research." He said no more.

Nebbie paled, horrified. "It's not in our kitchen freezer?!"

Gort: "No. Cold storage is in another closet. The only ITSE devices in my office refrigerator were for monkeys. They were going to be implanted in two weeks."

Jefferson offered his thoughts. "Someone. A monkey knew where they were."

"Watch this", said Gort. He magnified the monkeys in the closet. They had a backpack, removed a long screwdriver, and forced open a small freezer—one that the watchers could now see, with the open jimmied door across the room in Gort's office. Here, where they were, was the crime scene.

Back on the computer screen, the monkeys placed four ITSE boxes in the backpack and immediately jumped to the top of the breached closet door, preparing to jump towards the filing cabinets close to the entry door. "Watch the outside window. See this other monkey looking in." The computer, manipulated by Gort, enlarged the body outline. Facial features would be hard to identify. But not the scar.

"Edgar," said Roark, but only to himself. All interior movement ended. The computer screen showed only an empty, violated office.

RoarUni Fact

In the United Kingdom the leading political party stated they were going to "partner with scientists, industry, and civil society as we work towards the phasing out of animal testing". New plans include replacing animal testing for some major safety tests by the end of this year and cutting the use of dogs and non-human primates in tests for human medicines by at least 35% by 2030. Animal experiments in the UK peaked at 4.14 million in 2015 driven mainly by a big increase then in genetic modification experiments - mostly on mice and fish. By 2020, the number had fallen sharply to 2.88 million as alternative methods were developed. But since then that decline has plateaued.

DECISIONS OF CONSEQUENCE

They were at a crossroads. They all deferred to Roark on what to do about the robbery. The Security Team prepared the Incident Report (only one copy), which Roark placed in his own locked filing cabinet. Gort redoubled and tripled his security equipment. All areas of the University campus fell under an invisible bubble of electronics. All Admin Offices, the ARC Building, were thumb- and code-locked. The Security Team added two watchers of video security feeds, barn owls who enjoyed long hours of sitting and watching, hardly blinking. Unless a mouse made a mistake thinking they had found a safe space.

With a little help from Security's report, Orville's investigative review of activity at the Monkey Garden at The Herd confirmed that Edgar and four of his IA buddies had been reported missing from the apartment complex two weeks earlier. Team Member Jefferson discovered that one of the monkeys at the University, whose testing suggested ITSE would make them a valuable citizen, had been in Gort's office a week earlier. That monkey could no longer be found on campus and was assumed to be the 'inside' monkey scoping out Gort's office.

Roark would do nothing for the time being. Filing a theft report with local law enforcement would likely result in unwanted publicity. And that Edgar and his 'gang' were the culprits could do irreparable damage to the University, and again to The Herd's reputation. He could not inform the ITSE Committee of the loss, or the University might forfeit receiving future allotments. Again, his hands were tied. The good news, if true, is that Gort once said he could track the devices if and when they were installed. He had received serial numbers on all ITSEs and knew they were embedded into the ITSE device chips, but they only went active when inserted into a live monkey. Having that knowledge gave Roark no relief. Again, he had no retribution in mind to use the information. He could only guess that Edgar would increase his 'gang' by four new members and 'ITSE' them.

The robbery motivated new directions. Roark and Gort agreed that certain research funds be directed to the Research Lab to explore a method of disconnecting the tracking device from an ITSE so the Animal could be completely free of any human mind interference. And they wanted assurances, very hush-hush, that ITSE would not be eventually programmed with a dead-animal switch that could terminate an Intelligent Animal on some mad human's whim.

Gort felt it unimportant to tell Roark of his own maniacal thoughts. He meant to go a few steps further and research how to create an ITSE clone device without ITSE Committee control… and its distribution limitations. To bring intelligence to all animals reverberated as the unsolved mystery lodged somewhere in Gort's messed-up mind. He had already autopsied a monkey to understand brain and nerve functions. In his curiosity, he began asking Silent John a lot of probing questions about the human's larynx neck technology that John wore. No one knew, including Roark, that Gort's own ITSE beyond a scientific base re-programming at his previous employment (as the 'lab rat') he had been also endowed with the latest AI data computations to solve the impossible. Gort a walking savant but Roark from personal experience, and a lawsuit, had an anathema against AI wizardry.

RoarUni Fact

New Clinical Technology in Veterinary Medicine includes the emergence of personalized immunotherapy, such as autologous cancer vaccines, shows promise in targeting specific cancer cells in pets. And point-of-care testing and liquid biopsies provide faster and more accurate diagnostic results, aiding in timely treatment decisions. The mixed-blessing coming future: The integration of automation and AI technologies aims to make veterinary practices more efficient without replacing human expertise. Automatic note-taking is a prime example of how hospitals can utilize AI to save valuable time. A recent survey revealed that nearly 40% of veterinarians are already using AI tools.

STAR REPORTER

As a favor to Orville, Eliza attended a meeting of the Herd Executive Committee as a reporter for the newsletter. Orville said he was meeting with a literary agent who had flown in from California to discuss a book project on circus people. Eliza knew Orville had interviewed most of the major stars of the C&B. Of course, she would step in and help cover the meeting; she owed Orville so much for providing support as she learned and established her own direction.

She was unprepared for Chairman Balfour's rant. The Emperor Penguin strutted like a barnyard rooster and dribbled out putrid scorn like a squashed roadside skunk. His blustery speech revealed his mean spirit to the point Eliza thought he might fly to the ceiling, certainly a first for penguins.

First, he raged against the now fifteen or so Animals who had found their way to work at the Roar University.

"We cannot have our harmony be upset when our residents do not take advantage of all these amenities we have developed. We have over 200 television and cable channels all over this facility for anything they want."

His ire turned against the *Three Cool Cats,* whose wild 'free spirit' dances had blazed across the *Short Skiff News* front page and several regional media outlets. "Flaunting our Rules & Regs to return to circus-style dancing should be forbidden. I told everyone we would not participate in the human's Founding Day ceremonies. We did not pioneer this town. We owe them nothing."

Still on a rampage, he turned on one resident as the cause of all that had befallen The Herd tranquility—the interloper, the scoundrel, 'the disgraced movie star.' He concluded, spent of spittle, "I believe that this Roark does not meet the standards of The Herd. He is and was never a circus Animal. He now employs and consorts with humans, teaching Animals all sorts of radical concepts of human-Animal co-existence. Our way of life that we earned, the right to privacy and comfort as best being independent of humans, must be preserved at all costs."

Eliza wanted to dispense with her objective reporting and jump up and shout, 'Yes, Animals Only! Animals Equal Rights!' She refrained.

Balfour made his pitch. "The Herd must evict Roark as not conducive in merit or moral character to everything Intelligent Animals stand for."

Instead of an outpouring of support, silence permeated until Huntington the elephant asked, "Can we do that? I don't recall that we ever stipulated eviction since the government pays our stipend, so a resident can always pay the nominal rent. We would have to create new rules."

Hazel, the zebra Treasurer, warned, "If you go this route, Balfour, you cannot make rules aimed at one individual. With Roark's resources, he would probably litigate."

The Chairman raised his beak in confident defiance. "It is my opinion that The Herd, as a place of his residence, is now superfluous. I hear he spends most nights sleeping at his so-called University. His human servant has moved over there and is cavorting in lust with a female human, and they both take care of

Roark's needs." Balfour gave a disgusted squawk at the unknown illusion he inferred.

All this time, Eliza sat straight, taking no notes, and was somewhat startled. They were going to kick Roark out with no legal reason. Her pre-legal thoughts churned. He might indeed have a case against The Herd. But the Chairman smugly announced his strategy.

"I will submit some new rules for this Committee to enact. Rules that some residents may run afoul of. And when a certain number of infractions occur, the Association and its members may vote as a majority to remove said violator.

"It is the will of the Herd."

Chairman Balfour strutted from the table, believing he had found a proper and legal way to evict. Let the Rules and Regulations reign supreme.

* * *

Eliza saw injustice in the making. She told herself it was not Roark, the orangutan, but Roark, the aggrieved party of the first part, who should have the knowledge and right to defend himself and not be attacked without notice.

She could have told Orville everything and let him talk to the University Chancellor. But no, she could best convey both the threat and speak succinctly of possible remedies. She did not want to admit it, but Roark voluntarily giving up his apartment and moving over to the University would be the easiest solution. At the same time, the old memory of the bygone days of the two of them, three if counting Orville, four if—no, she had stricken Silent John from the close happy group—only Animals are important.

She asked Orville to set the meeting.

Roark insisted it be after hours at the banyan tree on the Roar Uni campus.

RoarUni Fact

Hummingbirds are the only birds that can fly forward, backward, sideways, and even hover in place. Their wings beat up to 80 times per second.

RETURN TO THE TREE

Early evening and a perfect winter night for orangutans. Florida-muggy, with a slight tolerable coolness in the temperature. The Herd van dropped Eliza off and would pick her up in one hour or less if she called. Her meeting should not take long. Impart news, depart.

As she walked, her head moved side to side, taking in the progress of a fully functional university. Animals, of all mixed species, wandered in all directions, to where she did not know. Perhaps night classes? Out to a late dinner in the student-run restaurant? Back to their dorm rooms for studying? What struck her was that they all suggested their directions had purpose; they were engaged, laughing, discussing class work, and gossiping.

She spied a few humans, probably teachers. She changed paths to avoid walking past them. In the distance, in the darkness, and in and out of the walkway lighting, a dog and a human strolled, surveying their surroundings. That's right, the University had watch-Animals who worked with human security guards. Those two probably made up the security team that came to rescue her.

She could smile at Roark's attempt, the whole campus thing, of humans and Animals co-existing. It could not possibly work, yet it seemed to, at least on the surface. If she could get a few Animal students alone, as a journalist, she might pry out self-loathing or resentment that Animals felt about human contact. She understood. She faced the same dilemma of how to interface with the human world. Avoidance, she was coming to realize, was nearly impossible.

As she approached the banyan tree at the back of the campus, against the swampy wetlands, the dark shadow swinging from branch to branch was the University Chancellor, Roark. Eliza guessed this was his 'quiet time' for exercise and 'me-time' for contemplation. Orville explained that Roark worked too hard, with little rest, and no moments to unwind, to enjoy a fun romp.

On one of his swings, he caught sight of her and looped in a circle down to the lowest branch, pointed to a dangling banyan root, and held out a hand to her. She made the leap, took one swing, and grabbed his hand as he pulled her up to a sturdy branch where they both could sit, out of sight of passing students or faculty.

"Welcome to my humble retreat. It's been a while since you have been here."

She wanted to say, 'too long,' but those days and nights were wistful times past.

"Yes."

He smiled at her. "I don't think you've been here since we launched operations?"

"No." The last time was when she was leaving on the bus to return the primates to Central America—such a fiasco.

"You can see the University is going full speed. We will have the graduation of our first class in a month. You should come and witness Animals making history."

She took his remark as a personal invitation. She was here to be gracious, yet behind that invisible wall, she remained unapproachable.

"No, I don't think so. I will probably be gone by then."

His disappointment looked genuine, so crestfallen.

"Going away? To where?"

"NARLAS, The National Animal Rights Legal Aid Society, which I have been communicating with online, asked me to be part of their litigation team on several legal filings they will be making. They say they will assist in fast-tracking me towards a law degree and that my activism will give their organization more, what's their word, 'panache.' Strange word. Looked it up. Means 'tuft of feathers'. Still, it will give me a more visible platform."

"Where does this Animal Rights group work from?"

"Virginia. Close to the power center where human national decisions are made."

"I thought you abhorred being around humans, saw them as despicable?"

Eliza realized it would be the first time she had vocalized her words and thoughts aloud.

"I have not changed my beliefs, as we had discussed months ago. I believe *all* animals should be treated equally to humans, free from their control, and have the right to an ITSE device. However, until that day, they must have a sponsor or advocate to speak for their cause, especially if they are not English-speaking. To achieve such advocacy, I must enter into the human legal system, so it is a sacrifice I will endure to carry the battle for animals and IAs to get the justice they deserve."

Roark laughed without malice. "Spoken like a great barrister might plead her case?

"Barrister?"

"What they call a lawyer in other countries. You know, perhaps I should have added a law school component to Roar University, but I focused on basic education. It looks as if Animals like you will soon rise to their own talent.

"So, congratulations. The Herd Animals will certainly miss you. Orville says you have become a great friend to all of them and an accomplished journalistic writer as well."

Eliza saw his sincerity. But for her purpose, she focused on his challenged rights.

"Thank you. But that is why I wanted to see you. At the last Executive Committee Meeting, Chairman Balfour boldly announced he would seek your ouster as a Herd resident."

"Did he? I do have a contract."

"He is planning something. New rules that he believes you will violate and force an eviction."

"A battle is what he wants?"

"Roark, please, I don't see that a fight is necessary. You have your University; you are probably living here most days. Balfour has power and control over Herd activities. He believes you're behind all the unrest he has been facing."

"Like what?"

"Herd residents teaching at the University. The dance ensemble put on by the lionesses. One of the small donkeys went missing, and the gossip is that she is an armed security guard working here. Mildred. Is she here?"

"Guilty as charged, counselor."

"And Edgar and his pack have gone missing. Balfour believes you are behind their wanting to leave the better life at The Herd."

Roark's levity disappeared in a solemn denial.

"I had nothing to do with Edgar and his ilk. Good riddance, though."

"But a legal fight between you and The Herd will do the residents no good.

"This coming from a future attorney defending noble causes."

"Roark, be serious. You can afford to walk away."

"Is that what you want me to do, Eliza? Walk away? Not contest if I am being wronged?"

She had to stop and think. She did not know the best position to take or the best outcome to fight for.

"I just think the Herd Animals do not need public injury or mockery."

"But you won't try to convince Balfour to drop his attack against me?"

"You are more reasonable in viewing facts and reaching the correct decision."

"I am reasonable?"

"Yes, and you have a good heart."

"Ah, yes, you have said that of me before. I am kind, gentle, and a good lover."

Eliza blushed, but he couldn't tell because of her skin pigment.

He continued, "Eliza, humans and my previous Animal fan base think I ran away from Hollywood. Do you think it is right I continue that perception by running away from those who wish to enforce their prejudices against me and, worse, are willing to change the law, the Herd Rules & Regs, merely to force their will over me?"

She had no answer. To argue further would be to take a position against protecting those wronged. What was that big word? *Conundrum.*

Roark silenced her vexation by pulling her into his arms.

She did not resist. The embrace, the rising passion. Natural. She took over and let The Act be everything. What he wanted. What she desired. And when it was over, while still in his embrace, her ardor cooled, and she could not find the right words to express those deep feelings; instead, she sought her own doubts and placed back the barrier between them.

"This can't happen, Roark. I have a new life, a career I want to follow."

She moved to put her body at physical arm's length, for an orangutan that was approximately six feet away. Roark looked at her, the animalistic smirk of the satisfied male. Her thoughts: *Could he not see that any sort of relationship they might have would be so wrong?* Yes, she had been reading up on it. Yes, she had doubts.

"This can't work. We are two different branches of the genus. You are Tapanuli, and I am a Bornean orangutan. The humans"--her words caught in her throat..." Their genetic researchers say that if we were to mate, any offspring would be 'hybrid.'

"Together by current science, we would be diluting our gene purity; in this country, we are banned from 'breeding' cross-species." She became intense, the fearful truth came out, still very much anti-human. "They could sterilize you, or me!"

"You would let that 62 miles of sea that separated our ancestor forebears separate the here and now of what two Animals feel about each other? We are compatible; you and I have just proved philology. And if it is wrong, it is, by human standards, their desire to control our biology, our future lineage. Plenty of hybrids exist in zoos, even if they are not pure. And they are loved within their family unit."

She felt the pain, the worry. Realizing he was right. Society—human society— was dictating. But she should not let internal heat drive her so quickly to want him.

"But a child would be a hybrid? Probably shunned.

Ostracized." The word felt repulsive on her tongue. She paused and felt she had to step back, had to hurt him to keep them separated.

"Someone at the Animal Legal Aid Society said if I had urges and to keep my hormones in check, I should just go over to the

Sanctuary for Great Apes, only two hours from here. There are orangutans of my species. They are not IAs but willing ones who will not ask questions, not challenge me, and afterward, let me go on with my work, not ask me to be part of their lives."

She was rambling; she tried a stabbing remark. "Maybe you should go over there and go ape wild. I am not going to be around. Get your jollies off."

She knew she was punishing herself, encouraging him to find some other primate to mate with. *Stupid. Stupid.*

"Is that what you want, Eliza? No, I don't think so. I don't think you have grown up fully. By that, I mean exploring your reasoning and seeing if you can exist within the world we have. Maybe you can make changes, I don't know. But above all, as much as you seek independence, you must decide if you also want companionship, to hold on to those who will really support you. In the wild, a male orangutan is a natural loner. I do not want to abide by what was or is. I am no longer of the wild. I can accept creating a family unit as humans do."

She dared not ask him if he was offering himself. But for her to answer might stop her career momentum. She could not let that happen. She must... She must…

She must go. And Eliza swung from the tree, her most favorite place, and scampered away back to the security of The Herd and then to be a confused *barrister* in the human world.

* * *

Roark watched her disappear. His loneliness returned. He had only one central thought: *Why must someone face all the tribulations and heartaches of the world when they could build a paradise around themselves and be happy?* He then wondered: *Who was he talking about? Eliza, off to be the heroic wanderer or himself, immersed in his secular world, no longer the stage and screen adventurer, but merely an educational functionary?*

RoarUni Fact

Dr Jane Goodall (1934-2025), primatologist and anthropologist and regarded as a pioneer in primate ethology, made her first field season at Gombe in 1960 where she noted a male chimpanzee over a termite mound poking stalks of grass into the termite holes to get 'snacks'. Her meticulous notes when published demonstrated that chimpanzees — and many other animal species — do make tools, solve problems and display emotions. Soon, other animal behavior researchers accused Goodall of losing her scientific objectivity and seeing human traits in animals that couldn't have such things. She proved them wrong.

A CLASS OF THEIR OWN

The first graduating class of Roar Animal University captured headlines, live-streaming worldwide. Ninety IAs completed their courses as required and walked the dais and received a diploma on a purple ribbon (better to put over the necks of the Animals) rather than 'handed over' in paws, claws, and beaks. The valedictorian, a Chinese Red Panda on scholarship 'loan' from the Smithsonian National Zoo, spoke eloquently of success, the future, and always going forward. Success from this tremendous accolade of graduating from the first Animal University means the future of going out into the world is the best prepared. Quoting Walt Disney, she said, "All our dreams can come true if we have the courage to pursue them."

One of the great surprises to all outsiders, one that would set a tradition in years to come, was that each graduate could pick their own last name. Animals had never been accorded a full last name, having either the Latin description of genus/species or a pet owner creating some gobbledygook coochie coo moniker, totally embarrassing to an Intelligent Animal.

This ceremony would become a significant shift in the Animal's modern culture, setting a tradition that would be intensely special to each graduating student when the Chancellor announced their name. Graduates chose to add a last name, some tied to the memory of a parent, or to an ancient habitat never visited, but the majority sensing history appended the middle name or initial –

'Roar' or 'R' to separate them hereafter from all others, a new class of the distinguished.

* * *

Roark ended the ceremonies by having the continuing classes, presently consisting of an astounding 300 students, stand and be recognized as future graduates, who then sang Debuchelon's *Animal Anthem*, followed by the *Roar Fight Song* (written by Gort's computer when put into AI 'create song' mode). The following is an excerpt:

Beasts, Beasts of Roar seize the prizes
See how our golden future rises
Our labor has just begun
For we Beasts shall move the sun.

Beasts, Beasts of Roar, off on a spree
Boldly going beyond eternity
Where no Animal has gone before
Beasts Forever! ROAR! ROAR! ROAR!

* * *

During the week immediately after graduation, Roark found himself overwhelmed, answering congratulatory accolades, and conducting a select few interviews with only those media outlets that would highlight the positive attributes of Animal education.

News of the graduation and the associated publicity renewed the analogy earlier used of 'drip, drip.' This time, the drips turned into a giant wave. A tsunami of new applications drowned the Admissions Office. From across the country, under a multitude of varied experiences, IAs sent in applications, followed by humans who were sympathetic in sponsoring non-intelligent animals to receive an ITSE implant to better themselves. Less altruistic were many applications from pet owners who thought a Roar ITSE graduate would give them cocktail party boasting rights, and their pet would feel grateful to return to a personal household and take orders. Such applications were screened and rejected.

One unanticipated surprise was financial contributions. Whether it was a few dollars or a thousand dollars or more, supportive individuals (and some wealthy IAs) sent in donations to the Roar Scholarship Fund. The generous outpouring of even small gifts from human children eventually endowed student scholarships for at least two years.

What further assured the University's continued growth and expansion was the legal action taken under the Testamentary Will of Mrs. Wellington Saylor, a late heiress to a candy fortune, whose estate was valued at over $125 million. The bulk of funds and property were left to her two cats for their welfare and care. Any annual residual income above expenses could be allocated to benefit any deserving animal care organization. With high billing rates, the human attorneys, who for several years had run the Trust overseeing their feline ward's health and expensive tastes of ground steak over meow chow and quail over chicken meals, made the decision, for favorable publicity to offset charges of estate management malfeasance, without notice, announced an unrestricted grant of $7 million for capital improvements to Roar Animal University, and that any educational building constructed with the Trust gift would bear the name of Saylor (and her precious cats would find on future student dormitories their names immortalized as *Cotton* and *Butters*).

RoarUni Fact

"There are two means of refuge from the misery of life — music and cats."

—Albert Schweitzer

MUDDLE ON

As the beginning of the third year approached, Roark felt bothered by his last conversation with Eliza, which had taken place over six months previous, when she had hinted that she might mate indiscriminately with a non-ITSE, non-intelligent orangutan—she, a Bornean (*Pongo pygmaeus*), to a male Bornean. She inferred that his family genus and species, the Tapanuli orangutan (*Pongo tapanuliensis*), would not be an acceptable match for her. Roark, being open-minded, did not bear intra-species prejudices. His earlier California lifestyle and hedonistic love life never developed into serious relationships, as he mostly accepted the loose debauchery that came with stardom back then. When accosted by an aggressive female, he couldn't care less, nor did he assert during passion that any female orangutan was ineligible. This roguish cavalier of celebrity attention later matured and diminished, his career focused on work-based celibacy, replacing casual conquests, only awakened by his chance trysts with Eliza. If he sought a family, he realized that Eliza made the most favorable impression on him.

Still, he needed to define his feelings and tried to see the world from Eliza's perspective. With stardom and then as University Chancellor, he developed a superior understanding that education made the Animal, and in his broadening thinking, he became more astute about what the human world imposed on the Animal world. He quietly developed the opinion (but kept it to himself) that humans sought to maintain animal purity and ban interbreeding between species. However, the country's entire human geo-population bragged about being a citizen of 'the great melting pot.'

Such head-throbbing machinations led him to have Nebbie schedule a tour of the Sanctuary of Great Apes in Florida, only two hours away from his office. On the trip, he took security team members, the human J-S, the team leader, and the falcon, Murray. Roark's recent fame as a pioneer of education for Animals had started a resurgence in tracking his new activities, post-Hollywood, and the kooks out there did not care that Roark was self-owned and not property. Not yet regaining his former wealth, the public assumption of such supposed financial success carried fears of kidnapping for ransom, which he could neither pay, nor would he ask any of his new fan base to do so collectively.

The Sanctuary was everything an ape, an animal with a small 'a' could hope for, under zoo-like conditions, consisting of ten large domed outside living habitats, all the latest in wild ape amenities from toys to tubs to devices, all to encourage exercise. There were dome enclosures for quarantining new arrivals and habitats for handicapped and geriatric apes.

The young human tour guide smilingly delivered her prepared speech with enthusiastic praise for all that was great for the apes: how they had been rescued from medical labs, entertainment shows, neglectful owners, distressed pet owners, and direct animal purveyors (the illicit kidnapping trade). The guide paid respectful compliments to Roark for establishing an educational system for animals who wanted to advance, but at the same time, made the point that zoos and sanctuaries like theirs dealt with animal conservation and rescue. And these primates were quite happy in their present condition, so she said.

Of course, the tour guide had no answer to Murray's question, "But have you asked them if they are content?" The falcon, looking intimidating, sat on J-S's shoulder. The guide adroitly switched topics when they came to the orangutan habitats. "The current population of orangutans is less than 60,000 individuals (53,000 in Borneo, and roughly 6,000 in Sumatra). Orangutans are critically endangered and threatened by the destruction of their habitat for palm oil cultivation, one of the ingredients of cookies and ice cream."

Roark questioned: "Have you had any IA apes here as outside visitors?"

The guide replied, "A few IA chimpanzee relatives, I believe."

Roark had a follow-up question: "No Animal visitors to the orangutans recently?"

Without sensitivity, forgetting she was speaking to an orangutan, the guide blithely answered, "Oh, we had a memorial service for one of our aged orangutans, who got too sick to eat. We had to put her down. It was a beautiful service, but no orangutan family members attended."

Roark to himself, steamed under his breath, "'Put down'? Let an Animal say that about a human!"

After that, Roark showed less interest in the guide's speech and more interest in scoping out the orangutans. There were thirty of the three species in all. He was not impressed, satisfied that not one orangutan stood out as a dominant male with attractive virility, regardless of their flange markings. They were tree loungers, enjoying a life of idleness dependent upon humans. Eliza had not visited, so the tour had merely been a distraction, masking his earlier pangs of jealousy. Still, he came away shaken with a new perspective.

Back at the Roar Uni office, he called a meeting with Petra and Keith, the call center sales lion. Nebbie took notes.

"This University is organically expanding, with a good chance of exponential growth. I think I have been, too... what's the word I want?"

"Self-absorbed," said Keith, trying to help, not helping.

"*Insular* is the word." It came to Roark. "The University is reacting to animals being brought to us for relocation or ITSE education. We have not ourselves been the instigators of defining what sort of candidate we wish to help. And I, for one, might be partially at fault. I must admit that I have an aversion to using AI special effects. I have also had an aversion to reaching out to apes, to primates like gorillas, other orangutans, and even chimpanzees. Beyond that, we will need more teachers in the future. Where is that pool of intelligentsia? Where all neglected animals are first placed—in zoos and research labs.

"Keith, I want to create a sales campaign to encourage the humans who control these animals and give them an incentive to let us educate them."

"Humans won't easily just give up a zoo animal," said Petra, trying to understand the mission.

"Agreed, unless the incentive is to the humans to let us 'rent out' an animal, say for a three-year period, we provide the ITSE implant, which a zoo is not able to apply for, we then educate the animal, and after three years the animal goes back to the zoo, or maybe there is a buy-out of the contract where we get to keep them. A zoo might have a duplicate inventory of animals, and selling an animal to make money might help their budgets."

Nebbie had risen from being the appointment secretary to a vital role as the Chancellor's Admin Assistant and gatekeeper, sitting in on strategy meetings to offer a human perspective. She had become invaluable, as Silent John could also attest to in a more personal regard.

Nebbie observed, "This sounds like a contract they used to have before this country was founded; they called it 'indentured servitude.' It might not be palatable for humans and animals."

Roark saw the comparison. "Yes, in a way, but it allows us to break the bonds of 'zoo imprisonment,' and if we have to pay the humans for Animal education on their behalf, it gives us three years of a new Intelligent Animal being on our campus, and during that time what do you think the odds will be that they understand what the Animal world is like beyond a zoo cage?"

Petra saw the big picture. "An indentured IA might rebel against going back, and a zoo might have to cut its losses and let us have them. Or if the Animal is forced by contract to return to a zoo, they might return and spread all the positive aspects of a Roar education and career opportunities. More Uni applications forced on zoo management."

"Exactly. Very good." Roark saw a strategy forming. "And do you know what a program like this is called?" Nebbie, Petra, and Keith waited for the expected enlightenment.

"Stealth Democracy."

Keith caught on. "If, while they are here, they suddenly see they have a chance to return to their former homeland, Petra's relocation program gains a whole new group of outgoing immigrants. IAs, with a Roar degree going worldwide."

"Let's not get ahead of ourselves." Roark turned to the campaign details and the new Admissions Marketing Campaign, discussing how best to disseminate the information. First, Roark wanted to target primates to increase their presence and give them a chance to prosper. Perhaps a new orangutan spirit can be created—a protected homeland away from palm oil cultivation and habitat destruction. He owed his species that much. And maybe something Eliza might approve of.

RoarUni Fact

"We have to speak up for those who cannot speak for themselves."

— Peter Singer, Animal Liberation

"We speak, therefore hear the simple wisdoms so long left silent to your ears."

— Chancellor Roark

NEW NEWS

On Roark's instruction, Gort had a stand-alone computer on constant news search for words related to current educational practices and a catch-all of the Chancellor's personal interests, such as *Animal Equal Rights Extremism, Eliza the Orangutan, and Animal Legal Rights Litigation.* They collected data and news, under no name that would come back on them or Roark. They even signed up for the National Animal Rights Legal Aid Society (NARLAS) newsletter. Gort also maintained a news clipping service on topics related to *Hollywood, Animal Star movies, Roar University, star Roark,* and *Roark as an educator.* Once a week, Roark received an indexed, summarized computer file with any related stories prioritized.

News items showed Eliza had become the darling of NARLAS, their poster child of animal activism, so to speak. She was not big on self-promotion, more concerned with assisting in passing laws that benefited animals while continuing to focus on her studies in preparation for her final law exam. One of the legal battles of NARLAS she had attached herself to dealt with the grunt work of library annotated case research on the subject:

No Intelligent Animal (ITSE) can be euthanized without the Animal's direct, signed, and notarized approval (unless the Animal is comatose and therefore requires at least the signature of three concurring doctors). Of course, Eliza lobbied NARLAS that euthanizing should apply to all animals, giving their lives such protection. But the Society's board had to point out to her that this would cause a national uproar since it would prevent any animal from going to a slaughterhouse, thereby destroying an industry and raising opposition from the carnivorous human population, let alone the powerful meat industry lobby. Again, small steps are best, she was advised. With an internal grump, she held her tongue. *Some day my quest will prevail*, she pledged.

She cited an odd incident where an IA llama, owned by humans, would be euthanized because the owners were moving abroad and merely didn't want the hassle of all the red-tape permits, quarantines, etc., if they took the Animal with them. They didn't even try to find a suitable home as an alternative.

On behalf of NARLAS, Eliza co-wrote the emergency injunction when a sympathetic judge (a pet owner) granted it. This embarrassed the human llama owners so much that they canceled the euthanizing procedure. Bad press against the 'attempted innocent animal slaughter' raised national outrage. NARLAS immediately filed a state suit barring all future IA euthanizing except under strict guidelines. The litigation was winding its way through the courts.

Eliza's subsequent involvement as a resource analyst concerned the national campaign to put voter rights for IAs on state ballots as a state-approved referendum. If passed, Intelligent Animals could vote in state races only. If enough states passed a constitutional amendment, this would jump-start the more critical national campaign of national election emancipation by encouraging two-thirds of each House and Senate member of Congress to pass this as the 'IA Voting Rights Amendment' into the Bill of Rights. Only five years prior, polls held this as an unrealistic long shot, showing humans, at the time, were uninterested in what Animals thought. However, by their strategic thinking, NARLAS believed one state's passage of a constitutional amendment would be a public relations victory to ramp up the struggle.

Hopeful of soon becoming a lawyer, Eliza received notification that she would lead the legal defense team during the upcoming off-year election to protect the ballot and voting integrity of the Animal Voting Rights Act proposal in every state—a significant compliment by the NARLAS humans regarding her abilities.

Her resolute intensity of constant action toward her causes had paid off, though the pressure put her body out of whack, or so she thought, and she ignored it.

On the eve of sitting for her bar exam, she discovered she was pregnant.

Immediately going to her computer, she caught up with the facts: Borneo orangutans show no signs of fertility and, with conception, will have a gestation period of 8 to 8 ½ months (274 days). Two months had already gone by when she discovered she had this hidden 'surprise.'

She knew who the father was. But did it matter? In the orangutan world, the mother watches over her child daily as the primary caregiver for up to one year or more.

Eliza, a lawyer-to-be, had progressed into a logical and pragmatic thinker since her time at Anndwell Farm. Her world was far too crowded. Did she want an infant brought into a world where human evil so easily transgressed into the Animal world? Mortality in the wild for orangutans was astronomically high. She knew the statistics. In just sixteen years, her species, the Bornean orangutans, had declined in numbers by 150,000 individuals. Did she wish to bear another victim into this world?

She had time. Yes, she would make the right decision.

TINSEL TOWN?

Good news came to Roark and Orville. A New York publisher had accepted the manuscript and was willing to publish *Mercedes, the Orangutan—Her Story,* if Roark would write the book's foreword. Unfortunately, the publisher was unable to fast-track the book to stores or online for the holidays, but would release it for the Spring catalog. Contractually, they agreed to allocate a substantial marketing budget behind the release. "A real tearjerker with an ending of hope," Roark's Hollywood agent, Leibowitz, conveyed what his firm's literary agent had said the publisher's rep called the plot after a reading. The certainty of the book being published gave Liebowitz the confidence to start shopping the rights for a 'book-to-movie' project to several directors to produce a documentary. All the elements were there to tug at the heartstrings: jungle nirvana to kidnapping, sale on the auction block, difficult births, separated families, the circus life, ITSE awakening, The Herd experience, and rediscovery of a lost grandchild who turned into a famous movie star and now a nationally recognized educator for the benefit of Animals. To die happy after a life lived fully.

A month later, agent Sammie Liebowitz, in full Hollywood matchmaking chutzpah, set up a conference call with Roark and an esteemed director, whose last film, a modernized version of Joan of Arc set in the 1930s Spanish Civil War, had won an Academy Award for Best Director [The Best Film Award went to an AI-generated musical drama of blind kids who rob a toy store on Christmas Eve].

The director's first words: "I don't want to do a documentary; too 'cut and paste' of old photos and newspaper clippings. No visuality. The story Sammie gave me was intense. A strong storyline. A morality play. I see it as a full-length theatrical release out by next winter, maybe during Thanksgiving. There is no rush to stream. The book is scheduled to come out in the Spring, I hear. Then my movie. And with luck and good PR, there's a good chance for Awards nominations and a February announcement in the following year."

As he recalled fondly the Tinsel Town speak, Roark could have let the director do his 'luv it, baby' spiel. He found it a welcome change that someone seemed to be captured by Mercedes and her complicated life. And the director had the creds. But Roark had been around the block in the biz, and he cut right to the bottom line.

"Do you have a studio to bank it?"

"I won them an Academy Award. Their checkbook is open within reason."

"Here are some firm points I would like to set out and put in place contractually."

Agent Leibowitz jumped in with pained laughter. "Don't be too unreasonable, Roark. This is a gift horse and not to be negotiated with a horse's head in someone's bed."

"I'll keep that in mind." Leibowitz and Roark had previously discussed deal terms.

"Let me rattle them off," began Roark to the director's silence.

"The book, of course, will have Orville and me as co-authors, my name beneath his. We want that recognized on the screen, me with co-producer credit. You can add other people if they help with production or financing.

"Your people can write the script. We want final script approval. No studio last-minute rewrites. For your creation, I will be the strongest advocate for your vision, within reason. Stick to the story.

"Next, I want final approval of the female orangutan to play the main Mercedes character in her youth and older, and the same with her family. They have to be Tapanuli. There is a recognizable difference in the Animal World."

The director started to object, but Roark interrupted with a verbal jab and his last and most serious demand.

"No AI digitization of the actors. You use real Intelligent Animals to play the roles. You can green-screen the landscape, of course, if you don't shoot on location. I will give you the full support of the Roar Animal University to look for possible actors among our students and faculty." The director whined, "But everyone's using AI production values, especially in animal-themed movies. It's a cost savings."

"I know how the Industry thinks. If you produce a masterpiece and maybe even grab an Academy Award, the Industry will hit the screens with multiple knockoffs, and there'll be a resurgence in real Animals back in vogue. And there's a lot of Intelligent Animal talent out there. I should know."

There was another gurgling protest from the director. Then Roark interjected, "To sweeten the pie and to give you and the studio confidence, I will guarantee the completion bond if you have completed 75% of pre-production and there is any hold-up or the Studio tries to bully you. But, if you accept, I get 2 points of the film's gross, audited."

This was new to Liebowitz. He never took risks; he was an agent. But he did not like seeing one of his best (past) moneymakers take a pure cash gamble, even if it sounded like merely doing the back-end movie's insurance policy. Yes, Roark would gain a premium on the money put at risk, plus the bonus percentage. The director and agent did not realize that Roark was putting the University into movie financing by pledging the Saylor Trust funds for the completion bond. Meanwhile, Leibowitz was calculating that the actors, the live Animals used in the film, would probably not be recognized as name-drawing talent, so their salary costs would be capped on the low side, with no participation points. A production expense savings there, but still…

The director wanted a tie-down. "Let me have the option. My attorney and your attorney can draw it up. Let me run all your 'demands' past the studio and see if they'll sign off." (The director emphasized 'demands' as if he was being tied up in a box and dropped in the river, mafia-dead style, not Houdini-escape style).

Roark gave his blessing. "I will work with you to find the right Mercedes."

"Jehovah and Allah help us all," said Leibowitz, praying that this property would get the green light. These days, bringing a concept to the big screen has only a .03% chance of success. Sammie silently thanked the Deities again that he was just an agent.

THE PITCH

All business opportunities undertaken require risk-taking and faith in the god of optimism.

The first week in the new year, two humans and an orangutan met in the ARC Building.

We have an idea," said Silent John. His girlfriend Nebbie sat beside him. Roark had known they were a couple for some time. John had finally made the declaration, so it was out in the open to avoid misplaced loyalties or conflicts of interest. Roark, of course, never had an interest in human relationships, but in this case, his imagination for a few long seconds wondered how their love-making might be accomplished; Nebbie lacked an arm and a leg—and did John remove his face mask? He never asked, and since they seemed to be professionals in public, what went on bore no consequences for him. He also kept silent about the fact that he and Eliza had engaged in their own trysts. To be no more, sadly, he reminisced. He turned to his two loyal staff employees.

To Silent John's declaration, Roark said, "Ideas are always welcome if they improve the bottom line and benefit Animals first, humans next. Or equally to both." Roark had perfected his entrepreneurial approach to filter out the many sales pitches and deal memorandums piling up on a second desk in the corner of his office.

More than anyone, Silent John knew what was driving Roark—to regain the stature and acceptance he was once accorded in his film career. In John's estimation, Roark rapidly overtook the bar he had set for himself. However, this movie-star-turned-educator did not realize he had entered an entirely different world regarding how he, Roark, was being viewed—less these days on the marquee as the movie idol he once was, but instead gaining kudos in national, even international recognition as a visionary, the Animal who was wisely giving Animals the tools to be more valuable contributors in overall society. John knew Roark would study what he and Nebbie were about to say by putting on his savvy, analytical hat and considering how it might mesh with his current business model of the University, Roark's proud toddler.

Silent John began.

"Nebbie and I have been reviewing the speed and the direction in which the University is going. As you know, we have recently been inundated with more applications than the University has the capacity to handle. And there are so many untested directions to gain new revenues, as you have told Nebbie, about the constant daily proposals thrown at you. We both see how overwhelming and damaging it is to the quality of time and work you endure while trying to prioritize against your fear of missing the 'one big idea' that might be the game changer."

Roark nodded. The thread of John's introduction had blunt merit. He was only one intelligent primate, but a bad judgment call could ruin everything and shatter his dreams.

"And your solution?"

Nebbie pulled out three copies of their proposal. Roark knew he would have to seriously consider whatever they had on their minds. These were the only faithful humans he directly worked with in the University management on a daily basis. He was dependent on them, as they were to his generosity, both tied to the success of elevating Animals.

"Franchising," said Nebbie, and she put a copy in front of him. "You need to delegate and, at the same time, maintain the quality of your goals. To achieve this, you need other people's money and effective expansion management so the University can turn out Animal graduates quickly enough to meet demand. Your preparatory school concept never really got off the ground. It's like a summer finishing school for those on the waitlist.

"Franchising is the future for Roar Uni."

"Okay, franchising works for the fast-food industry, but we are an educational institution seeking to establish a reputation for turning out Animal graduates who can enter the human workforce." He was preaching to the choir.

"Exactly," agreed Silent John, "But do you feel that Roar University can be, say, in 50 years, on par with all the Ivy Leagues and their billion-dollar endowment funds, who are cranking out fraternal cliques of snobbishness? If you look at what you have actually accomplished, Roark, you'll see you've started a movement, something no other Animal has even contemplated. Your movement is, as you've said, and as did Eliza before she left, the Equality of Animal and Human Rights.'

Nebbie added. "A movement and a crusade. We want to go along for the ride."

Roark tapped the proposal. The cover read, "Profitable Expansion of the Roar University Brand Through the Creation of Roar School Franchises."

Roar Schools.

Encompassing, thought Roark, and he waved his hand for them to continue the 'idea.' He guessed it would be a tag-team approach to keep him intrigued.

Silent John: "Roar University will be the ultimate brand; I believe it will be on par with the Ivy Leagues someday. Roar will be where one achieves their Master's and Doctorates, the post-grad for excellence among Animals. *Roar Schools for Animals*, the franchise we propose, could be established in every large, medium, and suburban-sized city in the country. Their curriculum will be what you are doing presently on a certain level, a training school of self-improvement and career development. Students would consider the schools like junior colleges, and the most brilliant graduates would compete to move up and enter the centerpiece, Roar Animal University. Graduates here will eventually be industry and political leaders as your goal of Animals' integration into the human world becomes a total reality."

Roark, ever the businessman, asked the all-important question: "How does a hundred pop-up schools help the bottom line?"

"Before John and I answer that," said Nebbie, "and before we open the first page of the proposal and go through the detail part, we want to broach an overall philosophy of what you have so far accomplished and suggest a change that must be made for the betterment of this movement."

"I made a mistake?" His face revealed more quizzical humor and mock disbelief. An expression saying, 'How could I be so wrong?'

"Not a mistake," intoned John, "but a part of the evolutionary process. We are part of the problem, and I say this with my heart full of love for the times we have been associated with you. But the time has come when those in your near orbit must be solely Animals. It is an optic to show that Animals in your sphere are listened to and not create the wrong impression that whatever is decided has a human behind it."

A sadness came upon Roark. The word 'dichotomy' came to mind. It had always existed there, known, yet sought to be melted into one. Human and Animal equals. *Was this an impossible quest, or must an attempt be required?*

Nebbie spoke. "We adore you; you must know it. But we feel it is time, at this moment of your success, that we move ourselves on a different path to protect you from the slings and arrows."

John quickly interjected. "But not too far away from you. And regarding your previous question on the bottom line:

"Roar Schools will have its home office here on the campus, and we will set it up and run it for you. We recommend that it will be 75% owned by your BT Enterprises holding company and 25% to Nebbie and me, hopefully as one voting unit, in the near future." They exchanged endearments through their eyes and held hands.

John continued. "Since a franchise will need owners with capital, and Animals don't yet have the financial power, each franchise will be set up so if a human provides the capital, there will be a 7-year buyout where the minority Animal shareholders can purchase a controlling interest, and the human owner receives their investment back plus a return well above the going bond interest return. If an Animal has the capital, they will be 100% owner unless they want to have human minority shareholders."

"Schools are not necessarily great profit generators."

"But some are like trade schools, and using the model you have been developing with Roar Uni, we see that the schools, in turn, would have subsidiary operations run by Animals, such as restaurants or repair shops. Maybe even financial institutions. So, the franchise is more than a school. Each franchise becomes its own mini-conglomerate. The parent company provides the educational texts, oversees scholarship funding for students, offers consulting services to the franchisee, and suggests options to open other spin-off profit centers. The parent company will hold a small interest in any of these attached subsidiaries.

Nebbie opened the first page of the proposal and pointed to the first paragraph. "We had a few investment bankers validate our business model and believe that in a five-year period or less, we could take the umbrella Roar School Corporation public with an IPO for a major return to you. Your initial investment is minimal, consisting of seed capital as the franchise owners will provide the funds for what you, in turn, will offer back to them as educational materials. It is the 'Roar' brand that makes franchising work. The brand and the unique idea that no one has yet developed except you. We only want to continue and maximize your direction."

Absorbing all, impressed at the pitch, the underlying hard hit was that they would no longer be there as day-by-day, side-by-side companions. New pangs of this separation seemed to create a mild stress attack, so brutal seeing the coming change. Roark placed his hand on the proposal. Silent for a solemn moment of contemplation.

Silent John sensed this was a new crossroads the orangutan must face alone.

"Roark, we will be here, around. Talking to you in meetings about our progress. Nothing has changed our friendship. And you are still the boss."

"Roark," said Nebbie, seeking to alleviate his uncertainties as they impacted him. "I have been identifying potential employees to handle your increased workload for some time. You need a staff of Animals, not just one human who might be able to type like a human but can't speak Animal to all those who wish to converse with you only in Animal-speak. I can bring this staff to you as early as next week, and you can see how they might help clear your desk." She smiled, and he smiled back. "And for John, he has wanted to say it, but with the first phase of construction finished in opening the University, he mainly walks the site with little to do. And to be your personal Assistant, you and he have grown beyond that. You have a security team for protection and division heads for the University's operation. Please give him a new challenge, which will be the best for all three of us."

Roark sighed at the inevitable changing of the guard. Because of his success, he also had to see the big picture, move forward with divergent ideas, establish new profit centers, and people or animals he trusted to run these related businesses, much like roots spreading out from a banyan tree.

"I will read your proposal and get back to you." He paused. He had to acknowledge creativity and spunk when he saw it. "There's something here, I believe." And he blew them a raspberry until all three were laughing.

RoarUni Facts

Research fellow Dr Richard Naylor from the University of Manchester developed a new method – now used across the world – to easily and quickly screen new drugs for treating different kidney diseases using zebrafish larvae instead of mammals. The model is a novel alternative to mammals which reduces the numbers of animals in research and drug screening and enhances the care they receive.

NEW OPPORTUNITIES

Fate or coincidence galvanized Roark's decision on the Roar Schools proposal, which occurred with a visit from the president of the First National Bank of Short Skiff Key. The calling of a banker on one of his main depositors is always good business. The University had deposited part of the Saylor Trust Grant funds with the local banking institution, understanding that proper community loyalty bears dividends, as the meeting would highlight.

After the perfunctory pleasantries and the banker spouting the proper obligatoriness of 'How we may assist you in the future to support your growth?', the real reason for the visit came to light.

"Two of your recent graduates, who also majored in business management and were active in the University's student-run restaurant, have approached us seeking a loan to open a food truck to serve the surrounding communities. Our loan committee reviewed their business plan and was impressed." He hesitated about what he wanted to say. "We haven't been able to decide if we bank this as an 'auto equipment loan' or a 'building loan—for a mobile building.' Our other concern is that their capital base and economic strength are not strong, and they have no personal history of credit borrowing."

"And how do you think we, the University, could help?" Roark responded cordially, realizing there was another 'proposal' seeking his blessing. What was it?

"The Bank could support them in applying for a government small business loan. Our risk is minimal, but we still have concerns about an untested business." To Roark, the banker did not have to say the unstated, 'a loan to Animals'. Of course, this discussion faced another ancillary issue on his chosen road of supporting Animals and their dreams.

"And you want the University or me to do what? Back the bank with our personal guarantee in some fashion?"

"Your credit and financial resources as co-signer, with guardian oversight, would certainly make our decision a *fait accompli*. That would benefit all—the bank and the University supporting Animal businesses. And certainly, we anticipate that with the University's success, there may be more of these requests in the future."

Roark reacted to what was being told to him, what he must do to meet human standards. *A guarantor, a guardian*? He was to be *in loco parentis* or a sort of *godfather* to all those he educated and sent out into the human world, because why? Were these graduates not to be considered as independent minds, reliant on their own life choices? He had to play the diplomatic role and look to the long game.

"May I get back to you by the end of the week, if that is acceptable? Could you send me a copy of the loan documents and the business plan? Who are these Animals, by the way?"

"Why, but of course. Our loan committee meets next week. And the loan applicants are Cosmos, a black bear, who was assistant manager at the restaurant, and Raffles, a kangaroo, who was a cook."

"Ah, yes, I know them. Graduated with honors, I believe."

The banker departed.

He put a call into Silent John. "You talked about subsidiaries that might arise through establishing Roar Schools. Put your thinking cap on, and let's look at banking to support Animals." Roark felt he was becoming like one of those circus Animals at The Herd: the juggler seal.

Nebbie poked her head into the office and walked in, followed by three Animals.

"Here is the staff that will make your life much more efficient."

Greta, a chimpanzee, Administrative Assistant; Marcus, a beaver, Bookkeeper; Lydia, a lion-tailed macaque, Internal Data Systems.

RoarUni Fact

Giraffes are the tallest land animal in the world, reaching heights of 19ft (5.8 m). They communicate with snorts and bellows and use low-pitched hums that are below the range of human hearing. The wild giraffe population has declined by about 40% in the last 30 years, making them a critically endangered species.

BALFOUR STRIKES

In a constant frenzy of activity since graduation and after the first of the year, Chancellor Roark had been spending most of his focused time at the University, now sleeping in a small apartment set aside for him on the top floor in the Administrative Roar Center, the ARC.

That night, however, for whatever reason, he decided to check out his apartment since Silent John had vacated it and was no longer part of The Herd and was off campus in his own housing, where he and Nebbie lived together. Roark decided to double-check on the vacant apartment where Eliza used to reside, on the fleeting chance that she chose to return.

As he entered The Herd and walked the hallway across the open space of the interior courtyard to ride the elevator to his floor, he passed a black swan and gave a friendly greeting, "Have a good evening, Swan."

"Whoa, there," said the swan. "You did not address me correctly?"

"Are you not a swan and a very striking one at that?"

"The new rules say that we must all be addressed by our known sex."

"Good evening to you, Mr. Swan, or is it Mrs. Swan?"

"I have declared myself to be He-She Swan."

"Oh, is that for this particular evening, or does addressing you change in the morning?"

"We male black swans live with other male black swans; we mate with a female swan, but then, as a 'she,' we take over the raising of our goslings."

"If I see you again, I shall say, 'Hey, *you*, good evening.'

"No, not at all. That would not be in accordance with the Rules. One must be defined as to preferred sex. Not to acknowledge us so is a Rule infraction."

"A new rule, I presume."

"Yes. And I must report this infraction."

Roak merely nodded his head and proceeded without any further comment.

So, his battle with The Herd Executive Committee had begun. He must hire local counsel and form a spirited response.

* * *

Roark tried to read all his incoming correspondence daily, which proved to be a vexing task. One document he scanned online and printed was a compilation of Animal stories nationwide, so he could be apprised of what was happening and the temperature of human response to the University.

Among hate groups, there are those weak, intelligent humans who will hate anything—their easiest bullying targets are those minorities they feel are inferior to them. Hatred against Intelligent Animals, according to national police statistics, was on the rise. All because of the recognition of the University and its goals. Roark wanted to be up-to-date on this subject, as prejudices against his students must be thwarted and opposed. A copy of what he saw also went to the Security Team, which had its own ranking of the groups to be concerned about.

Another online clipping service brought to Roark's attention a private update on Eliza's meteoric rise in the Animal Rights legal jousting against anti-Animal laws. Attorney Eliza's name began to appear on many legal briefs and filings as the representing counsel. He was proud of her, that she embodied what an Intelligent Animal could attain in the human world, though he knew her private thoughts were barely tolerable of human contact. Like having poison ivy to endure, but no alternative to the painful itching.

With this quick review of all pertinent daily news, Roark missed a snipped news report. *In Georgia, a zoo was broken into at night, and four monkeys were stolen.*

* * *

Orville, the soon-to-be-published author, visited Roark.

"I have some problems that I need advice on."

"Let me guess, I am one of the problems."

"I have been asked to step down from my position as Editor of The Heard. No real reason given, just that the Executive Committee wanted to move in a different editorial direction. But no doubt it is because of our friendship."

"I'm sorry, Orville. You are just too close to the falling bombs. Are they trying to force you out of your apartment? That's their goal with me; eviction and public animal society humiliation."

"No, I think it's different for me. I have a lot of supportive friends who would raise a stink. And my exit from the newsletter is not that bad. With the monetary advance from our New York publisher, I'm financially secure for a year or so and can devote my time to writing. And if you want, I could teach a class at the University on journalism or media studies."

"Of course, that would be a great addition to our faculty. But could you stay in place at The Herd for a few months and surreptitiously write articles, anything you want, for the University campus newspaper, say, under a pseudonym? I may have a greater need for you to stay in place at The Herd and the support of your 'friends' as I do battle with Herd leadership. I want to maintain my apartment, and I see this as a case of Animals being prejudiced against Animals. That's something our students may face in the outside world: career jealousy. And if I can, I want to set the standard of peaceful, if not legal, resistance.

"And can you get me a copy of the updated Rules & Regulations? As a resident, I was not notified of any Board action. The other day, I received a formal letter stating that my rent payment to them, which my bank automatically handles, was late because the bank had a holiday, and the payment reached the Herd Treasurer one day late. There's no grace period. And I am the only tenant not receiving the government stipend, which is automatically deposited into The Herd's banking institution. So, a New Rule infraction. I think I have two infractions and am unsure what triggers the eviction hearing."

"Okay, I'll keep tabs on what's happening at The Herd. Your own inside ape."

"By the way, have you heard from Eliza, by any chance?"

"I receive the NARLAS newsletter. And I got a nice email about a month ago. She's as committed and engaged as you are. I wish she were still around doing Animal relocations. But I have to say, Petra is doing a remarkable job, with multiple relocations simultaneously. SOCA leaders are quite pleased with your partnership. I hear Petra might be working with an African country to establish a new preserve solely for SOCA animals. Perhaps build their own resort village. A major accomplishment."

"Yes, with that program, we are doing well." They spoke no more of Eliza.

RoarUni Fact

Species helping one another. This year, researchers have gained huge new insights into pigs. New studies are providing an "atlas" of pig lung immunity, detailing how immune cells in pig lungs change after influenza infection or vaccination. Humans and pigs share a similar anatomy and physiology making pigs a useful model for understanding the immune system – among other physiological features – for both species.

BANKS, SCHOOLS, GREAT APES

In early Spring, Roar Animal University and BT Enterprises' publicity sent out two announcements.

One press release announced the establishment of the *National Bank of Animal Progress*, a joint venture between BT Enterprises and The Bank of Short Skiff Key. Details were not publicly available, but later filed annual reports with the State Banking Board would reveal that BT Enterprises held a 65% ownership interest and Short Skiff Bank a 30% interest, with 5% to a mix of Animal and human minority shareholders. The Agreement would establish, within the first twelve months, three mini-regional banks (better known as *Roar Progress Banks*) strategically placed in tourist-oriented demographics in Florida, the marketing aimed at supporting Animal's financial needs. As it turned out, initial deposits over the first two years were made predominantly by human pro-Animal supporters. Then, slowly, deposit and client percentages changed as Animals entered the workforce, deposited their paychecks, and sought business loans or mortgages for starter homes.

The second public relations announcement of great importance dealt with the national opening of franchise applications for the *Roar Schools for Animal Initiative* [Roar Schools]. The rush for franchise locations became an avalanche, with investor groups vying for supposedly hot geographic locations that would generate fast growth. Each new franchise owner would have a choice of subsidiaries tied to their operations that would benefit from a workforce graduating from a Roar School. Again, as Silent John and Nebbie had outlined, Animals would have carried an interest in minority ownership, with formulas for future buy-ins. The major business media wrote glowing reports of potential growth, further encouraging public interest in the investment franchise package.

Roark, for his part, had to hustle as spokesperson and chief marketing officer to gain new students to attend the school. He would have the downpayment of the franchisee holder for financial support, but he also extended his SOCA partnership to increase fundraising for Roar School scholarships (a finder's fee applied). For him, he was no longer dipping into his own pocket to finance his new projects.

* * *

During this time of burgeoning entrepreneurship, Roark and his new University staff had to set aside time to interview great ape applicants. Being very cautious, zoos were going to experiment with this temporary loan of large primates to be students in the University's educational program (known only to the University as the *indenture clause method)*. A vetting committee conducted personal interviews (at the zoos) and reviewed the primate candidate's origin history, noting any mental temperament issues and other qualifications that might direct the career choices of these great apes. The finalists were ten gorillas (eight accepted), fifteen chimpanzees (eleven accepted), and five orangutans (all accepted). Those not accepted were, for the most part, ill or elderly apes that zoos tried to rid themselves of.

Perceptive prejudice easily occurred, as even Roark discovered. He saw gorillas as strong-armed and fierce, maybe considering them for law enforcement, or televised wrestling leagues. Omar, an eastern lowland gorilla to be 'loaned' out from a Chicago zoo, wanted to come to the University to study art. Over the years, he had been an 'entertainer' at the zoo, scribbling watercolors. However, he told the interviewers he knew he had a greater talent for true ape impressionism that just needed to be guided by serious art teachers. He gained entry.

Brutus, a silverback western lowland gorilla from the Central African country of Cameroon, had an online following playing computer games. He wanted to be a games designer. Gort approved his acceptance, asking for Brutus as an intern in his Research Lab Department.

Roark realized he needed to alter his preconceived notions, giving the student applicants their choice, not some guidance counselor B.S.

And so, it went. The hardest decisions regarding placement were the orangutans, where two females, both ten years old, wanted to work as part-time clerical aides in Roark's office. Roark saw how they looked at him, that he was good enough to eat or at least nibble on. They were accepted as students but directed to the campus clinic on Animal health practices, hoping they might be motivated into medical specialization.

Finally, a Cross River Gorilla, the smallest of the species, a female with the Swahili name of Muuaji, had been trained in various forms of self-defense. The Security Team immediately approved her and would begin training her in a rigorous martial arts course. She could someday be a bodyguard to VIP clients.

After final approval as students, and with the candidate's approval, they were placed in the queue for a fast-track ITSE insertion, when the next release of devices became available under 'research' designation from the ITSE Committee. Despite his success, regardless of the positive public acceptance of a teaching school for Animals, Roar and the University were still held 'hostage' by the slow government process and the limited release of ITSE implants.

RoarUni Fact

The howler monkey is the loudest land animal. Its calls can be heard from 3 miles (5 km) away.

THREATS ON THE HORIZON

Everything is all well and good until it isn't.

Roar Schools for Animal Initiatives gradually expanded into openings across the national landscape. Roark had even traveled around Florida and surrounding states to participate in ribbon-cutting ceremonies and welcome new students. To his credit, his speeches at the dedications were seen as positive and not 'radical' and were reported widely in local media, and his more pithy quotations were picked up by the wire services.

The fledgling Roar Progress Banks, tested first in Florida, attracted a quick flow of early deposits, mainly from the curious with extra cash and Animals who were earning paychecks, small as they might be. Seeing this as new competition, several human banks recognized this new market and began to soften their credit red-lining restrictions against income-generating IAs.

This summer, the graduation of the second class at Roar University boasted 750 Animals of all walks, crawls, and flights of creature life. The ceremony had to be moved to the Short Skiff Key municipal auditorium because of torrential downpours. The rain caused some minor flooding, resulting in a rise in the swampland water level, but no serious damage to the academic buildings.

The… 'until it isn't'…began without anyone's conscious realization.

* * *

Over many millennia, the evolution of primates retained one trait of their prowess: the ability to take a long piece of straw or a thin wooden stick and collect ants and bugs out of holes for a tasty snack. This skill in modern times made monkeys proficient lock pickers.

Click. The back door opened just enough not to trigger the motion alarm. The overhead camera that covered this rear outside entrance area had been rendered useless, as it was disconnected from its supposed secure location on the roof. Three monkeys skittered across the floor and climbed the walls to cover the night cameras, which were concealed by small black bags throughout the store's interior. The sign on the back wall read, '*Welcome to the Best Damn Gun Emporium in all of South Carolina*". Two other monkeys entered, carrying medium-sized duffle bags, and eased open the glass front of the central showcase. The first three monkeys, who had blinded the cameras, scurried to ammunition drawers, jimmying them open with screwdrivers. Another monkey with a scar worked the chain lock on the automatic rifles behind the counter. When that snapped open, it was the signal for the smash-and-grab. The showcase glass broke, triggering the security alarm. The large AR-16s and heavy pistols were ignored, but the small weapons a small monkey could hold with two hands were snatched instead. The Capuchin monkey leader especially admired a snub-nose machine pistol that required not only both hands but operated on a shoulder. The other monkeys grabbed derringers and .22s and filled a duffel bag with appropriate ammunition. They were in and out of *The Emporium* in under seven minutes.

Local newspapers wrote of the break-in and the thefts, but no Animals were ever mentioned as possible suspects.

Edgar and his gang were now well-armed. And Edgar had a plan.

* * *

Roark's new staff had been miracle workers in bringing his jumbled list of tasks from the previous week into a minimal level of organization. That day, as he reached for the top of the pile, the hospital called, and he rushed out.

The food truck owners, Cosmos and Raffles, had been beaten, and their truck trashed. The story came out in the police report. They had set up their food truck to handle a weekend beer festival at the beach down the highway, several miles out of Short Skiff Key. The human muggers left a calling card with spray-painted anti-Animal slogans on the side of the truck.

Roark checked on their injuries; they were not serious, a warning-type beating. He gave them what confidence he could supply by saying the truck was insured and BT Enterprises would cover the loss of business until they were back and operating.

In the hospital waiting area, off to the side, he held a brief meeting with Gort, head of Security J-S, and donkey Mildred who had tagged along. Roark seethed.

"If we can't protect our students or their attempt to make a living after we encouraged them to take the risk, I don't know how the University can survive in the long run." He considered a political point he usually did not make. "We can't let the attempts at Animal success be destroyed by hoodlums."

J-S agreed but added, "More than hoodlums. The more you succeed with the University, the more we are seeing the anti-Animal scum rising to the top and becoming organized, as well as cowardly executives who fear change and businesses who feel threatened by the subsidiaries you are opening with the Roar Schools. Even zoos and wilderness park managements who fear that with your 'rent-an-Animal program' you might eventually attempt to free all animals. There are rumblings."

"I have been maintaining publicly that the University has no plot to push a policy of All Animals Must Be Free." That was Eliza's mindset, not his.

Chewing on a basket of get-well flowers someone had discarded, Mildred said, "Some humans want to hate, to create fear of those who have taken a brighter path." Roark looked at the donkey. It was a simple sentiment and correct. Mildred added, "And don't forget there are even Animals, like some at The Herd, who feel your University might cause humans to disrupt their monastic lifestyle."

Roark told the three key employees assembled, "I don't know if I really want to go in this direction, but I assume this attack is the beginning of the rise of these haters, the stupid who destroy progress, and the insidious and smart evil ones who will beat a larger drum to assemble the easily deluded.

"People have started calling what I launched with the University a 'Movement'; that is not my intention. I have only strived for Animals and humans to work together in harmony and peace. But it seems we may have to prepare to protect that ideal.

"We need to have a proactive campaign. Focus positive PR on our purpose and increase the Security Team's intelligence-gathering function. And to deal with any attacks, we need, what do you call it, where we can get to the scene of trouble as fast as possible?"

"A Rapid Deploy Force," offered J-S.

"Yes, let's create some version to protect our own and build up our current security team. But look and act as what?" He gave thought, looking for the word.

"Para-military?" again from J-S.

"More 'Minute Men' in style and look, not uniformed, not a National Guard. We can't have the haters, even the local governments, believe we are arming ourselves, or they will call us insurrectionists or worse. We want to employ a quiet hand but with a big stick."

As a result of this meeting, the University acquired a small office building across from the campus. It was built of concrete, two stories tall, with a small yard in the back that became a training ground. Added to the remodel was a secure room that housed an arsenal with enough weaponry to arm the enlarged force yet to be identified and hired.

CASTING NEST

In addition to these problems, Roark became deeply involved in the pre-production casting call for the *Mercedes* movie. He suggested only minor changes to the script, which surprised the skeptical director. They both agreed it would attract more viewers if he, as he did for the book, did the intro and the ending soliloquy, voice only (not to risk his non-compete agreement clauses on non-digitized acting).

For the last several days, he, along with the director and the casting agent, had been selecting the orangutans to play the different ages of Mercedes's life—the baby, the kidnapped youngster, the late youth primate surviving aging into the older female reaching the culmination of her struggles to start The Herd Apartments, protecting ex-Circus animals (the script leaned heavily on her heroics and less on Herd communal decisions).

Today, the 'late youth' actress appeared for the final audition. A 15-year-old orangutan, she had flown in with her agent for Roark's final approval and blessing. Her stage name was Carmen, and she was very attractive (to Roark), as she was Tapanuli to match Mercedes' species to maintain storyline accuracy.

She and Roark hit it off, she more so, being quite flirtatious. Roark had created in his mind a 'saint' vision of his grandmother, and this actress had her own idea on how she could secure the part. From her headshots and viewing her film reel, which featured previous television work in commercials for animal-only body deodorants, Roack admitted she had the talent and could carry off the range of emotional expressions the role required. Alluring teasing could be overlooked if she maintained professionalism. Besides, he was not going to look over the director's shoulder. When her agent left the room to take a personal call, Carmen made the play to what she thought could secure the part, star to star.

"I could spend the night if you want to talk more about the part. I noticed you had a large tree at the back of this place.

"We could go swinging together. I could show you my talents." The suggestion was too obvious: a director's auditioning couch now a tree fornication nest.

He would not be tempted, though the temptation might alleviate stress.

He ignored her. When the agent returned, Roark merely said, "If the director accepts her, Carmen has my blessing, and if all the contracts work out with the studio. Final question: 'Are there any deep, dark secrets that might cause embarrassment to the production or cast a shadow on the character of Mercedes we are trying to achieve?'"

The agent gave the standard, 'No scandals, no diseases, no exes, no children."

Carmen huffed, "Children, why would I want to stop my career for children, obnoxious little beasts?"

Roark smiled, complimented her past acting, said he would recommend her, and wished her well. Her parting included sultry eyes, a longing hug to him, and she licked his face.

Roark sighed deeply at her departure.. *If I had been in Hollywood and she was on set—that siren could have blown up the entire set—and might still.* He would ask the director to put a babysitter assistant with her. Her exit brought back memories of Eliza; time and distance felt bittersweet, the kind that could quickly turn negative. The mention of 'the tree' in the recent conversation reminded him of good times past. *How was she doing*? he wondered.

* * *

Eliza could not help but think of Roark; his face plastered inside one of those movie fan mags on the racks at the store check-out—an old photo of him in a strong pose as an orangutan about ready to do battle against the *Mad Monkeys of the Universe*. Primate stars didn't need to wear makeup, she considered. Maybe salon-blow his hair, but certainly not with that Rambo battle paraphernalia draped all over him. She didn't realize that his photo was an AI computer composite. What bristled her *own* hair was a photo of a striking female orangutan, identified as the actress Carmen, who had been signed to play Roark's grandmother in a movie about her life. All hush-hush, but the magazine had the scoop (through Carmen's publicist) and the quote from Carmen, "That Roark is such a hunk. I can't wait until he returns to the screen." So that's it, Eliza ground her teeth. He was on the prowl, not concerned with her or...she patted her tummy, her very expanding tummy. Her decision followed her beliefs and resolved that if she thought about what was best for all animals, all primates, then she must support the concept of family. Her passion for supporting any worthy cause was that, yes, she would bring a baby into this world, but by her actions, it would be a better life than she ever had. And she would be the protector. Her mind went to a darker place: a baby without a father.

GORT'S LAB

He had never been to Gort's expanded research lab, the Science Department, which had recently relocated to its own building. Roark was too busy and, if he considered it, had never been formally asked. An invitation from the brilliant chimpanzee meant something. Roark entered this labyrinth of cubicles, mostly filled with computers where various animals tapped away, and a couple of offices; the doors were open, revealing a lot of strange medical equipment, tubes, and even an operating-type table. And one door closed with a padlock, stating 'Do Not Enter. Sterile Room.

"Did I sign off on all this equipment?"

Gort could have voiced his normal fast-speed chatter, requiring a translator. However, in recent months, tiredness due to his workload had changed his demeanor and slowed down his talkative personality to more staccato sentences of short duration.

"Yes. Research."

"So why am I here?"

"Project API."

"API?"

"Application Programming Interface"

"And this…is?"

"Let me show you."

Gort led him to another locked door with a sign forbidding entrance. Opening the door, they stepped inside. Roark found himself looking at two small beds, with a Capuchin monkey lying in one bed playing a computer game, and a young baboon watching a show on a miniature wall television.

Both said, almost simultaneously, "Hello, Doctor Gort."

"Doctor?"

"Titles uplift responsibilities and provide a trust factor." Gort blurted the sentence out in mild gibberish. "I want to introduce you to King and Kong."

"This is Chancellor Roark; he is responsible for who you are today."

They stopped at their activity and beamed with worshipful faces.

Both spoke excitedly. "Thank you. Thank you. It is so wonderful. Doctor Gort is so good to us."

Then, Roark noticed each monkey had a white band around their neck, not a bandage but an elastic collar with a small metal mesh square embedded in the neck. It hit him: just like the one Silent John wore.

"What is this?" Roark asked, his curious nature begging for an answer.

Gort took a deep breath, and launched into an expansive rushed sing-song response.

"My version of ITSE. Less invasive. A pill ingested contains two microscopic computers placed by scoping into the internal carotid artery, which we then direct by external imaging guidance into the middle cerebral artery. The pill dissolves, and one part of the computer inserts itself into the brain in Broca's area, located in the left hemisphere. The other attaches itself to brain tissue in the frontal lobe. They have transmitters that send signals to a receiving unit inside the throat, depending on the Animal. One signal is from Broca's area, which handles speech, and the frontal lobe expresses thought. They meet in the lower throat where both convert thought into speech, and you guessed right, a speech device similar to Silent John's magnetic larynx translator into human English-speak. In time, I think we can do away with the outward band and place the mesh within the throat."

Gort had rattled this explanation, and Roark only gained half of what was said. What he now witnessed, if practicable, was a momentous new English-speak device with multiple applications.

"Is this ITSE? Do we face patent infringements?"

"All components are totally unlike ITSE. It is a different product with the same outcome."

Roark's brain whirled with what needed to be accomplished—patent lawyers, securing more funding, and plans for manufacturing. A real *Fantastic Voyage*. He turned to Gort.

"Could you program in languages other than English?"

"Slight modification, program language database. Yes, down the road. I need more testing on our present system. I could use another monkey corpse to further research."

"Could you insert a tracking signal, perhaps another pill the subject takes without knowing?"

"We can do that now; what for?" asked Gort, a little suspicious of a lay-ape's meddling.

"If this works and we don't use ITSE, we'll need to track our students and graduates against possible scenarios to protect them if we need to rescue them quickly, wherever they are. The system would be under our control. I want fail-safes. Very hush-hush."

"Watches and phones can do that now. But I can create an internal tracker, undetectable, I believe. More money, more time."

"Yes, let's go forward. Because of the threats I hear about, sooner the better." Roark turned back to King and Kong, who had returned to their games and television programming. He could not mask his enthusiasm for the possibilities with this invention of Gort's. "What do you see as the best application for what you've created?

Gort looked to his boss, a wide grin forming. He knew what he might do, but he also knew that though he was ultra-smart, he was not business or politically savvy. "You have to decide, not me. You could make a lot of Intelligent Animals for University and Schools. Make money, but then…"

"Then what?"

"Make free to all animals. Open license to all inventors to improve. Let Animal world speak for themselves."

"One step at a time. Let's first finalize a marketable product, *Doctor Gort*."

"Almost there," answered the crazy, not so crazy, chimp genius.

RoarUni Fact

New medicines. For treating cat diabetes *velagliflozin* is a once-daily liquid solution with the same mechanism of action as *bexagliflozin*. To help cats with nonregenerative anemia caused by chronic kidney disease, *Molidustat* reversibly inhibits hypoxia-inducible factor prolyl hydroxylase (HIF-PH). *Fuzapladib* is labeled to treat acute pancreatitis in dogs. Consult your vet.

SHIFTING CURRENTS

Sekhmet, the lioness, attended an emergency meeting of the town council, where she had been a council member for almost a year. The agenda limited this day to one item: *Town Emergency Preparedness.* The hurricane season was fast approaching. Storms were forming in the Atlantic, nothing definite, trajectories yet to be plotted. Better prepared than sorry. The Emergency Planning director went over the Short Skiff Key evacuation plan. Going north rather than across the Glades to the Eastern side. Storms were unpredictable. Sekhmet found herself concerned, thinking of her own animal living situation. She didn't believe the Herd had ever considered coordinating with humans to protect themselves. Their attitude was that the former Kure Steel Erectors buildings were solidly constructed. She began to take notes and decided to ask Chairman Balfour to create The Herd Emergency Storm Plan. "Preparedness is safety," stressed the Disaster Relief coordinator.

* * *

Eliza could not determine whether this next job assignment meant a fantastic promotion or if she was being shuffled aside for a more competent attorney with years of experience in political affairs. The head of NARLAS had called her into his office and praised her for the work she had completed so far, including filing papers to begin a state-wide petition drive to place Animal Rights on the fall ballot. She had gotten amendment language approvals for ballot petition circulation in five states.

The human executive kept trying not to look at her expanded belly. Eliza, in mild depressive moments, had compared herself to a watermelon-carrying ape. The due date was not too far off, and she had yet to schedule a veterinarian for a date to induce delivery. Natural childbirth, like in the wild, did not sound very appealing. She was at least that civilized.

Said the NARLSA president, "Your work of putting in place the legal structure for the petition drives will be used as a template for the other states. But to be perfectly frank, creating an enthusiastic campaign to file the petition numbers in a timely manner with the various Secretaries of State will require a significant effort from our volunteers. It was the thought, and you came to mind, that the one State where we have a favorable chance is a State with a strong Animal tourism industry, Florida. That's where you once lived? We would like you to take over Florida's entire ballot initiative campaign. What with aquariums, zoos, the Sanctuary for Great Apes, Roar Animal University, and even all the ex-circus Animals who have retired to Florida, I think voters would be empathetic, and it is our best chance for passage. And with you in charge of the publicity and the ground game, you should bring in a slew of volunteer campaign workers."

She felt the human thought expressed without saying: a primate pregnancy did not inure their reputation as lean and mean litigators. Truth be told, she was tired of the constant office hustle and the small legal fires assigned to her to quench and snuff out, many of them in neighboring states. Travel in her condition became exhausting, if not painful. In this one-sided conversation, she smiled at the right moments and took the proffered 'promotion' regardless of their reasoning.

She telephoned Orville. Why not use The Herd Apartments as her base? A familiar base, halfway in the middle of the State. A short jaunt to Miami and up the coast to the state capital in Tallahassee. Orville, upbeat, was truly pleased to hear from her.

"Of course, you can stay here. You can have my apartment and look after it while I'm gone. We have this project on the West Coast. Roark probably told you about it?"

No, he had not. She had left before the topic of the movie and this starlet hussy was mentioned by Roark.

Orville continued, "Anyway, I have to go and work with the director on script rewrites to be true to the story of Roark's grandmother. I'll be gone for about two weeks. I'll leave a key at the front desk. And don't mention my name around too much. It seems I am persona non grata with the Executive Committee. No longer editor of The Heard."

"No", she said, "I hadn't heard. I've been traveling a lot and haven't kept up with Apartment resident scuttlebutt."

"I'll tell Roark you're back and around."

"Please don't. I'll be on the road a lot. No time for renewing old acquaintances."

Orville said nothing but changed the subject to the latest gossip, to the parade that Roar University had participated in, and that Chairman Balfour was upset and was getting close to evicting Roark, so he heard. Sekhmet was on the town council, and the *Three Cool Cat* lionesses were upset that they could no longer perform in public and were themselves threatened with eviction due to a new rule that had just gone into effect.

She chose to return to The Herd Apartments, not because of Roark, so she told herself. It would be fine if they did not run into each other. What was critically important was having a top-notch on-call veterinary Ob-gyn who could be at the Apartment when she started feeling the pains. Until the baby arrived, she would remotely direct the petition drive campaign from Orville's apartment.

RoarUni Fact

"Dogs believe they are human. Cats believe they are God."

—Anonymous

MONKEY HERD GANG

Part of the arrangement with the First National Bank of Short Skiff Key required that, for educational purposes, a small satellite branch would be established on the University campus, where one or two human bankers would work alongside Animal trainees. When the Animals, usually Animals, those paws or claws could count money and make customer deposits, learned their jobs, these new tellers and bookkeepers would be assigned to the future Animal Progress Banks that BT Enterprises was establishing around the State.

One of these banks was located in Miami-Dade County, renting a former bank that had shut down during the human epidemic several years ago. The staff consisted of two tellers (a bobcat and a grey squirrel) and a giraffe manager.

The bank's front door opened, and when the squirrel teller looked up from her money counting, a monkey wearing a cowboy hat and a bandana over its face jumped on the ledge of her window, waved a miniature pistol in her face, and showed her a note with the writing, "All your money." To the bobcat, the same deadly interruption was taking place.

Two other 'cowboy' monkeys climbed up the glass barrier and over, dropping beside the tellers, and began emptying the cash drawers.

The bank robbers were long gone within five minutes.

The giraffe returned from her lunch break in the break room to find two inconsolable bank tellers with the strangest story to tell. But security cameras did not lie.

Roark received the call later that afternoon. He immediately had suspicions about the perpetrators. He had forgotten all about them and had considered them reprobates up to no good, never thinking that they could take monkey mayhem into criminal enterprise and against Animals.

Jefferson, the human Security Team member who handled University intelligence and was teaching a training class of ten new Animal recruits to consider forensics as a police career, brought him the news. He had contained it, seeking Roark's advice on how they should proceed. Should they contact the FBI and the FDIC authorities?

Roark's thoughts returned to the mess in Central America, which Edgar and the members of his monkey gang were mixed up in, what Roark thought, at the time, was malicious delinquency. That incident was serious; this robbery was catastrophic, rendering him unable to decide what to do. Again, humans should not hear about Animals committing crimes. The destruction of the reputation of peace-loving Animals could set back human-Animal relations and give credence to the cries of the anti-Animal Rights opponents, shouting: 'See, I told you, they can't handle our civilization.' Damned if you do, damned if you don't act.

Ignoring this problem would come back to haunt Roark. It would have been better if he had just taken the bad publicity and embarrassment and let the humans know they might have an Animal crime wave on their hands. He asked Team Leader J-S to form a 'flying squad' to privately track down the cowboy culprits. To top it off, they had only stolen $450. Not a big deal, so Roark thought, but he couldn't know that 'slim pickings' to Edgar only fueled his rage and set him to devise more diabolical plots. For some reason, Edgar's blind wrath bubbled with spite against all other Intelligent Animals.

STORM CLOUDS

A weather disturbance built itself to power over the Atlantic, dipped down, and passed over the Dominican Republic and Haiti, pelting the islands with lashing rains and 40-50 mile-an-hour winds. Rebuilding strength in the Caribbean Sea, the new storm graduated into a Category 2 hurricane, passing south of Jamaica, and heading up between the Yucatan Peninsula of Mexico and Cuba, flooding Havana as it headed toward the Gulf of Mexico. As it was early in the season, the World Meteorological Organization designated the hurricane with the male alphabet name *Demonio,* which meant *Devil* in Spanish. The latest forecasts had the storm weakening and dissipating somewhere in the Gulf, perhaps turning back into a rain system to lash the Louisiana coast. Florida meteorologists tracked it but saw little concern—until it turned, without warning, towards southwest Florida.

And intensified.

* * *

The Executive Committee met in special session to discuss strategies for planning the upcoming formal Board meeting, which would be open to all residents and be held the following week.

Chairman Balfour went to his pet project, which involved ousting resident Roark from the Apartments.

Those in attendance: Larry the lion (Secretary), Hazel, zebra (Treasurer), Huntington, elephant (Rules & Regs), Benny, black bear (Building Maintenance). Skye, the brown eagle, had an excused absence. As a realtor, he had an open house down the road in Siesta Key.

A rough draft motion circulated detailing the infractions against the tenant, and required notice was to be given (posted on his apartment door, which he seldom visited) that the tenant could formally appeal the decision at the next public meeting of The Herd residency. Hazel worried that the loss of two housing unit rentals would be unfortunate, but the budget could withstand the revenue hit. Huntington explained that the new rules of eviction, which had passed a month earlier, were proper and that they were now going 'by the book.' Benny wondered if they were moving too fast on this issue, as Roark seemed to be gaining a lot of favorable local mention about Roar University. "Could there not be advantages", Benny postulated shyly, "of Herd Animals taking night courses", or something like that?

Balfour immediately shot that down, emphasizing that Roark's concept of Animals learning to work with humans went against the core of The Herd seeking to be more aloof in their dealings. The Executive Committee had already sent out a letter reminding residents of the harmony and peace that The Herd amenities provided, and to dissuade any residents from participating in outside activities. However, as several board members knew themselves but said nothing, this letter did not seem to have had much effect.

The Chairman pressed, and the motion to set the Eviction Hearing with all tenants present passed with no negative votes.

Larry brought up the news that Roark's 'cousin' had returned but was staying in Orville's apartment while he was out of town.

Was she also an 'undesirable? Larry sought clarification on the Chairman's thinking. Balfour sought to be fair and magnanimous, saying that if she had no long-term plans to stay and did not upset any residents, he could see no problem. But he would withhold his opinion, and they may have to revisit having another outsider on the premises.

Before they adjourned, Hazel mentioned the weather forecast of a storm that might be heading towards Florida, although it was four or five days away. Balfour said they had weathered tropical storms before. Benny opined that the buildings were structurally sound enough to withstand any storm, although he admitted he had not reviewed any original construction engineering plans. And yes, the buildings were old and not up to current codes in some respects.

Larry mentioned that his mate, Sekhmet, had attended an Emergency Preparedness meeting at the Short Skiff Key town council, and it was her opinion that maybe The Herd should create their own evacuation plan. Balfour grew irritated about outside human interference and instead agreed with Benny that staying was the safest course of action. Balfour did not want to deal with the logistics of moving all those Animals and finding a safe haven, which would be a massive undertaking with exorbitant costs. He affirmed that staying put was the best way to ride out this storm.

But it was not a storm. It was much worse.

* * *

Eliza had been, as the humans say, in confinement, staying all the time in Orville's apartment, working on her computer, and mapping out her campaign to track the progress on the petition seeking Animal Voting Rights, which would be placed on the ballot for next spring's election. It was coming to her attention that Florida State Senator Harold Mumford had been making speeches around his rural constituency, speaking out against Animals having *any* rights, that it went against God and natural selection. It turned out he was a major gun-toting game-hunting enthusiast. The politician's condemnation even appeared in op-ed attacks against Roar Animal University, finding it inappropriate to encourage Animals to be educated and take jobs away from good, honest, hard-working humans.

At the same time that her petition drive was underway, she set up a small group of Animals to launch a grassroots letter-writing campaign to state-wide newspapers, political leaders, and the media in favor of Animal Voting Rights. The message sent emphasized that voting rights were only fair to Animals. All mention of Equal Rights for Animals had been downplayed as a political strategy; even Eliza had to support it to avoid human animosity in the signature collection process. But this new ERA movement found followers among a few solitary herds and migrating flocks. Even at Roar University, a very small group of student activists who sought out new causes perceived as unjust had formed an unsanctioned campus ERA club for 'discussion purposes only.'

During her in-bed officing, the Herd's outside human veterinarian looked in on Eliza, found nothing wrong, and said that mother and infant were doing well, with all signs pointing to a healthy birth within two weeks, a date well past the approaching bad weather. No discussion suggested that Eliza might want to find friends up north, with whom she could stay during the next several weeks, and a place close to a hospital.

Eliza read and accepted the latest Heard newsletter, reassuring all residents that it would be best if everyone sheltered in place as the storm warnings did not appear severe enough to cause concern.

RoarUni Fact

The word hurricane comes from the Taino Native American word, *hurucane,* meaning evil spirit of the wind. A tropical storm is classified as a hurricane once winds goes up to 74 miles per hour or higher. A typical hurricane can dump 6 inches to a foot of rain across a region. The most violent winds and heaviest rains take place in the eye wall, the ring of clouds and thunderstorms closely surrounding the eye. Every second, a large hurricane releases the energy of 10 atomic bombs.

DEMONIO COMETH

As everything unfolded in a calamitous rush, it will be hard to recreate and timeline the moments and events when Hurricane Demonio made landfall at Short Skiff Key.

Weather reporting is still not an exact science, but satellite imaging showed the hurricane making a sudden curving change back towards the Florida Gulf's west coast. There was uncertainty about whether the hurricane would move south towards the island Keys, maybe higher up to cross and hit Miami, or go further north to Orlando and into Georgia and the Carolinas.

Like a whirring cocktail blender, the rains pounded in, fierce gusts slapping all. Hurricane Demonio intensified from Category 2 to Category 3. Short Skiff Key was destined to be the bullseye center, and when it finally hit full on, the wind was recorded as Category 4, with winds of 130-150 miles per hour, a damaging blow.

The Short Skiff Key Town Council with one day warning promptly initiated its Emergency Preparedness Plan. Citizens were encouraged to evacuate up the coast. Those hunkering down were to board up their businesses and shelter only in buildings with steel-enforced concrete or brick walls. Frame buildings were most at risk. Most human citizens chose to evacuate. This included the veterinarian who treated The Herd residents, who was under the impression that the Animals would do likewise, being intelligent.

The storm came on too quickly to mollify Chairman Balfour's obstinacy and his constant assuredness that all Animals should stay inside. After all, as Animals, they were expected to tolerate outdoor weather. The truth was that they had never created an evacuation plan nor tied it to the town's storm warning apparatus. Oblivious, they thought they could watch the storm pass by, and most tuned their televisions to the news and weather or their other favorite entertainment shows—until the power went out, and the generators that kicked in only covered the main common areas and a few resident apartments.

Chairman Balfour decided to keep the residents' minds occupied by holding the residents' meeting, since the agenda was critical—to him. Plus, a group gathering ought to keep everyone calm.

His hope that the quick agenda would be rammed through fell apart in the early afternoon when Larry presented him with a two-page flyer.

"What's this?"

Larry seemed confused about how to explain.

"It seems to be a report on the beneficial economics and a call for a petition for all the residents to vote…to turn…The Herd Apartments into condominiums."

"What? Where did you get this?"

"It was put under my door around noon time. Others said they received the same thing the same way."

"Who did it?"

"Don't know, but everyone I talked to wants to discuss it at our meeting. I don't think you can table this without first answering questions."

Chairman Balfour was flummoxed, trying to decide how angry he should be. This stank of rebellion! Of his authority! He read the flyer and plotted how best to kill the proposal. Maybe he should postpone the meeting. No, the Roark eviction was paramount. He could handle it all. Only a challenge, and he was up to it.

As the storm hit the area and a rain curtain descended on visibility, Petra easily breached the grounds of The Herd Apartments. After removing her clothes, she looked like one of the Monkey Garden residents who were all hiding somewhere inside. She carried a backpack filled with flyers asking the residents to demand that the Apartments become condominiums.

Roark's strategy was to avoid suing Animals to fight the eviction, instead create by flyer misdirection internal dissension and undermining the Executive Committee. The flyer spoke about the benefits of providing every resident with a tangible asset: ownership of their residence. They could keep it or sell it. Suddenly, the Animals, the ex-circus animals, would realize they had created wealth for themselves. And freedom to choose what was best for the individual, not the collective.

Finishing her stealth insertion of the flyers throughout the complex, Petra had planned her exit near those vacant or unused apartments, where Roark and Orville had the only units. As she eased herself through the corridor, she heard a noise, more of a muffled cry. The sound was coming from Orville's apartment, but he was supposed to be in California, so Roark had told her. She put her ear to the door—someone in pain. The door was not locked, and she opened it, glancing in.

* * *

Eliza had felt the first pain an hour earlier. Like the storm, the pains built, and more recently, the sharp stabs were coming more frequently. She had called the veterinarian's office, then the Apartments' front desk. Her cell phone was dead. The lights flickered and died, then came on, went off again, and switched to low-wattage emergency lighting.

She had been stupid. A window of evacuation had been available, but no one chose to leave, and she followed suit, wishfully thinking that the baby would come after the storm as she had been told with certainty. She believed that. But that god, the one Roark told her about, Mother Nature, sets her own schedule.

Eliza gave a loud gasp as her expanded stomach pressed on her other biological functions. She felt that she couldn't walk to the elevators, and what if they didn't work? Stairs were out of the question. She yelled out uncontrollably in misery.

The door eased open, and a monkey poked her head in, cautiously.

Through her tears, Eliza recognized the Capuchin.

"Petra?"

"Yes, are you all right?"

"No, do you have a phone? I need the doctor now."

Petra reached into her backpack and tried calling for an emergency response, but it was not working. The storm outside raged. The rain was hitting the window, not downward, but horizontally.

Eliza sighed at the inevitable. "Shortly, I'm going to have a baby, naturally, like in the jungle."

"A baby?" Of course, she was, Petra noted Eliza's stomach.

"Can you help? I think with you here, I can make it. Just need some hand-holding."

Petra sat down next to the orangutan. She had seen jungle births. How hard could it be?

ENTER THE VIOLENT WORLD

The baby orangutan, a male, eased out in the midst of nature's violence of close lightning strikes and a hurricane's wrath of destruction. With the birthing over, after Eliza had cleaned her new creation, staring in amazement at what she'd accomplished, she slept, the baby clinging to the mother's breast.

Petra felt she had offered no help but accepted Eliza's weak smile at the end of the journey. She also felt exhausted and ready to take a quick nap when she heard a noise in the corridor, a repeated knocking on doors. She could not be discovered; Roark's involvement in these propaganda enticement flyers would wreck his plan.

Quickly, she moved to the door and locked it, just as the handle turned, with loud knocking. Eliza barely stirred, although the baby reacted to the new sounds outside the womb, but made no noise.

Staying silent, Petra held her breath as the ruckus moved down the hall with more pounding on doors. She waited until the sounds seemed distant and slowly eased the door open a crack, glancing out. She shut the door and quickly relocked it.

Angry monkeys were at the elevator, weapons in their hands.

* * *

Chairman Balfour miffed and a little disconcerted by the turnout. There were more residents than usual, but not an overwhelming number to support his plans. He surmised many had stayed in the upper apartments with their families to wait out the storm. Those in attendance wanted to feel there was safety in numbers. Others, with flyers in their paws, teeth, and under their wings, wanted clarification. Muttered questions surrounded the penguin: *Were they turning the apartments into condominiums? Is that a better financial direction to take?* Balfour had a solution ready to implement, referring this question of condominiums to a study committee and letting it languish.

His gavel came down, and the meeting opened. The atrium windows rattled.

A gunshot was heard above the storm's din. At first, Chairman Balfour did not comprehend. Then, he did: *A gunshot*? *In here? In the Apartments? Human terrorists*?

Suddenly, different groupings of Animal residents from all over the complex started coming in, all in fear, followed by monkeys pointing pistols at them.

Walking to the front and grabbing the gavel, Edgar the monkey, his body draped in bandoleros of ammunition with a miniature semi-automatic machine gun with a cut-down barrel, waving his weapon at the crowd, gaining control by terror, silencing the cries and mutterings: "I am here to say, 'The mad monkeys are now in charge!'"

* * *

When Petra heard the gunshot, she knew she had to act. Waking Eliza, she whispered, "I think Edgar is here with his gang.

I have to get help. You must lock the door behind me. If you can push a desk in front of the door; do so. I will be back with help."

Although panicked, Eliza felt her paramount concern in protecting the innocent, whom she shielded in her arms.

"But it's miserable out there. Flying debris. You'll be killed."

"I've got to get to Roark."

The name. "Does Roark know I'm here?"

"I don't know. I don't think so. Or he would've been over here instead of me."

Eliza masked her indifference but failed. "Doesn't matter. He has his world of movie stars; I have my world of political action."

Petra laughed. "You're post-birth delusional. Eliza, Roark is totally committed and busy with a hundred projects, but he has feelings for you. I see him often in his tree, not resting, not contemplating great things which he is capable of, but moping like a love-sick primate."

Eliza tried a weak smile. "You sure have gained full language capabilities since the last time I saw you."

"And I am one fucking Intelligent Animal who is going to help Roark kick monkey butt."

"Why do you think Edgar is here?"

"Who knows? Maybe fomenting, what's the word—'anarchy.' If he attacks humans, the Federal Government will send in the army, animals will become beasts to kill, intelligent or otherwise. And here, he's familiar with his past home and probably feels he can intimidate, rob everyone, and use it as a base for other attacks on Animals. Maybe even the University. Who knows?"

Eliza understood the ramifications. " You are right. Monkeys attacking monkeys might be forgiven by the humans, filed away as odd news. Knock down our intelligence. But, if he starts robbing humans, we become wild animals once again. All our efforts, the University, our voting rights, and our Animal-human equity open to all animals will be destroyed forever. I wish I could do something. I feel so helpless."

"Hardly. You have the next generation of IA leaders."

"But," Eliza paused, upset, confused. "But he's a cocktail, a hybrid."

"Bullshit," said Petra, heading to the door. 'That's human talk. What you are holding is Super Primate. The best of you both. Roark and you will love him as unique."

"Roark? He's not...."

"Oh, come on, Eliza, be honest."

Petra had put the backpack on and slipped out.

TURMOIL

Roark thought he had the storm preparedness under control. Most of his students who had family housing elsewhere were evacuated, with many taking their university roommates who did not. Teachers and faculty employees went home to care for their own families, many subsequently evacuating. Those remaining, those dependent on the University for their home, moved their bedding to the upper floors.

Silent John worked with local officials who informed him that the water in the swamp had risen during past storms, so surge flooding was the greatest danger. Roark could be pleased with the architectural improvements, similar to many Gulf-designed resorts, which usually had their ground floors as open spaces on concrete pillars, allowing water to flow through without submerging and stressing the sidewalls. Still, this Category 4 had to be carefully monitored. What caught him off guard were the human refugees from the neighborhood, whose nearby single-story homes were inundated with surge flooding or had roofs torn off. They had waded to the University and were made welcome.

From his office, Roark and John had been juggling all storm impacts and actions taken via the in-house short-range walkie-talkies configured, of course, by Gort's team.

Petra burst in, limping, her face bloodied. Roark knew where she had been, on an errand for him. Before he asked, she blurted out, “Edgar has taken over The Herd.” She caught her breath. “And you’re a father.”

Dumfounded. Merely saying, ‘What the hell?’ seemed insignificant to the news.

Petra slowed down, found control, and filled in the details.

“I don’t know how many monkeys he has with him. I did not see any guards in the outside areas, but there *is* this storm. They are armed.”

“And Eliza?”

“She is locked in Orville’s apartment. She’s fine. Baby boy. Gave birth while I was there. She has the door locked. Said she would not move.”

Roark immediately went to the walkie-talkie, calling in his Security Team leaders who remained on the property. He did not have a full task force. He did not know what he was facing, but he knew he and his group had to be the rescuers. He could not depend on humans, not with this storm. They would prioritize who to rescue. More importantly, he didn’t want the outside human world to know monkeys were running amok. He also realized it was his fault; he had not taken action or been decisive about the threat when he knew Edgar had robbed the University of ITSE devices, and later the bank. Roark’s mood moved from anger to retaliation.

He also placed another call to the medical team he had assembled to be on call.

“Did they hurt you?” He eyed Petra’s injuries.

“Storm injuries. People have to walk through the flood. For speed, I took to the trees but got hit by a lot of flying debris. I’m ready to go back.”

J-S and Jefferson entered. They had been in a temporary command bunker, staying on top of the weather’s impact. Roark had Petra relate to them what she had seen. A medical intern, a cat named Sheba, treated her cuts and bruises. On Roark's insistence, Petra left out that part about a female orangutan likewise trapped at The Herd with a newborn. Sheba volunteered to go with them to treat any other on-site medical issues at the apartment complex, although she admitted she hated getting wet. Could they rig a first-aid carry bag for her to dry-travel in?

J-S began to outline the team he would take into the Apartments. Roark stopped him.

"I appreciate you're the Rapid Response boss here, and you are. But I believe the retaking of the Herd Apartments has to be seen by Animals and humans alike as an all-Animal response. You can monitor everything from somewhere outside and send in the human cavalry if it's needed."

With that direction, a plan quickly formulated. Sober, realizing this would be an armed insertion, and Animals could be hurt. Animals versus Animals. Not what Roark thought his world would come to.

* * *

Edgar had intimidated everyone, so they cowered to his control. His great strategy was made up as he went along. He thought it would be a simple robbery: gather food and cash and head out into the Everglades. The hurricane changed his thinking. Finding shelter. He would make The Herd his base and stay as long as he could, maybe a couple of weeks. Loot them all.

By his takeover, he increased his 'gang' by three monkeys from the Garden who saw Edgar's dominance as exciting thrills. He took them in but did not give them any weapons. Let them prove themselves. His gang now consisted of twelve members. A strong-arm number to rule over these placid, lazy Animals. He held nothing but contempt for them. The strong and ruthless must rule. His mind wandered into his barely contained glory and flashes of Animal armies and conquests. *In good time, was it possible?*

Chairman Balfour, at first intimidated, then regaining a shaky confidence in himself, elevated his self-superiority as The Herd leader, sought to take on Edgar, challenging him to give up his foolish actions. Edgar pistol-whipped him in front of the entire Herd residency.

"As I have demonstrated, resistance is futile; please take it easy. No heroes. Just watch television—when it comes on again. We will get you fed. And we will gather up your cell phones. And we will search all apartments—no communication to the outside world. We will be here for a few days. And you can get back to your routine right after the storm. But no one leaves here. For any reason." Edgar, now emboldened, knew he could take over the operation of The Herd. Dictatorships work if you have the power. And he had firepower. Edgar gave his prisoners a mean, crazed smile that matched the onslaught of the storm's horror.

* * *

Skye, the brown eagle and realtor Employee of the Month, worked with Sekhmet in the central control of the Emergency Preparedness office for Short Skiff Key. According to weather reports, the eye of the storm would be passing over the town right about now. The hurricane damage assessment team would send up drones, but they were not as efficient in the turbulent wind currents as a flying bird with a voice transmitter around its neck, reporting back those critical places that needed immediate assistance.

After about thirty minutes of eye-in-the-sky reporting, soaring and being buffeted, he decided to swing by The Herd Apartments to see if there was damage. He had to get in and out before the eye of the storm moved on, and he was brutalized by the tail end of Hurricane Demonio.

From a sweeping pass, he could see the storm surge rising against the front of the building. Structurally, the roof and all buildings looked secure. A lake was forming in the circle drive entrance. Then, something strange and unusual—monkeys peering out of the front windows of the common area.

Another bird, a falcon, swooped down and buzzed Skye. The motion and the wing wave were not threatening, but a signal to follow. They found an eave on the underside of the main building. When both birds landed, Skye quickly identified himself.

"This is my home, just checking for damage."

"I'm from the University. I'm Murray. You've got a problem. Edgar, one of your monkeys, and his crew have taken over your home, the entire complex, I believe. I'm reconnaissance. We are planning a rescue mission."

"I can inform Sekhmet, the lioness on the town council, she's at City Hall. She can mobilize police forces."

"Roark feels Animals should take care of Animal problems. And the monkeys are armed."

Skye felt frustrated. He was one bird. And humans probably would not send the police, only Animal Control would be contacted. They would be shot at and not prepared to fight back against armed primates. A bloodbath for all.

"What can I do?"

"Let's take turns making runs on the building. Determine the best place to make our entry breach. Then head back with me, and you and I will arm up with claws and mini bombs."

"It could come to that?" Skye felt his perch shake. For a moment, he thought a gust signaled the end of the quiet center of the storm. But no.

"Look there, at the corner below us. That's where the common room and atrium are located. Watch that corner."

And both predator birds stared.

The water surge hit the building and swirled into a small whirlpool. The ground moved out from under the building and dropped several feet, enlarging the whirlpool. Skye, tuned into Florida real estate, the good and bad, squawked an alarm.

"There's a sinkhole undermining part of the building! We need to warn everyone inside!"

"And get shot? We must tell our team that's coming in. Let's fly back. Put everyone in fast-track attack mode."

Skye could only hope they weren't too late. He sensed the eye of the storm passing, the hurricane renewing its ferocity when both birds were only halfway back to the University. One of them would not make it.

CALAMITY

Edgar had two of his Capuchin gang take the lead in going from apartment to apartment, searching for valuables, more importantly, phones, and disconnecting computers by taking the connecting wires. He wanted all Animals in the main common and recreation area under monkey control.

It took nearly two hours, but the two monkeys, lugging bags of phones and wiring, had completed most of their apartment search. Edgar had forced Benny, the building maintenance director, to relinquish his master keys. They were presently on the top floor where Orville and Roark had apartments. Storm noise from the roof made the searchers nervous, afraid they might be sucked up into the void if the roof blew off.

They knew who Roark was, where he lived, and the hatred Edgar felt towards the movie star. So, they slowed down their search and spent considerable time trashing what they could find in his apartment. It was fortunate for Roark that all of his grandmother's papers and memorabilia had been moved over to the University for safekeeping months earlier.

At Orville's apartment, the door seemed stuck when opened; it could be pushed slightly but would not open fully. Both monkeys pushed together, the door gave way, and the blocking dresser moved aside. They knew that someone must be hiding in there, and in the bathroom, they smashed the door and, yanking back the curtain, discovered an orangutan in the bathtub. And a clinging baby.

Said one of the primate terrorists. "Oh, Edgar is going to love this. A valuable hostage. Roark's cousin."

"Come on, let's go," said the other monkey, waving his pistol at Eliza. "I'd hate to kill the baby by mistake."

"Hey, scum monkey!" Roark smashed the butt of his rifle into the threatening monkey. The anger came with such force that the monkey criminal could not respond as his head was smashed in, and he fell dead in front of Eliza, who was lying in the bathtub.

"No one takes over this planet!" said a triumphant, incensed Roark, his last statement one of his battle cries from *Mad Monkeys of the Universe.*

Eliza was shocked at her discovery by a demented pistol-toting monkey, then was unexpectedly rescued. She looked up to see Roark, a fierce warrior, whose raging expression seemed to be similarly demented.

Behind Roark, a small female gorilla held up the other monkey by one foot, upside down, both of his wrists broken.

The baby moving on his mother's chest attracted his rescuer's attention. Both mother and father exchanged looks before Roark spoke gently, "Edgar has seized everyone. They are on the ground floor, gathered in the common area. You and your baby are best to stay here. Petra is here with us, and we've brought a medical tech to check you over."

Regaining some sensibility, Eliza looked down at the lifeless body within her touch and said the obvious.

"He's dead? He was a Herd resident from the Monkey Garden." She grew more resolute in a core ideal, ignoring the reality before them. "Are you going to kill them all?"

The gorilla, one she did not know but who looked dangerous, replied, “If they point a weapon at me, I’m going to blow them away.” She shook the whimpering monkey in her grasp.

Said Roark, affirming, “We are here to save Herd residents.”

“Please don’t kill them,” but her new maternal instincts had kicked in. “If you can.”

Roark shook his head at her sympathy for her tormentors, gave her a hard stare, another glance at the baby she held, then moved aside and left as Petra helped Eliza into the bedroom, where Sheba, the pre-med nurse, began taking vital signs and prepping some injections, energy for the mother, protective vaccinations against a dangerous world for the baby.

* * *

Edgar was stuffing his face with fruit when the gunfire broke out. His monkey cohorts looked to him for direction. He grabbed his machine pistol and ran from the kitchen to the great room, where his prisoners were in a panic. The front windows had been blown out, and the loud noise of the storm began to swirl in, as did the rain. This forced all the captives to rush to the opposite area of the presumed attack, which was precisely what Roark and his team wanted.

The monkeys ran to the windows to defend the ‘castle,’ anticipating where their enemy might rush them—but this was all misdirection. The rescuers, four pigs from the University, had crept in. Lower to the ground, they quickly infiltrated the surprised Herd residents and began ushering the smallest of the ex-circus Animals to follow them quietly out into a side corridor to safety and a well-defended interior location.

Gunfire from outside peppered the building, and it took a while before Edgar realized that bullets were not flying at them but going above them to protect the hostages. When he turned, he saw half of his prisoners had disappeared, and only the large ones remained. Elephants, giraffes, zebras, and lions had been used as blockers to allow the others to escape.

Enraged, Edgar raised his rifle to find a target to make an example of, when Larry, the lion, always one to defer important decisions, took the hardest choice of his life. As Edgar pointed his wrath at the three lioness dancers, Larry launched himself to protect his female pride. Edgar cut him down in mid-leap as the automatic fire stitched Larry's body but saved the lives of everyone behind him.

* * *

Outside, in the storm, brave Mildred, the donkey, under explosive expert Cooper's direction, had previously walked through the rising waters and dumped a load of explosives at the edge of the sinkhole. Skye, the brown eagle, signaled those beyond the front gate to detonate the explosives immediately, squawking that inside, they were killing innocents.

The muffled explosion tore off the corner of the building's base, which the criminal monkeys were defending, and accelerated the sinkhole's collapse. The side of the building crashed inward into a large, dark hole, quickly filling with water. Three of the armed monkeys at the windows were sucked into the sinkhole and disappeared.

The pigs had returned and quickly herded all the large creatures out of a side door further back into the building, away from the surviving yet disoriented gang members, one of them Edgar, who, when he recovered his senses, found himself without a weapon, clawing his way out of the building's wreckage, to face armed and angry Animals with a lethal intent.

Roar Uni Fact

Animal adaptability to survival. The echidna, an Australian egg-laying mammal, employs skill at hiding (and immediate quasi hibernation) to stay alive during a wildfire.-- The favorite food for a mongoose is a King Cobra, who can even survive a snake bite.--Dromedary camels in the African and Middle Eastern deserts can live for around two week without drinking water. --Atomic bug survival: a lethal dose of radiation for humans is 1,000 rads (the measure of absorbed radiation), for a cockroach it is over 10,000 rads. Even crazier, the **little habrobracon** wasp has been observed to survive X-rays of 158,080 rads but only for a limited time. Just over 4,000 rads makes the females sterile, and their lifespan is less than a month in any case.

CLEAN-UP

The Rapid Force Team quickly departed, carting off the remaining live monkey outlaws. Approximately six of them survived, including their ringleader, Edgar. All culprits disappeared, shell casings and weapons removed. As the storm abated, shocked residents crowded in comfort near a deceased hero within a partially destroyed, storm-battered building, yet clear of past mayhem.

The Executive Committee could no longer function. Chairman Balfour sat, head battered and dazed. Larry lay dead, his pride, the three dancers, wailed, nudging his still body. Larger Animals protected the smaller ones and moved everyone to the higher floors, away from the collapsed part of the main building, fearful that the entire structure might collapse at any time.

* * *

Using the remote camera that Skye had been carrying, Roark contacted the Short Skiff Key Emergency Preparedness Hotline and asked to speak to Sekhmet.

When she answered, he was brief and to the point.

"Larry was killed in a building collapse in the main building. He was a hero. He saved lives. I am here at The Herd. We are fearful that the structure may be unsound. There is a sinkhole undermining the northwest corner. See if you can find human volunteers, engineers, and maybe some backhoes to move rubble.

The Herd Animals seem safe. If any boats or army trucks are available, I can move the most vulnerable over to the University; the others probably can weather out the storm."

Sekhmet said nothing, totally shocked and devastated. She had placed the incoming call on the speaker by chance, and everyone in the Emergency Preparedness office had heard the University Chancellor's voice. Her mate had been killed. The Animals were in danger, and the building needed to be saved.

The last of the storm pummeled Short Skiff Key, but it did not stop the human volunteers who rushed out into the tempest to save their fellow town residents.

Hurricane Demonio moved on, heading north, none too soon, becoming a lesser tropical depression of rain cells. By the next morning, a cleansing sun broke through the remaining cloud cover.

* * *

University students returned quickly to campus and, with those who had remained, volunteered their time and energy to the town's recovery efforts. Surprisingly, but maybe not, rescued residents of The Herd, saying nothing of their harrowing experience, also joined in with removing debris. After a while, there was no discernible difference between the University and Herd Animals. They worked in teams alongside humans. Where mechanized vehicles could not reach to clear away the rubble, elephants used their strength to shove fallen palm trees to the side. The dancing dogs carried water bottles, while the show horses carried away debris.

Engineers from the Short Skiff Key Public Works Department quickly appraised the structural damage to the Herd building. The sinkhole had to be filled, but the building's damage could be reinforced with new steel beams and would be returned to usability.

Hurricane Demonio lived up to its name. Sekhmet would hear the truth about Larry's heroism, and she would personally oversee Larry's cremation, and his ashes would sit in a prominent memorial on the grounds of The Herd. His death certificate read, 'Deceased from hurricane-related building collapse.' No human asked for more details. Animals from the University attended Larry's service. Students sang a wonderful African chant about a lion sleeping, though Larry had never been there.

Still, the eyes of most attendees watered or shed profuse tears without embarrassment.

When Sekhmet finally could no longer control her grief, she asked Roark about the fate of the monkeys. He replied coldly. "Nature will mete out justice. We must be the civilized ones. And you must represent us all in making this a great community." She was unsatisfied with his answer but saw deep determination in the primate's eyes that he would do what was right.

Murray, the brown falcon, had been found alive in a tree, having been slammed by the storm with a broken wing, but soon healed.

* * *

Silent John had been overseeing the sandbagging operation during the storm to hold back the rising swamp water when a strong gust of wind stripped off his mask. No one said anything about his facial deformity as students and faculty worked as a team to save the campus. Thereafter, Silent John, sans mask, no longer treated his face as a disfigurement, comfortable with who he was. To support her future husband, Nebbie would occasionally wear short-sleeved blouses and sometimes even skirts, accepting her prosthetics as an undesirable but unavoidable new extension to mobility and the importance of feeling whole to herself.

A day after the storm, the massive cleanup effort began with military-like coordination led by the University Security Team in the forefront, working with the Florida National Guard.

An odd story from all this: while volunteers John and Nebbie worked side by side clearing debris for truck disposal, they discovered, under the eaves of a blown-off roof, a small, wet, shaking dog, with no back legs, unable to move because of the little wagon harness trapping the poor creature. They could never find the owner among the living. John and Nebbie adopted and cared for the gentle mutt and named him 'Storm the Miracle Dog'.

* * *

Repercussions from the hurricane altered lives. Chairman Balfour was voted out of office in a special election. Several reasons seemed apparent, but the unspoken complaint was an arrogance against the reality of the world where all creatures had to live and cohabitate. He accepted a demotion to become the lifeguard at the penguin ice plunge pool.

So, as it came to be, when the Annual Regatta, three months after the storm, was next held in Short Skiff Key, it was seen more as a Survivor's Party, quite festive as possible with posters and messages of hope and camaraderie.

And the Herd Animals came out in force, all wearing their circus clothes pulled dusty from closets or traveling trunks. They marched in all their majesty with Hazel, the zebra, the new Chairman of the Executive Committee, leading the Herd procession. Their float, their first-ever entry, won—a mock circus tent playing calliope music, showing two small children, a boy and a girl, next to each other, facing the mock circus tent opening where stood a baby giraffe, and a small donkey with a small monkey on its back [Petra] waving a colorful streamer, the theme suggesting all could be drawn to that once mystical place of entertainment so precious still.

In response to public demand in preparation for the Regatta Day, Chairman Hazel had established a fan-based autograph area for those interested humans and Animals who sought a personally signed photo of their favorite Animal circus stars.

She had no problem convincing Orville to sign his first published book, '*Mercedes, the Orangutan—Her Story*,' just released to positive reviews on the national book scene. It didn't hurt the book's promotional stature when it was announced, on the book cover and other media sources, '*A full-length movie soon to be released*.'

Orville, in turn, persuaded Roark to stop by for a couple of hours likewise to sign the story of his grandmother and to allow the public a chance to see not only the movie star persona but the primate with the growing reputation of a forward-thinking educator who supported career-advancing Animals, and as the national news exaggerated, as usual, was said to have saved a group of hurricane stranded Animals at risk to his own life. Humans and Animals stood in a long line to shake his hand and receive an autographed photo.

The evening performances of Short Skiff Key talent drew the Regatta events to a close. The three lionesses were again a hit with new dance material. Town Council member Sekhmet beamed proudly at the persistence and training of the three felines, who gained loud applause. She noted a young lion in the audience, intently watching the trio's whirls and twirls. Later, Sekhmet approached the lion, who introduced himself as Keith, 'from Texas,' he said. When she politely inquired about what he did, Keith told her he worked at the University as Head of Sales, marketing Animal worldwide tour adventures. He said she and her sisters should visit the Serengeti; he could arrange a tour for them. Sekhmet and Keith had a pleasant discussion; she introduced him to her sisters, and he told them they were 'extraordinarily beautiful and talented. Why were they not in Las Vegas doing performances?' Of course, they welcomed such flattery. A week later, Sekhmet called Keith to 'come up and see them sometime.' After that, Sekhmet, who was too busy with town and regional politics, suggested Keith volunteer his free time to represent the *Cool Cats* trio as their manager. Three months later, 'Keith from Texas' became not only an impresario manager but male domo to the Herd pride—three dancers and a politician. Larry the Lion was never forgotten, but, as they say, Intelligent Animals are socializers and communal.

MOTHERHOOD

Eliza enjoyed motherhood bliss for three months, the center of attention from her friends at both The Herd and the University. She even brought her baby to the Regatta, and regaled with the attention as the proud mother.

She seldom saw Roark, did not try to avoid him, but made no effort to seek him out. Her baby was not part of his life, and he seemed too busy with University matters, post-hurricane, while she focused on the Animal Voting Rights State Amendment, which had gathered enough signed petitioners to be on the election ballot.

To run the statewide campaign, Eliza soon moved to a shared condo in Tallahassee, near the State Capitol, with another activist, a human, the girl named Jill from SOCA. Like most human women, after such a horrible ordeal, she bore repressed scars. Still in therapy, she forged on with the new assignment, lobbying zoos and wildlife sanctuaries in the Southeast to send some of their animals to homeland resettlement through the SOCA-Roar University partnership channel.

Eliza had her work cut out for her. State Senator Mumford had gone off the rails, a complete anti-Animal bigot, and to heighten his prominence, proposed a bill to halt all further ITSE operations and ban the education of Animals who would take all jobs from needy humans, especially after the hurricane shut down many businesses. A hearing on the bill would be held in a month, followed by a committee vote to advance the bill for a full vote in the State Senate just before the Voters' Rights election. The human public could be manipulated by fear-mongering, a known talent of the articulate, bombastic State Senator Mumford.

Eliza found herself trapped by her own words. She could not personally testify against the bill, as the anti-Animal opposition could easily search online for her many articles and speeches advocating for the rights of all animals. She would be tarnished publicly as a 'radical'. Where the Voting Rights legislation had been limited to Intelligent Animals only (a first step to complete emancipation, as she believed would someday come to fruition), humans in these times, where there already existed divisiveness between political beliefs, would balk at creating a powerful new voter block, that could—they might fear—subjugate humans. Incendiary selected clips of past animal domination movies, most starring primates, were released by the opposition.

Eliza had to walk a narrow line, which meant defeating the bill by emphasizing the value of educated Animals and demonstrating that their success would not threaten the human workforce. Animal voting would benefit improved conditions, including support for human issues. And this meant swallowing her emotions and asking Roark to speak on behalf of Roar Animal University.

He was well-liked and admired by his peers within the educational universe, and his popularity had not waned but, in the last two years, had risen to national recognition: first, by his starting Roar Uni; second, the release of the heart-wrenching dramatic biography of his grandmother, now a best seller, and finally, his rescue of Animals during the devastating Hurricane Demonio as portrayed in the local papers by the propaganda efforts of Orville to mask and revise the real truth, removing rumors where Animals allegedly went wild—against each other. There is nothing wrong with positive mythology.

This last event again estranged Eliza and Roark. She did not truly understand why she began the argument, except for a deep sadness that Roark was not all he seemed to be—he had human tendencies of retribution and callousness towards life.

A month after the hurricane, she confronted him while he was lounging in his banyan tree, which, being stout and multi-rooted, had miraculously survived with minor damage.

"Where are Edgar and his thugs that survived your attack? You executed them, didn't you?"

Affronted by the accusation, Roark looked down on her from his perch.

"You think I would so easily kill another Animal?"

"I have seen your movies. I know you are capable. And you did kill that Monkey Garden resident."

"Dear Eliza, those are all fiction. My last two movies weren't even me, but AI-generated facsimiles. And yes, I did kill but to protect. Of that, could you not see my motive, my outrage at what that creature threatened to do to your baby?" The 'our' almost slipped out.

Eliza knew she was not good at winning arguments without facts, but that did not stop her.

"Edgar is dead, isn't he?

"To my latest knowledge, he is alive."

"And you can't tell me the details?"

"Eliza, what would you do with my answer? For your causes, for all animals, how can I be assured you won't manipulate any news to fit your own ends?" He liked her, he did, but was unsure if her 'loyalty' and 'trust' were not yet a guiding instinct.

She became incensed. Probably by his comment, which had been valid in the past. *One molds truth to sculpt a victorious cause.*

She nearly yelled at him. "I see now. You turned him over to humans, and they put him down." It was an accusation, not a question.

"You know me better. I believe Animals and humans must co-exist, but there is a separation of species. No one species rules over another. Until we are all equal, Animal law must protect and defend Animals. You must see that. Bad monkeys must face Animal justice, which is the final arbitrator." He let that soak in. But he could not hold back his most important question.

"Eliza, your son, is he… *my* son?" A small body climbed onto her back to look over her shoulder.

"Does it matter to you?" She was not bitter but more confused, frustrated, and unsure of her emotions.

"Yes, it does. I would be a good parent."

She had no snappy response. They stared at each other, and then Eliza walked away. At this point, her career and caring for her son had equal importance. *Was her heart that closed off?* He did not see the watery turmoil in her eyes.

Roark watched her go, smiling at the little critter holding on for dear life, clumps of his mother's hair in his tiny fists. He considered, *I wonder who he will take after when he grows up, what he will become?* Roark did not yet monitor every Animal who graduated from Roar Uni, then track and support their careers. Some he did keep an eye on. He knew he was regarded as a father figure and accepted that they felt they were his sons and daughters—Roark being conditioned to be a good parent if he had the opportunity.

Eliza could create an anger against her baby's father, but she needed what he represented, for her cause, and connivance was not beneath her.

To gain Roark's public support in opposition to State Senator Mumford's bill, realizing this was a matter of politics, and as uncomfortable as Eliza felt (this self-guilt again), she had to secretly use his friends to encourage him to speak at the State Committee hearing. She would stay out of the picture and no longer put herself into his life.

Orville, Petra, Gort, and Silent John were those she sought out, beginning with general gossip, explaining what she was doing in Florida, how vital the Voting Rights bill would be, how bad State Senator Mumford's proposed legislation would shut down Animal progress in Florida, and then watch it ooze nationwide.

Of course, they were provoked by this injustice in the making. Yes, certainly, Roark was the perfect public spokesperson, if only he could be convinced.

After being swamped by his close personal friends who were pitching the extreme need for him to testify, he knew who was behind building the pressure. He politely declined all encouragement to be an outspoken advocate.

"I am merely a local businessman and educator, not a politician, like some," he told the media when they asked him if he would be a speaker at the State Legislative Committee Meeting. Roark detested committees but offered no comment.

ART OF POLITICS

Roark could play the game of political chess with the best of them. After all, he survived within the Hollywood meat grinder for years before journeying on this sabbatical escape meant to cleanse his integrity. And now his life would again change dramatically with a notable improvement in his own self-satisfaction.

Without anyone's knowledge, he hired a national public relations company to enhance his image, share positive stories about Roar Animal University, and then focus on the Voting Rights issues, the importance of the committee hearing, and whether or not he would speak. Public outcry to speak intensified. *Speak! Speak!* A week before the hearing, the news 'leaked' and became, in press release verbiage: *The citizens of the country have convinced him: Roark the Movie Star and University Chancellor Will Speak to the Nation.*

His goal was not aimed directly at the localized issue but to draw attention across the country to the onslaught of any further bad public legislation. He did have a vested interest. At the State Capitol, he only needed the committee to vote against moving the bill to the floor for passage; he did not have to sway State Senator Mumford to change his vote. His goal was to kill the bill, but it was not his sole intention. To that end, he had become a political animal, manipulating his strong suit for his advantage, his students, and the University, for the expansive Roar Schools, and most importantly, for the future of Animals, all Animals, big 'A', small 'a'. *Hear me Roar!*

* * *

His motives were not totally altruistic. He hoped that his speech, which had to be an well-written skilled presentation, must motivate. He needed the attention to attract more faculty and enroll more students in Roar Schools, which were now franchised nationwide, but growth statistics showed lackluster enrollment numbers. They needed an electrical charge. The same was true of career hiring post-graduation. The curiosity about hiring an Animal had cooled to normalcy in the marketplace, driven by demand for the best-qualified employees. More humans realized that Animal work ethics were an asset but not enough. Finally, he had to speak nationally to all pro-pet, pro-Animal lovers who must be challenged to rise and let their voices be heard for Animal parity with humans.

To himself, he allowed the truth, for better or worse, he must move a Business Plan into a 'Movement'. He must take possibilities to the next level. Lying low and declining to speak out would not purchase millions of dollars of free media coverage to pitch what he had envisioned. A movement required funding and supporters.

Eliza, he accepted, in her basic education, saw the ideals unfettered by compromise. She was right in futuristic terms. Roark saw, in terms of practicality, a need for realistic goals. They were both dreamers. Roark had grown internally to view achievement through a business model. Eliza believed that all that is good would prevail someday when what is right awakens the ignorant, and a business strategy would not be required. Could both philosophies prevail, jointly? Roark wondered.

* * *

To Roark's paid planning, fortune can come calling when least expected. The week before the hearing, *Mercedes, the Orangutan -Her Story* hit Number One on numerous book list tabulations, and reviews were positive. As if a coordinated feeding frenzy were upon them, the production studio released early teasers of the upcoming movie, and the public was primed to see the film around the year-end holiday release date. Any published news story or television comment on all related stories would be as relevant as the tagline, 'The grandson of Mercedes, the movie star Roark, will appear to testify on the Anti-Animal proposed legislation in the Florida Legislature next week. The hearing will be televised.'

The stage was set for his finest hour—until it wasn't.

* * *

From who knows where, a televised celebrity gossip show blasted 'allegations' that Roark had fathered an illegitimate child with an ex-office worker who was now actively promoting Animal Voting Rights.

It does not matter that Animals might mate, but they don't fill out marriage certificates like humans do to legalize their relationships. Accept the worst in human terms. Slimy gossip becomes news when headlines follow headlines and are assumed to be accurate, as there were no issued denials from either involved party.

Roark made no public statement except that he looked forward to speaking before the State's Legislative Committee. The press salivated.

New scurrilous headlines from anonymous sources said the 'love child' might be a 'mixed species,' inferring something tainted. In certain states, journalists reported (as if they cared) that sterilization might be mandated to protect 'species purity.'

Eliza went underground to avoid being outed as the unidentified 'female of interest.' Trying to be kind to her in this 'nasty' predicament, her employer, NASAL, asked her to take a leave of absence until the controversy died down. She saw it as humans protecting the organization's reputation, yet she understood, accepting that she was the author of this mess. And yet, when she analyzed all the circumstances, she felt no remorse in embracing motherhood. She also wondered, '*What was Roark feeling*?"

Roark was feeling fine. More controversy brought more eyeballs to his grand entrance at the State Capitol in Tallahassee. He even acknowledged on the Capitol steps before all the cameras that he had a 'love child,' saying, "Yes, and love conceived a wonderful Intelligent Animal.' He displayed pride to counter the vitriol.

That day of the committee hearing was a mob scene of reporters, television cameras, news drones, anti-Animal protestors, and pro-Animal supporters. State police had established barricades. Admittance was by special ticket, and attendees went through a double screening process, and yes, three weapons were confiscated.

Both for and against parties met to establish rules on testimony. Representatives of the pro-Voter Rights group were the most vociferous in opposing the Senator, and met with their counter group, which favored the anti-Animal bill. The Legislative Committee established a regulated agenda to preserve decorum. They all agreed that Roark, the acknowledged and most well-known figure among all the proposed speakers, would be allowed to deliver his prepared remarks first. There would be an adjournment for lunch, and then in the afternoon, speakers for both sides would testify, with the vote to advance the bill or not to be held the following day.

RoarUni Fact

The Bill of Rights spells out rights of citizens in relation to their government. It guarantees civil rights and liberties to the individual—like freedom of speech, press, and religion. It sets rules for due process of law and reserves all powers not delegated to the Federal Government to the people or the States. And it specifies that "the enumeration in the Constitution, of certain rights, shall not be construed to deny or disparage others retained by the people."

The currently proposed Amendment XXIX amends the voting rights of citizens in Amendment XV to include "Intelligent Animals" and amends other Amendments of the Bill of Rights to reflect the definition of 'citizen' wherefor stated as people now adds 'other intelligent speaking species'. Three-fourths of the states, which is 38 out of 50, must ratify a constitutional amendment for it to become law.

SECOND THOUGHTS

It would be remiss at this point not to interrupt and reveal the backstory that led to Roark's presentation and its aftermath, culminating with the reconciliation between he and Eliza.

Eliza was channel-changing to find the best television station to watch the on-camera live legislative proceedings when her apartment doorbell rang. Nervous at all the unwanted publicity, she wanted no visitors but still glanced out a side window.

Silent John stood at the door. He wore no mask. Reluctantly, Eliza opened the door and bade him enter. He took a seat.

"I can't stay long. Nebbie is in the car. We're going to a bar to watch the legislative hearing on television."

"You are not going to the State Capitol?"

"My face does not need to take away from what Roark has to say. Why aren't you there to give him support?"

She sought an excuse. "We mothers are constrained in our ability to go anywhere at the drop of a banana."

"Roark could use your support."

"He will survive. He has done very well to date."

"Eliza, I came here on my own. Roark doesn't know I am here. There are a few things that I need to say that he, being a stubborn male, usually finds it hard to express."

"I don't think...."

"Hear me out. He misses you, and I can see he loves you. He is a great leader, but when it comes to personal relationships, he really hasn't had any real relationships to speak of, and that gives him, let's say, a lack of personal experience."

"What about…this Carmen, the movie star?"

"Carmen is a shallow narcissist. She has a bad reputation, and everyone, even Roark, knows to stay far away. Because of his new standing as an educator, he has crafted a reputation through his accomplishments that are seen as sacrosanct to his students."

"Well, there's the media; they've muddied us up. He would want to stay away from me."

"Do you really believe so? Have you asked him? Today, he has acknowledged he is a father and is proud of it. He calls his son 'a beautiful, Intelligent Animal, the next generation of leaders.' He is very loyal to friends in distress, I should know. I think having a son would be the most important thing in his life, along with you. He needs family to be around him as a complete Animal. Do you know he keeps a photo of you feeding in that banyan tree? He took that over two years ago."

She wavered. She did have feelings, but was still uncertain.

"He has a dark side to his personality that I question. I have seen his anger, even if he was protecting me. But Edgar, what happened to him?"

John had to laugh but caught himself when she gave a harsh stare.

"Again, he was protecting you from what the press did to you with their accusations. He has kept anything possibly bad from you, even when you both think differently. You want all Animals and animals to be free; he believes that, yet he recognizes the need for political sensitivity so as not to upset the human world. You see free animals now, and he sees Intelligent Animals who vote for the future. You are both on the same page, but a page has two sides. He needs you to understand what he is trying to accomplish and needs you to support him, ensuring that his actions align with your shared goals. Have you heard about the work he is doing on the G-1000?"

"No. What's G-1000?"

"Again, protecting you from any blowback, he has been thinking of you. Anyway, G-1000. 'G,' by the way, stands for Gort. Let me tell you two quick stories."

After absorbing what she heard, Eliza quickly changed clothes, and John and Nebbie drove her to the State Legislature.

THE SPEECH

In the overflowing committee room, Roark was directed to the front witness table and microphone. Photographers snapped away at him. Two television cameras were designated as pool cameras at different angles to relay images to all other feeds. This was national news with a world audience.

Roark dressed impeccably in a dark blue suit and white shirt, with no tie or shoes. He held a folder with his speech.

The State Senate Committee members sat at elevated desks, mimicking their counterparts in Congress. Today, most of the audience were humans, but scattered among them were intensely serious Animals, all dressed and behaving well and respectful of the process. In the back of the courtroom, SOCA employee Jill had held a seat open for her friend, and moments later, just as the Chairman's gavel pounded for silence, a small figure, Eliza, slipped into the chamber and made her way over to the seat beside Jill. Eliza wore a flower-print skirt and yellow chiffon blouse, and over her shoulder, she carried an oversized shoulder bag, which she stored under her seat. Security scanning detected no dangerous metal within her bag, and such devices were not technically advanced enough to pick up the gentle sound of a tiny heartbeat.

* * *

After attending to various housekeeping matters and notice of the bill under discussion, the Chairman turned to the first speaker. Roark opened the folder before him.

"Chairman, members of the Senate Committee, ladies and gentlemen of the public, and to the people of this great country.

The bill before you today, which could become law in this State and perhaps produce similar legislation in other states, is a bad bill, and you must take action to ensure it never sees the light of day.

In fact, and I will not mince words, this is hate masked in fiction, not to protect but to mislead the public interest.

Let's go back to establish a few facts to put things into perspective.

As you have noted, this bill is aimed at destroying the welfare of all Animals.

The Animal World is, and has been, an integral fabric of the human experience. Animals have sustained mankind as food when faced with starvation, transportation when great distances needed to be traveled, and warmth from fur pelts or simply by lying next to a freezing human in the cold of winter. Above all, Animals have proven to be the most steady and loyal companions, the givers of love to humans when they needed it most, through tragedy or depression, and in moments of joy.

However, as human technology advances for the benefit of all, two major scientific breakthroughs have occurred over the last decade, and these were not to the detriment of humans or Animals, but only to the continuing advancement of the evolutionary process. First, scientific researchers were able to understand Animal speech by identifying the brain source of their thought processes. Second was the laboratory invention of the ITSE implant, which translated Animal thought into actual speech.

This bill seeks now to destroy mankind's curiosity and to limit the horizon by which science can lead all to better tomorrows.

With this progress, Animals awoke. We found we had a voice. We could now communicate our thoughts and our pains. This new freedom allowed us to tell veterinarians where we hurt, and more of us were saved. We could tell our neighbors if we suffered from animal cruelty, and more animals would be saved.

We owe humans so many thanks for protecting us. Now, we have come to a crossroads, and we want to return the favor. How do we do so? In numerous ways, but most importantly, we want to help humans run their businesses more economically and effectively by becoming valuable employees. To achieve this, Animals need to educate themselves through the creation of educational institutions such as Roar Animal University and Roar Schools. For example, we have achieved our goals, and you can now find Animals throughout the country who hold down jobs working side by side with humans in harmony.

The proponents of this bill aim to halt human progress and to deny Animals certain rights to support the human goals of prosperity. Keep in mind, and economics will soon bear this out, that Animals working adds to the increase of the gross national product and provides more revenue and bottom-line profitability to businesses.

Those who propose this bill are spreaders of fear, which humans have faced over the centuries, and that is marginalizing and holding down those minorities or selective nationalities that don't meet the standards of the majority. This country has fought wars, humans against humans, in foreign countries and on this soil, to maintain, as your document so plainly states, "All men are created equal..."

Ladies and gentlemen of the Senate, and to all humans at large, you have been given a tremendous historic opportunity, the chance to be remembered throughout the ages of those people who could put prejudice, hatred, and mistrust aside and welcome Animals not as some invading horde but as hand-in-hand companions to build this country to new heights, to acknowledge humans and Animals are citizens of a very small planet, and that you recognize that the future of Nature and human existence will come about when all of us speak to each other in friendship and the desire of mutual survivability on this fragile Earth.

You may have concerns that all animals will someday speak and think and, therefore, will wish to force upon you, in various instances, unwarranted demands or even suggest superiority. That is the farthest from the truth.

Animals do not all think alike. They consist of all divisions of differences, just as humans do not speak with one mind. Freedom of speech, as we all have, creates opinions, and by that great truth, we are not all the same in our thinking.

Animals have rights and should have human rights, but they also have limitations. Because of science, a new

Animal stratum has risen among Animals: the Intelligent Animal. This creature is a new variant and a valuable asset to mankind. Some animals do not wish to be intelligent, nor do they have the scientific capabilities of speech-thinking by this ITSE device. So, you have no fear. The Intelligent Animals, known as IAs, only want to be recognized as kindred spirits to human progress. And they can achieve this beyond speech-thinking implants or future new technology. It is simple. Again, it is the education of Animals. Education is selective, and the most intelligent learners will survive in the human-Animal world. They are limited in number, yet they are invaluable to mankind. They must not be held back if they are to be supporters of Humans in the continued leaps forward.

How do Intelligent Animals best employ their learned expertise? By having equality with humans, the most primary and sacred of all rights afforded is the right to vote. To an educated Animal, it has become an inalienable right and one well deserved. Remember that a hundred years ago, human women did not have the right to vote. They were deemed second-class citizens, and yet they had, through education, the intelligence to call for and demand equality for themselves. Today, I see two elected women sitting before us, listening to my statement. What makes us so different?

Intelligent Animals bring strength to the workforce, offer intelligence to solve problems facing us all, and in most cases, Intelligent Animals are free. They only want to exercise all the rights that each citizen enjoys, including the right to freedom, education, and, by voting, the right to select the best humans to protect them.

Let me make this very personal observation. Like your ancestors, ours are those of immigrants; many of our forbears were brought to this country against their will. This is still a travesty today that, over time, must be eradicated. There is a significant population today of Intelligent Animals who do not wish to see their brothers and sisters as property, bought and sold without the ability to speak up against injustice. This country fought a civil war to afford the downtrodden and chattel property the right to have the same freedom as their peers. This is all we seek.

In the future, perhaps zoos, aquariums, and animal parks will host volunteer animal residents who will be motivated educators. Who better to teach the world about protecting all creatures that are fast disappearing from the Earth? Let us think about what that progress might indeed mean.

My grandmother came from a foreign land; she struggled and survived in the circus world, which no longer exists. Her name was Mercedes. At the end of this year, her story will be told in a movie and on streaming television nationwide..."

At this moment, Roark stopped speaking. He heard a commotion in the back of the room. The politicians also drew their attention away from him, looking at the audience. Those sitting next to the walkway looked down, all wondering, until a tiny baby orangutan jumped to the railing, looked across the courtroom, searching, and finally, seeing an Animal like himself, jumped to the table and climbed onto Roark's shoulder.

Ladies and Gentlemen, as I was saying, but shall amend, my grandmother Mercedes inadvertently became a part of this great country. She had hopes and dreams. Here is one of them: her great-grandson. I hope this Committee, in their wisdom, sees fit to protect his future as you protect your own children and grandchildren. It is they who will lead in this coming human and Animal world.

Thank you.

Pandemonium ensued, with loud applause and cheers. Wet eyes were dabbed. Those favoring the bill turned out to be only a few and knew to stay silent, so no more testimony was heard. Roark and Eliza left the State Legislature hand-in-hand, the baby still on Roark's shoulder, playing with his hair—the perfect front page cover of a very photogenic family.

The following day, the bill failed in committee.

Roark, Eliza, and the baby, to be known as Roary, returned to Short Skiff Key and later that day swung into *their* Banyan Tree for hours of playful romping. And finally, as the baby slept, the parents, in a blissful nuzzling, heard the chattering sounds of students crossing the campus, saw the world accept a sleeping sun, a crimson sky fading, and stars emerging as trailblazers for the adventuresome.

EPILOGUE--UPDATES

One of John's had-to-be true stories to Eliza:

* * *

Edgar felt nauseous. Waking up with a fuzzy head, he discovered himself in a metal crate, along with five of his gang, all in various stages of regaining consciousness. When they were all back to normalcy, Edgar took control to study their surroundings, escape being his priority.

Muggy, jungle-type heat; night, the moon breaking through distant trees. They seemed to be alone.

Edgar scoffed at their 'jail'. He and his gang could not be contained. The locks were quickly picked, and they were free, only to discover they were on an island—a small circle of land with enormous bare dead trees in the middle, surrounded by murky water. The land surrounding the island looked reachable, except for the wire fence perimeter, which had signs that read, "*Electric Fence. Do Not Touch.*"

Another nearby crate lay open, stocked with food supplies; nutritious food for monkeys, but limited. Edgar knew that, as their leader, he would demand the most.

A ripple in the water brought Edgar alert.

"To the trees!" he shouted. And they all scampered to apparent safety, high up in the branches.

A large head appeared above the water and slid onto the land, followed by a lengthy form.

Snake. A large one.

In minutes, ten more snakes made their way to Monkey Island.

Edgar looked down at the largest reptile.

Manasa spoke. "Hungry." And then smiled, if boa constrictors could smile, with her row of curved fangs.

Edgar looked at all the snakes who looked up at him and his gang. All their beady eyes held famished stares. Horrified, he spied the rusted sign: *Anndwell Monkey Farm.* His new home, his prison. For how long? Who knew? Who cared? Intelligent Animals like Edgar can scream. Even if no one would hear or come to the rescue.

* * *

On the beach, Eliza and Roark spoke special vows of commitment, legally officiated by Sekhmet, Mayor of Short Skiff Key. Their son Roary was the ring bearer; the ceremony momentarily halted as they searched for the rings in the sand.

After the hurricane Gort fitted Storm the Miracle Dog with custom-designed AI robotic legs. This year he advanced the robotics to tie into ITSE, and tears flowed as the canine did its own form of running when John and Nebbie took their daily beach walks. Storm liked barking more than talking and still held to the old habit of sniffing out bottles and cans for recycling.

In their happiness and as pet owners, John and Nebbie established a foundation to help all humans and animals with physical disabilities to use the latest technology and become independent and productive members of society.

Chancellor Roark announced that his research lab had patented G-1000. This revolutionary two-pill preparation achieved Animal thought-speak at a 30% discount to the current ITSE model. Applications for Roar educational facilities tripled. Almost immediately, the ITSE Committee filed suit to protect its monopoly.

The movie, *Mercedes the Orangutan: Her Story,* was a major success and nominated for Best Picture (it did not win) but scored the Best Book Adaptation award. Orville accepted the award, received a standing ovation, and gave a very short speech. He has since started work on his second book, which will be based on Roark's success with Roar University and its franchised schools. To write this story away from distractions and with a significant monetary advance, Orville moved to southern France to write and teach Animal Literature at one of the International Roar Schools.

The Voter Rights Bill for Animals passed in Florida, and other pro-Animal groups began their political push to pass this legislation in other states.

Roar Animal University graduated one thousand students with nearly 80% employment placements.

Roar Schools went public and raised $300 million for further franchises and new company locations. John and Nebbie became multi-millionaires in the transaction and married soon thereafter, with Roark as Best Animal and Eliza looking lovely in her bridesmaid outfit. Roary was again the ring bearer, and again the rings were misplaced, soon sniffed out in recovery by Storm, the Miracle Dog.

The University won its patent battle against the ITSE Committee and received a settlement for damages of $35 million (which went immediately into its Endowment Fund). Roar Uni would then strike a deal with the ITSE operating company and sign a Use Agreement to share the two products on the market, where gross sales could occur with a profit split. This joint partnership lasted three years before BT Enterprises released its new, improved, and advanced product, the G-2000, making all previous devices obsolete. The internal installation was reduced to a one-hour outpatient clinic visit. As the human, Arthur C. Clarke, once intoned: "Any sufficiently advanced technology is equivalent to magic."

* * *

Roar Uni spun off its Research Lab under the direction of Dr. Gort, who though not easily understood, almost everyone appreciated all the new products he created for the betterment of Animals—and humans.

* * *

Roark returned to Hollywood rarely and only as a silent investor to underwrite Animal heroic centric plots. Behind the scenes he contributed to and supported all artists, actors, and screen writers, to protect their creativity against plageristic AI incursion.

* * *

Eliza found her relationship with Roark dynamic, the satisfaction in cherished mating, which Intelligent Animals defined as 'love'. She could be proud of him, but in no way wished to stand in his shadow when she saw so much in herself yet to be expressed. It came as no surprise to Roark when Eliza launched her own law firm, AAA [All Animal Advisory] Legal Services.

Being a smart female orangutan, she minimized financial risk by signing up many of Roark business interests as her first retainer clients, thereby guaranteeing her a base income to hire supporting staff. More importantly, it allowed her independent freedom to take on pro bono cases that she found would support her beliefs, that is, to protect the growing law in animal rights.

* * *

During these early years, Roark and Eliza worked both separately and together on those issues facing the animal world, agreeing most of the time, sometimes agreeing to disagree. Near Short Skiff Key, they discovered and acquired a fifty-acre estate with two young banyan trees with open fallow acreage where they planted rows of durian fruit.

Everyone who saw them could only speak of the happiness within this close-knit family, representing the best among Intelligent Animals.

And all was well with Roark, Eliza, and Roary until it wasn't.

THE FUTURE UNWRITTEN

State Senator Wilford Mumford announced his candidacy for the U.S. Senate, and his campaign would focus on his opposition to the Animal Voting Rights Bill which had passed in seven States possibly heading towards majority confirmation, meaning eventual inclusion in the Bill of Rights. In deft strategy to gain the national spotlight, politician Mumford challenged Chancellor Roark to a series of four debates (to be highly promoted) across the country in those contested States where the outcome was too narrow to predict. Roark, after much pressure from Intelligent Animals and supportive humans, found himself in a less than enthusiastic position, and reluctantly accepted the debate challenge. The entire country's social media apparatus hyped the coming verbal clash.

* * *

Charlie of the Safari Ranch would give all his support to the Mumford Campaign. Yet, he had been, watching from afar, caught up in his own brilliant brainstorm to re-ignite his lagging revenues, lately suffering from the rising anti-animal cruelty groundswell of which his ranch had received bad press. Under the table, with no fanfare, he secretly canvassed his most loyal clients: 'We have an extensive inventory of exotic animals for your hunting pleasure but what if Safari Ranch could offer the ultimate test: stalking and bagging Intelligent Animals'. And Charlie knew just where he could find the most evil and devious Animals worth culling, a university with a constantly generated pool of 'intelligent game'. He began putting his idea on paper and penciling out the economics.

* * *

Eliza found herself mad at herself. On one hand, she cheered that her mate, Roark, would take on that mean Mumford. Any national media exposure would bring attention to the plight of Animals. But his university work and this upcoming absence on this 'debate campaign trail, and with her own heavy legal work at the office, she would see him less and would miss his closeness and touching. She had chosen this hectic profession of legal activism. Supportive, yes, he had come to accept her crowded career, as she his, still there was the burden, both unable to set aside quality personal time for each other, with the added responsibility, mostly on her part, of their 5-year-old Roary, now a scampering handful.

During these days and weeks of constant legal juggling with corporate and legislative cases representing either Roar University clients or pro bono animal rights appeals, she was caught unawares, surprised by a public outcry of events, of injustice, which pushed her and her team into representing defendants in a murder case, who if convicted would be put to death by...slaughterhouse. A jurisprudence cliff-hanging challenge of such proportions to match the attention of the upcoming vitriolic politically charged Voting Rights Debate, and to inadvertently draw in Roark.

Eliza agreed to defend three large swine who *allegedly* murdered a Farmer Woolf and eaten him. To be hereafter remembered: ***In Defense of Three Pigs.***

Where all The Ends are just the Prelude

APPENDIX #1

New Science & Technology That Led to How Animals Came to Use Human Speech

Children's cartoons and adult action movies have showcased the visuality of animals talking for over two centuries. The science that finally turned this imaginary goal into a reality, of Animals understanding and communicating in human speech, followed a circuitous route from ethological* pioneers to eventual breakthrough technology employing modern brain stimulation and AI advancements.

Beginning in the Pleistocene period over 2 million years ago, early humans bonded with canines for mutual hunting advantages into present recorded history, where researchers observed various animal behaviors trying to interpret visual cues and vocalizations, defining patterns as 'communication.' Scientist Karl von Frisch explored the dances of honeybees, and Konrad Lorenz studied the social signals of geese. Niko Tinbergen's work on gulls established that different vocal sounds and pitches could imprint patterned communication.

* *Ethology is a branch of zoology that studies the behavior of non-human animals. It has its scientific roots in the work of Charles Darwin.*

Within this spectrum, it was accepted that animals could learn, albeit in limited ways, various human words; accepting these words meant specific actions were warranted. Seeking to enlarge and bridge communicative possibilities during the 1960s and on saw a rise in animal linguistic studies, as exampled by Andre Martinet, *A Functional View of Language,* ed1, 1967; Gardiner, R. A and Gardner, B. T, *Teaching Sign Language to a Chimpanzee,* .ed.1, 1969, pg.664 –72]. Demers, R. A, Newmeyer (ed.). *Linguistics and animal communication,* [ed.1, 1988]; Cheney, D. L. & Seyforth, R. M (1991). *Truth and deception in animal communication.*

In the comprehensive overview of such research, the glaring fact remained: Animals ten years ago did not have the physiological and mental capacity to implement human speech (without a futuristic caveat to be mentioned later). The roadblock to such an ambitious goal was found in the controversial **Theory of Mind** (ToM), where in one camp, it was theorized that some non-human animals have complex cognitive processes that could be interpreted as 'mind reading,' while an opposing viewpoint said animals learn by simple 'behavior reading.' At that time, the general scientific and ethnological community dismissed ToM animal communication, pointing out the obvious: animals did not have the body parts to make human speech, and within their brains, they could not process the attribution of 'perception/knowledge' and 'intention.'

In this country, it took a neuroscientist, Doctor Shanti Khorana, in the course of lab research on electrical stimulative impulses on glial cells (microglia and ependymal primarily) within animal brains (live monkey experiments), who discovered that ToM could exist (the caveat) by *manipulation*. Thus, finding two levels of animal intelligence could be layered simultaneously:

(a) the original animal core of all its genetic and trait behavior (and original communication), and (b) a new brain functionality, in layman's terms, a non-biological interface that mimics the glial cells related to learning and memory. Another five years of lab work would be needed to achieve the communication device made viable with the rise of microscopic AI implants, which could translate the brain's thought stimuli into human speech. (See Preface: ITSE, 'Animals Speak…and Write').

The AI implant also overcame the physiological deficiency of the required human voice box so that Animals were not mouthing specific mouth-movement words from their beaks or mouths but rather emitted a brain-generated thought to AI and out as a computerized audio voice, paired with the animal species' natural 'accent.' Unlike an animal cartoon, the lips did not form human words, yet by expelling air, most humans in observation assumed that animal-human speech mirrored the way they spoke. In the final process, since animals did not have an original understanding of the breadth of human experience, having been given a blank slate by ITSE, all implants required educational encoding, and in the first years of implementation, much 'knowledge' offered by the government committee overseeing ITSE was not maximized, and Animals could perform only basic requirements, initiated by human direction for human specific needs. However, within a short time, through further experimentation in testing the capacity range of Animals to learn expansively and by market competition, most notably by the Research Lab at Roar Animal University, revised educational programs brought Animals closer to 'knowledgeable' parity with humans.

Note: in a growing trend of recognizing AI technological advancement, several years after Demis Hassabis and John Jumper won the Nobel Prize in Chemistry, having developed an AI model to solve a 50-year-old problem of predicting proteins' complex structures, Dr. Shanti Khorana received the Nobel Prize in Science for his neurological work that led to ITSE, for the benefit of humanity.

APPENDIX #2

An Open Letter from Chancellor Roark

Roar Animal University
Short Skiff Key, Florida

Dear University Students, Faculty, Alumni, Friends, and Supporters:

Though we have made great strides today in the advancement of education and the life improvement of Animals within our campus system and communities, there are times when we must reflect and recognize that there are those who are less fortunate who do not have the advantages we have been given, and many who live daily for their very survival.

Beyond your support to our various programs and our Endowment Fund, we are appealing to your generosity to support non-profit organizations that directly and actively strive to improve the living conditions, welfare, and health of all Animals, not only here, but worldwide.

Please visit our campus, review our various course curriculum available to Animals as well as select humans. We look forward to a productive pro-Animal friendship with your participation.

Roar Animal University
http://www.RoarAnimalUniversity.com

Let All Beasts Roar!

www.ingramcontent.com/pod-product-compliance
Lightning Source LLC
LaVergne TN
LVHW100506110826
845146LV00002B/536

9798218888756